Paris!

The Autobiography of Calista Antoine
Book Three

Bongo Books

DIG IT

Paris!
The Autobiography of Calista Antoine

Published by Bongo Books
http://www.bongo.net
Publisher's Cataloging-in-Publication (Provided by Bongo Books)
Bondurant, Mark.
Edited by Sara George and Stacy Gordon
Paris! / by Mark Bondurant. – 1st ed. p.300 ; 16x23cm.

ISBN: 1-940995-15-9
ISBN-13: 978-1-940995-15-1

1. Teenage girls. 2. France. 3. Alternative histories.
4. Zeppelins. 5. Steampunk fiction. 6. Science Fiction.
7. (Fiction), American. I. Title.

I wish to thank my writer's group in California.

We met weekly in various coffee houses,

sharing our stories, critiquing, braking our works down.

I will forever miss the stories I never heard finished.

Contents

First Foreword

The time has come for us to part ways. This will be my last work. I am beyond retirement. The work, if it is to continue, will be taken up by my son Martin. He is young, but has made his way as an author. He accompanied me on many of our trips to visit the Princess Consort and she seems satisfied with him. These were easy interviews of course, Paris being one of the happier times in her life. Not like the old times when we worked our way through those first two bitter books, fighting our way through royal opposition from every quarter. No. Thankfully, this one was easy. I don't have the stamina I used to. I doubt I could have persevered as I did if it were otherwise.

This volume covers her ejection from Belgium and flight to Paris. The creation of their residence in Pigalle and her unfortunate first performance. And, of course, the start of her business empire.

She threw off, no, she broke the shackles imposed on her by the British and began reaching out to grasp her future. The foundations are all here. All that she became started in Paris. She could have landed in no more fertile soil.

This work will put to rights many of the apocryphal unauthorized biographies cluttering store and library shelves. Most are rubbish. Even the better works, such as the one by the John Walker mentioned in this book, are filled with inaccuracies. Her Highness' distain for journalists left them all in a difficult position. There has been so much sensationalist press that sorting fact from fiction is difficult. She is so hard to pin down that I suspect that there will be many who will contest her own memories of events.

Let me be clear. Her ability to recall events is remarkable. Her story never varies. My work involves little more effort than that required to transcribe her words and then join them together into a single narrative.

Second Foreword

My father has suffered a stroke. He is alive, but bedridden, no longer able to write. It robbed him of his words and now he awaits death. His last words precede these. I have had to go through the rewrites and negotiations with our Hachette editors alone in order to see the manuscript through to the end. You see the results here.

During editing, I read to him, going through some of the rougher sections. He lay there listening, nodding yes and no. He cannot speak. I have no way to explain to him that his choices make no sense. I can't tell if he really understands. The weight of his condition is crushing. It colors the air within our house. He was so robust.

He receives callers on occasion. She herself has visited twice, alone, without their children, journeying all the way from Brussels by airplane, then leaving in tears. We get only a day's warning, the street outside our house, the back alley, and the catacombs, filling with police. Now that they are first in line to the succession, her security has the full weight of the state behind it, and the British are, as always, looming large. They will not see an independent Belgium, even if means her death.

We can only wait for the end, cursing God for drawing it out. He was the best of fathers. He did not deserve this, the worst kind of death that could have been chosen for a writer.

Perhaps though, it is the best choice of time. He is missing the darkening skies. The gathering doubts for our country's future. The growing menace from both Britain and Germany. We are caught in between again. Only the arms dealers are happy. But none of this is the Paris here in these pages. Those were brighter, happier times.

I suppose this is where he would talk about the interviews, about Her Highness, perhaps adding an anecdote or two, but she is a very public figure now. You can read such as these anywhere. And I don't feel up to it. I give you instead the book itself.

M. Bondurant

The Autobiography of Calista Antoine

Book Three

As told to

MM. Mark and Martin Bondurant

In the fall of 1905

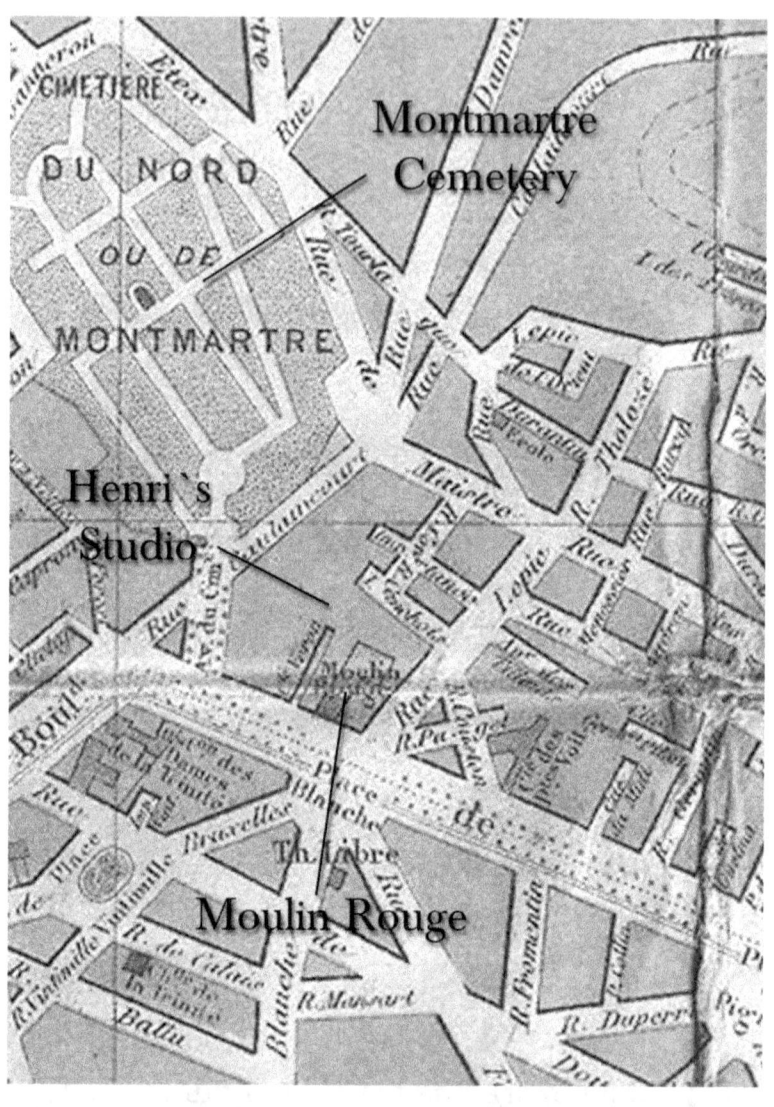

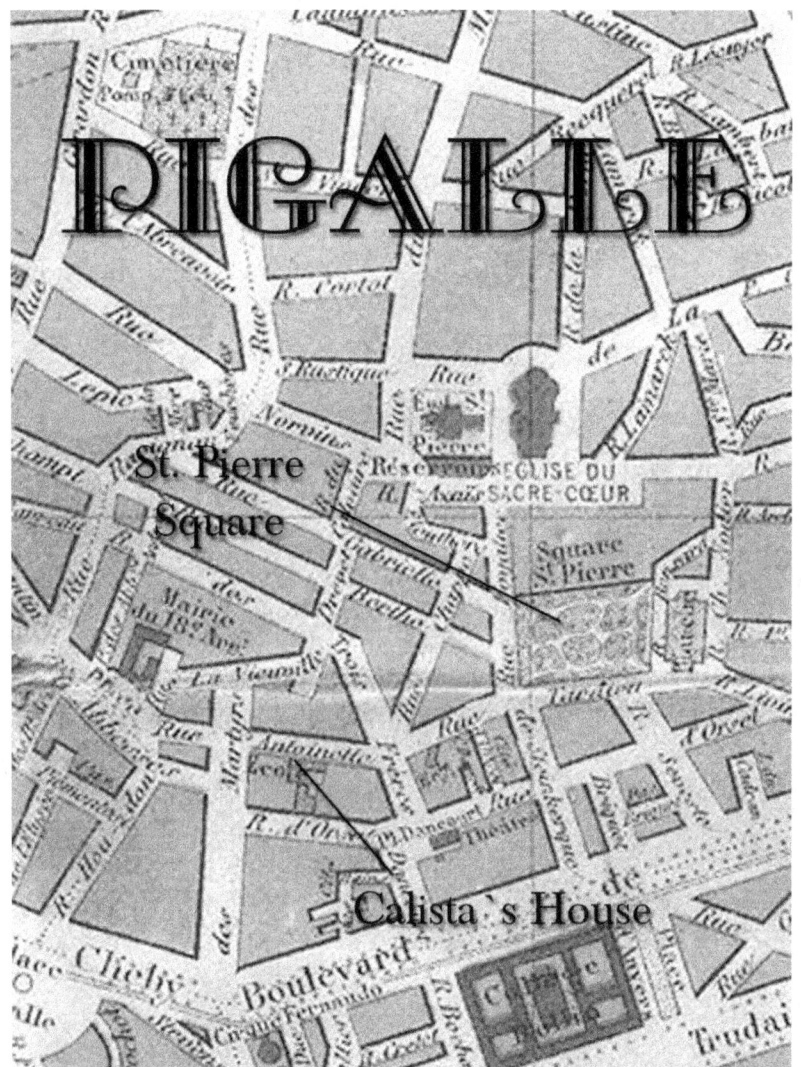

PIGALLE

St. Pierre
Square

Calista`s House

Chapter 1 - Brussels

"Absolutely not!"

We sat with our instrument cases in a paneled, well-carpeted office, in front of a large wood desk, behind which sat an elderly man with spectacles. Behind him stood a tall, thin man, looking down his long nose at us. The man at the desk spat as he talked, his accented English terrible. He rarely looked at us, but when he did, he squinted. He clearly felt our presence was unpleasant.

"We a telegram sent to you. Told you not come. Told you!"

"Clearly you sent it after we left," Aleta replied. "We received no telegrams."

"This is not important. You will not attend," he stammered,

finishing at the end of his breath, wanting to reach for the cigarette that he had already finished. He stared at the ashtray with distaste. Then drawing deep breath he hissed, "The scandal. The endowment. Our reputation is not worth this. Or our standing." Then he hammered in the last nail in the coffin lid. "Accepting street musicians," he sputtered. "Against it I was. And now the news. Your female . . ." and he trailed away.

He looked up at his friend and they jabbered until they came to an agreement.

"Proclivities!" he huffed. "Your immoral behavior of the royal family. How could you coming here think?"

I was sitting there, in shock, but Aleta lit into him.

"You have no idea what happened!" she yelled, almost in tears. "What we've gone through for the sake of Belgium. What you did to us!"

But he didn't care. "It is best. You leave now must. Go to Germany back," he sneered

But Aleta was on her feet, hands on his desk.

"We have no connection to Germany."

"I care not your plans. It will not happen here."

"We gave you the patents for cordite!"

"Leave."

I leapt up and grabbed her, pulling her back. I think she was about to go for his throat.

"Be thankful. We could the airfare repayment ask," he continued. Of course they didn't offer to pay our return fare!

"You have no idea what you're doing," Aleta yelled. That ended in a sob. I pulled her back towards the door. This was Aleta's one big chance in life vanishing in a puff of smoke.

"No!" she sobbed.

They looked smug.

I still remember the date of the appointment, November 14th, 1892, at 10 am. We had been offered a scholarship to the Royal Conservatory of Brussels to study music and had spent a harrowing three weeks crossing the Atlantic in a sabotaged zeppelin full of spies, barely making it across only to be kidnapped by Gustav Rothschild, possibly the richest man in the world. Everyone had been after Dr. Dewar's discovery, cordite. A new and apparently very dangerous replacement for gunpowder in artillery.

He died during our escape, but his daughter, Vic, had his notes and understood them as well. Lucien, the Duke of Tervuren, my beau, helped us escape and set her down with lawyers. They helped her file pending patents, contracts, and found her an apartment in Brussels three blocks from the palace. She had a new dual British and Belgian citizenship, or she would when her new passport arrived. The Belgian crown was very pleased with her, but apparently not with Aleta and me. The non-stop slander in the press, mostly supplied by the British, had blackened our names. I was the infamous German spy, "The Rabbit." I single handedly lost the Belgian Congo to the Germans. I even led the invasion! It was all crazy nonsense.

I expected it, to be unpopular. Leopold, the heir to the Belgian throne, could have stopped it all, but he would have had to admit he been wrong. That the fault was his, but I hadn't expected their displeasure would extend to our attending school. Coming from America, I didn't yet understand just how much the aristocracy controlled every level of society. At least they hadn't arrested me. The English would have loved to get their hands on me. A quick show trial was what they wanted, then me locked away in a dark corner – or even executed! Scandal under the carpet. Done.

We were staying with Vic. Her new apartment was only two blocks away from the music conservatory which, naturally, was close to the palace. Vic had a key and we just got off the coach and walked in. It was so big I had my own room all to myself! So much space. You should understand that I was raised on a schooner. My cabin was a three by six foot locker with two feet of headspace, but now I had a whole room with a big bed that I didn't have to share with anyone.

The apartment came furnished and we had barely begun to explore. There were cupboards with linens, clocks to be wound, candles, and paintings to ogle, but there was no place to cook. No kitchen at all. There was, however, a café next door. We didn't know how to turn on the gas anyway and we had no wood, so it was cold and Lucien couldn't help. He had been called away. . .

Oh! But he took me dancing back in Antwerp before he left! We waltzed. He bought me a new dress just to go dancing in. And we polkaed too. It was so fun! I love the way his clothes smell and the feel of his hand around mine as we flew swirling around and around. But I'm digressing again. I suppose it's because I don't want to talk about this part. Some things are simply hard to think about.

The day started with such optimism. We were going to report to school and start our new lives. We had breakfast downstairs, outside at a café on the *Grand Sablon*, which is halfway between a street and a square. We were wearing nice dresses, with corsets, coats, bustles, and horrible hats. We were definitely not wearing Paul's spy dresses. Then Vic had the doorman find her a carriage and left for the lawyers. Brussels doesn't have steam or cable trollies, but at least the streets are cobbled. The sweeps were very diligent, practically walking behind the horses, so everything was very clean there too. We were left to walk to the conservatory, which was around the corner, past the cathedral.

And as you know, it didn't end well.

Poor Aleta cried all the way back. And it was raining! We had no umbrellas. People stared, but we ignored them. I was so worried about her that I didn't think about what it meant to me until later. We climbed the stairs, the doorman asking if we needed help. At least I think that's what he said. Everyone in Brussels speaks Dutch or, in a pinch, French. Aleta's German and Spanish were still useless, except at court of course, where they all speak German. But it was highly unlikely we would be allowed near there.

Upstairs, we flopped down on couches in abject misery. We were alone. This was what Pa had meant by getting me to transfer money for contingencies. At least we weren't poor. I had over seven thousand French francs in cash and uncounted piles of German goldmarks, Belgian francs, and pesetas in my new purse. Aleta too. Most if it came from Lufthansa as payment for our hurts and trouble. And I had my bank account I transferred from home. I intended to go to the bank once we were settled.

I looked over at Aleta. She was laying on the couch across from me. They'd put a table between them, which seemed silly. You had to lean forward, practically getting up to reach it. She started crying again.

"We'll find another school," I said.

"How will I pay for it?"

"I don't know. We don't know how much they cost."

"I don't have any schooling. I can't read music. I don't know any classical music."

"We'll work on that."

Then she took up sobbing again. I felt so bad.

Eventually I got up and took off my wet dress and moved to my bed, laying there in the gray afternoon light. It was all too much. It seemed that the Congo would follow me for the rest of my life.

When Vic came in we had to go through it all again. It was her turn to be outraged. She came back with someone to turn on the gas. I had to hide because I was in my night dress, but we would have light and hot water that night. It would be a complicated evening as we had only one tub, but we really had nothing else to do. At least we didn't have to heat the water on the stove like we did on Red, my family's ship. When we finally adjourned downstairs for dinner and she told us all the news.

We were going to have servants. She was going to an agency tomorrow. They wanted to teach her Dutch as well, but she insisted on French. Dutch is useless outside of Flanders and she still wanted to move someplace warm. Aleta wanted to learn too, which wouldn't be a problem since her tutor was coming to the apartment. I think Aleta wanted to go someplace warm as well. I couldn't blame her. I just wanted to see Lucien, but he was gone and I had no idea when he would be coming back.

Lastly, Vic was going to see the King. She insisted she was going to plead my case even though I told her not too. I couldn't see any way for them to back down. It would only cause trouble and embarrassment. It might even prod them into arresting me.

No, your poor Cali was completely at a loss. I went to bed early not knowing what to do, which isn't hard when you're deeply depressed.

Our new help arrived on our fourth day in Brussels, the morning of the 17th, after Vic went to the agency. Aleta and I shared a maid, my first and only. It came as a complete surprise. Her name is Sarah and she's still with me. She barely speaks any English, but she does speak French. Back then she was a nice young girl with blond hair and a pale round face, about my age, but I couldn't get her to be friends, which was vexing. She kept calling me miss and ma'am even though I wasn't any older and she constantly insisted on rearranging my things.

"I'm keeping my bodices in that drawer," I would say.

"Yes Ma'am," she'd reply.

"No don't put that there. I'll never find them," I'd said, as she went to put something else away. As if I was supposed to! She was in charge of all of this. I had no idea.

"Please don't call me ma'am," I added looking at her with concern.

"Malady?"

"Cali."

"Yes Cali."

"Oh. That doesn't sound right."

Then I'd catch a ghost of a smile.

Looking back, I realize that she was very patient with me. I had no understanding. She lit the fire and put out my clothes, helped me with my corset, and shoes. She wanted me to buy more dresses, but that could wait for Lucien. Trying on dresses for Lucien is fun.

Apparently, the downstairs part of the building was where the servants lived. They just moved in. That's where the kitchens were too. We had no idea. It wasn't an apartment at all, but a house. And we weren't supposed to go downstairs! The doorman worked for Vic as well. He came with the building. We didn't know. Even Vic! She had a staff of eight. Apparently she had become very rich.

I got a letter from Lucien. He was reviewing the work on the King's palace at Laeken. Apparently it burned up. He missed me! Unfortunately, I had no way to write him back as he was living in temporary housing of some sort and he wasn't expecting to be there long. I think he was living in a tent. I did write Grandpa, airmail, to tell him our address and received a letter back a month later, it had to follow me to Paris, telling me Ma and Pa were still at sea. He was amused once he knew I was alright and wanted to know everything.

Brussels is boring. I now understand what M. Marmontel meant about it being "stuffy." We visited the cathedral, which seemed kind of small and plain, the air thick with old incense and shadows, thus said Cali the worldly critic of cathedrals. But really, it was. We went to the parks, but they were just trees and benches. And then the art museum, which wasn't nearly as interesting as the one I saw in France. We looked at the palace, but as you might guess, it was much like the rest. There was nothing to do when it wasn't raining but walk and try to explore. Walk in my corset and awful shoes. Eight weeks before I'd been able to skip down the streets of Boston in my school uniform, but now I was a fine lady in a corset in stuffy Brussels.

Life was pretty bleak until I found the music store on High Street. Don't look at me like that! It was *Hoogstraat*. I'm not completely ignorant. I was picking up Dutch.

Aleta and I were working on her reading music, which was why the music store was a godsend. The owner had instruments too. I finally got my bow rehaired. All he had for violin and flute was Vivaldi which, except for having to adapt it a bit, wasn't terribly challenging. It took some thumbing through the pages to find parts that were fun.

So as I said, life was pretty dull with us just sitting about listening to tutors or practicing. That was until Vic went on her visit to the palace.

She had a new dress made just for the occasion and they came for her in a gold carriage with men in livery and horses with feathers.

Oh, and I received another letter from Lucien. He was in Ghent negotiating with the Bishop. It's always been like this. They never leave him any time. This time though I had an address and I wrote him. How do you mail a letter in Belgium you ask? I have no idea. You give it to a servant and it just disappears. I've always found not knowing to be very uncomfortable.

Two hours later Vic stomped in through the front door. She had walked home. I told her not to try. The Queen had actually yelled at her.

Two days later I received an anonymous letter, although I was pretty sure who sent it. It contained ten thousand francs and two zeppelin tickets to Boston leaving in two weeks. The hand written note in French said:

> *This is for expenses. I'm deeply sorry for all of this.*
>   *L.*

Vic, shocked, asked, "From Lucien!?"
"No," I replied with a laugh. "It's from Leopold."

Leopold is not very bright when it comes to people. I say this even though, as you know, he's now my brother-in-law.

"The King?" Vic exclaimed.

"No, his son. The one I told you about."

"I don't want to go back to Boston," Aleta moaned.

"I don't want to accept anything from him," I replied, but I wasn't sure what to do.

"What a cretin," Vic observed.

I laughed again. I'm sorry, but it's the truth.

Vic looked at me and added, "Then again, I could think of a lot worse I could say." Which got us all laughing.

But I really didn't know what to do. I stared at the tickets as my smile died away. I couldn't leave Lucien, but I think that's what they wanted me to do. They were trying to buy me off.

"Cali," Aleta said, carefully. "Maybe we should try for Paris. You have offers there." I think Aleta was worried that I would leave her or perhaps drag her to Boston. Would she come with me if I went back?

"Maybe," I said. "But it's so far from Lucien."

"You could write M. Marmontel. Maybe he has advice."

"That's a good idea, but what's wrong with Boston?"

"The war. I'd never make any money. There's too much competition and too little pocket change."

"True, but you like Chinese food."

"True too, but I bet they have it in Paris. And more."

"Brussels -is- a bit boring," I said wistfully. Then I added, "We could go to Paris anyway." Which got a smile out of her.

"Now I want to go to," Vic whined.

So I wrote M. Marmontel. Then I fretted about it. I didn't want to be that far from Lucien, not that he wasn't far away already. At least in Brussels he had a chance of visiting.

I was sitting on my bed with my violin case on my lap, thinking about working on Saint-Saëns when Sarah timidly asked me a question.

"Pardon, Miss."

I looked up at her, "Yes?"

"If you don't mind, when are we going to Paris?"

"Going to Paris?"

"Yes, Miss. I need to make plans. We'll have packing and travel arrangements. The cook needs to plan for meals."

"We haven't decided yet," I replied. I hadn't thought of what would happen to the servants if we left. Clearly, I had to talk to Vic about it. And how did they know?

I caught Vic in her room.

"I have no idea," she replied. "I don't know what happens if I go away. I'll ask M. Deprez."

"M. Deprez?"

"My lawyer. I'm seeing him tomorrow."

M. Deprez requested that Vic not take any vacations until at least the start of March. He would be needing signatures as he crafted business contracts and set up accounts. Vic had new business interests all over the world.

If she left, the servants would stay behind with the house, except for her maid and await her return. That is, unless she wanted to close the house and take them with her. Some people did that when they went to Italy or Southern France in the winter. But then they rented entire villas, or even owned them! The alternative was to dismiss them, which could be a hardship. It was that European class thing. It had Vic trapped, and might even trap us too if we let it. Another reason to leave. It didn't occur to me then that I was already caught. I just didn't know it yet. Sarah was already teaching me the things I needed to know to survive. When I later married Lucien, I would end up caught even tighter than poor Vic.

So we decided that rather than sitting around Brussels we would try to find a school in Paris. We would come back if we failed or Vic could follow when she could. We would trade our Lufthansa tickets in for tickets to Paris. But naturally, my life couldn't just proceed peacefully. There had to be an explosion.

Vic had just left for the lawyer's and we had gotten our instruments from our rooms to work on Vivaldi. We hadn't even taken them out yet when the windows burst in and the building jumped. I was on the floor under a painting that had fallen off the wall. There was screaming from somewhere, perhaps outside.

Those pictures are a lot heavier than you might think, especially if a table and vase follow it down. I had to crawl out from under them. The room was a mess.

"Aleta?" I moaned.

"Cali," she moaned back. "What happened?"

I didn't know. I stood up. Aleta's chair had been knocked over backward with her still sitting in it. She had to roll to the side to get her dress clear.

"Vic," she snapped, her eyes suddenly wide.

"No!" I hopped up and ran to a window. Below, the street was torn apart. They were pulling people out of the café, from under bricks and masonary. The screaming was coming from one of the carriage horses. The other was dead. The carriage itself was kindling spread about the street. Aleta stood beside me cursing. We ran for the stairs.

Most of the house staff were already there, some kneeling next to a figure laying on the front steps. It was Vic.

"Vic!" I wailed and ran to her. Part of her head was crushed in. She had hit a wall. I could see blood darkening her dress, but none flowing.

"She's dead Ma'am," someone said.

"No." I was sobbing. "Damn them, damn them!" I repeated, as I sat curled up on my knees next to her. This was their revenge. The British had to have the last word. I should have thought. I could have known. They'd waited until her patents were public record but not yet granted. She had no heirs and no will. It was now free knowledge for the world to use as it saw fit.

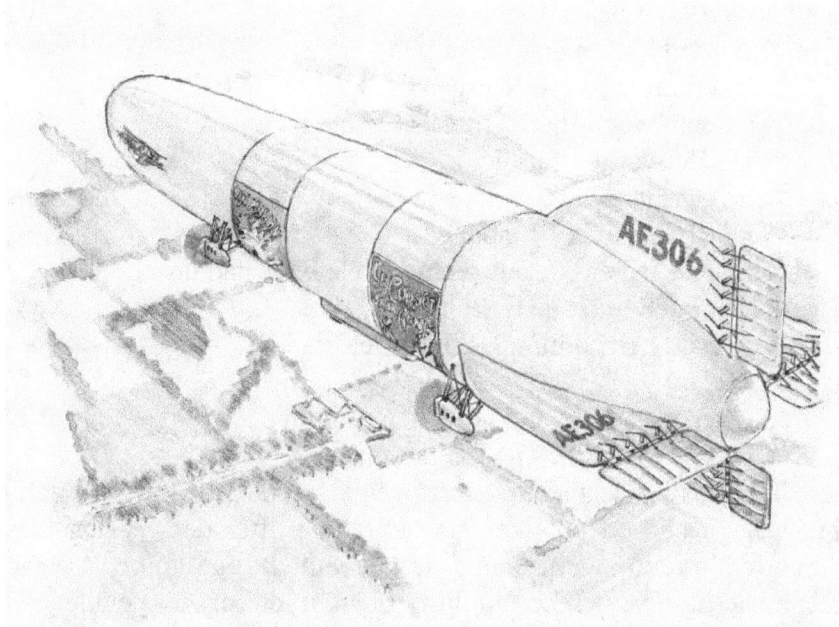

Chapter 2 – A Punctuation Point

The police, naturally, arrested me. After all, I'm the infamous Rabbit. I'm the cause for all the world's woes, especially the ones caused by the British. They picked me up off the ground, still crying and literally tossed me in the back of a van. I was handcuffed and pushed into a corner by two rough men. Thankfully, they left Aleta behind.

They left me in a lone chair in a bare office.

"And why are you in Belgium?" asked a looming man in a suit. I could see Vic's ghost behind him, which made him keep glancing back to see what I was staring at. She looked concerned.

"To go to school," I replied. I'd already told them at least six times.

"I thought you were here to take care of the Dewars."

"They wanted to go to Belgium."

"Victoria Dewar died," he snapped.

"They killed her."

"Her father died as well."

"It was an accident." I was so tired. They'd been at me all day

11

with no meals or water."

"You told him to go on that boat."

"No. I didn't. We were escaping."

"The man who killed him was German."

"Yes. He worked for them."

"The Germans?" he snapped.

"The Rothschilds," I moaned.

He hated that answer. It seemed to leave a bad taste.

"He wanted to come to Belgium," I said.

"And you helped him. He and Victoria."

"Yes."

"You helped them and now they're both dead."

"It was the British. The Institution."

That answer seemed to leave even a worse taste, but I wouldn't budge. We carried on like this until long after dark, when they "escorted" me to a cell. I suppose he wanted to go home. At least Aleta had my violin. They couldn't break it looking for "evidence". I was pushed into cell and onto a cot, which I gratefully collapsed and slept in. Vic was sitting on its edge. They gave me no dinner.

I opened my eyes past the remains of tears and a bad night. There crouching in front of me with a look of concern, was Lucien.

"I always seem to find you in trouble," he said, attempting to smile.

"I don't ask for it," I mumbled. My mouth was so dry.

He could see my predicament and stood to get the cup and pitcher they left on the shelf above the chamber pot. He looked at it and frowned, then sniffed the water.

"Get her fresh water," he said to the guard.

"Sir."

He returned with a fresh cup and pitcher. I drank it greedily, then rubbed some on my eyes.

"They killed Vic," I said, my voice dead. I could see her standing in the hallway, a thin shadow. She was looking at Lucien.

"I should have set guards at the door."

"I think they kept you away," I replied.

"Perhaps." He sounded tired too. "It's an unpleasant thought."

"We have to leave. We're going to Paris." At that Vic gave a slow nod.

Lucien said nothing for a moment. "Can you stand?" he asked.

I felt terrible, but that got a snort out of me, and rose slowly from the cot with a groan.

He was thinking. "It will be harder for me to help you there."

"They're not in the pocket of the British."

"Cali. I'm sorry I started this."

That surprised me, mostly because it was so wrong.

"You didn't start it. I did. I sent us to the Congo. It was my idea."

"I put you on that zeppelin."

That was true. He put me on that zeppelin, but with the best of intentions. I was there to help Vic and her father.

"We were only trying to help," I said, half to myself as I stood.

Max had warned me. The British Foreign Office wanted this all cleaned up. Vic was just another correction. I was destined to be the next. Somewhere, soon, there would be an anarchist or an accident waiting for me.

We were walking through the jail hallways. There were no gendarmes to be seen. Looking down at my dress I could see that it was hopeless. More blood.

"Another one gone," I said. "I can't seem to keep nice clothes." Spooky, tall tales, bloody, and now prison Cali, I thought.

"Were they difficult?"

"I'm getting used to it," I replied. He winced.

We walked past the desk. I didn't have to sign anything. Outside I blinked in the sunlight, a rare occurrence in winter Belgium. He had a carriage waiting, which I fell into, my head resting on Lucien's shoulder. That helped. Then we clopped back to Vic's house.

Of the original thirty eight passengers and crew that left with the Bremen on October 14th, with Vic's death, only fourteen lived to see the Christmas of 1892. I need to add Éléonore to the list. She died on the operating table as they tried to fix her hip. So many of us died on that voyage. We kept on dying long after we made shore.

We stopped on the way to Vic's and had a late breakfast, but I'm afraid I wasn't the best company despite my having not seen Lucien in almost a month. It wasn't just grief. I felt a deep unresolvable anger. Vic had done Britain no harm. She held no malice towards anyone. It had been pure spite on their part, an example. Examples are the last resort of the small minded.

The servants had left except for Sarah. Gone. Back to the agency. The front of the house was cupped out, broken glass and loose scattered brick everywhere. The front door lay on the floor in the hallway, the house open to the street. The gendarme guarding the house saluted. I ignored Vic's blood as we stepped through.

We found Aleta pacing upstairs. Lucien had told her to say and watch the house.

"Finally," she said, when I walked in. "They let you go."

"Yes," I sighed.

She took my shoulders and held me at arm's length. "Ooo, you don't look good," she said.

"I'm not," I agreed. "I need a bath. Do we still have hot water?"

Aleta nodded.

"I've had Jacobse removed from the case and the case itself closed," Lucien said. Then he looked at Sarah, "Who is this?"

She curtsied and replied eyes down, "Sarah, milord."

"I think she's my maid," I replied.

Lucien seemed to shrug and moved on to asking about the state of the house and our place in it. It struck me that he seemed to take Sarah for granted, but really we knew nothing about her. It was a big blind spot. Were all the upper class like this?

Back in my room, Sarah helped me out of my dress and into the tub, which was gloriously hot. I soaked the jail out of my bones. I even washed my hair. Sarah laid out a dress for me. She'd been packing.

"Sarah," I said, when I came in from the tub. "You work for Vic, not me."

"Not any more, Miss. I could use a new placement." She gave me another of those infuriating curtsies that I'd yet to manage properly myself. Then I realized that she was asking me for a job. Me!

"Sarah, you don't know who I am."

"Oh but I do. We all did. You're the Rabbit."

"Then you know you could get killed." I shuttered as I thought of the bomb. I didn't even know the doorman's name.

"Oh, I know, Ma'am."

I squinted at her. She seemed to relish the thought. I walked to

14

the door and called, "Lucien. I need some help."

He stared at me for a second in a daze. It was my night robe. I guess he liked it. He helped me buy it!

"Is there a problem?" he asked.

"Sarah wants to be my maid."

He looked at Sarah, I think for the first time.

She looked back anxiously.

Then he looked at me. "Cali. You want me to make this decision for you?"

Oh! I thought. *Lucien, you are worse than Pa.*

"Honestly, Miss," Sarah pleaded. "I want the position."

Aleta poked her head in. "What's going on?" she asked.

"Sarah wants to be my maid," I replied. Then I asked Lucien, "What do maids earn?" Perhaps I couldn't afford her. But apparently they earn very little. A full lady's maid earns about three thousand francs a year. I had that much in my purse. Of course it's far more than that because I would have to clothe, house, and feed her. She'd need airfare to Paris. And I had no income, although people did seem to be constantly thrusting money into my hands, but that was to make up for their trying to kill me!

"I can't, Sarah. I have no income and we want to go to music school and we're going to have to pay for it. And they may call me the Rabbit, but I'm not really a spy. If I was, I'd have money and protection. I've just made some bad enemies."

"I'll work for free," she replied.

She was desperate. She was crazy. We all looked at her.

"Please," she begged.

Lucien rolled his eyes. "I'll hire her."

"Lucien?" I asked.

"Really?" Aleta added, a little incredulous. I think she liked having a maid.

"Then you'll have to stay in touch," he said with a smile.

We had a chance to bargain. My inner merchant leapt up. "Then you should pay her more. She'll be in danger." I knew this was pocket change for him.

"And she'll have more to deal with than a normal maid," Aleta added.

He was halfway between a frown and a laugh.

15

We settled on four thousand francs and I realized that I might not have to pay for airfare either. I could cash in the prince's Lufthansa tickets. They had to cover three tickets to Paris. For once it was all going to work out.

"Lucien? How do I find Lufthansa?"

He frowned. He was wondering what I was up to. I think he caught on to that about me fairly quickly. It's strange, but I think that it was something he liked.

The next morning, at breakfast, we saw the papers. They said the explosion was the work of anarchists. It had been covered up.

We spent the next week at the Hotel Metropole. I saw no sign of Vic ghost. Not with my eyes at least. Just in my dreams.

The hotel wasn't far and it was brand new. It even had electricity. Lucien booked two adjoining double suites, picked a room, walked in and fell asleep. He'd been up for two days.

I wasn't much better. I picked the room next to his. It was so romantic. When I woke, I remembered Vic and cried. It was late afternoon. It took supreme effort of will to make myself get up. I was becoming so familiar with these things. Familiar with police interrogations, the sight of blood, the sound of guns and explosions, and, worst of all, the death of friends. Heavy in melancholy, I stumbled back from our bathroom towards bed. Aleta followed along trying to entice me into eating food. Halfway back I realized she was right. I'd had only one meal in the last two days, but I didn't feel it. I felt nothing but a dead numbness.

"I'll eat," I said.

It helped, but I still went back to bed. I won't kid you. There were times back then when I thought seriously of suicide. But fear not. Paris is coming soon and for a time, all will be right. Just wait!

I woke again at six in tears. Vic had been there trying to console me. Her arms had been warm. She made sure if it. She had put that extra effort in for me even though it hurt her.

Lucien was up when I woke and we had dinner downstairs.

Sarah couldn't come with us! Apparently she shouldn't even be sleeping in the rooms with us, which is crazy. The hotel had a special section for servants, with their own place to eat. Sarah claimed not to mind. In fact, she seemed strangely eager to get down there.

Our hotel restaurant was lovely, the ceiling painted with angels and hung with chandeliers. I was down to one dress again. That is unless I wanted to go formal or wear one of my spy dresses. The spy dresses would announce the presence of the Rabbit to the press, which was something we wanted to avoid. It might even have gotten us thrown out of the hotel, not that we hadn't already been identified. If we had looked, we would have seen that the Rabbit was again in the papers.

Lucien took time off. I think he was as bitter as me and I'm not really sure if he actually asked permission from the crown. We both suspected that the Belgian Sûreté and perhaps even the Crown had been involved.

We picked a day that promised sunshine and took a car out of town for a picnic. I would like to say that the outskirts of Brussels were an adventure, but it was mostly tenements and factories. I supposed we were living in the much nicer center of town. Eventually, it gave way to sweet fields of hay nestled between woods and fences. Hay is soft when it's under a blanket and the sun warm, even in fall, when you're nestled within. Rain though, drove us back to the car and its leather top where we snuggled in our wet clothes under our blanket. We sipped wine and ate sandwiches packed for us by the hotel. These were the moments that kept me alive back then.

Lucien does nothing without reason. He and Sarah seemed to have an understanding. She was bent on teaching me how to behave around servants. It's very hard to let go when you've been raised to do when you see things that need doing. The only time she relented and joined us was when we included her in our self-defense practice. We moved the furniture back to make room in the center of the floor. Sarah somehow made sure the hotel staff didn't put it back.

Those two weeks until our zeppelin flight were two of the most beautiful of my life. Lucien worked to bring me back to life. He took me to salons, stores, and dance halls. I deposited my Goldmarks and transferred half my money to the Bank of France.

We visited Duchess Baudouin! She huffed when she got up to move about even without her corset and finery. It was good to see her again and to know she had escaped the Congo too. So many

17

others hadn't.

"My dear, how can you have lost weight?" She asked as I sat.

"I guess I've been a bit busy." Looking down, I asked, "Do I look bad?"

"No," she smiled. "It's raw jealously. I hope you don't mind while I look you over."

I must have looked surprised because she added, "I'm looking for scars."

I grinned. "It really is amazing isn't it? I'm surprised myself."

She laughed. A deep gurgling thing. "It's your youth. I'm sure I wouldn't have made it out of the palace grounds."

"I had help."

She glanced at Lucien. "I'd need a wheel barrel and two strong men."

"You could have shot while they pushed."

She laughed again. "That would have been a sight." Then she looked up. "Oh good. Here's the tea."

Two servants put trays down on the table.

"Try the orange ones. My doctor has forbidden me from eating these things, so naturally I stocked up in case they cut me off."

I do love her. We carried on like that for an hour. I think she was a surrogate mother to Lucien. I caught her eying me curiously, taking inventory I think. Or, perhaps she was assessing the damage I would cause. She told me Omama had escaped as well, along with her evil assistants. They were in Brussels too. Before we left I had to promise to visit again, but it would be a long time before I came back. After Lucien and I were married.

The day before we left for Paris, I received a letter from M. Marmontel telling us he would be delighted to have a visit, which was a huge relief. I had little hope of friendly advice in Paris without him.

Did you know that Zeppelins are life's punctuation marks? They represent endings and beginnings, leaving one place and moving on to another. The world that you knew is left behind and shortly an entirely new one unfolds before you. They are not to be treated casually. Our world ended on December 2nd, at the Brussels Aerodrome. A Friday I believe. Our next world would be a new, different place.

I couldn't hold back the tears as they were calling for us to board. It's like we had grown roots that tore and hurt as we pulled apart. I could see tears in Lucien's eyes, damn the British for making us go. He promised to follow soon.

With Lucien at my back, we boarded. We looked around as we climbed in through the side door. There were spartan wood seats in long rows, windows down the sides, and nothing else. No tables, couches, big windows, tea, coffee, or cookies. Huh?

Aleta listened to me griping and replied, "It's what you get when you fly small-hub carriers." She shrugged. "We're lucky to not have to sit next to livestock."

We were flying Aero Europa, an Italian firm. The best we could find on short notice. Apparently they went for maximum profit and that meant maximum bodies packed under the minimum envelope. We sat in our thinly padded seats elbow to elbow. Aleta got the window, Sarah and I the aisle. The whole cabin turned breezy each time the crew opened the hatch to go up top or someone opened the head door.

We flew much lower and much slower, with individual details such as cows and wagons clearly visible below us. I had an elderly French woman next to me who was very chatty.

"You play the violin?" she asked. I was holding my case, having refused to check it.

"Yes."

"My son is learning, but he's very headstrong and doesn't practice."

"I can understand that. It can be hard to practice sometimes."

"I tell him you must practice to learn, but he says he doesn't want to learn." She looked about. "I don't think you could practice in here."

"I don't think I could open my case, let alone draw my bow," which got a guffaw.

That was what it was like. It wasn't just the hard seat that kept me squirming. But all flights end – eventually. Ours took four long hours.

Paris Aerodrome is amazing. We came in under gray skies, threading our way through a maze of airships. Looking past my seatmate, I got a glimpse of the Eiffle Tower through the window as she told me all about her little dog Philippe. It was the first time I'd actually landed normally in an airship. It's a lot like our landing on the Liberté, the ship that rescued us. We got pulled down by a big steam winch, pulled down until we were close enough to the ground for them to lash us down to big buried concrete blocks. But, once tied down, we had, instead of a swaying ladder and a pitching deck, pleasant level steps.

In Paris they drive you to the terminal in big steam cars that carry twenty passengers each, and then cable trolleys take you to the aerodrome train station. It was all very organized.

Porters helped us with our baggage onto the trolley. Sarah watched them carefully to make sure there were no mistakes. It's something you should remember when flying second class carriers. Their baggage handlers can be quite careless.

The airfield around us was an endless meadow of mud and wet grass grazed low by wandering sheep. It slowly rolled by as we chugged along the gravel road. Above us, mixed with the clouds was a forest of cables and airships, all painted in a bewildering mix of colors, sporting flags and advertisements.

When we arrived, we found the floor of the Aero Europa terminal was littered with cigarette butts, candy wrapping, and old newspapers. Soot gathered under the seats. Their windows were covered with hand and nose prints. This was definitely not Lufthansa. Our cable trolley to the main terminal though, was clean, although open to the cold wind. It did, however, have a helpful roof as it was raining.

Perhaps it's because of the rain that women wear such big hats in Paris. It can't be because of the wind which constantly threatens to sweep them off. We held ours on as we rolled into the trolley wing of the main terminal, just as the rain really started rattling down, battering the glass and iron roof above us. It was fascinating. It made me think of Gustav Rothschild's skylight in the kitchen on his ship, the Octave. That had to be crazy fun during storms. The station ironwork was beautiful, cast to look like plants and trees.

Sarah had our luggage checked in the station, keeping the chit. The trolley wing led into a main gallery with buildings actually inside under the station's glass roof! It was past lunch and we were hungry, so we picked a café, its tables spread out across the marble floor under seemingly unnecessary umbrellas. As we sat, I noticed pigeons begging despite our being indoors. Perhaps the pigeons were why they had the umbrellas.

We were surrounded by sound, the roar of a thousand conversations and thousands of shuffling feet. Our eyes darted this way and that, trying to see it all.

Aleta laughed, "I never got to come in here." She used to work crew for Lufthansa.

"Never?"

"We were always busy with maintenance. And catching up on sleep."

I was looking at the menu card. "What are you going to get?" I asked.

"I was thinking *croque-monsieur*. It's all I recognize," she replied

"Hmmm, Miss," Sarah voice tinged with disapproval. "I suggest the sole."

"Really?" Aleta asked.

"Yes. *croque-monsieur* is for the lower classes. I'm surprised it's on the menu. I suppose they must cater to all sorts. I suggest white wine as well."

We smiled. This had become a running joke with us. It was her lessons in upper class etiquette. The sole was good though. We finished with coffee.

Sarah would not let us pay, pulling notes from inside her purse, which she hid from us. She purchased the train tickets too. She now controlled the money although I had no idea where it was coming from.

"Ladies do not pay," she said. The money in my purse sat untouched.

She dealt with the luggage too, then she pulled us along to the platforms, which were in a separate building. We got to them by going up sweeping marble steps, then through big brass and glass revolving doors, which are a hoot. You could just keep on going around and around. Honestly though, I didn't. But I might have if Sarah weren't there.

The train platform building had a great arching ceiling open at both ends, with the trains sliding in beneath. We stood on a long bridge that let you walk over the tops of the trains, with stairs leading down to the platforms. The train's steam flared around you from beneath as they passed. But I should warn you that before you go anywhere in these sorts of terminals, you must first open your umbrella. Sooty water drips down from the roof and it's best not to linger on the platforms if you value your clothing as well.

Luckily, trains left for Paris every few minutes. We had no reason to linger. Our train was a very nice one too. They built a blue and gold shell over the engine so it fit with the rest of the cars. It made it look far less forbidding. Inside we sat in a parlor car with pleasant seats and a man offering us tea and milk.

Outside Paris grew until, fields suddenly gone, we were engulfed by it. A sea of black smoke rising like seaweed, merging with the gray sky. Our train cut between endless dirty brown tenements and rude rutted streets, suddenly ducking though a dark tunnel in the brown stone of the outer city wall, then into the paved streets and better parts of the city inside, finally pulling in to North Station. The trip had taken only thirty minutes. A porter appeared with our baggage on a pull truck to escort us to the street, leading us to one of the waiting steam carriages. Once settled, enclosed, out of the wind, we rolled into the dim wet streets of Paris surrounded by the first flakes of falling snow.

Chapter 3 – A Party

Lucien suggested some hotels so I showed the list to our carriage driver and asked if any of them were near the *Paris Conservatoire*. He took us to the Hotel Scribe and Sarah went in to book us a room while the porter and the driver moved our bags from the back locker onto his cart. The car was about to leave when Sarah came storming out, back down the steps.

"They won't give us a room!" she said.

I was infamous. I knew what was coming.

"They want no bombs," Sarah snapped.

"Oh! I might plant one myself!" Aleta spat.

Which got me to laugh and took out some of the sting. Then I looked at the doorman, "Can we load this back on?"

It was the same at the next, then the next wanted triple rent, which was unacceptable. So we were sitting there stumped when the driver said hopefully, "My family has a house you can rent, but it's probably not up to what you're used to."

"Does it have indoor plumbing?" I asked.

"Yes, of course."

"Is it furnished?"

"Yes, it is."

"Ask if it has hot water?" Aleta asked.

He paused. "No, but there's a bath house four doors away."

It seemed suspiciously cheap, but not far away, just on the other side of the river, so we decided to look. We headed west towards the hill where they were building a church. You can't miss it. Paris is so flat that anything that sticks up stands out.

The street was clean, although a bit bare, lacking shops and carts, and the nearest trolley was two streets away. Most of the shopping too. We'd have to haul things over from there.

"It can be noisy at night," he said as he unlocked the door. "Most of the businesses are not open this early." I didn't see much in the way of business at all. There was a tea shop, and then a produce stand at the end of the street, so I thought this strange. Looking the other way I saw the bathhouse and then a cabaret on the corner.

Inside, it seemed nice, at least to me, although a bit musty, having been closed up for some time. It was large, three stories. It had a parlor, living room, and kitchen downstairs, and four rooms upstairs. On top was a large attic loft. We could even open a door to the roof. I mean it wasn't great. It was dark, the carpets were worn, and it needed cleaning. It was clear we would need someone to help with that. That or a cook, or something.

The day was wearing on and we had no place to stay so we looked at each other and pretty much shrugged. The driver, whose name was M. Palomer by the way, suggested we try it for a week at double rent first, which still seemed cheap, so we agreed. He wrote down his address, took our money, and then he gave us two keys.

And there we were. In Paris without a clue.

We began with an inventory. There were clean linens. There were dishes and pots. We found an untried door that wasn't on the tour that led to a basement with an iron cistern and coal scuttle, but no wood. No ghosts, which I've come to learn is unusual for Paris.

Perhaps they were polite. The pump in the kitchen coughed out clean water, but there was no tub. There would be no hot bath after our trip, no easy dinner, and it would be dark.

"I think we should try the cabaret and the bathhouse," Aleta said.

"I vote for the boulevard. We can eat and then bring back food."

We looked at Sarah, who seemed surprised. "I will do what you decide."

I kept staring, waiting.

She grimaced and added, "We should shop for lamp oil and matches at least. I suggest the boulevard."

"True," Aleta added. "Then we better go before it gets dark."

"We'll need bags to carry things," Sarah added.

"Do we have any?" I asked.

"No, Miss. I've been looking."

On the corner there was a sign. We were living on *Rue Antoinette. Clichy Boulevard* was two blocks away, wide and tree-lined. It probably looked very pretty when the sun was shining and you weren't tired and a little afraid and confused. We saw carts, and stores, and a plaza a block down. We found bags and oil. There were potatoes and bath salts, which I considered until I remembered we had no bath. We worked on Aleta's French, naming things as we went.

We purchased eggs, ham, bread, butter, onions, tea – and oranges! The oranges were expensive, but I would not be dissuaded. One for each of us. We found a coffee house that sold it toasted or baked, or whatever they do to it and then ground, but we didn't know if we had any way to make it drinkable. Even boiling it in a pot, we'd need a cheesecloth or something to strain it with. And what would we keep it in? We would be back the next day, and the day after that, buying all the little things it takes to get through the day. And, we needed to find our bank.

We ate in a little café then carried our loot home.

The noise started as we were thinking about bed. We'd been working on Vivaldi, but it was hard to see the music. We hadn't bought candles yet. It was just the wall sconces, lit with our new matches. We noticed our street had become somewhat noisy. Standing outside, looking about, we saw that the streetlamps had been lit, and lanterns had been hung in doorways. Carriages navigated the streets dropping off people, mostly men, dressed in every fashion, which had attracted push carts with people selling things. Everyone stood about smoking and chatting until a window across the street banged open and a naked woman followed by several equally naked friends leaned out and called, "Come one and come all. Antoinette's Boudoir is open." Then she cooed at a customer she knew below in the street, her friends calling to others. Down the street someone hung out a sign and music began to drift about from several doorways. Even the bath house was lit.

I was pleased to see a strong gendarme presence. Our house would be difficult to defend if we were alone with its bare windows within easy reach at street level and no back door. We had only the roof for escape. This was something we needed to discuss. Maybe we could dig a tunnel!

I suppose I'd been gawking because a man spoke beside me and I jumped. I guess he'd been waiting in the shadows, away from the others.

"I agree. Antoinette's is a bit brazen, even for Paris. But *pause dîner* is over."

He was short with a beard and spectacles, but his voice was quite deep. His suit and derby looked expensive.

"What did he say?" Aleta asked.

"Ah English. Then this must be a bit of a shock," he chuckled. "I wondered who would move in after the old lady died."

"We just moved in today," I said, and then explained to Aleta.

"American?" He looked surprised, then he squinted at me.

"Yes."

"My friends call me Henri."

"Cali."

He squinted at me even harder and then blinked, and reached in his vest pocket.

"My card."

I took it and thanked him.

"I'm afraid I have none," I replied.

He chuckled. "They're pretentious anyway." We stared at the street for a moment. More brothels were opening their doors.

"Here," he said. "Give me the card." He wrote on the back with a fountain pen. "There will be a party, tomorrow, if you and your friend would like to join. I think you might find it interesting and it might help you make a few friends."

"I'll ask Aleta."

"Do."

"What's all this?" I asked, waving my head at the men in the street. It was pretty clear what was across the street.

"Obviously that and that are a *manoirs fermés*. There, is a games parlor. The cabaret adjoins the bar around the corner. Sometimes Lefebvre will put out his latest on the sidewalk, if he isn't too drunk. But it's too early for him, or the carts. The rest are private merchants and parlors. We're just off Montmartre. You should walk up the street sometime."

He paused, then gestured at the crowd in front of the bordello across from us. "These are men who like to get in first, myself included. You pay extra for that."

I really didn't understand most of what he said. What I did understand was that our street was going to be noisy, probably all night long. When I'd said goodnight and we turned to go in, I saw Sarah standing in the doorway staring across the street with wide eyes. Clearly she'd never encountered this before. Most docks have a red light district somewhere nearby, usually near the navy. These were merely a bit noisier than usual.

We went to bed. I had foolishly jumped to claim the second floor room when we arrived with its view of the street and now the noise, having ignored M. Palomer's warning. And of course my pillow let out a cloud of dust that left me sneezing. It was old, the feathers past all use. So I rolled up a petticoat and used that, drifting away, too tired to notice the music wafting through the streets.

I woke, yellow sunlight reflecting off the walls of the buildings across the street. Our windows were very dirty and brown. I think the previous owner had smoked a lot. I lay in the bed and stared at the cracked ceiling with glee. It was all mine. All that space and a bed so huge I could spread my arms and legs. And I didn't have to share any of it with anyone! Our crazy maid Sarah had gotten up early and cooked us breakfast. She came in with a tray. We had tea, eggs, toast, and my orange, already sectioned! I would have spun on

27

point if it wouldn't have endangered my tray and its blessed orange. It was clear that I was going to love France.

I looked at the man's card while I ate. It said: *Henri Marie Raymond de Toulouse-Lautrec-Monfa, Société des Artistes Indépendants.* Society of Independent Artists, I understood. He was an artist. That might make the party fun, but I would ask Aleta about it first. I'd never been to a party before. Not like this. I would definitely need her advice.

But first we had to decide if we were staying, then I had to write Lucien and Grandpa. Of course we needed baths too, and then what would we wear? I needed to go to the bank. We needed food. And where was the post office? Coal and wood, a new pillow, the list kept getting longer. I took the tray downstairs to the kitchen only to be intercepted by Sarah.

"No, no, Miss. That's my work," she said, as she took it from me. "I'll be going out later to buy food. Tell me if you need anything."

I started. "Christmas!" I needed to get Lucien a Christmas present! I had three weeks. And my parents too! Back on Red we didn't really buy presents but had a big dinner instead, but I was so far away. I had to do something. Maybe a picture.

I think she saw my panic. "Don't worry Miss. We'll get it all done."

I took another breath and said, "We may be going to a party tonight."

She frowned. "You've no clean dresses."

We didn't! They'd all been put off for way too long and nothing dries willingly in Paris during the winter. Not in a day.

She saw new panic rise again and cooed, "Don't worry. We'll see what can be done."

Downstairs it was warmer. My breath no longer fogged. Of course, Sarah had lit the stove. She cooked breakfast after all. She must have hauled coal up from the basement. When I had walked in, she had been washing the dishes and pots.

"I can help with that," I said.

And she stared back in horror, "Oh no. It's not a problem. But I think we could use a housekeeper."

She was right.

"What do they cost?

"In Belgium it depends on their duties, but here I don't know. This isn't a normal household."

"Then I'll leave it to you."

She beamed. "That's the right thing to say, Miss."

"We're going to need our bank. Do you know where it is?"

"No."

"The post office?"

"No, not yet, Miss."

Now she was fretting, so I shrugged and smiled. "We'll find them all and everything else. I wonder if the neighbors know where to find a coal man?"

"I knocked on their doors this morning, but no one answered."

Maybe later in the day, I thought. "Judging by the street last night, I think most people sleep late."

"Hello," Aleta said, in French, as she shuffled into the kitchen with her tray.

"No!" Sarah wailed, and went to grab it.

"We're going to get a housekeeper," I said.

"Can we afford it?" she asked.

"I think so, at least for a while. And I want to ask you about the party."

"Party?" She brightened.

"Yes, we've been invited to a party," and I pulled Henri's card from my pocket.

She eyed it, turning it over. "This sounds like fun."

"Do you think? I wanted to check with you."

"It's better than listening to the noise in the street."

"I slept through it."

"I don't have anything to wear," she frowned.

"We could wear our Rabbit dresses," I suggested. That seemed to vex Sarah, but we thought it silly. We were young. I didn't want to announce that the Rabbit was about, but then again, what good was it having incredible clothes if you never wear them? Especially to parties! And it was just a party.

"We would stand out," I said.

"Yes we would," Aleta grinned.

Sarah would not go. She actually crossed her arms. "I will not have the Rabbit bringing her maid to a party. It's not done."

And so she stayed. We had no trouble finding a carriage as there was a constant stream of them letting people on and off up and down our street. There were doorways with music on the next block and we could hear the cabaret. The street that looked so plain and rundown in the daytime was beautifully lit and full of people at night. We caught stares as we showed the driver the address and clopped away.

"Cali," Aleta said. "I want to stop for some coffee."

The moment she said it, I felt a yawn coming. It had been a long day with a lot of walking and hauling. Our first full day in Paris and already a party!

"That's a great idea." So I asked the driver.

He turned left at the next street down from ours. We could have walked! There were three coffee houses. When we asked how much, he waved us away and said, "It is nothing."

Inside, the waiter's eyes widened as we approached. We ordered two coffees and milk. People stared as we drank. When we tried to pay, the owner waved us away. "Anything for an enemy of the British," he said. And, our carriage driver was waiting outside for us! All this was nice, but I could see these dresses were clearly going to draw trouble.

The party was across the shining boat-lined Seine. Along its edge were brightly lit boats with smokestacks billowing smoke. I could see piles of clothing on their decks.

"Excuse me," I asked our driver. "What are those?"

"Laundry barges, Miss," he said as we rattled across the cobbled bridge. "They drag them upriver to where the water is clean." My dresses were down there.

We rode through traffic into a much nicer part of town, right by the Louvre. Across the river we clopped into a maze of narrowing streets, each one smaller than the last, until we came to a covered alley going right through the middle of a building. A tunnel really. A carriage and a car had just let people out and were pulling away, luckily going in the same direction we were because there was no room to pass. The covered alley was too narrow for carriages. We would have to proceed from there on foot.

I could hear music so we paid the driver, hoping we would find a carriage when the time came to go back. I wasn't sure I could find my way if we needed to. Even if it wasn't cloudy, I could barely see the sky between the buildings to get a baring.

The tunnel opened into an alley, or maybe a narrow courtyard, facing a tall whitewashed brick warehouse. The street sign at the end said it was the Street of the Dragon and according to the sign painted on the warehouse wall we were facing the Julian Academy, an art school. Milling about out front were young men and women dressed to varying degrees of formality, holding an odd assortment of cups, mugs, pipes, and cigarettes. I could see threadbare second hand suits mixed with the best silk finery lit only by the light spilling from a single doorway. I wasn't sure what to do. Aleta stopped with me and we stared together at the throng.

"This is going to be interesting," she said. "Artists can't be that different than musicians, can they?"

And here I was looking to her for advice! "I can hear people playing so there have to be musicians." I heard at least four. A violinist even.

"The worst that can happen is that they throw us out," she said.

"That would be unpleasant."

She sighed. "Come on," and she dragged me forward.

"I wonder if there's dancing?" I asked.

"You and your dancing."

"You just say that because you don't dance," I replied.

"True."

We walked forward, people looking up, many showing surprise, staring with frank attention. They parted to let us through.

I heard Aleta sigh to herself, "Maybe tonight."

I think she was lonely.

Inside, through large sliding wooden doors, we faced a large lantern lit room with several desks and file cabinets, an open office. But leaning against the walls were stacks of paintings, most seemingly unfinished or neglected, and shelves and the floor piled with a bewildering array of junk. Things like stuffed birds and pieces off of statues. A large block of stone sat on a pallet in the middle of the floor with a table cloth draped over it. On top was a punch bowl and an eclectic mix of cups and mugs.

In for a penny, in for a dollar, I thought. I walked up, several young men stepping aside, to reveal the woman manning the ladle. She stared at me, stopping halfway into a pour.

I held out my hand. "Bonjour, I'm Calista Carmichael. Henri told me there was a party here."

"Really?" She was blinking furiously.

"Yes." I looked at her with what hoped was sincerity. I mean, why would I lie?

"Really." She put down the ladle and shook my hand carefully. "Émile Sabouraud. This is Tony, Robert, and Jules." They shook our hands.

Then she poured me a mug of punch and asked, "Did you really bang Leopold?"

I broke out laughing, then answered, "No, but it was complicated. He really tried." Then I had to explain to Aleta who rolled her eyes.

"Does anyone speak English or German here?" Aleta asked.

"Germans and English aren't very popular around here, but there are a few Americans," she replied.

"Charles is Australian," Jules added.

"Yes, he is," Émile said.

Soon Aleta was being led away by an American named Frank to be introduced around and I was left to my fate in a gradually growing crowd of people with questions, many of them complicated. People had so many crazy ideas about me.

I would never have made it out of the front office if an instructor at the school, Susan, hadn't wanted to give me a tour. They had large glass roofed galleries for classrooms, the walls covered with mostly excellent artwork. I had to be careful as I moved about as everything was dirty. It was quite a trick in the bathroom. The sinks were full of paint despite the sign saying no washing brushes.

The musicians were set up on a platform in the center of the main gallery and I was watching them while trying to follow the conversation, and on my third cup of punch which tasted vaguely of licorice, when I realized that I was just a bit drunk. I suppose that's why they call it "punch". The musicians had seen me eying them because the violinist held his violin out and said, "Care to give it a try?"

"I'm not sure I can. I've had a bit to drink."

Then people were telling me, "Go on," and "We won't laugh."

"Maybe not much," someone mumbled.

So I said yes if someone could get me water or coffee. And I was up on the platform and Aleta was looking at me like I was out of my mind. I think she was thinking it was time she dragged me home, and she was probably right.

His violin was different. It was only the third one I'd ever played. It was shorter than mine, but it wasn't the size. It was definitely its soul. I could tell this wouldn't be love as much as a Sunday dance. I asked if they knew any jigs and we negotiated until we settled on *The Flowers of Edinburgh*, which is all about emptying chamber pots if you didn't know. That's what being drunk in front of strangers will get you.

We played, poking at each other, completely silly. But people danced anyway. Then it was *The Penny Wedding* and someone brought me more coffee, which helped a lot.

"Play them something serious," Aleta said, sitting on the edge of the stage. She was always setting me up for the crowds. "Play Bach."

"I'm tired of Bach," I whined. But I thought about it and decided on Grieg. I don't generally like Grieg. The piece is way too happy. Repetitious too, which is good because no one knows if you cut parts out, especially in a crowd like that, and it has is lots of spots to stop if you get fed up. I hadn't played it in a couple of years, but I was drunk enough to give it a go, Saint-Saëns be damned if I wasn't going to play with it.

I announced, "Drunken Edvard Grieg." And everyone cheered. I could see Henri in back standing on a table. He smiled and made a face, which made me laugh. He was sketching. There are paintings of me, which what comes of performing in an art school.

I launched into it.

The thing is technically complex, but it's all wasted. No one knows you're being clever. It's all lost in the safety of major chords. It's that way because it's supposed to be charming, which is fine if you're a young girl reciting for the school's board members but this was a party! I chopped and played with it and frankly made some of it up because I couldn't remember exactly how it went. And people seemed happy, which is the point.

And that was it. No more for me! I climbed down and accepted my refilled coffee cup, and then another cup of punch after. I do love licorice.

I have no idea when we got home. The street seemed less busy. I had no way to tell because we didn't have a clock.

Chapter 4 – Independent Women

We made the papers again, not that I saw them. We didn't know how to buy milk let alone newspapers. But I have since learned that there was great speculation about why we chose to go to that party. Julian is a fringe school, quite out of favor with proper society. One of few that will seriously teach women. Perhaps I was in Paris to lead a women's revolt! And who was that mysterious German-speaking Brit who's always in the background?

The next morning, judging by the stray rays of sunshine peeping from between the clouds, we didn't get up until noon which threw off my whole day. It's funny because I not only didn't know what time it was, I didn't know what day it was either.

"It's Sunday, Miss," Sarah said as she brought in my tray with my lunch.

"I've got to get up," I moaned.

"Yes, Miss."

I really did. I'd gotten some suggestions for photographers that were nearby from people at the party, written on the backs of cards mixed in the stack I'd collected. How late do photographers stay open? I also had no idea how long it took to make a photograph, but I was already past sending it to Boston by any means but airmail. And I was sure it was going to be expensive.

But first, most of all, I really needed a bath.

"I'm hoping to see a photographer today."

Sara frowned.

I realized why. "My dresses!"

"I sent everything out with the laundress. Nothing will be ready for two days at least. Most will take three."

I frowned. I felt ill. I could tell it would be a difficult day.

"Wait. Someone's cleaning them? How are we paying for this? We haven't found the bank."

She looked worried. "Your Lucien left you a housing budget."

I growled and flopped back on my pillow, "Lucien!" Wait, pillow? There were two.

"I wasn't to tell you, but we had to have clean clothes and I can't do your dresses in the sink. I couldn't wait for the bank. And it wouldn't be right for you to be walking around in dirty dresses."

"How much did he give us?"

"I'm not to tell you." She had started cringing, which is not pretty.

"Lucien! This is just kind of thick headed thing Emma warned me about!"

So now I was spooky, tall tales, bloody, prison, kept woman Cali! Without clothes to wear, we had to take the day off. Really, I had to send the picture air mail anyway.

"A picture." Sara looked worried.

I stared at her.

"Well, Miss. We'll have to get your hair done."

And then I thought, what dress would I wear? Maybe my ball gown? How did I want to look for my parents? What would cause the least worry?

"What can I wear to the bath?" I couldn't wear my spy dresses.

"You still have a dress from the trip that wasn't too bad."

Not too blood-stained. At least not much. Just tea down the back.

Walking around brought distress, but according to Aleta I was hungover. She agreed a hot bath would help. I hoped so, because I wasn't sure I should have eaten lunch.

And so, to that end, we found ourselves walking down the street, crunching sweet yellow apples from *Limousin* we bought from M. Gagne, our grocer. But I haven't told you anything about our street yet have I?

The first thing you should know about Paris streets is that every street is a village, with everyone knowing everyone else's business. I couldn't have picked a better city or better street. Rue Antoinette was already long awake, showing its day face, its citizens out and about. Mme. Touchard, who I didn't know yet, was out on her balcony smoking. She lives with her brother and sister, both of whom dislike her Turkish tobacco, thus she stands on the balcony. I was not yet a real member of the neighborhood, but she gave me a little nod anyway. M. Pretre's wine shop was open early. He and his wife had probably had a fight. It was still way too early for red light shops like the lingerie shop and massage parlors, but M. Delattre's tea shop was open, if I wanted to stop and read the paper. M. Barnier's pastry shop was too. I'd had pastry for breakfast, a croissant still warm from the oven with sweet butter from Normandy, and steam pressed coffee. Sigh. I saw M. Cazal and his dog down the street, but he was walking rather than begging. It was early for him too. My never seen neighbor had a wagon parked in front. The door was open and I was tempted to look in, but it was for the best that we hadn't. We really didn't understand yet. They were smugglers, just another set of neighbors.

Many people grew things and kept livestock in their courtyards so you always heard a rooster or two in the morning. Sometimes it was pigeons racing overhead. And then there were the cats and dogs. The city issued tags and came through every couple of years to clean out the strays, but they missed a lot and many wandered the streets. Even unowned, they made friends and begged food. Every morning at dawn, the sweepers came through to clear out the dung and trash. Followed by our gendarmes who kept order, but also worked for whoever would pay them, but always with the best of intentions and the interests of the neighborhood at heart, bless them.

The entry to these communities was through the shop doors. They were the neighborhood's meeting places. The bathhouse was four doors down, two houses joined with apartments upstairs, the sign in front said it was closed from four to eight for dinner and from three in the morning to eight for cleaning. It was our very first shop door, where were would make our first introductions.

They had a waiting room and desk in front, in the lobby. There were no men present that first time, just three women.

"You're new," said one.

"Cali," I replied with a smile.

"Lilli," she replied.

"You're the ones who moved in down the street, aren't you?" asked another.

"We did," and then I had to translate for Aleta.

"She doesn't speak French?"

"No, she's English."

"My English is very bad," said another.

Aleta brightened, "You speak English?"

"A little."

And then Aleta set to work trying to milk that little she had out of her, coming up with quite a bit of French on her own as well. She had clearly been working on it.

"You're American?" Lilli asked me.

"Yes."

"Are you here looking for work?" she asked.

"No. We want to go to music school."

"You chose a house far away from them. They're all across the river."

"We didn't know where to go," I shrugged. I wondered if we'd have to move.

"Most girls come here looking for work. That or they're bohemian artists." Then she smiled. "Or both."

"Bohemian?" I asked.

"Free spirits. They fight with society."

"Then I suppose we're bohemians."

"I thought so." Her voice trailed away.

"So, what are you?"

"Oh, I'm definitely both."

"Any ones?" the man at the desk called.

"What's a one?" I asked Lilli.

"Fresh tub. They call them first because they can charge more money."

"Oh, us!" I called back, pointing at Aleta and me.

She smirked at me and said, "Maybe not so bohemian."

"Bohemians like dirty water?" I asked. Being bohemian sounded fun but now I was worried I'd committed some sort of faux pas.

"No," she laughed. "Bohemians have no money."

"Oh." I thought for a moment, then asked, "So you're here to work?"

"Yes." Her answer sounded tentative.

"Where?"

"Across the street," she replied.

It took me a second. "Really?"

She nodded, looking a little worried.

"That's incredible!"

She looked surprised.

"We had bordellos on the docks, but Pa never let me go near."

"A bordello is a *lupanar*?"

"I don't know. They don't teach you street French in class."

She laughed. I think she was relieved.

"I think Henri called them closed mansions."

"Henri? The short one?"

"Yes."

"He's funny. I enjoy his visits."

Thinking about the face he made, made me smile. "Yes, he is."

"Ready!" called the man at the desk.

We stepped up.

"For the two of you?" We nodded. "A franc."

"Don't overcharge them!" Lilli called. Then others piped up in outrage too.

The man rolled his eyes. "Fifty centimes." Then spat at the woman, "No visits from me if I don't make money." We gave him some of our worn coins. Their money still had Napoleon on them! He handed us two chits and towels.

We said thank you to them all and then walked in through the hall curtain to a corridor lined with doors. The air was warm and damp. An older woman had just stepped out through one of the doors carrying a bucket and brushes and motioned for us to come.

"This way," she said. "You have thirty minutes or we charge you extra."

We walked forward with her holding a door open.

"You in here and you are over there."

Inside my room it was dark, damp, and too warm. The sconce flame in the small room overwhelmed the narrow space, but steam still rose from the tub so it was hotter. The tub was concrete with two steps leading up to it. I guessed you sat with your back to the door. They had hooks for your things to keep them off the wet floor and a bench to sit on while you took off your shoes. It's wise to wear old clothes when you go to these things. You need to bring soap and a towel too. They give you cheap ones. My towel was very thin and scratchy from too much washing. And bring a hair brush too. But at this point I was just learning.

Bad soap and scratchy towel aside, it felt glorious to be clean, and cold as we walked back with our wet hair.

That evening, when they opened, we saw Lilli at the window and called out to her, "Hello Lilli!"

She smiled and waved, calling back, "Hello Cali! Hello Aleta!" No Henri waiting in the shadows though. I suppose he was hungover too.

I felt so much better the next day. I avoided the punch at the ball in the Congo and now I knew it was for the best. It's far worse than wine.

That morning we heard the coal man out in the street calling "*Charbon!*" I jumped to the window. He was clopping slowly along, his horse as soot black as his coal. It came bagged, the sacks piled in the back. Sarah came out to meet him and he lifted one almost as big as himself. They took it under the window where I couldn't see, to the coal chute.

A lot of things are sold from wagons in Paris which saves hauling things home. They travel up and down the streets, calling out their wares. Over the course of the day, we bought bread, produce, sundries like lilac and baking soda, and especially wood! We would have a fire that night.

I was homebound and it was hard to sit still. We had all of Paris out there and I was back to sawing at Saint-Saëns. Aleta and I practiced self-defense without Sarah, who was eternally busy. I was pretty much completely bored out of my mind until, finally, relief came in the form of callers in the late afternoon. My first ever!

Aleta and I were working on Vivaldi in the parlor.

"You can't push those like that. They need to be crisp. Precision." I was chiding her just like Mrs. Hartnoll!

"But it's boring that way."

"People will know. There are ways you can play and ways you can't."

She rolled her eyes, just like me!

We heard a knock at the door. My first thought was Lucien, but then I remembered the bomb and jumped into the hallway to stop Sarah.

"No, Miss. It's my work!"

But I held my finger to my lips and shook my head. Aleta had gone for the window and was peeking out at the street.

"It's Henri," she said in a loud whisper, which brought a grin from me and we all relaxed. "But he has friends."

It was enough that it was Henri so I retired to the parlor, letting Sarah go on. She came back with one of Henri's cards. It was just like in a dime novel. We laughed.

"Let them in," Aleta said. In French! She is so good.

"Oh no, Miss," she chided. "You're hardly dressed to meet callers."

I thought about the messy art school and laughed.

"They're artists. I don't think they'll care." I looked at Aleta, who shrugged, then added in English, "Let's see them!"

Sarah fretted for a second, but turned to get them, coming back with Henri and two friends. I stood to greet them and we visited. They were women, Cecilia and Fannie, both Americans! They were from Pennsylvania and Virgina. Aleta had met them at the party. Cecilia was a painter and Fannie did photography, but was learning to paint. Language is such a chore. Poor Henri spoke no English and

41

poor Aleta spoke little French, so someone was always left out.

We all compared bits of our lives and made small talk. It was wonderful making friends without something exploding or someone getting killed. Sarah brought tea. The best part was that Fannie could help me with my picture! She would drop by the next day to tell me when. She had to make sure of studio space and make plates, and I needed my dresses. By the way, Fannie wasn't wearing a corset either. I knew I would like her.

Cecilia was incredible too. She came to Paris all by herself to study art because they don't allow women to study anatomy and figure painting in the U.S. She worked her way over as an artist all by herself!

"Painting dishes!" she spat. "It was horrible. But we have a studio here. Four of us, just for women."

"I want to see it!"

"Me too," Aleta added.

She had taken a sip of tea, setting her cup down. "Any time you want. Ask though, just to make sure we're there."

Then she gave me a hard look. "I think it's that touch of red in your hair." I must have looked surprised, because she continued, "That makes you fight. What we are is in our flesh, given to us by our parents and ancestors."

"That makes sense," Aleta said. "You haven't see her Ma swing an ax."

Which got us laughing. They thought Aleta was joking. Then Henri said he wanted to take us to the theater on Friday, which had to be fun, so we said yes.

Sarah set up the fireplace. It's called banking, I guess like a river bank. Anyway, when she lit it, the room began to fill with smoke. Damper be damned, our chimney was blocked! Sarah ran in from the kitchen with a pot of water and tossed it on, letting loose sooty steam which ended our visit. It was a mess, but funny, at least that's what I was thinking as we aired out the house.

That evening I saw Lilli again and said hello across the street, my window to hers, which was maddening. What good is it waving hello from windows, especially when one of you is naked? I got up and walked downstairs.

"Where are you going," Aleta asked, as I walked by the parlor. I think she was as bored as I was.

"I'm going to leave a note for Lilli," I replied.

"You're going in there?" She looked surprised. I supposed I was too, but I'm not used to sitting around. It was driving me crazy.

"There's no other way to talk. I want to ask her out to lunch."

She frowned, then said, "I'll go with you." I think she wanted to see inside too.

"Okay. Do you have anything to write with?"

Neither of us did. There wasn't a pencil or piece of paper in the house, which reminded me that I needed to find the Post Office and tell Lucien and Grandpa my address. Setting up a house from scratch is very complicated.

"Can I help you find something Miss?" Sarah asked, as I rattled about the kitchen.

"There's nothing to write on," I complained. "Maybe I'll go up to the boulevard."

"It's dark. Everything will be closed." Then she gave me a look, "Why do you need it now?"

"I want to invite a friend to lunch." I was being evasive, which kind of bothered me.

"Can it wait until tomorrow?"

"I suppose," I mumbled. "I bet they have some."

"Who?"

"Across the street."

"Miss, you shouldn't be seen in places like that."

"Sarah, we can't be bohemians if we're afraid of bordellos."

"Bohemians?"

"Free spirits," I said flightily.

"Is that why you hate corsets?"

"Definitely."

She laughed nervously. We left to cross the gas-lit road with Sarah watching us from the door. I think she torn between propriety and wanting to go – and afraid too.

The men who waited for opening time had already gone in so the doorway was clear, except for one man who looked at us and turned away for some reason. Perhaps we embarrassed him. Inside it was warm. Maybe too warm, but then we hadn't had any heat in our house yet, so maybe it was us. There were sofas, chairs, and a bar. Really, it wasn't that different from our house except that the front door went right into the parlor. Like a hotel lobby.

A small thin man with a high pitched voice that practically sang met us at the door and said, "Hello, may I help you?"

"Yes. We would like to leave a note for Lilli."

"Really?" He seemed pleased. "You're from across the street aren't you? If you give it to me, I'll make sure she gets it." The men sitting on the chairs, some with drinks, were trying not to stare at us, and us back at them.

"The problem is that we've nothing to write with yet."

"Oh! I can take care of that. Sit down and I'll be right back."

"Would you like something to drink?" the man at the bar asked.

Aleta caught that and replied in French, "Café ou thé?" That made me smile.

The man seemed caught off guard and shook his head slightly no. Two men came walking down the stairs adjusting their clothes, giving us stares as they left.

We plunked down on a couch. Another man came in, passing the two going out. Then he stopped and looked around with a frown.

Clearing his throat, he said, "Ladies," tipping his hat. "How can you possibly have been ignored? My name is Maurice."

"Cali," I said to him with a smile. He seemed nice.

"Cali," Aleta mumbled, poking me with her elbow.

"What?" I said.

"Tell him we don't work here."

Maurice clearly didn't understand English and blinked.

"Oh!" I think I blushed. "It's a pleasure to meet you, but we don't work here," I stammered.

Now it was Maurice's turn to blush. "Goodness."

Some of the other men chuckled.

"I found paper," the small man said, walking back into the room.

Maurice looked so taken aback that I couldn't help but smile and said, "But I appreciate the complement."

Maurice took a seat and several women came downstairs wearing entirely flimsy night dresses and began sitting on laps. I recognized one from the baths. She shot me a smile. We wrote our note, which was easy: *Lilli, Want to go out to lunch? Cali.*

Then it was back across the street where we sat laughing with relief. It had been fun.

Chapter 5 – Photographs

It didn't take long to realize the shortcomings of our house. The obvious lack of heat and hot water. But then there was the state of the carpets, paint, and woodwork as well. We didn't even have a way to hang a door lamp. The hook had broken off sometime in the past. At least we didn't have rats, bugs, ghosts, or scary neighbors. Or perhaps they hadn't shown themselves yet, which is practically as good as long as they stayed that way.

People were always walking or rolling down our street during the day yelling, hawking their goods and services. It was late morning the next day when I heard, "*Ramoneur!*" I didn't know the word, but Sarah did. It's chimney sweep. She jumped up from her sheet folding and ran for the door. We put down our instruments and hit the windows. He'd been walking down the street with his pack, chain, and poles.

He was a big thick man, already sooty from an earlier job. Sarah bravely bargained with him. She was small and blond, practically shining next to his big black frame. He had to bend over a little to look at her. They settled and he came in.

He saw us and tipped his hat hello. "Ladies."

Setting down his rucksack, his torso still wrapped in chain and brushes, he began pulling out smudged bedsheets.

Stopping with a sheet half out of his bag, he eyed us both. "Best if you leave," he said.

"I'll watch him misses," Sarah said from the doorway.

So we retired with our instruments to the warmer kitchen, sitting at the table amidst the laundry racks and drying clothes. We'd barely begun when we heard a knock on the front door. Sarah had gone upstairs with our sweep so we jumped for it. It was Fannie.

"We're getting our chimney swept so we can't invite you in." She was smoking a cigarette too, which are difficult to avoid in Paris. Impossible in restaurants.

She smiled. "It's about time, I think."

I saw several girls hovering about across the street. I was wondering if they had come to Antoinette's looking for work.

"About the day . . ." she started.

"Lilli!" Aleta called.

I realized that one of the girls was Lilli. She didn't say hello. Had we done something? She looked angry, but she walked over.

"*Bonjour*," she said. She didn't look at Fannie.

"Lilli, this is Fannie. She's going to take my picture," I said.

They greeted, but seemed reluctant to make eye contact. Weird.

"We're going out to lunch," I added, then tried to pick a neutral subject. "And maybe I'll find out where the Post Office is."

The Fannie continued, "I'm thinking Friday, in the morning?" We had switched to French.

Henri was taking us to the theater on that night, but otherwise we were free.

"Our laundry should be back by then. What should we wear?"

"Several changes I think. Those dresses of yours at least, and your instruments."

I rolled my eyes. Aleta did too after I explained. "Why those?" she asked.

"It's part of the deal with the studio," Fannie replied.

"Oh," Lilli chimed in. "They want to sell your picture!"

47

"Really?" I asked.

"You would get a cut of the profits naturally," Fannie explained.

"How much of a cut?" Lilli asked, suddenly frowning, finally looking at Fannie.

"The usual 20%."

"20%?" Lillie snapped back. "That's nonsense. You know these will sell."

"Sell?" I asked.

"They sell them. I've done this before."

"30%?" Fannie countered. She clearly wasn't a bargainer.

"Better," Lilli responded.

"I'll have to ask." It was Fannie's turn to frown.

"Do," Lilli replied coolly.

"Do you have ball gowns?" Fannie asked.

"We do."

"Bring them."

"Look out," Lilli whispered.

All I wanted was a picture to send to Ma and Pa. But then again, it might be interesting and we could always use money. But I asked Aleta as well and she agreed, so I did too, and Fannie left leaving us an address, a time, and a smile. She'd written it on the back of her card. We really needed to have some calling cards of our own.

Please judge us with care. We were very young, stranded in Paris with fistfuls of money and people offering us more. How could we not go a bit crazy? We thought they were just pictures. We didn't know they would change everything. That they would turn us into commodities.

When Fannie had gone I asked Lilli, "Are you angry at us?"

She beamed, "No! It's just that she's a customer."

That threw me. It never occurred to me that women might go to a bordello. Lilli didn't mind about soot and she wasn't smoking, so we invited her in to tell Sarah we were going out. The sweep worked fast. He had already poked out my fireplace and was working on Aleta's and Sarah's. Sara said she would be fine, but then Aleta had a thought.

"How are we going to know when to go on Friday?"

"Sarah. We have an appointment on Friday, but how will we know when to go?"

"You need a clock," Lilli replied with authority. "I know where to find them, but they're expensive."

"We do need a clock," Sarah added.

"How much is expensive?" I asked.

"Maybe twenty five to as much as you want to spend."

She seemed to feel that that was a lot, but I had two thousand francs in my purse and lot more upstairs.

"Well," I replied. "Then that's what it costs."

She looked surprised, but said nothing. We left and went east towards the park, which was only a block away. Up on a hill, nearby just above the park, they were building a big church. The street in that direction had less business and more houses with lots of kids playing in the street, despite the cold. They block the sidewalks with their games, when it's not already blocked by vendor wagons, and construction equipment. Between there and our house, down on Antoinette, we had a grocer on the corner, who I told you about, and a cheese shop, a butcher, and further on, a baker. All very handy. You smell the food all the time. In the morning they're making bread and in the evening it's herring and cauliflower. The smells fill the street.

"Did you know you live in Pigalle?" Lilli asked as we walked.

"Is that a red light district?" She didn't know the English reference, but got the meaning.

"Yes," she sighed.

"I don't mind. But we're far away from the music schools."

I noted a *quincaillerie* as we walked, which is where you buy pieces for houses and surely would be handy.

"But you are near the music stores," Lilli replied.

"Really?" I asked. "Where?"

"The other side of Clichy."

This I had to explain to Aleta who was rapt in concentration, trying to follow our conversation. She really is good at languages.

"When it's warmer, the park is full of artists and musicians." Lilli added.

It sounded worth waiting for, but that afternoon we were there for the shops surrounding it. I saw a stationary store, but Lilli was aiming for the pawn shops. She said there used to be a windmill on top of the hill, which must have been fun. But then my stomach rumbled. It turned out we were all hungry, so we ate first. It was our treat for her help. She offered no objections. She was and still is, after all, a bohemian and what kind of bohemian passes up free food?

Afterwards we were walking to the stationary store first, because that's easier than carrying a clock around, when she asked me, "So you aren't going to ask me about me being a *putain*?"

"Why? I figured it was a job."

"Some seem to feel they need to lecture."

"A job is a job. You have to eat. I've been living next door to them most of my life."

She thought on that for a bit, then asked, "Are you the Rabbit?"

Then it was my turn to think.

"Yes."

"Are you hiding?"

"I don't know. I guess we're not doing a very good job if we are."

She smiled. "No."

We bought a mantle clock that didn't make too much noise. It was low and wide, which in my estimation made it hard to knock over, and it was beautiful. Red wood with brass numbers on its face and carved swirling leaf patterns. Sure, it had a "dent", and the back was missing. But, it wound and it ticked, and we paid only a hundred francs.

We proudly carried our purchases home. Of course we didn't know what time to set our clock to. We set all our ship's clocks every time we docked. Pa would carry the time back from the harbormaster with his pocket watch. The harbormaster got it from the train station. It's important for navigation, but here in Paris, according to Lilli, everyone set their clocks on Sunday with the general consensus of the church bells. We used M. Gagne's best estimate when we set it. Once wound, it filled our silent parlor with ticking.

That night we had a fire in our fireplace and we were warm.

Friday was our photo appointment. I took my letters for Lucien, the Carrigan School, and Grandpa to drop off at the Post Office on the way to the studio.

We had clean things to change in to. The laundresses pick up and deliver clothing in big long flat baskets on Mondays and Thursdays. Your clothes arrive folded and clean, then you fill the basket back up with dirty things for her next pickup. We took our ball gowns, nice dresses, and spy dresses, all crisp and neatly folded, packed in our shopping bags, along with shoes, brushes, jewelry, and Sarah to help us change, together in the carriage.

The studio was off Avenue Maine on the other side of the river, in a very nice building, in a very nice part of town! The road out front was full of steam cars – nice ones. And men came out to help with our things, which was a little surprising. We were met by a man with a clip board.

"You're right on time," He said. "Which of you is Calista and which is Aleta?"

We raised our hands in response to our names as we climbed the stairway.

"Excellent. And this is?"

"Sarah, our maid," I said.

"We have maids and hairdressers already, but she can help."

All I could think was, *what was going on?* Did I want to be involved in this? But they were moving us along so fast.

We were given contracts to sign. We were getting crazy forty thousand franc advances! I had to put my foot down on exclusivity opting instead for three months. What if we were in another country? I couldn't not get my picture taken!

And the studio itself was like half a parlor within a parlor. I mean it was a fake parlor, just to be in the background. The studio had a high ceiling, which was a help because the limelight was very warm. We had a hairdresser with an assistant and a maid for each of us, which we insisted must defer to Sarah. They couldn't let my ponytail alone. I got a better ribbon – pink that curled like my hair. They said the color would look better on film.

Fannie brought in some men, our *investors*, to say hello. I will describe them as old, well dressed, and non-descript. I wouldn't have looked at them twice on the street. But I only just got a look before it was time to begin.

We stood apart, together, sometimes playing our instruments in the "parlor". Fannie said she made "fast plates" for us so we wouldn't have to sit still. We sat for portraits, me smiling for Ma and Pa. And then came their surprise. They had someone dressed up like Leopold, white uniform, moustache and all. How had they known? They wanted me to waltz!

"This is out of the question!" Aleta snapped, in English.

I was sitting staring at him in shock. All I could say was, "No."

"It says clearly in the contract that we get three poses of our choice." One of the men had my contract.

Aleta looked at Sarah. "Tell them she has nervous shock." But Sarah didn't understand. "The soldier's terror," Aleta tried again.

She tried, calling it "soldier's fright."

I couldn't speak. I just stared at him.

The fake Leopold stared back at me with a perplexed look. "Honestly my dear, do I really look that much like him?"

"Don't call me that!" I snapped with venom. That's just how he would have said it. All I could see was him standing there, our dance, the war closing in, the darkness pressing all around me. Black stick shadows were running back and forth across the burning walls. I wasn't even in the same room with them.

"Honestly Fannie, we should have warned her," Leopold said, with a worried look. "I think we've struck a nerve. I think we should skip this one." But it was too late. I was gone.

"Cali." Aleta kneeled next to me drying tears, trying to get my attention. But my eyes were locked on a Leopold in another world.

"I'm convinced," one of the men sitting in the back said.

"Me too," said another.

Fannie snapped a picture.

When we got home, there was a card stuck in our door. It said, in English, "Aleta, would you like to go out to lunch?" It was from someone named Frank. Aleta had a gentleman caller! But then I realized that he couldn't have known our address unless Henri told him. We couldn't have everyone knowing where we lived. We needed to find Henri. The problem was that although he knew where we lived, we didn't know his address or how to contact him.

Fannie came by with prints the next day. Apparently she had

been up all night. She wanted our opinions and permission.

"I'm so very sorry about the Leopold model," she stammered. It was her third apology.

I laughed them off, but it had been a nervous laugh.

"Honestly, I'm no judge," I replied, holding the stack of pictures. "I trust your judgement. But I think I would like to send this one to my parents." It was one of Aleta and me, playing together. It was nice. We'd forgotten the studio and seemed so happy. "May I have this one? I need something for Christmas."

"Of course you can have it. I can always make another. Take any you want." Then she stopped and thought. "Take them all," and she gave me the stack. "But there's one I would like to keep for my personal collection. I didn't show it to the studio. No one will ever see it." She reached in her bag and pulled out another.

"I'll destroy it if you ask."

There was a girl in a ball gown sitting in a chair, Aleta kneeling next to her, Sarah reaching for her from the side. She looked so small. Her eyes had a haunted look, staring at something not in the room, tears running down her cheeks.

As I looked at her, I could feel the tears again.

"No," I said. "Keep it."

"Really?" Aleta said. "Are you sure about this?"

"It's just a picture."

Fannie frowned, but put it back in her bag, then pulled out several sheets of paper.

"We need you to sign this so we can deposit directly to your bank account." I had an account, but I'd never been to the bank.

I read it. It was straight forward. A standard form.

"And this." She slid over a second sheet. "This authorizes us to use outside printing houses."

This was more complicated.

"We anticipate sales outstripping our capacity."

The contract stipulated that additional costs incurred would be split between Fannie's company and me. When did Fannie have a company? *Johnson Entreprises.*

"No," I said.

Her eyebrows went up.

"But I would be willing to invest in expansion."

Then her eyes filled with shark-like amusement. I was reminded of Vic.

"A partnership," she replied, as if testing the word. "It would be nice, but I can't."

She reached out and took my hand.

"I have nothing to expand. Everything belongs to someone else." She squeezed it lightly before letting it go.

Chapter 6 – Stepping Out

We had no idea what to wear to a theatre. Not having a lot to choose from, we finally decided that it was going to be formal and chose our ball gowns. But when Henri showed up, he just laughed.

"I should have told you!" he said, then broke out in a smile. "If you don't mind, I can help you select."

Allowing a strange man into my closet. Even I know that's a bit forward. But considering my upbringing, I didn't blink an eye.

"Sure!" I said.

Aleta gave me a squint, but followed. Sarah gawked at us as we went upstairs. I threw open my wardrobe doors and showed him my meager selection.

He gave them a round of serious inspection and then pulled them out one by one until he settled on my sea blue dinner dress Gustav had made for me. "This is far too nice." He seemed clearly torn. "But it's too good to miss. Just be careful backstage." He stared at it for a second more, then thrust it towards me. "You'll stun everyone."

Backstage?

"Tell him to pick one for me," Aleta said. "Stunning people might be fun."

He picked another Gustav, her midnight blue one. I was going to skip my pearls until Aleta pulled out her necklace and earrings. I considered that a challenge.

We clopped towards the boulevard with Henri sitting between us, top hat in lap, looking smug, until his smile dropped and he sat up. "This won't do!"

"What?"

"It's nothing. A change in plans." He pulled out his watch and squinted at it.

I hoped they were quick plans because our dresses were not built for warmth. We had only lite wraps.

We pulled up at a café and got out. Paying the driver, he said, "No more tonight."

We were going to need transportation to the theater and I thought this unwise. The café looked unremarkable as well, and the street was dark. Dark streets are generally unsafe for women to travel in Paris.

Wait. You think I mean the streets are full of crime? Nonsense. It's the cobbles and our heels. You can twist an ankle.

I heard music coming from *below* the cafe, which was strange. Henri saw me look at the café and smirked, shaking his head.

"One must explore to enjoy Paris," Henri said. "In this case we must descend." He held out his elbows and we laughed and put ours through his, walking down a stairway that led to a basement. "Besides, if you're going to live in Pigalle, then you, of all people, are going to need to know him, and he you."

We should have asked who.

We met a couple coming up, leaving, and had to turn to the side to let them pass, which was funny. Henri is so short and poor Aleta had the high side. But Henri wouldn't let go of her. He wanted to make an entrance. Above the door, lit by a lone lamp, it said, "*La Pègre*", a word I didn't know at the time but would not have been reassured by if I had.

Henri knocked with his cane, the man opening it nodding to Henri. The landing inside was very small and crowded, a walled in bit of basement. Especially crowded with the man watching it occupying most of the space. He was very large.

"Ah, Henri!" he said. "It's been awhile."

"Paris is such a wide plate to sample."

"Yes, of course. But you know ours is best. Who are your lady friends?"

"Cali," I said.

"Aleta."

The doorman answered, "It's a pleasure to have our lowly . . ." Henri snorted. ". . . establishment blessed," then rolled his eyes. He and Henri had been through this before. But then he frowned and looked at me again.

We stood for a second, Henri smiling back at him like he knew some joke. Aleta was looking back and forth at everyone.

"Benoit," Henri said, gently. The doorman blinked. "We'll need a car."

"Of course," he smiled at Henri. "Have fun."

Henri was definitely smug.

We walked down rough stone steps, cut through raw limestone, with echoing music and warmth drifting up from below. At the bottom was a crude candle lit stone room edged with wooden coat racks. A man took our wraps and Henri's coat, hat, and cane. The restaurant entrance was carved through what had to have been the base of a very old wall. Inside, a flat stone quay stretched around a stretch of water punctuated by arched stone columns. It looked as old as Cadiz. We had only the candlelight from the tables to light things. The room echoed with the murmur of voices and music that drifted across the water from a string quartet.

"*Très bon*," Aleta said.

Henri grinned. "This is one of my favorites. It's part of the catacombs. The undercity. You could die getting lost in the tunnels."

A waiter with a table cloth over his arm and menu cards bowed before leading us to a table, tossing the tablecloth over it as we arrived. He and Henri held our chairs for us as we sat.

"Henri," I said. "This is really too nice." It had to cost!

He shook his head. "It isn't nice enough."

"And weren't we going to a theater?" Aleta added.

"It's far too early."

He was looking at the wine list as he talked and started.

"An 88 Bordeaux! A Saint Croix. Roman roots surviving the second grafting after the great blight. It will be soft, slightly sweet. Perfect with this stonework and you two."

I actually tried to translate that for Aleta.

"How did he learn this?" Aleta asked.

"It helps to be French, to be raised with it," He said. "And it helps to be a count who can afford it."

"You're a count?" I asked.

"Did you think I got this name that can hardly fit on a card by making chairs?"

That got me laughing and Aleta impatient because she wanted to laugh too.

"How is your French coming?" Henri asked Aleta.

"It is coming, but I will need time." She said it French. I was grinning. If only she could get Vivaldi that fast.

"Ah, French with an accent," he said wistfully. "So exotic."

To be clear, she knew some already before we came to France. But her grasp of languages has always been remarkable.

The waiter came and Henri ordered the wine. They brought us bread, still warm. It was those funny tasting long thin loaves I had in Le Havre. But they tasted good with wine, which was as perfect as Henri had predicted.

We were laughing at Henri's jokes, which he seemed to weave out of thin air, when we were joined by an elderly man. He still had all his gray hair, which he combed back from his forehead. He was trim, wearing a clearly expensive suit.

"Do you mind if I join you Henri? My evening could use some brightening."

"Jean-Paul! It would be an honor. This is Calista Carmichael and Aleta . . . I don't know your last name," he said, wincing at the last.

"It's just Aleta," she replied.

"Ange was right," Jean-Paul said with wonder in his eyes. "It really is you. I'll have to hang a sign on the wall. And you both are everything I've heard and more." Then he bent down and kissed our hands, his lips just missing the skin, as is proper. All these complements. They clearly knew how to make girl shine.

Aleta said something to him in Spanish and he smiled and replied.

Henri laughed. "Now we all have someone we can't speak to."

Jean-Paul left when they brought our food, which was for the best because he had a cigar he clearly wanted to light. He owned a lot of restaurants, including the one we ate at. Henri called him a *Parrain*, which I regret I didn't ask him to explain. He seemed to find our landing in Pigalle and our claim of being bohemians to be very amusing. I had to admit that I did too, but it had advantages beyond the constant police presence and friends like Lilli.

Waiting in the street for us was a steam carriage, this time with a closed top. I guess he wanted to make an entrance at the theater too. He was making it a big night.

The *Théâtre des Variétés* , the Theatre of Variety, is a tall gray stone pillared building lit by big lamps hanging down between the columns in front. Upstairs, above the columns, is a balcony where we could see people in beautiful clothing smoking and drinking.

Pulling up in a jet of steam and the clatter of ratcheted breaks, we were helped out by a footman who had been waiting for such as us. The sidewalk and tree lined street around us was full of people, the street itself a bouquet of carriage and shop lights. We were adjusting our clothing, getting ready to walk, when Henri again stopped.

"I've made a mistake!"

"Oh Henri," I said, and then "he's made another mistake," to Aleta.

"This is a comedy theatre. Aleta will understand nothing!"

"I'll be fine, Henri," Aleta said.

"No, no. We can do better. But we can go in and mingle for a bit. It's early."

People seemed to be mingling out in front too. It was like a big party with more and more people joining as cars and carriages pulled up. We sighed, and followed him up the steps, holding his arms, drawing stares.

I have since come to understand that it wasn't a large theater by Paris standards, but it was my first and to my eyes then, it seemed huge and magnificent. Part of its draw was its intimacy, specializing in comedy. The players and the audience are never far apart, each as one with the humor as it unfolds.

Checking our wraps at the cloak room, we entered the lobby, which was covered in red velvet and great single pane mirrors. Bigger than I'd ever seen. They blazed in reflected light like crystal doorways, pristine and pure.

"Downstairs," Henri said.

"Can we see the theater?" I asked.

He blinked, then smiled. "Of course!"

He took us upstairs to the second level. They had a lounge there too, but it seemed Henri thought it second best. The open doors to the theatre glowed with red and gold, and beckoned. Henri went to buy wine, but the moment he turned his back we were drawn in. Inside was a golden heaven.

We stepped down red carpeted steps past gilt Greek columns, each topped by small gas chandeliers, past rows of red velvet seats towards balconies that swept to the sides around us. We stood in the center, under the great chandelier, basking in the warm glow. Henri came walking up behind us balancing three glasses.

"Henri, it's beautiful."

He shrugged. "It isn't the Opera."

"The Opera," Aleta sighed.

"Where do we sit?" I asked, taking my glass.

"If we were to stay, we would be on the first balcony on the left. But trust me. What I have in mind is much better."

"It couldn't be," I said.

He laughed. "You are the strangest women I've ever met."

I tried to smile, but it only made him laugh again.

"We're you really raised at sea?"

"Yes."

"Then this is your first theater?"

"Yes."

"That explains it." He looked around with appreciation, then nodded as if it fit his expectations. "Trust me Miss Carmichael. Hold on to your hat. You haven't seen anything yet." He waved us forward towards the stage. "Come. Let's go look."

We stepped down into the orchestra pit then under the stage, down some steps, and through a door. Blinking away the darkness, we could see light falling between the cracks in the floor of the stage, making lines that fell across crates and men. They sat about in their tails, orchestra members smoking cigarettes in the dim light.

"Ah, Henri," said one. "I'd ask if you came looking for models, but I see you found some." The tip of his cigarette etched a glowing line as he gestured.

"These are no models my friends," he said, looking smug. "This

60

is Aleta and Calista Carmichael."

Eyebrows went up. Several said, "Really?"

Henri nodded. "Really."

One stood up. "I wouldn't believe it if it weren't Henri," and he held out his hand to shake.

I beamed and took his hand. Aleta took the hand of another.

"Amazing," someone said.

"You haven't come to perform have you?" asked one.

"No."

"We're doing the town," Henri replied.

"You're showing off," rumbled another.

Henri laughed, "Naturally."

"You're shameless," he rumbled back.

"All the best artists are. So long, my friends," he called as we made our way to the back and the stairs up.

Upstairs, backstage, all was in chaos. We stood in near darkness as people dashed about, Henri making his way forward between women in unseemingly short skirts that flared like hazes of fluff. They all seemed to have the same destination in mind.

"There is someone I want you to meet," Henri said. Men were hauling a big wood wall towards the stage and we had to dodge to get around it.

"Henri," a man with a stack of paper said. "After the performance, not before." He looked at us and continued, "Really, we all love him, but we are very busy."

"Fernand, I would, but I had no choice."

Fernand gave him a piercing stare. "I must deliver these."

"May I introduce you to Miss Calista Carmichael and Aleta?"

He choked. He actually choked!

Henri laughed. "Fernand. Calm yourself!" Then he said to me, "He is the director."

"You're pulling my leg," Fernand said.

"No sir. He's not," I replied, and I held out my hand.

"What are they saying?" Aleta asked, and I had to explain.

"She is American," Fernand stammered, paper forgotten.

"Yes, I am."

This was fun. So many people knew me! I had no idea, but it was crazy. The word spread and they had to delay the show. Actors are drawn like a magnet by fame and we drew them along as we went upstairs to meet the show's star, a woman name *Polaire*, which means Pole Star. She was seriously beautiful, but wore the tightest corset I've ever seen! She eyed us with frank curiosity as we were introduced. She was eighteen at the time, right between Aleta and me, and she was actually shorter than I am which was a new experience for me.

"Miss Carmichael, what brings you to Paris?" She asked.

"We were thrown out of Brussels."

She laughed in her throat. I think it was the corset.

"I haven't tried that yet," she smiled. "Neither of you is wearing a corset. I wish I had thought of that too," she added. "I went the other way," she sighed.

"It's a striking look."

"You think so?" she asked.

"I think you're beautiful." She was too. She had dark hair and huge dark eyes.

She smirked at Henri. "You know Henri. I think we could be friends." Then she asked, "Perhaps we can have dinner sometime? I've no time to talk now."

"She wants to have dinner with us," I said to Aleta.

"Sure. She looks like fun."

"I'm afraid I don't speak English, but I speak Spanish and Italian."

Aleta picked up on that and they were rattling away in Spanish, which was great. Aleta told me that she stole money and left Algeria as a child to come to Paris – all by herself! When we finally left, to great disappointment that we wouldn't be seeing the show, both Fernand and Polaire had given us their cards. We really needed some of our own.

Henri insisted on a steam car when we left, nothing else being "right."

I sighed. But this time it had a heater which is a crazy good idea! It blew in warm air from little holes around the edge of the floor. Right up under your dress if you wanted it. I learned later that horse carriages sometimes have them too. You have to look for the extended back and stack. But they're expensive and cherished during the winter, when found at all.

We chugged along through streets full of people, cars, and

carriages. Paris is so alive at night, even in the winter. I think one could spend one's whole life trying new things. This time Henri was taking us to the *Moulin Rouge*, which was right near our house, up on the boulevard on the other side of the square! That Henri – we could have walked.

The Moulin Rouge sits squeezed between tall buildings, just a one story front. It doesn't look like much except for the cars and dress of those entering. It's what's inside that's important.

It starts with a windmill sitting on its roof, its vanes gas lit, the illuminated millhouse itself painted bright red. Light flared up behind as we drove up, silhouetting the windmill for a moment, lighting something large that moved accompanied by the cheers of an unseen crowd nestled among trees in back. Behind all that is a strange tower. Just a stack of draped roofs each smaller than the one below. I had to blink and then stare. I wasn't sure what I was seeing. All sorts of unearthly music drifted out.

Henri had been watching us with that sweet grin of his. We'd been staring.

We waited in line with other cars, each unloading. The dresses! Flares of silk, flowers, and brocade. Hats that could have floated fleets. Henri saw us look at each other's dresses.

"Fear not," he said. "You will slay them my dear Valkyrie, and the society section will certainly recount the battle in lurid detail. It's past time for a few towers to be toppled."

Yes, Henri did have a cruel streak, but I was better than that. Honestly, I wasn't nervous. Stop laughing. We didn't know we were leading a campaign of conquest, yet another revolution. Not then. We were completely naive.

Some had to pay to enter, but apparently we didn't. I think there was a pecking order, or perhaps Henri had an account with them. He insisted on locking arms, leaving no doubt we were there with our dear, smug Henri.

The lobby was covered in more red velvet, gilt carved wood, classic statues, and big mirrors. These though were at eye level so we could see ourselves and the crowd multiplied over and over. I sneezed. It was the cigarette smoke. Eyes everywhere turned and stared. Perhaps it was the bare skin or the simplicity of our dresses. Maybe it was that our hair was down, not up. We had no hats too.

And, of course, our natural figures. We couldn't have gone wrong in more directions at once. We stared back.

The spell was broken with a bang of a drum that went off like a gunshot and in danced two men and two women followed by two horns, a flute, and a drum banging out *Ta-rah-rah-boom-de-ay*. They proceeded to prance about in a quadrille, the women lifting their skirts to show their bloomers and one man actually doing a split! I really didn't think that was possible for a man to do that without injury. We stood still, practically in the doorway, having forgotten we were holding Henri's arms, laughing, practically floored. Then the dancers started in again, but Henri pulled us towards a door on the other side of the room.

"Come. Let's get drinks."

Henri and his drinks. I wanted to watch, but Henri led us on. We stopped to check our things, then went to one of the two lounges they have there. This was the dark one, lit twilight blue with dim yellow globes hanging from the ceiling that made me think of fairy lights, which is what Henri ordered; something called a green fairy. It started clear, but bar tender poured water over a cube of sugar and it clouded milky green! Aleta wanted one, but Henri held up a finger.

"Careful. They're very powerful."

She still got one. She gave me a taste. They taste like licorice, which made me wonder about the punch at the party. I thought of perhaps ordering Champagne, but I could drink a whole bottle of that, so I settled on a glass of white wine. I wasn't interested in getting drunk again. I realized though, that what I really wanted was coffee.

"Henri. Is there coffee?"

"They have everything here."

"Can we sit?"

"Of course. Come."

We could have sat in the lounge, but instead he led us back through the now quiet lobby, past averted stares, through another pair of doors to a small theater where it was dark and the floor was full of tables, all full. On stage, women were dancing in frothy white skirts that showed their legs and bloomers. Henri impatiently eyed the tables until someone got up.

"Ah! We must grab it."

And grab it we did, edging out another couple. The man eyed

us with distaste, staring down at us through his monocle until the woman, after a long glance and a frown, pulled him back. The band was only two tables away and it was loud, and vigorous, and the dancers put effort into it, but they couldn't compare to the flamenco in the Canaries. This wasn't art.

A waiter showed up and Henri ordered coffee all around, despite our already having drinks. I wondered if Aleta's licorice drink would mix with coffee better than white wine.

The dancers were followed by a magician who popped balls from a woman's ears and threw cards at a target. He finished and we waited for the next act, which seemed to be late. The coffee was good and very welcome. I was ordering a second cup when we heard a man hunting about for a table. His shoes had the worst squeak and he knew it. His distress was very evident and everyone was laughing at him! He tried walking carefully, the squeak drawn out to absurd lengths, until he gave up and squeaked up onto stage.

Someone had put a stool there and he appeared to put down a case on it. Opening it, he pulled out something. Tucking it under his chin, he reached in his case and pulled something else out and then commenced to play his ethereal invisible instrument. It was a violin! Everyone was laughing, and then I got it. The sound was coming out of his bottom! Then he looked sideways down at me and smiled. *Oh dear lord no*, I thought. But yes!

"He's got to be kidding," Aleta said. But he wasn't.

He danced down to our table and held out his hand. I was laughing with embarrassment, but I took his hand. He insisted and I couldn't refuse. Everyone was watching. Leading me up on stage to everyone's applause. I gave him a look. I'd make him regret this, but all I got back were eyes full of fiery mischief. He handed me the "violin", helping me take it. Rolling my eyes I "tucked it" under my chin, then held out my right hand and snapped my fingers impatiently for the bow. In for a penny, in for a dollar. When I posed ready to draw, he had to take a moment to correct my form, my impatience clearly hysterical. I let out a growl to the audience's pleasure, then drew it down and damn if it didn't make a sound. I threw in vibrato and it worked! We played around for a little bit, then I thrust them back at him before climbing down.

"That was good," Aleta said. "I wonder if he can do a flute?"

"He can do anything," Henri replied. "You should see him blow out candles." Which was funny.

Tired of coffee, Henri led us to a small gallery full of Impressionist artwork, some of it beautiful. It hadn't occurred to me yet that I could buy it. That I had walls now. Henri had two pieces there, but they were not to my taste. Too dull. Too much brown. That's why, Henri, I didn't buy any of your work until years later. By then the absinthe had taken its toll on you. You were and still are not easy to be around when you're drunk, which is too often. But it transformed your work, transferring all that boundless wonderful cynical fun to your canvases. They had become beautiful.

After that, Henri wanted to skip the other theater and go to the garden. He led us down a hallway and out into the night. Out into a fairyland. The garden stretched away into the night, surrounded by a long porch with doors and, sometimes lit windows. Ambling between streams, flower hedges, and ponds filled with floating tea lights, were couples and groups, some sitting on islands with tables under strings of paper lanterns. Beyond the bubble of running water was the thoughtful strum of some stringed instrument and flute.

"Oooo . . ." Aleta said. "I want to see that flute."

"It's in the pagoda," Henri replied.

"Pagoda?" she asked.

"The tower in the back."

It rose nestled amidst immaculately cut trees, but between us and it stood an elephant. It moved.

Chapter 7 – Making Friends

I reached for my gun, but met empty air. Not even a holster. Where was it? I couldn't see my rifle.

"My gun. Where's my gun!" I yelled.

Ghostly hands were clawing at me, slowing me down as I tried to shake them off. Thank God it hadn't charged. It was just standing there in the brush. I was telling them we had to back up slowly, but they wouldn't go. Instead they dragged me down to a chair, but it took four people to do it. Aleta was telling me to breathe, which was crazy because I was breathing. Someone had given me a cup of something that turned out to be water. With real ice. And lemon.

"Cali, stop." Aleta insisted.

I had stopped, but the elephant was still there. Why was it in a restaurant? It took a while before I could see that it was mechanical. Powered by steam. Which was obvious when you looked. Everyone was speaking French. I realized I was in Paris.

She cupped my face in her hands and peered at it. "Are you back?" she asked.

"Where is this?"

"The Moulin Rouge," Henri said.

"I know that," I realized.

"Does this happen often," he asked Aleta.

"No, but it's been getting worse." Who was translating? It was a woman.

Someone brought me a drink, but Aleta sniffed it and sent it back saying, "Anything but that."

No one questioned her. Instead they brought a wine glass with something brown red. It was sweet.

"What is that?" I asked.

"It's a mechanical elephant. It performs a show," Henri replied. "I was hoping to show it to you, but perhaps we should skip it."

"No," I said, drawing a ragged breath. "I want to see it." Now that my eyes were clear, I wanted to look closer, just to drive back the fear.

"Are you crazy?" Aleta asked.

"I'll never be able to come back if I can't face it. Help me up."

We walked towards it, slowly, tentatively. It raised its trunk and I stopped, but it only let out a jet of steam.

"It does that every few minutes," someone, a man said. He was holding my arm.

"What did they do to you?" Henri asked, concerned.

"They charged," Aleta answered. "Two of us died. They say she killed three of them."

"May I touch it?" I asked.

"Of course," Someone said.

We stepped over the knee high fence and I put my hand on its metal side. It was unexpectedly warm. I shivered.

"Enough." I downed the rest of my drink.

We backed away to the far side of the garden, under the pagoda and found a table, sitting with the man who had held my arm, a M. Tremolada. He was the manager.

"I would like to apologize for causing trouble," I said.

"Don't worry. It was actually somewhat amusing. Your shout had half the men in the garden reaching for their rifles." And then he added half to himself, "Myself included."

"It was the surprise. I'm braced for it now."

"Fear not. You're surrounded by veterans. We're all familiar with it."

"It will make the papers," Henri said.

"Yes," Tremolada sighed. "That is, after all, the reason for this place. To see and be seen."

"I didn't intend to complicate your life Cali," Henri apologized.

I gave him a sad smile. "You couldn't make it more complicated than it already is."

"Well," said M. Tremolada, as he stood. "If the young lady is settled, then I must get back to watching our cashiers. Half of them would rob us blind if I didn't."

Alone again, we sat and looked at the pagoda. Sitting in a small room, the outer wall composed of sliding doors that had been slid back to expose it to view, like a stage, sat three ladies playing strange instruments. Their jet black hair immaculate, held in place with sticks, their faces painted white, wearing strange brightly colored robles.

"Aleta. I think they're Japanese!" I said.

"I wonder if those are the kimonos Emilia told us about," she replied.

"Henri, are they Japanese?" I asked.

"Oh yes. The real thing too."

"They look Chinese," I said.

"They're beautiful," Aleta added.

"Look at the fabric!"

"Stroud was right," Aleta said. "Now I want one too."

"Don't jump too quick," Henri chided. "Wait until you see the shoes."

"They can't be worse than these."

Henri just snorted.

Of course our exploits ended up in the society columns. I understand the Moulin Rouge, but how did they find out about the Variety Theater? It turned out newspapers pay for snitching! Hungry actors.

We had been in Paris only a week and already we had friends! Our house had just about everything we wanted except hot water. But if it had that, we would never have met Lilli, Dior, Bijou, and Jolie. I doubted we could have made so many friends so quickly in a rich district. They gave us so much help. Those aren't their real names by the way. They are their working names. Their real names are my secret to be kept.

Aleta went out with Frank. He just dropped by. They talked at the door for a bit and then she grabbed her coat and called "I'm going out!" I was so curious as to what they would do. I'd never stepped out with a man, at least one I didn't know.

Sarah came up beside me. "Where are they going?" she asked. "I don't know."

That afternoon as we were waiting in the bathhouse, we decided we wanted to have a tea party, next Tuesday. We were all sitting around waiting for our tubs when I floated the idea. Yes, that was Cali humor. But none of us knew what one did at one. I would have gone to the library next to the *Palais Royal*, but I didn't know it was there yet. Sarah, of course, was our savior, not that she had that much experience either. But she at least had seen them.

The ones she had seen were outdoors. The only outdoors we had was the roof, but it being winter we decided that was a bad idea, which left our parlor. It, at least, had windows. People dress up for them too, but that seemed silly. How can you relax? Besides, not everyone had nice clothes. We needed a table too, but all we had was the kitchen table which had seen some rough use. So we bought one, a hardly stained table cloth, and some tea things. The tea pot was beautiful, tall and slim, all pink and gold. The silverware were mismatched from the pawn shop, but so was everything else. Really, what better way to relax. I mean, what would you do if you had a matched set and something got broken?

We baked all Tuesday morning, ham, bread, cookies, and a cake. We had pears and apples too. Sarah wanted to do it all but there has to be a limit. Besides, I like baking. To help her feel better, I let her clean the parlor windows.

The girls from across the street were arriving when I noticed we now had four strange girls across the street staring at us.

"Who are they?" I asked Jolie.

"We don't know. They won't talk to us."

Exasperation! I had no patience. It had been a busy early morning so it was out the front door. I stomped straight for them. I'd clearly taken them completely by surprise judging by the panic that followed. One was about to bolt when I yelled, "Hold it right there!" in my best storm watch voice, in English of course. I can't do it like Pa, but it still pinned them, English and all. And drew the attention of our street's gendarme as well.

"Why are you watching me?"

"Aliz Goutier, Miss, Ma'am." She curtsied as she stammered through that!

The others were Joy, Natalee, and Cloe.

"We were hoping to see the Rabbit," Cloe said.

This made no sense to me. "Why would you want to do that?"

"Because she's incredible!"

"You're out of your minds."

"My Papa says that, and that I should be married. But I'm going to run away just like she did."

"I didn't run away." Which raised a very annoying squeal. "If you want someone who ran away from her father, you should go see Polaire."

"But you fought lions and pirates."

"No. Just elephants and people. All the others either left me alone or I kept out of their way." I practically mumbled this. This was the most confusing conversation I had ever had. These girls made no sense. Did they think that somehow I could change their lives? What was I supposed to do?

"Miss." It was our gendarme. "Is everything all right?"

"Cali, what are you doing?" It was Aleta. "We have guests."

"We're fine," I smiled at the gendarme.

"Very well, Miss." He tipped his hat and went back to his walk. He knew we lived there.

"It's Aleta," one of the girl's eyes went wide.

"Aleta ran away from her father," I said. Precisely the wrong thing to say.

"Huh?" Aleta replied.

"Umm. We're having a tea party. Would you like to join us?"

"Cali. What are you doing?" Aleta asked.

I hadn't really thought about it until then, but now that I was safe in Paris it occurred to me what I'd been through must look like adventure to people. I'd become a penny dreadful.

I looked at Aleta. "I need to talk to them." Looking back at them, I said, "You need to understand the truth."

We took them inside, but it wasn't my story that had the impact. It was Lilli's, Jolie's, and the other girl's stories. They had all run or

71

been driven away from their homes. It was the cruel facts of the street and the truth of the bohemian life for girls alone in the world that made the difference.

Our new housekeeper came the next day, just in time. They have agencies in Paris just like Brussels. Her name was Mrs. Roche. Both she and Sarah insisted I was to call her by her first name, but I would not do that to someone three times my age. I'm an American after all and we must be given some leeway.

The moment she came in the front door, I could tell she was in an abject state of horror despite, I'm sure, Sarah having warned her. Frankly, I thought our house was completely fun, but I guess we all have different standards. Luckily, she wasn't a live in housekeeper because we were out of rooms. That very morning she knocked through our pile of dishes and managed to put them all away. We'd just bought them without thought as to where we'd put them. She was displeased with the kitchen as a whole and I had a feeling we would be making changes.

So our poor Sarah finally had help, which was why she had time to notice the noise in the basement.

"Cali," Aleta called. I was sawing at Saint-Saëns. The problem was that I'd never actually heard the piece played so it was hard to know if I was doing it right.

Oh, and I forgot to tell you that we had cards printed – finally! Aleta's were funny. It just said "Aleta". A complete contrast to Henri's. And we had two kinds. One with just our names and one with our address on the back. Women's cards are bigger as well. I suppose it's because we have purses instead of wallets.

"Come down to the basement. Sarah's found something strange."

"Okay." Really, I was making no progress.

Sara had her hands cupped to the floor, head pressed against them listening.

"Shush," she said. "I think they're voices."

All three of us did it. I couldn't hear it at first. Only by moving around could I find them. I could almost make out voices and shuffling, with an occasional thump.

"That's very . . ;" I couldn't finish, at a loss for words. What do you call someone tunneling under your house? Then I thought of Brussels!

"They're tunneling. It's a bomb!"

Aleta's and Sarah's eyes went wide. We ran up the stairs and out on the street to our gendarme.

"You have to come," Sarah wailed.

"They're tunneling under our house," I added.

"Are they now?" He replied. "Let's see." They really are the best, and very dashing in their winter capes.

We adjourned to our basement where we found Mrs. Roche listening at the floor.

"I can hear them too, Miss," she said, as she stood. "It's definitely unsettling. Rather have rats."

Then we heard knocking, which was strange. But it was coming from upstairs. The door.

"I'll get it, Miss," and Sarah bounded up the steps, clearly keen to beat me to it.

"I think, Miss," the gendarme said. "You have a case of the homeless."

"The homeless?" Aleta asked. I thought it sad that she knew that word.

"Yes. They live down in the catacombs."

"Under our house?"

"Yes, Miss."

"We need to be sure," I replied. "Someone tried to blow us up once before."

"I'm aware of that and we'll check to be sure."

"How do they get down there?" I asked.

"There's an access door down the street towards the park. It's supposed to be locked, but they break it as soon as we fix it."

Then we heard footsteps coming down and I looked up into the hazel eyes of Lucien! He'd come for Christmas. I leaped past everyone and jumped up the steps into Lucien's arms, knocking him back onto the steps, making him drop the flowers.

"I wish the Missus greeted me like that," our gendarme said with a chuckle. He was blushing!

"You came!" I was crying.

"Merry Christmas," he said.

"Oh, Christmas. Who cares? You came!"

"Is there something going on?" he asked, eying our gendarme.

"Noises. People under our house," Aleta answered.

Lucien frowned at our gendarme, "Is this true?"

"Yes sir, but it's probably the homeless. We'll check naturally. At the next watch change, when we have extra men."

"Good."

"Well misses," the gendarme said with a smile. "I have to get back to my station."

"Thank you," Aleta called, as Sarah showed him out. I was too busy to notice.

We received an invitation to an art opening and two notes from our bank in the post that day. It's really fun getting mail. It was an invitation from Henri's *Salon des Artistes Indépendants*, an artshow, only two weeks away on New Year's Eve! They were crazy. Throwing it on a night with so much competition, and it was short notice too. But it was another party! This would be fun. Lucien though, didn't seem pleased.

"It will draw more publicity."

"Everything I do draws publicity."

He sighed. "It keeps reminding the crown of your existence."

"I won't hide from them. Especially after Vic."

Lucien didn't look happy. "Unfortunately they have a great deal of say as to who I can and can't see."

"I won't hide from them. Besides, it's going to be fun. Artists are great!" Then I said with mock severity, "And why do you care about them? They won't even recognize you are a relative. You owe them nothing."

"A good point. One you seem to inspire me to exercise more and more."

I opened my note from the bank. It looked so official. My first! I stared. There had to be a mistake. Deposits were coming through from Fannie. I had over a hundred and fifty thousand francs! That included my Lufthansa settlement, but still. Aleta was certainly in a better mood after seeing her's.

Lucien's reaction was natural. "It's only been three weeks. What did you do?"

"We let them take pictures."

He laughed.

"What?" I asked.

"It's just that I'm going to have to get used to it." Then he frowned. "You need a manager. Someone to keep you from making mistakes."

"A manager? What do they do?"

"Exactly my point."

We argued over our living in Pigalle, but I wouldn't budge. I liked our house, although we could use another bedroom. Maybe we could put a bed up in the loft. It was huge. We could put a lot of beds up there. I liked our friends too. I liked the gendarmes who walked our street. I liked having carriages waiting outside our door. And that no one ever told me to leave because they were afraid of being blown up. To be fair, I didn't like the lack of a back door. The possibility of being trapped on the bottom floor or basement bothered me. Hot water might be nice too. But then again, I'd miss the girls at the bath. Lucien had no idea how to install hot water or even whom to ask, but offered to find out. He's very good at that.

Lucien was right though, I did need a manager to help me make sense of it all, but if I left it to Lucien I'd end up with some stuffy lawyer. Polaire would know all about managers. So I wrote her and gave the letter to Sarah to send, as I should.

And that leaves Christmas. We let Mrs. Roche have the day off to be with her family and decided to cook for ourselves. Well, actually, it was mostly me. Mrs. Roche made the gingerbread the night before. It tastes better the next day. After that everyone helped. We had a ham with molasses and cloves, candied walnuts, bread, cheese, figs, gingerbread, chocolate, pears, apples, and naturally – oranges and melon shipped in from the south by train! Champagne, wine, and coffee too. Lucien hammered apart a small block of ice to chill the Champaign and wine. We put them in some clay cook pots we found. He helped us haul a carriage load of stuff back from the pawnshops too without even blinking an eye. Mrs. Roche said we would need another cabinet for the new dishes, but that would have to wait until after Christmas.

We had most of the girls from the street over. They had no place to go! And poor Lucien was the only male there. Some had left boyfriends at home, for which I've come to learn to be thankful for. Some boyfriends aren't nice. Some had children too, which I would have liked to see. I sent food for them home with their mothers on extra plates wrapped in newsprint.

We sat around and ate. We played songs, some of the girls being musicians too. Female musicians are not any more welcome in respectable orchestras in Paris than they are in the U.S. Life can be very hard for them. They needed to head for Spain! So all together Christmas was definitely one of the good times.

Before Lucien left to go back to his hotel, he pressed a small box into my hand. He told me that wheels were turning and that I should have faith. Like I needed that! When I opened it, it contained a silver watch pendant and a note. It said, *this belonged to my mother.*

M. Marmontel lives on the nice side of the river, upstairs on the third floor of a beautiful building covered in statues and curls of stone. We chose to call in the late morning, taking a polished brass elevator up. A butler took our cards on a silver tray. We waited perhaps a minute before M. Marmontel himself came marching out to meet us.

"Cali, Aleta!" He looked genuinely happy. "It's good to see you alive," he laughed.

But that reminded me of all the death, and I think he realized his error.

"No, no. None of that. Come in. Farrin, we'll have coffee. Let's sit in the studio."

He led us to a big beautiful airy windowed room lined with carved wood, thick carpet, and a mix of seats and chairs. Music stands too, which were pushed up against a wall. He had a room just for practicing. One wall was entirely filled with bookshelves filled with music! My hand involuntarily reached out to them before I pulled it back. I wanted to paw through them!

"Take a seat," he said, motioning towards a sofa. "So you both live in Paris now."

"We do."

"In Pigalle." He gave us a smirk.

"We're happy there," I replied.

"A day doesn't go by that I don't see you somewhere in the papers."

"We don't read them," Aleta replied.

"That's probably for the best. Tell me. Do you really know Annie Oakley?"

I shook my head no.

"I thought not. It's hard to wade through the papers to look for the truth. I'd love to hear the real story."

"It's very long."

"I have time."

"No one believes it."

"Try me."

It wasn't just that I liked him. We needed him as an ally, so we gave him the full story. It took an hour. I actually heard some of Aleta's story I hadn't heard before. They had all been very brave. M. Marmontel just sat there, sipping coffee, occasionally adding an "amazing," until we got to the Bremen and we started comparing notes. He had been incredibly ignorant of all the things going on! Maybe that's what saved him. He knew more than he should about Gustav's villa. Apparently he and Camille are associates, if not friends.

"You must not judge him too harshly," M. Marmontel said. "He has not been at his best since the last of his family died. He spends months away overseas, trying to regain his composure."

"We didn't know."

"How could you? I warn you, though. Since you moved to Paris, he's been looking for you."

Now our house really needed a back door!

"I'm not sure what to do," I said.

"Be firm and truthful," Aleta said.

"Precisely. He's a good man and I think you have little to fear other than unpleasant conversation. Which brings us to the point of your visit. Paris was a logical choice. Perhaps the only one. But it will not be easy. You have no chance of entering the National Conservatory. Not under Thomas. I hear his health is failing, but I doubt you want to wait for that. It could take years." That ended with a little smile. He clearly had something in mind.

He took a breath, then continued, "Have you given any thought to enrolling in a regular university?"

I hadn't.

"The Paris Sorbonne, although less prestigious, has an excellent music staff, they accept women, and they won't dictate where, when, and who you can play for. I could write you a recommendation. I bet I could even squeeze one out of Camille. And I might be willing to work with you on your entrance exam."

We told him about Vivaldi, which he wanted to hear, so we pulled out our instruments and gave it a try, but he rolled his eyes halfway through.

"Stop. You have it completely wrong."

"We've never heard it before. We don't know what to do."

He squinted at us, thinking.

We waited.

"How are you coming along with reading music," he asked Aleta.

"Cali is teaching me."

He stood and went to his shelves, thumbing through sheet music until he pulled one loose, *Au Clair de la Lune*.

"Play the chorus please."

And she did, with no embellishment! I was so proud.

"You haven't been wasting your time. Good." Then he called, "Farrin! I need my appointment book."

Farrin brought it along with more coffee. Thumbing through the pages, he picked one.

"Can you both be here ten AM on the third?"

"Yes."

"We'll have lunch. Bring your instruments. Be prepared to spend the day."

Chapter 8 – Parties and Plots

We came back from M. Marmontel's to find workmen pulling out our carpets. Apparently, Lucien and Mrs. Roche had come to some sort of agreement. It was a mess. I swear our carpets were half dirt! They pulled them up and dragged them out into the street and piled them onto a wagon. Our house seemed so empty without them. Everything echoed. We swept the floors, leaving the dirt in the dust bin for takeaway. Then they came back with new carpets, their colors bright, with no bare spots or holes. Lucien had picked them, but how did they know what sizes we needed? Many things went on behind my back. But they did look nice and they kept Mrs. Roche happy for a little bit.

Did you know that Lucien bought the house for me? I didn't know for months. This was just the start. It all went on behind my back. From then on I couldn't put a cup down without being surprised that the table had been changed or the chair had been replaced. As our staff and my list of employees grew, I found that I gradually lost control of the environment around me, what I would wear, when I would eat. For a time I futilely tried to fight it, to fight for scraps of privacy. But this was where it all started.

Aleta went out with Frank again. We would probably have seen more callers from the school, but we warned Henri about our address. No more passing it out. Aleta seemed, at the time, to be happy with Frank, which was enough.

On New Year's Eve we dressed for our party. I wore my other Gustav dress, pale blue. Lucien made the mistake of coming to get us in a steam car. Our street was full of people, carts, carriages, and street vendors, Lefebvre included. So we made our way through the street in our nice clothes, drawing stares, including Lefebvre's.

Lefebvre's work is not to my taste by the way. He's static, entirely in line with the Salon, and often panders to needless sentimentality as well. But that is the public Lefebvre. There is the other artist, the one the girls love to pose for. I didn't, despite the rumors. He might have drawn me from memory though, but if it's the one I saw, it's not that good. Really, he liked dark hair better. He did a series, nudes that look just like Aleta! It was embarrassing when he put them out and worse when they sold! Who was looking at them?

On the way to the party we talked about our going to the Sorbonne, which Lucien thought was a good idea. He never attended university, opting instead for the Navy and then civil service. He was as curious about it as we were.

The show was in the *Ville Pavilion*, right on the river, which was that night full of party barges instead of work boats. Their lights and those of the Eiffel Tower, which I had yet to see up close, reflected in the rippling water. Our entrance faced the river, on a wide street. There were many carriages and some cars, but no one was there at the curb to help us out but Lucien, which was not surprising for artists, especially independent ones.

The City Pavilion is wide and full of columns. Originally, it had been built to house the displays for the City of Paris for the World

Fair, but after the fair it had been taken over by several organizations, including the Society of Independent Artists. But, as you will soon see, they mainly camped next door in the basement of the *Grand Palais.* At least they did when they weren't having shows.

I had an odd thought as we were adjusting ourselves before making our entrance. It was one of those small things that lead to great change.

"Lucien," I said.

"Yes?"

"Vic didn't have a coal man and she had hot water. We just had gas."

"That's true," Aleta added.

Lucien pondered as we began our climb up the steps. "You're right. I think I've been misinformed," he said. "I'll look in to it." Really, he's so good at that. Little did I know that that would lead to the eventual near-destruction of my little house.

A banner hung over the entry saying *Sans Jury ni Recompense,* Without Jury nor Reward. It sounded both defiant and a bit depressing. But their parties seemed to draw a crowd. We made our entrance along with the rest, entering a vast vaulting gallery containing a maze of alleys with walls covered with paintings. A large open space had been left at the entrance, one side of which was obscured by a crowd. Behind it was a long extended bar. Those manning the bar and even some standing near were wearing blue hats that looked like letter envelopes draped in gold braid. At the bar Lucien gave the man an odd handshake, which was strange because who shakes across a bar?

"And who might we have here?" the bartender asked.

"Lucien Antoine," Lucien said, omitting his full name and titles, which are worse than Henri's. "And this is Calista Carmichael and Aleta."

The man's eyebrows twitched up for a second. Something I was getting used to. Then he seemed to want to shake our hands too, which was weird.

"What can I get you?"

I started to say champagne, but changed my mind to white wine. Aleta had the same.

"Can you pick it Lucien?" There, see? I was getting better at letting people do things for me.

"Of course."

"American and British?" the barman asked. As if he didn't already know, but before I could answer, someone called.

"Cali, Aleta!" It was Henri. Of course he was near the bar.

"Henri!" we shouted.

"You made it," he replied. Then he caught an eyeful of Lucien.

"Who is this?" Lucien asked.

"This is Henri. He's an artist," I said.

"Do you have art here?" Aleta asked, in French!

Henri looked smug, "Naturally."

"Then we have to see it," I said. I would later regret that. As I said, I am not a fan of his early work, but I've since more than made up for it.

"Henri, this is Lucien," Aleta said. "Cali's . . ." then she ran out of words.

"My beau," I said. Henri and Lucien stared, confused. That's French isn't it?

"Hopefully *amour*," Lucien said.

I winced. "They don't teach you anything useful in French class," I replied to everyone's laughter.

We received our drinks and then walked the aisles with Henri introducing us to artists. We ran in to Cecilia, but she wasn't in the show and she was with friends. She said we could visit her gallery on Wednesday. The show itself was a mixed batch ranging from the childish to the sublime. Our purses were full of cards. People kept thrusting them at me, wanting me to know them. Painting after painting, artist after artist. One can get a bit numb after a while in large shows. The eyes grow tired.

Halfway through, Lucien took our glasses and excused himself, leaving us to Henri. We had just been looking at someone named Van Gogh who, to be frank, I was rather intrigued by. It was the emotional content of his work and the colors. Especially the colors. Each brush stroke was like a little jewel. Henri was telling me while we were looking that this show was rather small, which was crazy. An informal showing! The spring and autumn shows were twice as big. My feet already hurt and I was thinking that I probably would not be attending them. Lucien came back rather a bit later, carrying more wine from the bar. The bar must have been crowded. Henri explained that the real party was in the basement of the Grand Palais and asked if we wanted to go.

"Does it have paintings?" Aleta asked. She sounded tired too.

"Of course, but nothing formal. Just what we've left lying around."

I'm afraid that party, though it had far more important people, mainstream artists, government ministers, diplomats, and businessmen, was far more boring. Lucien got along well with them though. He knew quite a few by first name. One can get tired of having one's hand kissed. Aleta had wandered off with someone and I was just sitting on Lucien's arm while he traded gossip. Oh, excuse me, diplomatic and political news, which I was at that time sadly ignorant. So I was bored. That was until I saw a familiar face.

"Pardon me," I said.

They all mumbled their "of courses" and a few even gave a bow. I wondered off through the crowd like a torpedo. Yes, this was mean of me, but I was terribly bored and a little bit curious. She was holding court with half a dozen other young wives.

"Marguerite," I said as I snuck up behind her.

She turned. It took her a moment to focus, then a frown that she carefully put away.

"Calista," she replied. "You're here. But then you seem to have a way of turning up."

Some of the others teetered, which can be just annoying.

I met Marguerite at the ball in the Congo. She was not pleased with Lucien's interest in me, even though she was already married. She tore my dress by the way. My first ball gown, out of pure spite!

"I am hard to kill," I replied, with a smile, mostly because of the shock I knew it would draw. "So are you apparently. You made it out."

"Yes. It was a terrible business." A flash of pain in her eyes, which surprised me. Then she took a hard look at me. "You got me out, didn't you?"

"I saw you leave, but I wasn't sure," I said.

She blinked, then asked, "You knew?" I had found out about the impending revolution and invasion, and had given warning, giving them time to quietly evacuate as many as they could.

"Yes," I replied. We paused for an uncomfortable second.

"You live in Paris now," one of her friends said, picking up the conversation.

"I do. I have a house."

"In Pigalle," she replied, which the others seemed to find funny.

"Yes. I like it there very much," I replied levelly, their mirth clear.

"I suppose we all find our places," another added.

"People there are good. We take care of each other." It was clear this was heading for a joust.

"And other people," added another.

I was about to reply, "Like your husbands?" when Marguerite interrupted.

"Cali," she said. "I need to introduce you to someone." She took my arm and said to her friends, "Pardon us." We turned and she led me away into the crowd. The other women seemed surprised, which provided some satisfaction.

"Who are we seeing?" I asked.

"No one," she replied. "I had to stop that."

"I wasn't worried."

"I was worried for them. And the last thing you need is to make enemies here."

"Okay." We were heading for the bar. "So why are you here in Paris?" I asked.

"The same reason everyone is. Brussels is hell."

It was my turn to laugh.

"It really is. I'd get thrown out myself if I could." She smiled. She looked at the bar tender and said, "Another glass of *Chignin-Bergeron*."

"Is that good?"

"It's . . . unique."

"I'd like one too please." It was five francs! Marguerite frowned just a bit when she saw the money in my purse.

"This is all new to you isn't it?" she asked.

"Yes. I usually let Lucien pick them," I answered, misunderstanding.

"How is he?" she asked.

"Not well. The crown is applying pressure."

She paused, "Cali, you need to be careful."

"I know. The King is in the British pocket."

"Try not to say that out loud." She put her hand on my arm.

"What more can they do that they aren't trying to do already?" I answered.

"A lot. Something's brewing," she warned. Then she abruptly changed the subject as we were interrupted two men.

"I tried to tell him it was my time of the month but he wouldn't listen!" she said to me, loudly, ignoring them as if she hadn't seen them.

One of the men exclaimed, "Oh my." The other almost snorted his drink. They turned away abruptly.

She waited a second, then continued. "Count Humbolt. Mother wanted me to marry him just because he has some mountain named after him." She rolled her eyes, then she pulled me away from the bar. "Come," she said, and led me towards a corner.

"If you're going to tangle with Lucien, then you need to know what's going on." Her eyes darted about, assessing those near. "Leopold has foolishly announced that he's pro-navy."

"The King?"

"No, your Leopold."

"He already has a dreadnought. Why does he need more?"

She rolled her eyes again. Maybe it was a habit. "Don't be a fool. He might as well pin a target to his head. The British are not pleased."

"I wonder if an alliance with Germany combined with a navy might give him back the Congo?" I wondered aloud for her sake.

"That's better. Marrying Lucien will put you in the middle of it."

"I'm already in the middle of it."

"More in the middle," she said. "You'll be attending his funeral."

"You're not trying to talk me out of marrying Lucien are you?"

She stomped her foot and growled, "I'm trying to thank you!"

"Oh."

"Besides," she continued. "It would be a shame if something ruined that eccentric dress of yours."

"Do you like it?"

"I'm not sure."

"It's very comfortable."

She had warned me and that was clearly as far as she wanted to go. So our conversation was far more benign after that. Marguerite was the last person I would have thought would have been a friend in court, but there we were, chatting away over a glasses of very expensive wine.

Marguerite had to leave, lest her acquaintances start wondering, so I was left with a M. Carnot who was in the government. He had joined us, wanting to talk to me about something, but we were never left alone. People were quite brusque. It was always about problems in Panama. Everyone wanted a government bailout. I was finally rescued by Lucien.

He and a group of people were going up top, into the *palais* itself. We were led upstairs by one of the building's architects, jingling keys, opening doors as we climbed. Above it was huge and brand new for the next world's fair, empty bare concrete when we were there, stretching out in four directions. It's covered in a great vaulting lacework of iron and glass. You could park a zeppelin inside with no trouble. The moon had risen and we could see the Eiffle tower through the windows, the floor lined with shadow and silver moonlight. Others had taken the opportunity to look too, following us up, but we were tiny figures in that vast space. Its size killed any attempt at partying or conversation. It drove us to silence.

Come New Year's Day, the next morning, Lucien had to leave. They actually sent someone for him. Two men in immaculate suits topped with derbies. They arrived in a steam car just before lunch. They had been to his apartment and packed his trunks and had them in the back, which was very rude. But Lucien said nothing. We said goodbye with me dripping stupid tears all over his clothes. Apparently the crown was having a crisis, or maybe the English had withheld their tea supply. Before he left, as he kissed me, he whispered, "Be careful. This could be a trick." They had called him away the same way just before they killed Vic.

Polaire

Chapter 9 – A Deal with the Devil

I spent the morning, the start of 1893 heartbroken, lying in bed. But, I was not to be left to rot in peace as I so wanted. I heard the hardware seller below my window. Mrs. Roche was talking to him when I had one of my thoughts and ran downstairs, outside, clutching my purse, still in my night dress.

"Excuse me," I asked.

They looked up at me. I think Mrs. Roche had been flirting.

"May I buy that?" I didn't know the word for it.

The hardware man's eyebrows when up and Mrs. Roche's went down. I could see it in her mind. What is she up to now? And she was right!

"*Un choix?*," he said.

I pointed. "Yes. That one."

"Yes, of course," he said. I paid him from my purse, something I rarely seemed to do despite my having thousands of francs in it. I had to wade through the notes to find coins.

Taking my new choix, a stone pick, I walked back inside with Mrs. Roche following.

"What are going to do?" she asked. A valid question.

"We need a back door," I replied.

"Someone lives there," she said, pointing out the obvious.

"I'm not going in that direction."

We were inside. She called for Sarah.

I had my hand on the basement door when she arrived.

"Where are you going, Miss?" *It should be obvious*, I thought.

"Down," I replied as we clomped down the stairs.

"I can see that," she said, and she whispered for Mrs. Roche to get Aleta.

Aleta arrived as I was examining the floor. I wanted to start were the cement was weakest.

"What are you doing," Aleta asked.

"Digging a tunnel. We need an exit."

"The catacombs?"

"Yes. It can't be too far down." Then I looked up at her. "They called Lucien away before they killed Vic."

Aleta smiled and nodded, then she said to Mrs. Roche in her bad French, "It is good," and shooed her back upstairs.

"Maybe we should hire someone to do this," she suggested.

"Yes. We'll need a door with a lock. Probably a ladder too."

I took a swing at the floor, digging into the mortar. It was surprisingly easy.

"I want to see how far down it is."

Two more whacks at it, then I looked up at Sarah. "Do you understand what we want?"

"No, Miss."

"If they come at us through the front, we've no way to escape except over the roof."

"Oh my!"

I took two more whacks.

"They may be coming soon," I added.

"Can I try?" Aleta asked. "I was thinking they might even come in through the roof."

I can tell you now that she is dangerous with a pick. We hacked a cobble loose and then another. There was only a foot of soft stone beneath the cobbles which made me wonder about the stability of the house. When the pick broke though, it stuck and it took both of us to pull it lose. It left behind a fist sized, black hole.

"How deep is it?" I asked.

Aleta grabbed a stone and dropped it down the hole but we couldn't hear it hit. We would have to wait for the workmen. I drew a square around it to show where we wanted the door.

And then we had to go. We had our lunch date with Polaire. It was in a beautiful golden restaurant domed with green stain glass roof. In hindsight, I realize that it was very much like a greenhouse. The air inside was warm and moist with fresh flowers blooming everywhere. I suspect that it might have been heated. Polaire was just as beautiful as I remembered. It reminded me how plain my day dresses were. We kissed.

In Paris you kiss a lot. It's for friends, but not too close friends. Foreigners think you actually kiss, but you only come close, sometimes touching cheeks.

"Hello Cali, *hola* Aleta" she said as she found our table. She moves her rump as she walks. It makes men stare. "I'm sorry I'm late." She wasn't late and I doubted she was really very sorry.

"Hello, Polaire. You look amazing. That dress is incredible." It was a leopard print with black fir trim.

She laughed. "Now I remember why I like you. How was your New Year's?"

"We went to an art show."

She rolled her eyes. "The Independents. I was on top of the tower. The view was, as always, amazing, but the company was dreadful. What one must do for success."

She picked up the card and stared at it like it was a pit trap. "What are you getting?"

"The sole," Aleta said.

"It will be oily. Just a salad for me." She did have that corset to fit in to.

We ordered and then it was on to business.

"I need a manager," I said.

"You don't have one?" She seemed genuinely surprised.

"No."

"Then you're doing very well on your own."

I smiled. "Now I remember why I like you, too."

She laughed.

"The truth," I said. "I have no idea what I'm doing."

"You may want to leave things as they are," she replied.

"Why?"

"Everything in Pigalle is run by the *Milieu*, The Society. But behind them are the Italian Camorra."

It hit me. "Jean-Paul."

She looked surprised. "Yes. He's a *Parrain*, a godfather. My manager works for him as do the owners of most of the theaters I work in. It's a comfortable arrangement. I always have work and in return I do favors for him."

It was my turn to frown. "Favors?"

"Oh yes. I go to parties, like the one on New Years. I perform at events for free sometimes, usually for his friends, but I'd watch his kids if he asked. He takes care of legal problems and I get protection."

"Protection," I said, half to myself. Protection would be nice.

"If you hurt me and they catch you, you'll lose your kneecaps or maybe end up floating in the river."

"That seems like a very good deal."

"I assume he takes a cut of my wages as well, but I'm very comfortable."

"So tell me about your tailor," I asked. We really needed clothes.

"The papers said you had one," she replied.

"Paul Poiret?"

"Yes."

"Do you know where he is?"

She didn't, but said that if I asked enough carriage drivers, I'd eventually find out.

The next day was our appointment with M. Marmontel so we left it up to Sarah to ask M. Martin, the hardware man down the street, about finding someone to build us a trap door. He was the only one we knew that had any sort of connection to that sort of thing. It would probably take precious days to find someone, then even more to get it done. I hoped the British were patient.

We had more girls in the street in front of our house. This could be a problem. What if one of them was someone like Stroud? Mme. Touchard was up above, smoking on her balcony, eyeing them.

When we got to M. Marmontel's, we found he already had company. Two men, a flutist and a violinist. He had set up music stands and chairs in a circle.

"Ah Cali, Aleta. Come in. Farrin, keep the coffee coming."

"Yes sir," Farrin replied.

"Aleta. If I remember right, you don't know French."

"I am learning," she replied, in French.

M. Marmontel broke out in a smile. "Good! We'll give it a stretch today. Probably not too many music terms yet, eh?"

"No sir."

"Ha. Let's dispense with that too. Call me Antoine. This is Mathieu and Gaston." They nodded their heads. "We're waiting for Grégoire. We've been talking and the point has come up as to why you chose that particular piece?"

"It was all we could find," I shrugged.

He nodded his head sagely. "Not that Vivaldi is bad. It's really intended for an orchestra. I was wondering if perhaps you might entertain an alternative."

"Want to try something else?" I asked Aleta, as Farrin set down coffee cups.

Aleta's nodded.

Antoine nodded too, reaching back to the piano top, pulling down a stack of music.

"This is Mozart," and he passed it out. "Listen first." Then he turned to the two men, "Gentlemen?"

We set the music on our stands and they commenced to play. They were excellent and the piece was simple, clean, and beautiful. I was entranced. Gaston's violin work was crisp, exact, and pure.

The best I'd ever heard. They harmonized, their tone almost indistinguishable, then danced apart, circling, only to come back together again. I could see the notes skipping across the pages as they played. Aleta's fingers were moving unconsciously, her eyes locked on the music. I think the Mathieu saw it too, his eyes smiling.

Then it was our turn, just the first line. We stumbled through it note by note. Grégoire came in and sat, but didn't take out his violin. They played it again, and then us, around and around, correcting and explaining until, by lunch, we could make a passible go of it. We were still thinking of the mechanics of the music and not its expression, but that would come with practice.

We had an excellent lunch in his dining room, talking about us mostly. What we'd been through. M. Marmontel had his own cook!

"Now, I was thinking that if things went well you might want to think about a second piece," he said.

I know I must have looked surprised.

He smirked. "One should always have an encore in reserve. What do you think?" he asked, looking at his fellow musicians.

They mostly expressed mischievous amusement and general affirmation.

"Then *Boismortier* it is! We'll work on that this afternoon and send you home with plenty to think about."

And we did, and at the end of the day as we were leaving, he pressed a piece of paper along with the sheet music into our hands.

"We'll hold the next lesson here," he said.

It was next Tuesday and the address was at the Paris Sorbonne! Aleta saw it and started crying. I had to help her out the door, much to the amusement of the men.

Naturally, the next morning someone had to spoil everything by trying to kill us. It was inevitable. Anything to fill a Wednesday.

Sarah had visited M. Martin while we were away at M. Marmontel's and he informed her that the catacombs were forbidden and we would find no one to do the work. We had to ask permission. Who, you ask? The man you had to ask permission of for everything in Pigalli, Jean-Paul naturally. But what really made me angry was that our gendarme lied to us. There weren't homeless down there!

But we were talking about murder weren't we? Someone knocked on the front door and naturally Sarah answered it. I could hear them talking.

"Delivery for Calista Carmichael," I heard from the parlor. He had a box.

"I'll give it to her," Sarah replied.

"It's from a Lucien Antoine and I'm to give it to her personally." He smiled. "There's something special to go with it."

"Oh. I'll get her." She hurried into the parlor where we were practicing. "There's a package for you from your Lucien," she said.

It was the morning of the fourth. He left just before noon on the first. How did he send me a package? He didn't know he was going and he couldn't send it from the zeppelin.

"They're here," I said to Aleta.

"Oh!" Sarah stammered, taking a step back.

We could see a carriage parked out front through the parlor windows. A nice red one.

"We can't keep him waiting," Aleta said, worried.

I got up, "Let's see what they have for us."

"Hello?" the man called.

"Coming!" I called back.

There was nothing we could use for a weapon, unless perhaps I wanted to throw the clock at him. One more thing to add to the list. He was standing at the door, polite as anyone. He even gave me a friendly smile.

"Package for you Miss," he said, holding out the box. It didn't look like it weighed very much so I felt sure it wasn't a bomb, but I had to come forward to reach out and take it.

"And there's something extra," he said reaching in his coat pocket.

I was already moving, slamming the door, but he was incredibly fast. The door caught the knife blade – long thin and nasty – in the door jam. Catching the door on the rebound and flinging it back open, I kicked out and caught him at the base of the knee with the point of my shoe. Something cracked, the blade clattering to the ground beside me.

And then he just stood there, the color draining out of his face. Something had definitely been broken.

Stooping down, keeping my eyes on him, I picked up the knife. Then I pushed him over, which drew a shriek from one of the girls across the street.

"Got him." I called. I started yelling "Police!"

At this point I was angry. I could feel Aleta behind me.

"We need to check the carriage," she said.

I growled and threw the knife at the carriage where it stuck with an impressive thunk, which drew even more shrieks from the girls.

"Where are the police?" I yelled.

Our attacker was trying to sit up to little effect, tears streaming down his face. I stomped past him and out to the carriage, and that's when I saw him. He was far too nicely dressed and out way too early. He scowled at me.

"And who are you?" I was livid. I practically screamed it at him.

Picking up a rock, I threw it at him, missing. It hit him in the chest. I'd been aiming for his face!

He looked down at his chest in disbelief, the next rock denting his bowler hat. It would have hit his face if he'd been looking up.

"Who are you!?" I yelled again, I was so angry. Honestly, this isn't like me. I have no idea where it came from.

He looked up and caught a rock on his cheek. Finally our gendarme showed himself, coming around the corner, and our suited bowler-topped friend turned and walked away speeding up to a trot, catching another rock in the back without stopping.

"Arrest that man," I yelled.

"Yes Miss," our gendarme said, and he blew his whistle, two short and one long then taking off after him. But the man had already ducked around the next corner. Our gendarme came back a few minutes later with a couple of his friends. Their quarry had vanished. I looked up at Mme. Touchard on her balcony. She shrugged.

The carriage and package contained no bombs. We sat and explained while the police wrote notes. They took away our attacker and his knife in a wagon. He was unconscious, fainting when they picked him up. I guess I broke his knee. They took the carriage too. And then it was me upstairs in my bed sobbing. Aleta came in and lay down next to me, putting her arm around me, picking it up with me, sobbing together. We had to testify in court two months later. He had to heal enough to stand on the platform.

That evening we went to visit Jean-Paul at his resturant. We didn't dress. We missed Cecelia, by the way. We were supposed to visit that day.

"And what can I do for you ladies?" the doorman asked. This one was new and didn't know us.

"Tell Jean-Paul that Calista Carmichael and Aleta need an audience."

His eyebrows went up. "You're sure about this?" he asked.

I scowled back.

He nodded and sat back, writing a note and then pulling a cord that hung down behind his desk. A man popped out from around the corner at the bottom of the stairs hopped up to take the note. Then we waited.

Finally, the man who had taken the note appeared below and nodded.

Our doorman looked surprised and said, "You can go. Good luck."

We were led to an alcove in the back. It looked like it had been created by a small cave-in.

"Cali, Aleta. A pleasure to see you again." We did not kiss. This was strictly business.

"We've come to ask a favor."

He snorted, then said, "Sit first. I get few unescorted women visiting. Especially two as beautiful as you. Give me a little time to enjoy the moment before we get to business. Wine perhaps?"

I couldn't help but smile and nod yes.

"Besides, I already know what you want."

"You're watching us."

The wine came. He had already ordered it.

"How could I not? So much excitement. So much potential profit." And then with a mock frown, "so much liability!"

He poured. It was that same white wine we had before.

"You crippled *Fitz le Couteau*," he said. "He was good. I used to use him myself sometimes. Now he'll probably get the guillotine."

"We lost our housekeeper. I think we're even."

He laughed. "We are."

We sat quietly for a minute, sipping excellent wine. Then he asked, "How is the music going?"

"We are going to the Paris Sorbonne," Aleta said.

"And picking up French. She watches while you talk. A good strategy." He glanced around the restaurant at the customers, unconsciously keeping watch himself. There were quite a few customers, despite it being early.

"The Sorbonne," he continued. "A good choice. You'll be able to play wherever you want."

"A friend said that too."

"Students at the conservatory are considered employees of the state. The state controls their careers while they attend. But you two going to the Sorbonne; that could be useful." He thought for a second. "I think I'm beginning to see." His smile grew. "Yes, I think I'll bank my favor. We'll deal again. For my part I'll send you workmen, for a reasonable price." He took a sip of wine and looked at the glass with admiration. "Henri really is a genius. You'll get your bolt hole and maybe more, but you'll owe me."

I felt like I'd lost something important.

Then he started. "You need a housekeeper?"

"Yes," I replied. "Someone tolerant of violence."

Jean-Paul laughed.

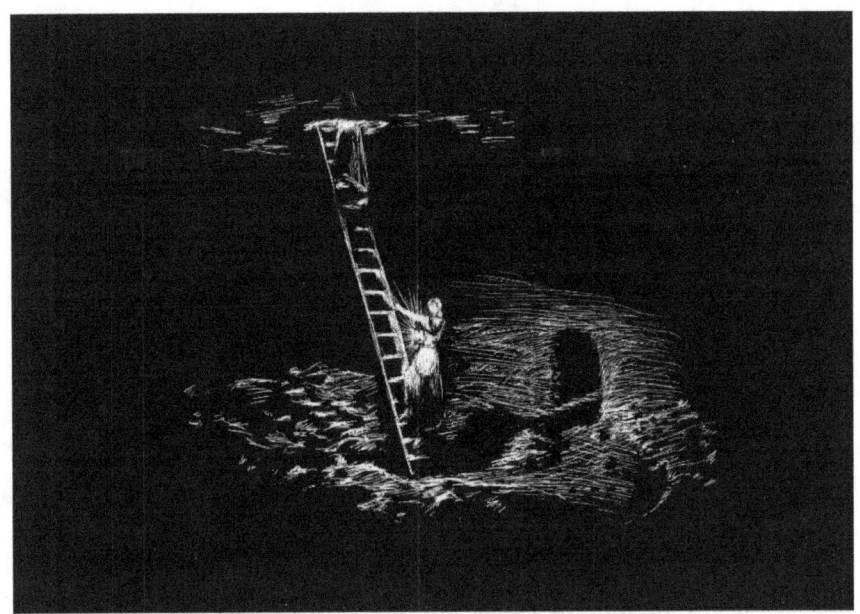

Chapter 10 – Our Bolt Hole

Sarah knocked on my door, which was strange. I woke with a start. What was wrong!

"Excuse me, Miss," she said. "There are workmen here."

"Already?" It was too soon. It was only Thursday. I slid out of bed and went to the window. Below was a wagon with flat iron square things in it.

Let's flank them, I thought.

I opened my window, looking about for watchers. "Hello," I called.

One of them stepped back from the door and looked up. "Hello," he called. "We're here about the window bars."

Window bars? I mean, it was a good idea, but I didn't order them. I just wanted a door.

"I didn't order them."

"No," he called back. "But we are to install them anyway."

It was Jean-Paul. What was this going to cost me? He clearly had something in mind. I looked down at the wagon. They were pretty. All curls and leaves.

"What do you need?" I asked.

"Your signature," he replied.

I sighed and closed the window. I bumped in to Aleta as I ran down the steps.

"What's going on?" she asked.

"Jean-Paul."

Out front were two workmen. Looking in the back of the wagon, the bars were even nicer up close. How could they have known they would fit? We had just seen Jean-Paul last night. He knew this was coming all along. I signed and they stoked the boiler on their wagon. Plugging in hoses and hammers, they began pounding holes in the stone around our windows.

"I don't have breakfast ready yet, Miss," Sarah winced.

"We can wait. Whatever you do will be fine," I replied, the racket from the front of the house deafening. I was sure it would upset the entire street.

"Thank you, Miss."

We were eating in the kitchen when another workman poked his head in. We'd left the front door open!

"Excuse me ma'ams, but I need access to the roof and the basement."

"I'll show him," Aleta said.

"No!" Sarah wailed, and skipped out of the kitchen to help the workman.

We finished and put our dishes in the sink, even though we knew it would upset her. We really needed a new housekeeper. Mrs. Roche was upstairs during the attack. She didn't even see it – and she quit!

We were looking at the bars as they worked when Sarah found us.

"Excuse me, Miss, but the door man needs to talk to you about the basement."

He was waiting downstairs.

"Ma'am," he said. "I need to know more about the door size." He had knocked the hole larger so he could peer down.

"Oh."

"Smaller will be stronger, but too small and you won't be able to jump without injury. Are you expecting to carry things down?"

"Like what?"

"I have no idea. Trunks? Bigger means weaker, although it's harder to batter a door in the floor than a door in the wall. And then again, small might mean a large man might get stuck."

Lucien needed to fit, I thought.

"It might be nice to be able to sneak out sometimes," Aleta suggested.

"Room for a reasonable formal skirt?" I asked.

"It's very dirty down there. There's been some cave-in so we're going to have to dig it away to find the original floor so we can anchor the ladder. Or did you want steps?"

"A ladder will be fine."

"They're really better for this sort of thing."

"How is the house foundation?"

"Don't know yet."

This was going to cost, even with a discount.

"You've built these before," I said.

"Oh yes. Mostly for the *nouveaux riches*. You can make a lot of enemies getting rich."

"Hello?" someone called from the top of the steps.

I looked up. "Hello Lilli!"

"May I come down?"

"Naturally."

"What are you doing?" she asked.

"We're fortifying the house. It was too easy for them," I replied.

"I don't think Fitz thinks so," she said.

That got a laugh out of us. It was funny that she knew him. It was a small neighborhood. It had only been a day and everyone knew what had happened.

But then I had to say, "You know they'll send better next time, and I will not run." I have a big mouth.

I doubt it was Lilli. It had to be the workman who was probably overheard reporting to Jean-Paul. That person said something to the next and thus are rumors born – but this one made the papers. "The Rabbit Will Not Run!" I defied the British. No! Challenged them.

I really didn't know what to do except to go on living. The truth was that I would gladly run if I had somewhere to run to. No one was pleased with British expansionism and this fanned the resentment, crushing any hope I had of a pardon from King George.

99

All gone in a whiff of newsprint. A seventeen year old girl alone defying the British Empire. You'd think I was Joan of Arc. I'm not, but apparently they did. She only lived to see eighteen.

So I was cornered with no choice but to get ready for a siege. We needed weapons. Perhaps boiling oil pots on the roof and cannon in the loft. Perhaps Paul could stitch me a knight complete with gatling guns to wear to parties.

I was hoping to go see Cecilia's studio, but, to be honest, we were both too tired and I was still crying over Lucien leaving. Besides, we had workmen all over the house and Lilli was there. Bijou and Jolie dropped by later. We all sat around until they had to go to work. Sitting about made me realize that some of our furniture was in pretty poor shape. You replace one thing and then everything else looks bad. We needed something to put our new dishes in too, although our future housekeeper might have something to say about our choices.

That evening we went to see our cabaret on the corner. It was burlesque, although I didn't understand that then. Comedy skits, lewd jokes and songs, punctuated by women jumping out and taking off their clothes. It wasn't to my taste, but at least we knew. A man in the bar wanted me to go with him to the Inferno Cabaret down the street, which, from his description, sounded interesting, just not with him. So it was an early evening.

We were walking back when Aleta said, "I've been trying to figure how long we've been gone." Then she began counting, "Three weeks crossing, a week at Gustav's, six weeks in Belgium, and now four here." We'd been gone a little over three months. Three months ago I had been skipping along in my school uniform and now I was going out to nightclubs without blinking an eye.

"It's been a really long three months," I said, my voice catching. Homesickness hit. I missed my Ma and Pa. I missed Red, and Lucien. "I'm never going back to sea am I?"

"After the war you will. You and Lucien."

We would, but it would never be the same. We are all in such a hurry to let go of childhood. What fools we are.

Aleta reached over and held my hand and we walked together, just two kids alone in the night.

The window bars were all we had for several days. Our doors didn't arrive until Tuesday, while we were at the Sorbonne. But the bars did help. I think I slept a little better. I hadn't realized how much those open windows bothered me. But we needed weapons, so what I was thinking were baseball bats. Only no one understood what I was talking about. Aleta was all for guns, but I figured that if we had them we might be inclined to stand and fight instead of running and someone would get killed. What if they sent someone like Stroud? She wouldn't give us a shot. She only showed herself on the train when she knew we were helpless. Then I remembered how she had climbed along the outside of the train. All our windows needed bars! I was worried about the windows again. Our only hope was to lose her in the maze of the catacombs.

Aleta was out with Frank with me beginning to wonder if this was serious, when I decided to go out on my own. I asked the carriage driver for a cabinet maker. He took me north towards the city walls near the rail tracks, to a street lined with them. I picked one and got out. With lots of seemingly idle men standing about and no carriages in sight, I asked him to wait.

Inside, it smelled of fresh wood. A glorious smell. It was a large, open shed, the ceiling filled with spinning pulleys attached to belts that powered the machines below. I found an office. An elderly man looked up at me from behind a desk.

"Do you need help?"

"I need something made."

"Of wood, right?"

Did he think I was an idiot? "Yes, of course."

I explained the situation. I wanted a club, maybe three feet long. Three of them. He had no idea what baseball was and I'm afraid I wasn't much help there having only seen it in books. He replied twenty francs. I bargained him down to fifteen. He didn't seem pleased, which meant I'd hit the mark. Then we went out into the shop, digging through a pile of wood.

"I'm thinking cherry," he said. "Strong fiber. Not brittle either." He pulled out a thick board. He called an assistant to help carry it.

"It has to leave a grown man on the deck."

He squinted at me. I don't think he really believed I was serious.

"Two and a half inches. It should work," he replied.

He took me to a saw with a big round spinning blade, and then another. Then we took one of the long blocks to a machine that spun it while we trimmed it down with a chisel.

"Narrower," I said. "I have to be able to grip it."

"It will be too thin. It might break."

I sighed. "Very well."

When we were done, he handed it to me and I gave it a swing. It had reassuring weight. I swung it fast and it made a nice whiz through the air. His eyes widened as he took a step back.

I handed it back to him with my card and the cash.

"I want them smoothed and varnished. Deliver them here."

His eyes widened when he saw my name. Then he looked up at me and gave a little nod.

On Friday morning Fannie came by with more contracts for me to sign. They wanted to sell our pictures in Germany and the U.S., both north and south! I made far less from these as there were more companies involved, tariffs, and taxes. More ways to divide the money. She said she might have a deal to make hard wax spool recordings of our music. I had no idea you could record music, but it sounded interesting. She also had a note someone had given her to give to me. It said:

Paul Poiret
14 Rue Dupin

Paul! It's crazy the things that will make me cry, but when I last saw him the Sûreté was dragging him away. He made it to Paris too.

"Aleta!" I yelled, making Fannie jump.

"What?" she said as she came downstairs.

"I've papers for you to sign," Fannie said to Aleta.

"No! I know where Paul is!"

"Oh good," Aleta sighed. "I need new day dresses."

"He really is your tailor?"

"Yes," I said.

"In a way," Aleta corrected.

"Thank you Fannie."

"It's nothing. You're making me rich you know."

I didn't care. I gave her a hug and said, "I'm glad."

She looked around. "My house is a lot nicer than this. Have you checked with your bank lately?"

"No, and I like my house."

"Suit yourself. The new rugs are nice."

I mumbled a "Thank you," and then said to Aleta, "We need to dress. I have to go see him."

"We've nothing to wear," Aleta said with a smile, like I should already know.

"That's why we need to see him," I answered.

Of course Aleta had to try to spoil it. "Then again," she said. "It might be a trap. Who gave you the note?"

"He did. He looked me up through the studio."

I squealed and spun.

Aleta smiled and Fannie looked at me like I was crazy.

"I'm going. Today," I said, quite firmly.

Aleta shrugged. "I'll get my purse."

"You're wearing your day dress," Fannie pointed out.

She laughed. "It's better than most of what I have."

True. Mine had hardly any coffee stains yet.

"Sign these papers," Fannie called up to Aleta as she was running upstairs.

She did, before we left.

Paul's shop was on the fashionable side of the left bank, down a side street. But when I saw it, I scowled. The arrondissement was correct, but the shop location was poor. The street was small and dark.

I should explain this. Paris property is valued by physical orientation as much as location. East west streets have a dark side and a light side. Narrow streets that get no sun at all are just dark. My house was on the dark side looking north. Paul's shop was just a dark hole. I paid the driver and we went in. He had a bell on the door! This was wrong.

"May I help you?" a young woman said. She'd been sitting. She was wearing my dress!

"Where's Paul?" I said firmly.

I heard something fall in the back.

"Paul!" I yelled.

He came tumbling out through the back door only to stop in mid stride, his eyes locked on me. Then he frowned. "What are you wearing?"

No hello. I laughed. Then he laughed. I think he was close to crying.

"Paul. Your shop is awful."

"Not anymore," he replied.

It was clear we needed each other. So I proposed a partnership. I would invest in his shop and in return he would keep us in clothes. First, he had to move to a proper location, preferably a corner. And his shop interior! Something had to be done. I needed a designer. I could only hope I had enough money. Perhaps Henri could suggest someone. And Paul wasn't going to sell my dress. How can someone so brilliant be so dense?

I promised to send a lawyer with a contract while he doodled and listened. When he showed me a sketch for a day dress, I deemed it to be uncomfortable. How could I move in it? He made adjustments. And then we adjusted it again with less ornamentation, rubbing pencil away with his eraser. He would make me one to try on.

Aleta had been silent throughout. Outside, she said, "You're out of your mind."

"Did you like the design?"

"Yes, but you're going to lose all your money."

I said nothing. She was probably right, but I didn't care. I would do this. "I probably won't live to spend it anyway," I replied.

"Cali!" She was angry.

We argued. It's just that sometimes I think I scared her. But I was going to do this. I needed to see Henri.

So we went to see him. He had given us his address. He didn't live very far from us. He had a little house like mine, but he wasn't home. His butler said he was at the studio. So we went there, but it wasn't a studio, it was a school, Atelier Common. It's right behind the Moulin Rouge. It never occurred to me that he was a student.

You had to crawl through a maze of little alleys to get to it and then it was up dark stairs. *They couldn't teach sculpture*, I thought. *Things would surely get broken if they had to carry them out.*

The school had no desk or reception. You just walked in. Walked in on two dozen men making paintings of a naked woman.

Most were lost in concentration, but a few looked up.

"Here for work?" one asked.

What? To pose naked? "Ah, no."

"Oh." He sounded disappointed.

"Cali, Aleta." It was Henri. Lots of heads turned to look at him. He looked back and forth at them and then got up, stowed his brushes in a can, and said, "They're friends." He led us out. We sat on the steps.

"What can I do for you?" he asked.

"She's crazy," Aleta started, in English.

"I need to set up a store," I said, ignoring her.

Henri's eyebrows went up. "What kind of store?"

"A clothing store."

"Why a clothing store?"

"Because I need clothing."

"Why don't you just buy it?"

"Because I don't like what they sell."

He nodded to himself, then asked, "What does this have to do with me?"

"You have to talk her out of it," Aleta said.

"I need a designer," I continued, pretending to ignore her. "To create the interior and exterior. It must look amazing."

"You can hire those anywhere."

"I need a modern designer. I need one cheap."

"How modern?"

"As modern as I can get. It must be art."

He frowned. "I'll think about it."

"Henri," Aleta said. "You're not helping."

"What is she saying?" Henri asked.

"Oh, nothing," I replied, Aleta growling, pushing me over as I laughed.

When we got home a kid, a guy no older than me stepped up to our carriage and offered to help us stand against the British. I didn't know what to say.

"*Allez-vous en,*" Aleta said. "*Vous nous ferez tuer.*"

"No no," I said. "*Vous allez vous fulre tuer,* You're going to get killed."

But I saw him still standing there later.

Under the house, the workers formed a bucket brigade, moving the dirt. I could see them through the new hole, down in the lamp light. The roof-fall in the catacomb under our house had been bigger than anticipated, but apparently the foundation stone under our walls was still intact. You might not know it, but houses sinking in Paris is common.

Our house was built on top of a relatively shallow gallery, the limestone having been cut away at an angle sloping towards the river, putting the house behind us at risk. Our east wall was built on the foundation of an older wall which had a mining passage cut through it that led to a Roman sewer that was no longer used. The dirt was going out that way.

It's funny, but I never saw any ghosts down there. I think it's because, unlike the catacombs on the Left Bank, ours were industrial. The remnants of mining or just foundations. No burials. But you really have to get used to them in Paris. Things will blow without wind. Out of place smells. The brush of cold on hot nights. It's what you get for living in a city that goes back before the Romans. You just have to ignore them. I've tried to talk to them when I see them, but mostly they fade when you approach.

We didn't go out that evening. As tired as we were, we practiced the pieces M. Marmontel had given us. The Sorbonne might test us on Tuesday.

Sunday was difficult for me because most things are closed in Paris. We dearly wanted to explore under our house, but we had no ladder. The hole though gaped open and inviting.

"If only we had a rope," I said.

"There's nothing to tie it to."

There wasn't; nothing that I would trust. The coal scuttle was just sheet metal and the stairway nailed wood. Above, there were pipes but I wouldn't trust them, and it was about twelve feet down.

"We could dangle, then drop," I suggested.

"The way out is probably locked," she replied.

I sighed. She was right.

"Maybe the river," I said, half to myself. "Lots of ships there. They would have rope."

"Still. . ."

"Yes."

We didn't even have Sarah. It was her day off and she was out doing who knows what. Probably shopping for the house.

"It's only twelve feet. If the rope was long enough, we could tie it upstairs. Put something across the doorway."

"True. So you're saying . . . ?"

"Let's go to the river."

We told the carriage driver to take us to where ships docked. He said ships don't dock here. They dock in Le Havre or Rouen then the cargo comes by steamboat. So we went to where the steamboats dock. He took us to the *Embareadére*, which is where passengers go to take passage. It wasn't what we wanted.

"No. We want to go there," I pointed to the other side of the river. Where the cargo was loaded.

"There?" He seemed to find that difficult to believe.

But away we went. He took us past an interesting garden, which I vowed I would explore. It had a maze! We clopped along until we found a steamer with an obvious deck watch. They were stacked two and three deep against the docks, their bright yellow and orange stacks poking up.

"Wait," I said, and hopped out. "Pardon," I called. "Do you happen to know where we could buy some rope?"

He blinked at me. "*Ich kann nicht Französisch sprechen.*"

"Aleta!"

They were both clearly happy to have someone to jabber German at. But the rope alleys were closed and the boat had none to spare, so we went down the dock until we found a barge with extra rope. The rope was old and a bit brittle, and showed some chafing, but it would work. I bummed a ball of twine off them so I could fix the bad spots and fretting, giving them a sour look to show I knew they hadn't taken care of it. I repaired it on the way back, borrowing the driver's knife.

"You know," Aleta said. "We should get some smaller rope, just in case we have to tie people up."

"Definitely." I wished we'd thought of that sooner, but I didn't feel like going back.

Chapter 11 – The Underworld

We pulled one of our couches over across the basement door and tied the rope to it, tying knots in the rope to make climbing easier. Then taking our brand new bedroom lanterns down with us, we shimmied down to the stone floor. Checking our pockets to make sure of paper, pencils, matches, and lanterns, then away we went!

The tunnel led to a cobbled passageway big enough to stand in. It looked like it was probably a sewer, but was dry. Our basement dirt had gone that way. We found it dumped in someone else's gallery a little ways down. But that way was a dead end.

The sewer though was clear, so we followed just to see where it came out. A short ways on, a basement had collapsed down into the tunnel, partially blocking it. Over the dirt we could see daylight. Crawling over left us very dirty, but we found that someone had knocked a hole in a wall, which led to a stairway up, which led to a door around which daylight leaked. The door was locked, but we could see street on the other side through the cracks. So that was the way out. We sat on the door landing and drew it all on the map we were making.

But the sewer still continued on in two directions. The hole past the basement collapse was small and full of loose dirt so we decided to save that for later. Besides, we heard those voices again. They came from the other direction, towards the river.

The sewer sloped down towards the Seine with occasional holes off to each side. We had two kinds, ancient inlets for the sewer and tunnels to limestone galleries like the one that went to our house. They were more limestone mines. So, unlike the left bank, our catacombs were pretty boring. No skeletons or weird carvings. But, the sound was coming from down the sewer straight ahead.

We followed it until at last, we came to a pipe that crossed over our heads. It was brand new. Every once in a while something would shoot through it – fast. Then, sometimes, bangs would come through them. It was crazy. What were they doing with it? We had no idea, at least not then. Over time we ran into more of them as we mapped and explored.

Then we saw a side passage that showed light. Creeping along as quiet as we could, we peered around the corner. Of course the passage bent so we couldn't see anything. It always seems to work that way. Leaving our lamps in the sewer, we crept down the passageway. Aleta poked her head around the bend, drew a breath and then pushed backwards, knocking into me. I fell backwards right into the man who had been sneaking up behind me! We landed in a pile. In front of us stood a short moustached man holding a pistol.

"What have we here?" he said. He stared down at us. "Interesting." I didn't like the way he said that.

There were three of them. They tied us up while the man with the gun stayed out of reach. And they all smoked!

"You'll regret this," I said.

"We will see," he replied.

"Call Jean-Paul."

He said nothing. The rope was rough. It hurt. The room wall and floor had sharp bumps. They hurt too.

"He'll have your skin if you hurt us."

"And why would that be, little girl?"

"Because he likes us," Aleta said.

The men laughed.

"He may or may not like you, but that makes no difference in business."

Business. That was something.

"He will because we owe him a big favor."

I could see the man with the gun's brow twitch. That gave him pause.

"Maybe so. But he won't be pleased."

It gave us a reprieve until Jean-Paul passed judgement. We spent all day tied up. We even heard Sarah calling for us and talking to someone, probably our gendarmes, but I knew they would do nothing. Sound really travels down there and I suppose I could have called back, but I didn't want to give our captors a reason to gag us. And just try using a chamber pot in front of strangers! But thankfully, that was the limit of our indignities. The men went on with their work.

"What are you doing?" I asked, just because sitting there was boring. You get over the fear pretty quick and then you are left with nothing to occupy your time but discomfort.

"Quiet," he snapped

"You might as well tell us."

He frowned at me. "And why would that be?"

"Either we're friends or we're dead. So it makes no difference."

The logic of my argument seemed to have impact, which clearly annoyed him, but still he answered a very firm, "No!" So all I knew was that they were tunneling up at an angle.

"You're either smugglers or robbers," I said as he walked by hauling buckets.

He said nothing.

"This is Pigalle so I don't think Jean-Paul would let you rob someone."

He grunted and went back up their hole.

110

When he came back, I said, "So, you're smugglers using the river."

He just sighed as he walked by with his buckets.

"So that's a storage house up there."

He growled and snapped, "Quiet!" And walked on.

"You shouldn't poke at him," Aleta said.

"I'm bored. But it's not like it isn't obvious."

"How do you say obvious?" Aleta asked.

"*Évident. Comment dit-on obvious*," I answered.

"We are not obvious!" he said as he stomped past with his buckets.

I ignored him, continuing with my French lesson. As he passed, I mused out loud, "It's not like Jean-Paul couldn't have us killed later. We live just up the tunnel."

"Then we could get some things done this afternoon," I called out to him down the tunnel. "We could even send down lunch sometimes."

We fell asleep after many hours.

"My dear girls,' said a voice.

It took a moment to remember where I was.

"Jean-Paul," Aleta said.

I squinted up at him. Our smuggler leader was standing behind him.

"Hello," I said. "Glad you're here."

"You sure about that?" he asked.

"If we're to die, then really Jean-Paul, I'd rather you did it," I replied. He, at least, wouldn't make a mess of it.

That surprised him, but he rallied and laughed. "Maurice," he said. "The rough rope."

"It's all we had."

"If you let us go, can we keep it?" I asked.

Aleta said something in Spanish and he laughed again.

"Then it really is them?" the smuggler asked.

"Yes," Jean-Paul sighed and knelt down and began working on our knots.

When my arms were free, all I could do was fall over on my side, which was heaven because my behind really hurt. Heaven until my arms began to wake up.

"I told you not to stray," Jean-Paul said.

"We need multiple escape routes," I replied through gritted teeth. "The Institution will cover as many holes as they can find."

"The Institution!" Maurice said. He stared at Jean-Paul. "You invited them down here?"

"They don't care about you, Maurice. And I see your point Cali. It makes sense. Ask first."

I would have said something, but at that moment Aleta and I were in agony.

Eventually he led us up to the street. He let us keep the rope, too.

"I apologize for making you walk home, but I shouldn't be seen here. Maurice will leave you alone from now on. But be more careful. There are others down there that aren't so nice."

"We need to thank him," Aleta said.

"Maurice? Why?" Jean-Paul asked.

"For not killing us," she replied.

Jean-Paul thought. "Yes. That might be good diplomacy. You might need him."

Sarah jumped into our arms at the door.

"Miss! Oh dear, Miss!" She was crying. "Oh dear God, your wrists."

"We were captured by smugglers," I sighed.

"And you escaped," she wailed.

"No. We made a deal," I replied

"And spent all day . . .," Aleta tried to add in French.

"Tied up," I finished. "Is there any food?"

"No, Miss. I was so worried."

"Let's go out," Aleta suggested.

"You are coming with us," I said directly to Sarah.

"Oh no. That would be wrong."

"It's an order."

She was close enough fit to me that we managed to put her in one of my dresses. We went to the Moulin Rouge. It wasn't fair that she never went out. What good was it being the Rabbit's maid if she didn't get any adventure? All she did was gawk at everything. Which said to me that she needed to get out more. To be clear, we also wanted to let the gossip page print lurid stories about our rope burns. I wanted to work on watching the elephant too. And while we were there, we could hear the Japanese musicians. They were not using a normal scale and this time I was lucid enough to notice their audience. Some looked like musicians too. They were taking notes!

The workmen not only put in a trapdoor, but replaced our front and roof doors as well. They had peep holes covered with iron grates, with little doors that could be opened and closed. Unfortunately, the peephole on the front door was too high for me. I needed a stool. Something else to find. The doors were thick heavy oak. My bats came too, but Sarah refused to touch them. They were beautiful. The grain of the wood shone a sweet red honey-brown under the varnish. Aleta still wanted a gun though.

Our new trapdoor locked from both sides. You needed a key to get out and in. They gave us only two, but I asked for two more. Of course, now we needed some sort of cupboard to keep matches, lanterns, spare shoes, and maybe even weapons in at the bottom of the ladder.

Sarah was afraid of it, like everything. It was funny. She so wanted to be the Rabbit's maid and at the same time she was so afraid. But she never quit, so, in a strange way that made her very brave.

"Give it a try," I said.

"Really, Miss, I'll just follow you. You can unlock it."

I rolled my eyes. "What if I'm going over the roof and you're trapped?"

"Then I don't think they'd worry about me."

"They know I care about you. What if they wanted to take you hostage?"

"They wouldn't!"

"They would do worse."

"Oh." She looked shocked. "Yes, Miss." Then she poked the key in and gave it a halfhearted turn, like it was made of glass.

"Twist it," I said. "The bolt is stiff."

When she finally got down the ladder, she looked around, eyes wide, like she was in some pit in hell. Gustave gave us copies of the key for the street door and I led her through the tunnels, up and out on the street, locking the door behind us. Then we went back the same way. I realized we'd need a lantern by that door as well, in case we wanted to go in that way. Yet another thing to buy, although, as you'll eventually see, we had to learn to navigate the tunnels in the dark.

We took Maurice, Ulf, and Ransu beer and sandwiches the next day. They were all apologies and helped us with our gradually growing map. They also warned us about some areas and some people. Not everyone worked for Jean-Paul. There was one man called "The Ghost", who was utterly mad and quite violent, but he only attacked lone travelers, and he constantly muttered and sometimes shouted so you could hear him coming. He stole things that were left out and they advised us not to leave anything at the bottom of our ladder. Especially not weapons.

Maurice's entry for their goods was an outlet on the river that was completely submerged during the winter. It was cold too. They were working towards summer operations. Their descriptions of the contraband they "imported" were too much like cargo. Aleta gave me the eye while we were talking about it. She knew that look. It would be difficult for me not to get involved. But, fear not. There was no danger as, as you will soon see, other events took complete control of my life.

That afternoon our new housekeeper arrived, completely unbidden. I was sitting in the parlor with Fannie and Dior, telling them about my ideas for the store. I couldn't help it. I kept thinking of new things to add. It couldn't be about selling Rabbit dresses. Those were mine. It had to be about creating individual styles for each woman. Paul had to do for them what he did for me. I already knew the name. *Le Femme Moderne*, The Modern Woman. We were interrupted by Sarah.

"There's a woman at the door. She says a M. Stefani sent her."

"Jean-Paul," I replied.

"You know *them*?" Fannie said, eyes wide.

"Yes. He rescued us." I got up, picking up a bat from beside the door. "Let's see what we have here."

In the hallway, the girls peering out from the parlor door. I couldn't reach the peephole and I needed room to swing if I needed to, so I decided to take a chance and open the door.

She was standing there, holding her purse. She had dark brown hair, not as old as Mrs. Roche, maybe in her mid-thirties.

"Are you Miss Carmichael?"

"No, but she'll be down shortly. And you would be?"

"I'm to report directly to Miss Carmichael." I thought I saw a ghost of a smile.

"Then you will have to come back on a different day."

"What have you got behind the door?"

"A friend."

Yes, it was definitely a smile. "Miss Carmichael, my name is Aline Bernard. I believe I'm to be your new housekeeper."

"And why would that be?"

"Because you'll get no others."

I sighed. Jean-Paul. "Come in. Sarah, take her things."

Aline surrendered her umbrella, hat, coat, and purse without complaint. She was wearing a conservative pale green dress with simple white blouse, her hair up as was proper. On the other hand, I was wearing one of my old blood-stained travel dresses, hair down, and no shoes. We gave each other the eye and then I let the bat I had behind my back down.

"Ooo, that looks interesting," she said eyeing the bat.

"I had them specially made."

But then her eyes darted around. "But you have no fallback. No one is covering you."

Apparently she had already discounted Fannie and Dior.

"I've never needed it," I replied.

"Not yet," she snapped. "But that will change," she said, then her look hardened. "As will your wallpaper!"

"It is kind of old and stained," Fannie said from the doorway.

It was, but I really didn't care.

"Don't tell me," she growled. Then she stomped past us towards the kitchen. "Let's see it!"

I followed alone, just a bit stunned, still holding the bat. She had gone in ahead and I heard a growl, "This will not do. It's older than Napoleon! Jean-Paul seems to be expecting miracles!"

I stopped in the corridor, Sarah standing next to me.

Aline's voice echoed out a stream of complaints, "No hot water? Coal? These are dishes? Lanterns?"

"What did we let in our house?" I asked myself.

Sarah let out a little nervous laugh. I think she was close to hysteria. I wasn't far behind.

Aline did, however, like our new trapdoor.

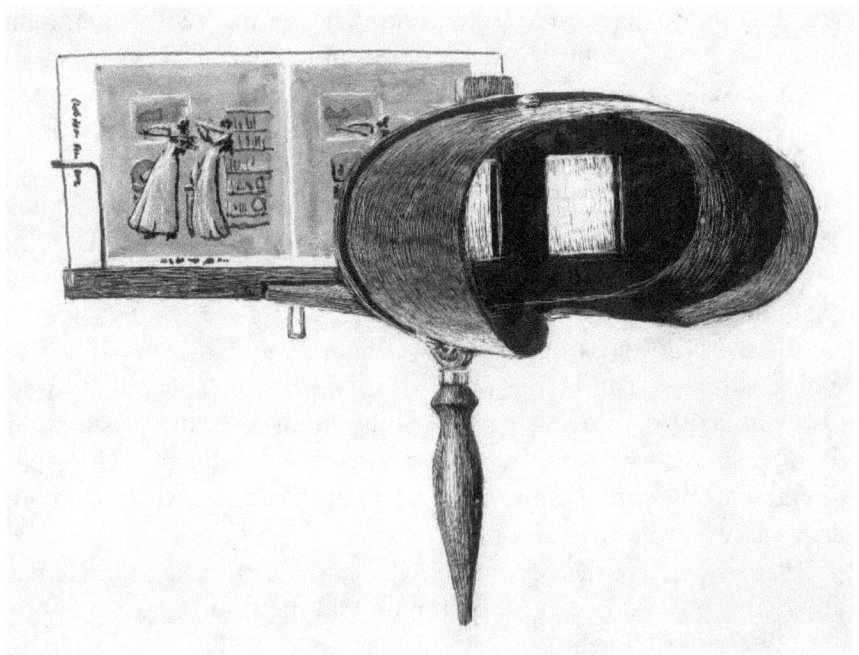

Chapter 12 – We Enroll

"Miss, Miss, it's time to get up or you'll be late."

"Late?" I jerked up, Sarah stepping back with the tray.

"Don't worry. Aleta needed waking too."

"We have school," I muttered, still blinking away the sleep.

"Yes you do. Now eat your breakfast."

Our new live-in housekeeper – we were converting our loft – warned us to expect workmen calling. She moved in that night. It's amazing how quickly things happen with Jean-Paul. We would not see them until Friday. We were going to be at the Sorbonne all day, all week.

Breakfast was different. We had toast and the coffee was better. Sarah never makes toast. As usual, I had nothing to wear. *Oh – where was Paul*, I thought as I dressed. *We need him.*

Aleta wanted to do nothing but practice that morning, even while we were eating, but Aline made it hard for me to concentrate. She stomped around the house poking at everything. I could hear her exclamations and footsteps echoing as I chewed. Nothing

117

seemed right to her, and to be honest my house was really more than little run down. But it was comfortable. So why did I feel embarrassed?

We had to walk up to the boulevard to find a carriage, it was so early. Sarah waved goodbye before shutting the door. We carried our instruments, umbrellas, and music, all clutched in our hands because we had yet to find out about proper school satchels. The sky was dark and heavy with threatening rain. It was a long ride with Aleta fidgeting all the way.

The driver let us out on *Rue Saint Jacques,* in front of a gate with a statue. It had begun to rain and we had no idea what to do once we arrived. We saw several young men in a similar situation dash in so we followed, but they split up and headed in different directions. We finally picked a door at random and hopped in, dripping water on their floor.

"Hey there, what are you doing?" said a gruff old man. He put down his apple and newspaper, pointing at the floor.

"We're lost," I said.

"Then you've come to the wrong place. This is the construction office. I can only tell you about places yet to be built."

"Do you know where this is?" I showed him the address.

He pushed his glasses up on his nose, squinting and holding the paper nearer and further to get the focus. "You've got the right building."

"There's more than one building?" Aleta exclaimed in English.

"The room number starts with a two, so it's the second floor." He seemed to feel that was sufficient.

We stared at him. The question should have been obvious.

He coughed, then said. "Go outside."

"Outside?" I asked, dripping.

"Yes, outside. We're trying to fix that. Down that way," and he pointed with his thumb. "You'll see stairs on the right. Go up."

Back under our wet umbrellas, back in the cold rain and wind while holding all our things up at eye level, we ran to a hallway that contained a stairway up to the second floor where we asked a passing student, but he didn't know.

"They didn't give you a map?" he asked.

"A map? No."

"An office you say?"

"That's what he said."

"These are all lecture halls. Perhaps on the other side," he said, frowning. "But the offices are all up a floor. Try going around."

We were, at this point, running and the numbers weren't getting any better. We saw an elderly man. He had to be a teacher.

"Do you know where this is?" We were out of breath.

He took a look and chuckled. "That's the old loft. They made it into offices a century ago, we were so short of space. It's on top of the theater."

"Where?"

"Go back, turn left, and follow the corridor. Turn left when it does. Halfway down you'll see double doors. Go through there. Then the numbers will make sense."

I doubted it. Address numbers making sense is the last thing you should expect to find in Paris.

We frantically ran through miles of corridors, finally going through the double doors only to find . . . more corridor. These though, were smaller.

We split up. I went left, Aleta went right. The numbers I was seeing seemed to be going in the right direction.

"I think it's this way," I called, but she didn't hear.

They were going down, down, but they were odd and we wanted even! At the end it turned right. Aleta came panting up behind me.

"This isn't right." She shook her head.

"This way," and I took off around the corner. It turned again and this time the numbers were even.

Up, up, up, and yes! We were fifteen minutes late. I knocked while Aleta prayed, "Oh please, oh please."

From inside we heard a "HA!" and then chairs moving.

The door opened on a dour face, Mathieu from M. Marmontel's. "It's them," he sighed.

"Ah ha, ah ha! Pay up." It was Grégoire.

Mathieu didn't even invite us in, but instead pulled out his wallet and started looking for money.

"Come in, come in," said a happy Grégoire. "Mathieu bet you'd be at least a half hour late."

"Everyone gets lost," Mathieu shrugged.

They appeared to be sharing the office. It was just two small desks and shelves, everywhere piled with sheet music, books, and stacks of papers. Every conceivable flat spot in the office had something stacked on it. There wasn't a lot of room to come in to.

"You're wet. It's raining?" Mathieu asked.

"Yes," Aleta replied. Apparently teachers don't get out much.

"Well then, let's get started," Grégoire said. "We thought you should know a bit about how things work before you decide if you want to attend."

"Know what you're getting in to," Mathieu added.

"You'll be enrolling in the College of the Arts, specifically the *Collegium Musicæ*. But that doesn't mean you'll be studying just music. Everyone will get a whack at you."

"Except the College of Theology," Mathieu noted.

"That, I'm afraid, got the axe." Grégoire rolled his eyes.

"In some cases literally," Mathieu muttered.

"Didn't make it through the revolution. Not that we don't have priests on campus, but they don't have their own school. The government doesn't pay much too, so you'll probably have to find outside income to make ends meet. There's student housing, you can live on campus, but there's a waiting list."

"You won't starve though," Mathieu said, brightening.

"No. The food's free. Better than the army," Grégoire smiled

Mathieu blew through his cheeks, "The army."

"Best not to remember that, Mathieu."

"No."

"You mean, we don't pay?" Aleta asked.

"Pay? Why?" Grégoire asked.

"We thought . . ." I started.

"No, no, we pay you," Mathieu finished. "You have to pay in America?"

"Yes."

"Huh?" Mathieu looked perplexed.

"That's crazy," Grégoire snapped. "The state's investing in you, not the other way around."

"Anyway. The campus is in shambles. We're completely rebuilding it for the world fair. Reorganizing, rolling back the revolutionary reforms."

"They were well meant," Grégoire added. "Let's be clear."

"Yes. But they knew nothing of higher education. And we'll have no embarrassments like last time," Mathieu said.

"Embarrassments?" Aleta asked. I think she was wondering what the word meant.

"No, no, we don't talk about it," Mathieu said, whisking it away with a wave of his hand.

Aleta blinked, but wisely kept quiet.

"So let's go look at the studios. Maybe they'll scare you away," Mathieu continued.

We walked down corridors while they complained about lack of funding, appreciation, and the distance between the music offices, which were all on that side of the loft, and the studios and practice rooms which were on the other side of the building.

"You'll have to pass the minimum requirements of all the schools, a bit of math, French, rhetoric, philosophy, history, science, law, and theology."

I think that went over Aleta's head, which worried me. Without French and some basic skills, she was going to have a hard time.

The studios were everything they said and twice as wonderful. The floors were worn through by centuries of scuffing students. They were dingy and poorly lit, although should the sun ever shine, they might be nice in the afternoon. And as we would find out, every ancient wood seat creaked in its own individual way as the day wore on and the patience of student behinds thinned.

We sat and played our pieces and they listened, or at least pretended to, and then Mathieu said "You're not using your music."

"It's wet," I replied.

They nodded, then Grégoire said, "Keep at it. Let's go see administration."

That was down on the south side. They took us through the chapel, which is beautiful. We filled out paperwork and were given classes, times, and thankfully – student handbooks with maps! It took some negotiation, but we managed to get our classes together along with a suggestion that we find solid flat shoes. Then it was off to the library to get our books. The Library was brand new and beautiful, huge and cavernous, with many of the shelves still empty.

Our books were just as I suspected they'd be. The university wanted basic math and French skills.

121

"Do you have a beginning math book?" I asked.

"Of course."

"Do you have one in English?"

"No, but you can go to the *Anglicus Collegium* library. They can help you."

"There's an English college?"

"Yes. And a German, Swedish, Dutch, Scottish, and Swiss ones too. We welcome foreign students."

"Where is it?"

"It's a ways away. I suggest a carriage, if you can afford it."

We left Grégoire and Mathieu behind and clopped in a carriage towards the English College, Aleta grew more and more depressed as she thumbed through our text books.

"I'm going to die," she said.

"We're going to work on it. Let's hope they're patient." Then I looked down at the book. It was math. "I know you can do that! You just don't know the symbols. It's no different than reading music."

She sighed with despair.

The English College shared a building with several other foreign colleges. It was six blocks away and upstairs. Their library made us fill out more paperwork. We had to show our passports again and our paperwork to show enrollment, but we got Aleta's books, everything in English. She would still have to write her assignments in French, but at least she would know what she was writing about. We even got a French-English dictionary and some recommendations on where to buy books in English. Apparently there was a book market down near the cathedral, next to the river.

We clopped back home only to find it destroyed!

They were knocking holes in the walls. And the wall between the bathroom and the closet was gone! And they were poking holes through the floor upstairs too!

Everywhere things were pulled apart and no one had asked me anything!

I was staring at the ruined wall next to my bedroom when I heard a voice behind me. "Either your housekeeper has magic powers or you have acquired some powerful friends."

Lucien! I spun and almost fainted in his arms.

"You're here," I sighed.

He chuckled. "I left. Walked out. They're angry, but I don't care. But I'm going to have to buy some clothing because I couldn't pack."

"All that matters is that you're here." Then I looked up into his eyes. "We're going to the Sorbonne."

"So Sarah tells me."

"It's amazing, but we have to help Aleta. She needs more French."

"Maybe it will help keep you out of trouble."

"Do you think so?" I smiled. "You should see our books, but we're going to need a place to work. I don't think Aline will allow us in the kitchen."

"She's very formidable.

"She just came yesterday."

"And all this so soon?" Lucien looked worried. "What did you do?"

"I owe the Camorra a favor."

That was the very first time I saw my Lucien truly surprised.

I tried to explain to him. But when he heard Aline was supplied by them, he lit out towards the kitchen and now they were having words. I sat in my room knowing I would be next. We really didn't need this. Aleta and I needed to get working on her math. It's just that he needed to come to terms with the situation we were in. I needed Jean-Paul to get things done. The next attack could come at any moment. We didn't have time for niceties. Despite her coarse nature, Aline was exactly what we needed.

"Miss," it was Sarah. "You have a visitor."

"What now?"

"It's Miss Johnson." It was Fannie.

"Oh."

She was waiting in the parlor.

"Is this the right time?" she asked. They were quite loud in the kitchen.

I gave her a grin. "As good a time as any. I'm testing the mettle of our new housekeeper and so far, she's doing quite well."

"I'm surprised Sarah could hear me knock."

"Are you here to say hello?"

"No. Well yes, but I've brought business." She had a bag.

"I hope you brought a pen. We've lost ours."

"No."

I gave her my brightest, grimmest smile and stood.

"Aline," I said as I entered the kitchen. "Do you know where our pen is?"

Her eyes on fire, locked on Lucien, she reached to the side without looking, opening a drawer to pull forth our pen. Lucien then plucked one from his coat pocket. They both held them out.

"I'm to choose?" I looked back and forth. "I'd accept neither, but I really need a pen." So I grabbed both.

"Wait. What are you signing?" Lucien asked.

"Contracts."

"I want to see them," he replied.

"You think I don't understand them?" Here it comes, I thought. My turn.

"I think . . ," and then he wisely stopped. This is why I love him. ". . . I'm curious."

"Me too. I haven't read them yet."

So we adjourned to the parlor, where waited a somewhat fearful Fannie.

"Let's see them," I said.

They wanted to open sales in Brazil, Russia, and Spain. And Fannie had something new. Double pictures you put in a lensed viewer so you could see depth! She brought me one too. That's what was in the bag.

"These are wonderful!" I exclaimed.

"I took them, but then we had problems. They're new and the machinery is tricky. Only a couple came out right. We're going to need to try again."

They actually got Lucien to smile.

"Sarah said you needed me," Aleta said, as she came in.

"Contracts," I replied.

"And we need to set a date for the cylinder recordings too," Fannie added.

"You found a studio?" I asked.

"Yes, but it's in Rouen. With travel, we'll need at least two, possibly three days if there's trouble."

I looked up at Aleta. "We can take a steamer!"

"Train would be faster," she said. She was thinking of school. "What's that? May I see it?" Aleta was reaching out for the viewer.

"It's incredible!" I said. "Wait until you see."

"Hello!" It was Jolie and Dior. They dropped by before work. It was another temporary reprieve from conflict.

We all said hello. Then Fannie added, "And I've been thinking about that store idea. May I get in on it?"

Another partner, but maybe one with time – which I no longer had. "How much?" I asked.

"I don't know. Maybe a hundred thousand?" I was thinking a hundred thousand would be the whole budget! How much did I have in the bank?

"A store?" Lucien asked, just as a pipe fell out of the ceiling behind us, bringing down lathe and plaster with it. Luckily no one was under it. Upstairs, someone yelled an apology. My house was being destroyed.

"You're opening a store?" Jolie asked.

"I want to," I replied.

"Cali," Aleta said. "After this can you help? Ratios make no sense."

"We need a place to study," I said to Lucien.

But all he could reply was, "A store?"

"Go to the library," Fannie suggested. "It's not far."

"There's a library?" I asked.

"It's huge," she replied.

"And pretty," Dior added.

"Lucien, can you come with us?" I asked. "Aleta needs help." And then we could spend some time explaining as well. It was that kind of day.

But before we left, I asked Aline if she was okay. She only growled, which I took as yes.

"Tell me about this store," Lucien asked. I think he was going to save my new Milieu connections for when we were alone. We were clopping towards *La Bibliothèque Nationale*, The National Library. It's, as I think I've already said, right next to the Palais

125

Royal, which is next to the Louvre.

"She's crazy," Aleta said.

"Oh thanks."

"You're going to lose all your money just to get some dresses."

"Tell me your idea," Lucien said, dropping Aleta a little smile.

"I want to do for other women what Paul did for us. I want him to create personal clothing lines. Individual styles for individual women."

"Oh, so it's your store now," Aleta said.

I gave her a wry smile.

"And tailors already do that now," she added.

"I'm not sure how to say this because I'm still figuring it out, but no they don't. They make clothes. There are designers like Omama, who work for the very rich, but even they only predict. They don't lead. I want to lead. I don't want a store. I want a work of art and I want great women to be a part of it."

"See?" Aleta sighed. "You're trying to save Paul."

"I want to save what Paul started. You have to admit, so far we've been leading."

Lucien templed his fingers to his lips and looked at me. I wasn't sure what he was looking for, so I waited.

Finally, he said, "You'll need a business plan."

"I know. There are so many pieces missing. I want a corner location, but I don't' know how much they cost or even if there are any to be found. I need an architect, but not a normal one. I need furniture. Unique furniture. I can't advertise in any normal way. How much can I charge? I'm thinking a lot. If I don't, then people won't respect me. But I don't know what a lot is."

"Kimonos," Aleta said, brow furrowed, like she couldn't believe she said it.

"Kimonos," I said. "If people want them."

"Kimonos?" Lucien asked.

"Now that you're back, we can show them to you!" I grinned.

The library, by the way, looks like a prison. A Big gray featureless block that rather abruptly abuts the sidewalk. You enter through a gate fit for Dracula and then have to cross a dreary grey stone fountain courtyard to climb the colorless, unadorned stone steps that all great buildings have. You could be entering a courthouse to await your death sentence. But there it stops, because inside it opens up and changes into cavernous fairyland of books.

The National Library has galleries lined floor to ceiling with books, four stories, opening to vast glass and stone vaulted theaters and atrium filled with desks! They were old then and still gas lit at the time, but that was changing. It's the largest library in the world. And the best part is that anyone can come in, rich or poor. This is why I love Paris. Of course it was half in shambles. Like all of Paris, it was being rebuilt in preparation for the 1900 World's Fair.

We sat down and got to work. It was hard because I wanted to run off wild through the shelves. I vowed not to leave empty handed, but I did. I needed proof of residency to check out books. They wanted to know where I lived, I guess to make sure they got them back. A gas bill or bank statement would do. I would have to ask Sarah.

Lucien is good with both math and French. Aleta knew the basics of math. I mean she could add, subtract, multiply, and divide. But the idea of expressing it as graphs was alien to her. And fractions are never easy. We didn't even touch algebra. As far as French went, with no formal education she lacked basic academic language skills. She didn't know what adjectives and verbs were. It didn't help that she had to learn it in English as well as French. And it was me who was lost in geography. It was all European. It wasn't even clear to me where Paris was. Despite her devouring one concept after another, we were going to be doing this every night for a long time. I hoped for patient teachers. We didn't have much time, less than a week. The new term started on the 16th, next Monday.

We were riding back home. It was dark.

"How am I going to remember all this?" she moaned.

"Repetition," Lucien answered.

"According to the school catalogue," I said. "We only have to pass the basic levels."

"I'm so dead," Aleta moaned.

"Maybe they have special classes for musicians," I replied.

Lucien laughed.

"No really. I'm not sure about a lot of this myself."

"I think," Lucien mused. "That it wouldn't be teaching if you already knew it. But I'm having a hard time believing they don't require Latin and Greek."

"Latin and Greek?" Aleta slumped down in her seat.

"That's in the catalogue," I said. "They were dropped as requirements during the Republic to make way for more modern subjects."

"Oh thank you," Aleta moaned.

"Which is why we have philosophy, law, and science," I continued.

She moaned again.

We decided that unless it was absolutely necessary, we would speak only French. It was also clear to me that I would need help starting the store. Thanks to school, I wasn't going to have much free time.

Chapter 13 – First Day of School

It was really cold, but Lucien and I took a walk when we got home, just to talk alone.

"Lucien, it's a sensible move," I said.

"They'll never let go of you. Not until you're of no use to them," he replied.

"I need allies and Jean-Paul owns this neighborhood. He can protect us."

"But he'll own you." Lucien sounded bitter and worried.

"I will go when he calls."

"What if you don't like what he asks?"

"I know what he's going to ask. He wants to manage my debut."

"Debut?" Lucien had stopped.

I looked up at him and smiled. "My first performance," I replied. "You said I needed a manager. He's one of the best."

He sighed. "I did say that."

We started walking again, with me starting to think that maybe going home was a good idea. It really was cold.

"I was hoping for someone a bit more reputable."

"I don't think it's a business that attracts honest people."

He was quiet for a bit, the stupid breeze blowing up under my skirt. "It's maddening not being here," he said finally.

"It sure is. What could they do to you if you stayed here?"

"They could strip away most of my titles and holdings," he replied bleakly.

"But you'd still have some," I said.

"I'd have my mother's family title and estate."

"So you wouldn't be broke."

"No," he said. I thought I saw a ghost of a smile.

"But you wouldn't get invited to parties."

He laughed. "No, I wouldn't. But at least I wouldn't be working if I did. It would be hard to do. My obligation to the crown has been bred into me. It's everything I've ever known. It would go against a thousand years of family tradition."

Which was something I could understand, but still resent.

"It's just like the Congo," I said.

"How so?"

"They won't change. It's all they know to do." Then I looked up. "What's *Le Neant*?"

"The Nothing. Where do you see that?"

I pointed.

"It's probably a peepshow."

"Peepshow?" I asked, genuinely confused.

"You look at naked women through little windows or holes."

How did Lucien know that? I smiled.

"What's a *Baudet*?" I asked.

"A Donkey. Where do you see that?"

"Next to the lingerie store."

He stared at it, then shook his head. "It can't be good."

I laughed, then said, "Lucien. I'm cold."

"I can fix that."

He hailed a carriage and we hopped in to clop the three blocks back with Lucien's arm around me, helping me to warm me up.

Back at home, our house was a disaster, but we still had chairs and a fire and Aline made mulled cider, which is incredible! It definitely went on my list of things to be careful around, just like campaign. I wanted to show Lucien the catacombs, but we were too tired. He needed to know the escape routes. I did show him the map, which I really needed to make copies of.

Please don't ask me what was going on with the house. I no longer had the energy to care. I let Lucien and Jean-Paul fight it out.

No, we sat in the wreckage until I couldn't keep my eyes open and Lucien left to go back to his hotel, which brings to mind something I probably ought to explain to you.

Lucien and I were by then as good as engaged, but we weren't formally engaged. Formal engagement for royalty, even for royalty once removed like Lucien is a very big thing. It requires a lot of family and even government approval. And one requirement that had to be met was that I be a virgin. I would be tested. I mean, in Lucien's case, it wasn't an absolute requirement. But everyone would want to know. Everyone would know. It might even be in the papers! So Lucien wasn't sleeping anywhere near me. The temptation to say forget everything let's move to Brazil, would have been tremendous. Besides, my being a virgin would give the story, when it hit the papers, that I walk around seducing people a big punch in the nose. But that didn't mean we couldn't have fun.

Paul dropped by on Wednesday – with dresses! We talked about the store and my ideas. He was naturally enthusiastic, especially since I was supplying the money. And I still hadn't been to my bank. I still didn't even know where it was! I asked him to scout for better locations. South facing on a street corner.

He smiled at my wrecked house. "I like what you've done with the place."

"It looks like a war zone!" I said, incredulous.

"Exactly. And in Pigalle too," he replied, looking about. "That was brilliant."

"You think so? It was luck."

"Luck is so important," he sighed.

"A friend once told me that."

"Don't tell me." He looked at me. "He was a spy."

"He was."

Paul laughed.

"No really," I continued. "A German one."

The dresses were light, simple and breezy. Probably not the best thing for winter in Paris, although they did come with light jackets, gloves, and small hats with netting that thinly veiled my face to just below the nose. I would have to put my hair up for it to look right.

"Why the net?" I asked.

"It's to shade your face. So you don't squint and to highlight your lips."

I grinned. "That's brilliant."

"Yes. It is isn't it? Try a little rouge with it."

When Aleta came down, her poor eyes were bloodshot from studying.

"Oh dear," Paul said. "The wars have taken their toll."

"We're studying for the Sorbonne," I said.

"Why?" It was Paul's turn to be incredulous.

"To study music. That's why we came here."

"The last thing you need to do is study music," he said.

"I suppose we'll see," I replied.

We were late for our first day so we took a steam carriage. Up on her balcony Mme. Touchard was smoking her first of the day and said hello as we passed. Even the sweeps, who were cleaning up last night's messes, popped cheery hellos. The warmth from the carriage's boilers was great, it was a cold morning. At least it wasn't snowing. This time we had a map and marked the locations of our classes. Sadly after such a great start our first class was math!

At the Carriagan School for Young Women we had sixty to seventy students enrolled all together in the entire school, so classes were pretty personal. There were never more than eight or nine girls in a class. Walking in to a lecture hall was quite a shock. They are as big as theaters with rows of desk seats sloping down to a stage with maybe a big counter, desk, or a podium, and giant slate boards behind. And because it's France, above the slate boards, they fill the wall with a big painting or paintings, I guess to give you something to stare at as you fall asleep. Your desk folds down. It's small and you bring your own ink well, so it's a constant danger. We didn't know about book sacks yet so we brought a shopping bag each. They were sturdy ducking with handles and they worked fine, but kind of made you stand out as clearly clueless. Our paper was wrong too, we were using stationary because that's all we had. We had to write small.

I mention my prior school and its size because in lecture hall you don't raise your hand, which I was doing, at least until the boy two seats away told the boy next to me to give me a shove.

"Ow!"

"You don't do that," he said.

"How do I ask questions?"

"In the classroom. Don't be daft."

I wasn't daft, but I was ignorant. That explained why we had math twice. One was lecture and one was class.

I had just spent the last three months being treated as an adult and here I was a kid again. Most of these boys were at least a year or two older than me and out of a class of eighty seven, including us, there were only ten girls. Thank goodness the first week was review. But I could tell from Aleta's notes that she was missing half of what the professor was saying.

We were let out early. Normally we would have ten minutes to get to our next class, but this time we had twenty eight.

"I'm dead," she said in English. "I'm so dead. I couldn't understand anything."

"Tonight," I replied in French.

"We will have tonight every day," she replied bitterly in French.

"We will learn," I sighed.

We were hardly in the hallway before someone thrust a piece of paper in my hands. Aleta stared at her's.

"Student what?"

"A student march on the National Assembly. They want to protest the new censorship law today at noon. Anarchy is a right?"

"Where is the National Assembly?" she replied in French, reminding me that we were supposed to be using it.

"It doesn't say." I replied.

"We had class."

"We have class." I was trying to tutor her. "*C'est la vie.*"

"We should see our class."

"Yes, we should look for our classroom. It's so easy to get lost."

I wasn't kidding. With all the construction, the school had turned into a maze. Construction both at home and at school. It was clear our star had moved into the construction constellation.

We found the classroom down a floor. It was a smaller version of our lecture hall. We sat on long benches at long tables. The sky had clouded over and the always present wind had picked up, which didn't bode well for the protest and limited the light from the windows. This is why, I think, paper is white. So you can see it in the dark.

Our teacher was young, with one of those awful pencil moustaches. He was not the one who had given the lecture. He came in late too, plunking his books down on his teacher desk.

"Hello. I'm M. Bongard and I will be your math instructor. My office is," and he wrote his name and then a building, room number, and hours on the board. "I doubt anyone could possibly have any questions at this point." He glanced around the room eyebrows raised. "So let's break early." Which brought a cheer.

"Excuse me," I called as he dashed for the door.

He pulled up short and turned to look at us.

"Yes?" he asked.

"We have a problem."

He sighed.

"My friend . . ."

Aleta said, "Hello."

". . . is just learning French."

"But you speak it," he said to me.

"Yes."

"Then you'll translate. Anything else?" Again with the eyebrows.

"No," I replied, confused.

"Excellent," and he turned and dashed for the door, leaving us standing there in the now near empty classroom.

"That was . . ," Aleta started.

"Abrupt," I finished.

We gathered our things. Class had lasted, according to my watch pendent, eight minutes, which left us close to two hours before music.

I saw one of the rare women students in the hallway and asked, "Pardon?"

"Yes?" she replied.

"Where can we find food here?"

"You're new."

"Yes."

"The cafeterias are in the handbook, but the nearest is straight downstairs. I'd go with you, but I'm late."

"Thank you."

"Solidarity," she replied with a smile and ran on. *How curious*, I thought.

They had given us meal cards when we registered, only the cafeteria wasn't open yet, but the courtyard outside was full of students and tables, many making ready to dash for cover if the sky broke. They had signs with Greek letters on them or sports, or things like *The Socialist Youth, Impartial, The Lampoon, The Turd*, or *The Voice of the Student*. Most of these tables thrust small newspapers and broadsheets into my hand. Some tables looked interesting like, *The Society of Women Academics (Solidarity!)* and *The Night Club*, with *night* spelled out *La Club de Nuit*. It was a club for musicians and music! Perhaps someday, if I found time.

When the clock struck noon, half the yard jumped for the cafeteria doors and we were left at the back of the line. They gave us soup, brown bread, meatloaf, and a choice of coffee or tea, which were all surprisingly good. Better than the Navy to be sure. But silverware without napkins! Students apparently brought their own. The tables didn't have tablecloths either.

We read our newspapers. I learned a great deal about the politics of Paris. The demonstration that day, for instance, was in response to the new anti-anarchist laws which did sound a bit strict and definitely needed to be withdrawn.

Our next class, music theory, had twelve students and it was deadly dull – except that we were working on pianos, which were new to me. I mean we had one at school, but it was for Mrs. Hartnoll. It was very hard to stay still and not go crazy on it, scales, intervals, and chords. But we could practice on them later.

One boy, though he was trying his best not to, was coughing and the teacher sent him away to the Office of Student Health. I asked our teacher after class and he said that it was a new rule. The school was tired of losing students to consumption.

We finished the day with Music History. There were only six in that class. They had a storage room full of instruments, most of which I'd never seen or heard of. This was Aleta's area to shine. She had so much more experience here. We were going to start with medieval and renaissance music. By the end of class we were bubbling with anticipation! I was so going to love this. All we had to do to stay in was to pass math and French.

The smaller class meant we all had a chance to get an eyeful of each other and introduce ourselves. There was Jacques, Gérald, Paul, and Aubert. We were going to be playing together on various instruments. Aubert and Jacques wanted to go out to a coffee house after, but Aleta and I really needed to get back home and study. Aleta was going to need all the help she could get if we were going to survive.

Back home the workers had pulled even more apart! Plaster from our walls and ceiling were gone everywhere. They were replumbing the entire house! The stove had been pulled away from the wall, with a pipe stuck between it and the chimney so we could cook. And Aline was still finding things to scowl at!

There was a big package for me and my first thought was Ma and Pa had sent it, but it was from The Society of Independent Artists. It was a painting. Lucien had been watching me at the show and I guess he'd seen me staring at it. It was by an artist named Van Gogh, a man sowing seeds in a field. It was the colors I liked and it seemed so happy. Henri though, told me later that the artist had died only two days before the show. Nobody had heard the news yet. They sent it to my house after the show closed. It was the start of my collection. *Perhaps someday*, I thought, *I'll have plaster on my walls to hang it up on.*

Lucien came by shortly after we got home, wanting to go out to dinner. This was one of those live or die decisions that you get from time to time. Go out to dinner or study? We chose to study and Lucien didn't blink an eye. We caught a quick bite at a café and then went to the library.

Every day starts with math, four days a week. We got Friday and the weekend off. We turned in our homework written on stationary because we still didn't have any paper. Aleta had to give the university her real name, because that's what was on her passport, but she didn't want to write it on her papers.

"Aleta?" he called.

"Yes?"

"Do you have a last name?"

"No."

He put her paper down and looked at her, eyebrow cocked, clearly saying, *Oh really?*

"I don't."

He squinted at her. "You know we have a store where you can buy supplies." He held up our stationary.

"We do?" we both said, almost in unison, which got a laugh from the class.

"We do. Look in your catalogue. And I need your last name or you won't get your grade."

We hadn't thought of this. And a store?

She told him "Smith."

But after class we told him her real name and pleaded with him not to tell anyone. He raised his eyebrows at us, but agreed. We were going to have go through this for each and every class.

French was a disaster. They wanted us to read books, real books, and write essays about them – in four weeks! We were going to need a tutor. I mean it wasn't just Aleta. I wasn't sure I could do it either! We asked our teacher M. Brun.

Well, we had to anyway. We had to fix Aleta's name, but we also explained our language problem. We needed a tutor. He nodded sagely and said this came up every year and he had some names. He had a list and we added our names and addresses to the bottom. Apparently there were people who made a living at this.

The university had a store. We bought paper, pencils, ink, pens, envelopes, folders, erasers, three newspapers, a hat, two umbrellas, candy, necklace chains, a trolley map, and in general went crazy. We got the good kind of school satchels, the ones with the shoulder strap.

Our new trolley maps told us the trolley stopped only two blocks from our house and would be a lot cheaper than carriages every day, however it turned out to be a lot slower and we rarely managed to find the time to take it.

Next was piano! We had to learn the piano to study violin, which is crazy! Maybe we could fit a piano in our house, because practicing at school was going to be a time consuming chore. And then came Music Studies were we learned how to study and *write* about music! We really needed that French tutor. What were we going to do when we got to rhetoric?

Chapter 14 – An Old Friend

School demolished our lives. It was non-stop all the way through until Friday, then they loaded us down with homework that promised to eliminate the weekend too. Henri dropped by on Thursday, but we were away at class. Fannie wanted us to come in for a shoot on Friday, but come the morning of the shoot we were pretty sure it wouldn't go well. We were both dead tired.

At the photo shoot, Fannie let us sit for a bit before we started pouring cup after cup of her strong coffee. Lucien came that time, which was nice and helped me smile. She had costumes for us too, and they were funny! We were Arab sheiks, cowgirls, and jungle explorers. She had backdrops with jungles and pyramids, and props too. I was definitely going to send these to Ma and Pa.

We went home to lay in our chairs to watch the workmen welding pipes in our parlor ceiling. We really had no security at this point. The front door was wide open for the workmen. The British could have walked right in and we would have been too tired to fight.

Oh, and outside, first one and then two of our followers showed up in Rabbit dresses. They were obviously homemade, but it was incredible! What do you do when you face something like that? You go over and give them hugs and laugh with them of course! You tell them they're crazy, but really it's both humbling and worrying. What kind of trouble will this get them in to? The British might shoot them by mistake!

Tired or not, Lucien wasn't going to let us rest. He had afternoon lunch reservations at a restaurant, which was good since our kitchen was useless. We were filling the toilet with buckets from a cistern on the workmen's wagon. It was a very rare sunny day and he wanted us to dress, so we wore our new dresses. Their maiden voyage. We wore our jewelry by the way and we looked, in my opinion, quite fetching. Sarah even put up our hair!

And now we come, finally, to the Eiffel Tower. How long had I been in Paris without seeing it? Four weeks? My days kept filling up.

So we were, and let's be clear, sprawled in the carriage, clopping along toward the river. Naturally we got a heated one on the one day we didn't need it, which didn't help with staying awake.

"We're are we eating?" Aleta moaned. We were all speaking French.

"On the *Champ de Mars*," Lucien replied. He looked smug. It was probably nice.

"What's that?" I asked.

"It's where they had the World Fair," he replied.

"Oh," your Cali replied, too tired to be curious. All I wanted was to lean up against Lucien and sleep. We clopped across the river and rolled through nicer streets, towards what remained of the 1890 World's Fair grounds. Most of the buildings had been torn down, but some had been reused, one of which was the *École Nationale Supérieure des Beaux-Arts*, the School of Fine Arts where I would soon be spending time. The carriage driver let us out next to the river, which is as close as you can get to the tower.

I had been asleep, so the first thing I saw was the tower going up. It's really, really big, and it's red, and it just goes up and up. The second thing I noticed as I was helped out by Lucien was that the cement underneath is all brown and stained with rust. They have men sweeping underneath all day, every day. But it really doesn't matter when you're standing there with it stretched out above and around you. It's so big that your mind can't grasp it. It can't quite believe it's real until you touch it and you're riding up in the elevator with a dozen other people.

The Tower has three levels. Naturally the ride to the top level is very expensive, but that's where the restaurant is. The first level was, like all of Paris, a mess of construction. They removed Tesla's equipment after the fair and left it bare concrete, but when we visited they were busy building foundations for pavilions for the next fair, and you could still look down the center. It's a long way down to the ground.

We couldn't see directly down the center on the second level, which is too bad, but there were holes and gaps so you could see little bits of it, but we couldn't get to the side to look directly down, which was disappointing, because there was yet more construction all around the sides.

Did you know that people actually take the stairs! Apparently it's free, but it's insane. From the second level up the stairway gets very small, spiraling precariously up the center. People have to squeeze by each other to pass with only a thin railing between you and the abyss. The climb can take all day.

You can eat stand food on the second level and people stop to rest and eat before going on. I bought some post cards there when we stopped. We were in no hurry. We had the elevator when we wanted it, at least when there was room.

The top was all brand new, just finished when we visited. During the fair, the tower had been used to broadcast Tesla's electricity, but after the initial fun, people had gotten tired of getting shocked by their doorknobs and had it torn down. It had apparently been able to send music through the air to anyone who wanted it as well, which you must admit is an intriguing idea.

So the city got smaller and smaller as we rose up and up, the girders going by and by, the climbers on the stairs shooting us looks of venom as we passed. The ticket up from the second level costs same as the whole trip from the bottom, which I think is a bit mean. It's things like this that cause the French to have so many revolutions.

141

But the top is worth it. You're so high that the people on the ground are practically invisible. You can see everything, the entire city between the wisps and trails of coal smoke, all of it drifting away into the countryside long before it rises to the tower top level. We had clean bright blue sky. A rare day in winter. Lucien had timed it perfectly.

We stood at the railing looking out. There weren't even any birds. It was too high for them.

I whispered, "Lucien, I love you."

He smiled and whispered "I love you too" back.

"You are embarrassing me," Aleta moaned, in French. Aleta and I had looked up embarrass up only two nights before.

"Where's Frank?" I asked. I hadn't seen him in ages.

"Frank is no more," she sighed. Then she switched to English, "I'm not Frank material. I will never be a *Housfrau*."

"Maybe we should tell Henri to start handing out our address again."

"I don't think I'm artist's wife material either," she said.

I sighed. "I'm not captain's wife material. Not anymore. Too much has happened."

Lucien just chuckled. He's always been a good diplomat.

The waiter called, "Antoine. Antoine," just as another clump of people tumbled out onto the platform from the stairs, too tired to appreciate the view.

The restaurant at the top is small, as was our table. Its roof is glass and iron, letting weak winter sunlight in. We unfortunately had to sit away from the edge and the view. They had a walkup bar which saw a steady stream of people ordering something to ease their pain. The menu was short, only six choices, as everything had to be hauled up. I ordered the fish.

"It might be nice to come up here at night," I suggested.

"Polaire did," Aleta said.

"In the Summer," Lucien smiled. "The wind tonight will be freezing." Though it had been relatively warm below, up high it was very cold.

The wine was very nice which is why I leave that to Lucien. His taste has been trained from birth.

We looked at the view some more, stepping over the people trying to survive the cramps in their legs, then went back down.

I asked to go to our bank but the driver said it would be closed. They close at three. So we went home. Sarah showed us the calling cards that had been left. They'd been multiplying as our address leaked out. Apparently two more publishers wanted to talk to us. This was before the British realized the danger a book would have represented to them and clamped down on it. I've thought and pondered, wondering what would have happened if we had accepted a book deal then. I suspect it would never have reached completion. The image of me that was slowly developing through my pictures, sound recordings, and movies, only helped support their cause.

"And there was a man. It was hard to understand him. He spoke no French."

"What did he look like?"

"Big, dark skin."

"No card?"

"No, he wrote a note." She handed it to me. It said:

Hello Missy,
Your Pa sent me to make sure you were
all right. He was worried despite your
letters. But I guess you knew he would be.

Crow

I'm at the Hôtel Molière. Not sure of the
streets here, but it isn't far.

I was crying and smiling before I finished. It just jumped out of me in a sobbing breath.

"Cali?" Aleta asked.

"He's here."

Aleta took the note, scanned it then whooped. Which brought a tentative Aline out of the kitchen, glancing around, holding a bat.

"I'm going," I said. "Sarah, give me my coat back please."

"Yes, Miss."

"Me too," Aleta said.

"I won't stay here alone," Lucien added.

So it was back into a carriage in the twilight. I could see the

143

moon, which I hadn't seen since the Bremen. The streets were just waking up.

Hôtel Molière was across the street from the library. Not much of a view, but it was nice. The lobby was wood paneled and carpeted. The dining room was small, but tidy, painted with green enamel. Despite the lack of an elevator, he'd made a good choice.

I asked the desk for Crow, which didn't work, then Takchawee Wachiwi.

"The American," the desk man said with a little smile. "I'll send someone up to get him." And he called the bellboy.

Crow came barreling down the steps at a run, but stopped when he saw us. We were still wearing our new dresses and it must have thrown him.

"Missy!" he called, then rolled forward even before I could jump back at him. He pulled up short of a hug, unsure maybe. But that didn't stop me.

"Oh Crow," I was crying again as I hugged him. "I missed you."

He pulled back and looked at me.

"Me too, but I wasn't worried, except maybe for those Belgians. They don't know who they're messing with."

"How's Ma and Pa?"

"They're fine. They'll be better when I tell them I found you. I'm gonna have to telegram them so they'll stop wasting harbor fees."

"They're waiting in harbor?" We had to put a stop to that. They'll come in late on their second run. But then I realized it didn't matter because I wasn't in school, which kept the tears coming.

"Fraid so. Those zeppelins are somethin aren't they?"

"When they work." It was like it had been bottled up and I didn't know it. It all came pouring out. I was holding him sobbing. People were looking at us from the dining room.

"Cali," Aleta said. "Let's go somewhere."

"When did she start speaking French?" Crow asked.

"There's so much to tell you."

"Come," Lucien said, motioning towards the door.

We lost our carriage and, unlike our street at home, they were sparse there. We had to walk to the corner, passing the men with their poles lighting the lamps. After such a lovely day, we seemed to be heading towards fog.

144

"It's strange seeing you all grown up," Crow said. I think there was a catch in his voice.

"I'm not grown up."

"Maybe." Then he smiled, "When did you get a maid?"

I laughed. "She's been working for us for . . ." I looked at Aleta.

"Two months? No three."

"Is that all? Sarah is incredible," I said.

"And a house," he continued.

"A rubble pile," I replied.

"They're fixing it. I suppose Lucien's helping you." He glanced at Lucien.

"Yes," I sighed. "And others. But I could if I needed to, I have my own income."

"See. That's the thing. Last I saw you, you didn't know what to do with money."

"Spending money is easy," I said, with a laugh.

"But I bet you know what to do with it. Your Pa saw to that."

"Maybe."

"Did you find a school?" he asked.

"Yes. We're going to the Sorbonne, the National University."

"Probably a lot better than some royal one."

"A lot harder."

He laughed.

"We have to take math!" I whined.

"And rhetoric, in French!" Aleta added.

"That explains the French. It sure is hard to get around here without it. Nobody speaks English or Spanish."

"Nope," I said. To be fair to my dear Paris, we hadn't yet discovered the American Left Bank.

"Where are we going?" Aleta asked.

"It's early for dinner," Lucien finally spoke.

"And too cold to sit around outside," I added.

"It sure is," Crow said. "At least it isn't snowing."

We decided to go to a coffee house. Really. Our house was a mess of dust and broken plaster despite Aline's efforts to keep up. We'd been in this one before and the owner recognized me. We picked a table at a window, away from the door and the draft. It was mostly full of men waiting for Pigale to wake. Aleta and I really needed the coffee. Crow laughed and accepted coffee, but it was the middle of the day for him of course. I recognized some of the newspapers on the racks from school.

"I'm getting used to it, but moving around the globe so fast sure throws a man off."

"Things were so crazy when we crossed," I said. "We didn't notice it."

"Now that's something I wanted to ask you about."

"The crossing?" I asked.

"Yup."

"It was hard."

"That's what they said."

And we had to recount it again. To his credit, Crow didn't show any sign of disapproval toward Lucien as some have. It wasn't his fault. We were all trying to help, but the world, as it often does, just bowled us over.

Then we went to dinner. I think Crow noted my drinking wine, but said nothing. I guess I was feeling self-conscious. I think it was that he represented my family and I suppose this was inspection. It made me question things as I did them. I wondered about the decisions I'd made up until that point.

Before we left him, Crow went up to his room and came back with a small box and three photographs. One was of Red, another other was Ma and Pa, and the third the whole crew! I broke down right there in the lobby. I couldn't even close the box. They were such a relief. I hadn't realized how deep the homesickness ran. They are my most treasured possessions. Inside the box was a gold locket as well. It opened to pictures of Ma and Pa, and Red.

We had yet another photo shoot the next morning and Crow agreed to eat breakfast with us and come along. It wasn't going to be fun, but I didn't want to let go of him. When I warned him it would be boring, he said he had nothing else to do anyway. But this was Paris. Nothing to do? That's crazy.

Crow sat in back of the cameras drinking coffee while we posed and played for Fannie.

When we got home, it turned out that we'd missed Henri again so Crow and I went to visit him. Aleta wanted to study and I realized we hadn't been practicing. I'd do that when Crow and I got back. When we got to his house, we found he was out again at the studio, which left me in a quandary. Do I take Crow to the studio or not? I decided that hiding things would just cause trouble. Besides, he'd see the kind of neighborhood I lived in soon enough.

"Who are all those kids outside your house?" Crow asked as we clopped along.

"They're kids who think I'm some kind of hero. It's the newspapers. I tell them to go away, but more and more keep coming. It's why I won't talk to book publishers. Turning things into adventures will just make them do stupid things." He seemed to accept this.

When we got to the studio, I took a deep breath and started up the dark stairs. They were all there again and so was the naked woman.

"Henri?"

They all looked up at me of course, but they knew me now. Henri nodded and put his brush in his can. We whispered in the hallway.

"I may have an architect for you," he said.

"Ooo . . . I didn't bring anything to write on."

He frowned, then looked up at Crow.

"Who is this?"

"He's family," I said.

Henri's looked up at him with disbelief. "You're kidding."

"He helped raise me."

"That explains much."

"What's he saying?" Crow asked. We had been speaking French.

"I'll explain," I answered.

Henri thought, then said, "Wait," and went back inside. When he came back, he had painted a name and address on a piece of posterboard:

Henri Sauvage
Somewhere on the second floor of Beaux-Arts
most days except Sunday not too early

I had to carry it, the paint being wet and it being too big to fit in my purse.

147

"So who was that?" Crow asked.

"That's Henri, a friend. I'm looking for an architect."

"Your house?"

"No. I want to open a store."

I realized, we had missed lunch. I asked the carriage driver if there was a decent restaurant on the way to Beaux-Arts.

"How decent?" he asked.

"Today is special. Very decent."

"Very decent it is."

He took us to *Le Grand Véfour* which turned out to be very decent indeed. A bit more decent than I intended. Looking around, I realized that this was the feeling I wanted in my store, although I doubted I could afford it. It was all gold, painted panels, and glass. I would need freshly arranged flowers too, perhaps every day. But at what cost? Lunch had been expensive. I guess it was shallow of me, but it had been worth it to see Crow's expression when I opened my purse. I wanted him to know that I wasn't hurting. But all I did was to make him worry.

Beaux-Arts is the visual arts school of the Sorbonne. It's right next to the Eiffel Tower, in the Old Exposition Park. As such, it faces the park, not the street, so you have to go in the back door. It also used to be a display hall so most of it is big and empty. A great place for large sculptures, but kind of sad too as they look so little in all that empty space. The ends of the wings are split into two floors and this is where the classrooms and work areas were. Of course, which second floor did Henri mean? The east one or the west one?

"Excuse me," I called to a student, pounding away with a chisle on a huge block of stone marked all over with charcoal lines.

"Yes," he groaned.

"Which way to the architecture department?"

"That way!" he spat.

"I'm sorry," I said.

He growled, then said, "It's just that everyone asks me directions. I wouldn't have let them unload the block here if I had given it any thought."

I tried to give him a look of sympathy, "You should make a sign."

"It will be my next sculpture."

I laughed, which got a begrudging smile from him.

Upstairs we found classrooms with big leaning tables for drawing and deep shelves filled with rolled paper like sea charts. I stopped a student, "I'm looking for Henri Sauvage."

"In the breakroom. Where else?"

The breakroom was filled with old furniture and a small coal stove. A woman was making herself tea.

"Pardon, I'm looking for Henri Sauvage."

She rolled her eyes and tipped her head at a couch.

I peeked over the couch back and looked down. There sleeping, was a young half-shaven man in dirty rumpled clothes. I gave him a poke.

"Pardon, but, are you Henri Sauvage?"

He grunted, so I poked him again.

"Stop," he mumbled.

"Are you Henri Sauvage?"

"No. He's down the hall."

I looked at the woman. She pursed her lips and shook her head no.

"M. Sauvage, Henri the painter sent me."

He opened his eyes. "Strange. I don't owe him money." Then he looked up with confusion and blinked at me, trying to clear his eyes.

"Who are you?" he asked.

I held out my hand to shake, "Calista Carmichael."

He stared, confused. "The Calista Carmichael?"

"Yes, and I would like to see your work."

"Really?" He took my hand and shook it slowly, absent mindedly.

I nodded my head.

The more he looked, the wider his eyes grew.

Chapter 15 – An Enigma

His hand reached towards the shelves of rolled blueprints, but stopped and moved down a bit, and pulled out a roll.

"This is an interior for a wallpaper factory display shop," he said, somewhat indifferently.

He rolled it out on a table, holding the corners down with small shot bags, then adjusting the flame on the hanging lamp a bit higher so we could see. Despite the shadows from the lamp's arms, I could see nothing that seemed remarkable about the design. It was just display tables. I mean the racks for the papers were interesting. Footed sloped shelves, allowing the sides of the individual rolls to be seen and a rack of little pockets to hold sample pieces. It was beyond my experience really. But still, it seemed common. And yet, he extolled its virtues.

"This is very nice," I interrupted. "Thank you."

Then he said, as I was beginning to turn, "Perhaps you might like this." And he pulled down another, laying it over top of the previous one.

It was a candy shop, long and narrow, with glass cases. Two rows of lights hung from the ceiling over the counters. It was pointless.

"Yes, thank you," I said, perhaps too brusquely.

"Then again," he said, in a sly tone as I was turning. "Perhaps you would like to see one of mine?"

That stopped me. My frown turned and I began to laugh.

"Yes. Very much," I replied.

"We live . . ," he paused as he chose two rolls. "In an age of speed. Trains, airships, and cars. We go faster and faster every day." He set the shot bags on the corners. "The world is cluttered with ornamentation that no one sees. It clogs our eyes. This is a bank."

It did look interesting.

"A bank is not a place to lounge and sip tea. It is a place of business. Its design is simplified to fit its purpose. Solid, fast, elite."

It was definitely all of that.

"And yet you do have decoration," I said. "Here and here."

"Yes. The windows are meant to look like Japanese sunrises. Their simplicity of design has always inspired me."

"I can see that."

Then he rolled out the next.

"This is a doorway. It's meant to look like music."

That, I must admit, hit me. It really did look like music. Without actually portraying them, he had managed to turn a pair of rectangles into a couple of cellos, their music flowing from within.

"It's beautiful," I said, half to myself.

"Ha! I got a fail on that. Monier said make them doors, not rowboats."

He had begun muttering to himself about making people dizzy, when I asked, "Do you have any more?"

He brightened and began pulling down more rolls. It was clear to me as we progressed, that this was the man for the job, if I could afford him. Henri the artist had been, as always, entirely correct. So I explained the project. He agreed to meet Sunday after tomorrow. He should bring some of his work to show. Free food. How can a

151

bohemian turn down that? Paul would be closed and thus most likely free too.

Crow listened stoically throughout all of this. I wasn't sure how much he was understanding.

Outside he said, "That guy's designs sure are crazy."

"You should see the painting Lucien bought me. The artist died trying to commit suicide."

"That does sound crazy."

"The funny thing is, the painting makes me happy."

"Now you sound crazy."

"Maybe."

I had no more time to play with the shop that weekend. We had homework. Aleta needed help and we only had that night and Sunday. I told Crow he should go see the city, but he came by anyway and laughed and laughed at my painting. Art is so often joy born of misery.

We had no workmen because it was Sunday. The library was closed too. We worked at home laying on one or the other of our beds with books and paper piled around. Then we practiced before working some more. I told Crow he could explore the catacombs if he wanted and left him the map. Even smugglers and crazy people have Sunday off in Paris, but I don't know if he did or not. He came up and said bye. I told him when we get home from school. That night, it was two very tired college women who fell into their beds and slept.

Of course, just as I was going to sleep, I remembered that next Sunday we were going Rouen to record. How was I going to find the time to tell our architect Henri? As it turned out, we had a new employee that I didn't know about – Jacques, a boy from down the street. Our household was growing. He was ten but almost as tall as me and he ran errands for Sarah and Aline. I was learning. When there's a problem, just ask Sarah! She sent him off with trolley fare and a note that I was pushing the meeting back a week. I'm sure he didn't spend the trolley fare on candy!

Lucien showed up early to escort us to school, which was sweet. He clopped with us there, complementing our new book bags. We looked so academic. Poor Aleta's eyes were red already. She had been up early. I told her she should have woken me, but Sarah had been helping her with French.

We needed to get books to read and write about, but Aleta needed one with an English translation. This was a real problem and we didn't have much time. The girl at the student store counter had the solution. We needed to go to the *Bouquinistes* near the cathedral. They sell and trade books on the street.

School days go better when you've done your homework, and we had. That would change as the week progressed and we had less and less time to do it. We took off for the booksellers after school with only an hour or so of daylight before they started closing. Notre Dame, by the way, is a really big church everyone is supposed to see, but we had no time for it. Besides, everyone says you need to go when the sun is shining to see the stained glass, which we would probably not see for at least three months.

Finding books in English turned out to be difficult and, not for the last time, I wished I had brought *Dracula* with me. We hopped from one table to the next, scanning the spines, asking vendors. So and so carries them. Where is so and so? That way. On and on. Until, finally, they found us.

"Pardon, but do you speak English?" a man said in English. He was tall and too thin, but his grey suit was well-tailored. He looked down at us over his long nose and well-kept moustache. I think he looked to be in his thirties, but it was hard for me to tell ages at only seventeen.

"Yes," Aleta replied. "I do."

"Oh, you're English," he brightened.

"I guess I am."

"We aren't terribly popular in Paris are we? John Walker." He held out his hand to shake. So un-Parisian.

"Aleta," Aleta replied, taking his hand.

"Aleta?" he asked, frowning.

"Aleta," she replied with a little smile.

"The Aleta?"

"I'm the only one I know."

"And this would be?"

"Cali," I said, and held out my hand to shake.

"Cali."

"I see." I think he had noticed our dresses. We had clearly been identified.

"You wouldn't happen to know where we can find English language books?" Aleta asked. "We've been looking and looking."

"I'm afraid you just have to look. Don't bother asking. They'll give you the runaround."

"I was beginning to get that feeling," I said.

"We're running out of time," Aleta said, with urgency.

"What are you looking for?" he asked.

"We need books in both French and English for school."

"And the Sorbonne English library is no help," he said, with a knowing smile. It was our book satchels that gave us away. "They only have reference and textbooks." Then he thought for a second and said, "Look. You can borrow some of mine, but we'll have to find the French versions here."

"Do you have *Dracula*?" I asked.

"Yes, but the French translation isn't out yet. But I bet we can find *Frankenstein*."

"I get it first!" Aleta said.

Find it we did, and *The Picture of Dorian Gray*. Mr. Walker seemed to have an affinity for horror. We had to take him back to his apartment to get the English versions, so we shared a carriage in the freezing twilight, sadly unheated. It was getting dark with many streets around us yet to be lit.

"I've been here eight years," he said. "Came to study and decided to stay. It beats London."

"It's just as cold," Aleta said.

"Oh but wait until spring. Then you'll see something." Then he looked at Aleta, "You might want to flip for Dorian Gray. The preface is practically your report prewritten."

"Then you should have it," I said to Aleta.

"I'm just learning French," Aleta added.

He winced. "A hard start for school. I did that, but I was going to the English School. Starting the Arts School that way is aggressive. Maybe you can put rhetoric off until after summer. Law too."

"We have math and French this quarter."

He nodded his head in sympathy. "I'll tell you what. I'll lend you Jekyll and Hyde too. Then you can compare and contrast them. Your teacher will love that. They love controversy."

"Controversy?" I asked.

"Gray's been banned, reprinted, and then banned again," he chuckled. "You'll love it."

"It sounds fun," I said.

He nodded absentmindedly, thinking. "Listen. There's a party this weekend. Expats."

"We're going out of town," Aleta said.

He gave a little frown. "Too bad. Maybe the next one?"

"Sure," I smiled.

"Sure?" He looked puzzled.

"Yes," I said.

"That must be American."

"Yes."

Then he dashed upstairs and came down with the books, and we swapped cards. When he saw ours, he gave a little nod, as if they confirmed his suspicions and said a cordial goodnight. We clopped home only to find Crow and Lucien sitting in the parlor sharing a bottle of wine.

"I'm so sorry!" I said. "We had to get books for school."

A laugh burst out Lucien when he saw our choices.

"These look good," Crow said. "Maybe I can borrow them when you're done."

"As long as we get them back. The English ones are borrowed and are very hard to get here."

Somehow we acquired one of those tables you put in the middle, in between the sofa and chairs. Things like that kept appearing. Our busy dueling protectors. We did our math and French downstairs in our new parlor on our new sofa table, sitting with Lucien and Crow next to the fire, with Aline bringing us food.

I didn't get to look at John's card until bedtime. Under his name it said he was a reporter for The Illustrated London News.

I showed it to Aleta, standing in our night dresses in the hallway. We were completely conflicted. The British press had created so many stories about us, all pure slander. And yet, we really needed the books. John had been nice too. But I was pretty sure that even if he didn't stab us, his employers would. We might as well invite Nigil to tea. But we kept the books. They were really good too! I did Frankenstein and Aleta did Gray because he was right about the preface, and she needed all the help she could get.

Oh, and I have to tell you. Lucien was in negotiations with Jean-Paul to buy the house next door. I didn't know. It would bump me up a tax bracket – twice the windows – but it had access to the courtyard! It was so quiet because Jean-Paul was using it for storage. He had a lot of places like that because he has a lot of things he needed to hide, mostly to avoid inspections, taxes, and tariffs, which is something I understand entirely. But, who knows what was in there. Bodies? Opium? Tobacco?

My house though, had been deemed to be too small. It was fine for Sarah, Aleta, and me, but our little family seemed to keep growing and it would be nice to have guests stay too, like Crow, who moved in to our loft next door to Aline. His room was under the roof door hatch so I guess he was guarding it. It was rude of them not to consult me, but then with school and everything else, they might have and I didn't remember.

Our French tutor showed up Tuesday night with no warning. He just came calling, which was also rude, but we needed him. We were working on homework at the parlor table, sitting on pillows while eating dinner. So we offered him some, which is probably why he came then and not later. Crow decided to learn French too, so we were definitely getting our money's worth out of our tutor.

Those were busy days. So many things were happening. I remember it all as a great whirl. Fannie dropped off our new pictures and they were great! We were at school when she came by, but we saw them when we got home. They look so real when you can view them with both eyes. And they fired up our hot water heater! It ran on gas. That and the generator, which ran the pump to the roof cistern. Our house was as crazy as Gustave's boat. We had separate hot water faucets everywhere and eventually we would have our own tub. A big claw footed one you could sit in!

So does this all sound as fun to you as it does to me when I sit here and tell it? That was one of the happiest times in my life.

"I'm going die," Aleta moaned.

It was Thursday, our first math test. Aleta's first school test ever! We practiced and practiced and I think her biggest enemy was fear.

"Doomed, doomed. I didn't sleep," she mumbled as she headed for our partially working bathroom.

To be honest, I wasn't exactly sure about myself either. This wasn't boarding school. We had no idea what to expect except that it was probably going to be hard. We would at least get it over with first thing, when the coffee was still fresh in our veins.

Crow and Lucien just sat and watched us mill about, trying to eat and find our things. I suspect they found us amusing. They had no help to offer. Neither of them had gone to college and had no advice.

We had a frost that night and our windows had pretty patterns in the corners. Our breath came out in white plumes in the blue morning twilight. Naturally, there were no carriages! We had to trot up to the boulevard lugging our book satchels to find one. Being early, before most of Paris wakes has its advantages. We got our pick. One that was heated.

The classroom's mood was subdued. Normally there were clumps of students or at least pairs making noise, but there was nothing but the rustle of papers and the creak of seats.

We were never part of those clumps of students anyway. We had yet to find friends at school. People gave us a wide berth, probably because of who we were. It was funny. Everyone wanted to talk to me in the street, but it's different when you're locked together in a classroom. But that didn't matter to us because we were so worried about just surviving.

When class time came around, the professor didn't even bother to show up! Instead, we got a student assistant.

"There will be no talking or I'll take your name," he said. "No books on your desk. Pencil and paper only. You have until the end of the period." That was it. Then he started writing problems on the board. Really, hard, problems.

"Oh God," Aleta whispered.

We set to it. Very few left early. I think most of us had discovered a new level of hell. Aleta was practically in tears in the hallway. It was that bad. The worst was that we wouldn't find out our scores until next week.

This tainted our weekend. My beautiful plans to take a boat to Rouen were squashed by practical considerations. First and foremost, it was really cold. Sitting on the water in the open no longer held its former appeal. Second, it would take us a day and a half to get there. After our performance on that test, we clearly needed to study. So we took a lovely heated late express on Friday instead. Three hours and we stayed in a hotel.

Poor Crow and Lucien. They listened stoically as we whined, griped, and moaned all day long, trying to study and practice, but accomplishing neither. We were sure we had failed and we were tired. But we read on the train. It's a shame we left late because Rouen is really pretty. I could see we made a mistake as we clopped down the narrow medieval streets to our hotel.

"Lucien, can we stay another night?"

"We have homework," Aleta chided.

I growled. We both felt the same way, but this was Aleta's big chance. It was very important to her. And she needed to work. Perhaps we had taken too many classes.

"How about going back in the evening?" Lucien suggested. "We could see a cathedral or two."

I looked at Aleta, who was clearly conflicted. She was frowning, but she nodded.

We stayed in a hotel that used to be someone's mansion. The wine at dinner went right to my head and I started nodding off before we were finished. I was exhausted, and so it was straight to bed.

The studio was set up by Thomas Edison, manned by Edison technicians from the U.S. The people who had just tried to kill us! They were the ones who sabotaged the zeppelin took from Boston. They had converted a storefront on a side street into a sound studio. No big rooms this time. Just the opposite. The room was small, the walls covered with plane heavy cloth drapes.

When we walked in, they introduced themselves, my hand stopping in mid shake.

"You're kidding," Aleta looked at Fannie.

"No. They developed and own the process," she replied, looking worried. "Is there a problem?"

"They tried to kill us," I said.

"Fannie," Aleta glared. "They're the ones who blew up our

zeppelin."

Fannie looked at Lucien. He nodded. Then we all looked at the technicians.

"Honestly," the lead said in American English. "I don't know anything about that. We just work on the recording team." He glanced back and forth at our glares. "It's a big company," he shrugged.

"Innocent people died," Aleta said.

"I read about that. That was us?"

I was turning to leave.

"Wait, wait, let's talk about this," the lead said, skipping forward to follow.

"Cali," Fannie called. "Please don't leave. This is important." She ran to follow too.

"Why?" I snapped, waving my hand in the air.

"Because we have a contract. I'll be ruined," Fannie replied.

"What?"

"I didn't know about Edison. I'm so sorry."

"She wouldn't," Aleta said, frowning.

"We can't work with them," I said.

"I didn't know," Fannie said. She looked frightened.

I could see the technicians looking out the door at us as we stood in the street. Lucien was watching me. His face told me no answers.

"How much will it cost to break the contract?"

"The kill clause is fifty thousand. But that isn't the problem. It's the damage to our reputation. I should have reviewed the final contract with you."

I saw Crow look at Lucien. He looked surprised. Lucien just gave him a little nod.

I asked Aleta. "How are you?"

"I don't know," she replied. She looked confused and hurt. This was money out our pockets, but her pockets weren't deep. Fannie and she were starving artists before this. Me? I had Ma and Pa and Red. I'd be fine; maybe even better than fine. I stood there thinking, trying to find an answer. Crow and Lucien were watching me, which they had been doing a lot of lately. They weren't going to help. It was my decision.

"Let's look at the contract."

"It's inside," she said. She almost winced.

I took a breath, just to build up steam, then walked back in. Sitting down, I began to thumb through it. Edison knew what he was doing when he set it up. Unlike the contracts I'd been signing for the pictures, this covered the entire planet and it was bullet proof. I couldn't see anything. That was until the end.

"Where's my signature? Miss Johnson has signed, but I haven't. Although she's my representative, she doesn't have signing rights."

"We were expecting you to sign when you arrived," The tech said.

We were off the hook, except for the damage Edison could do to our reputation and of course the loss of future contracts.

"Then we need to talk to someone with authority." I needed to know how far Edison could go with this.

"He's late," the tech said. I think he disapproved of his boss. "He was out last night."

"Can you send someone to where he's staying?"

He rubbed his chin. He looked worried. "Yes, of course."

Of course he can wake up his hungover boss for some cranky artist.

"Then let's do it. I need to talk to him. And after you've done that, can we go over your equipment? I'd like to understand what we're doing. I've never seen anything like it."

He looked relieved. This was something he understood. It sounded like progress. The lowest tech went out the door to run for wherever they were staying.

"It's all brand new," he said with pride. "The latest thing. You're our first customer in Europe." He picked up a bright blue tube and handed it to me. "Look. Feel it."

Their first customer, specially requested, I thought. We had leverage.

I hefted the tube. It was strange. Not wood or metal. "What is it? Some kind of linoleum?"

He smiled. "It's celluloid. The stuff is incredible. Cheap to manufacture. We can cast it. We can even cast a fingerprint. As far as we know, it never goes bad. Not like the old wax cylinders. It won't melt either. You can play them and play them, and we can make as many copies as we want."

"You can record sound on them?"

160

"Can we! Here, let's do one."

He picked a clean tube and we adjourned to the sound room. On one side there was little table with a box and a big cone.

"This is the cutting machine. We slide the tube on here and clamp it." Then he put a hinged piece of metal on top. "There. It will start recording when we turn it on."

"Okay," I said.

"Ready?"

I nodded.

He flipped a switch on the side and the tube started turning.

"Say something."

I thought for a second then said, "Hello, this is Calista Carmichael and I'm recording this on January 28th, 1894." I looked up at him and he turned it off.

"Now to play."

He lifted the metal piece off the tube and put another smaller one on, then flipped the switch again. Out of the cone came our voices! I was floored.

"That's me?" I squeaked.

"Yes," he smiled.

"Amazing," Lucien said. "The sound quality is a huge improvement over the old wax tubes." He seemed genuinely intrigued.

"Yes, except you can't shave and reuse them. But the tubes are cheap."

"Shaving is handy in the office," Lucien replied.

"But the tubes are so cheap it doesn't matter."

"And you can use them to start your fireplace," another tech added.

"Well . . . yes," the head tech said. "They burn well."

Their boss chose that time to intrude. His hair and beard were still wet. He had stuck his head in the sink.

"What's the problem?" he asked.

"We want to amend the contract before we sign."

He frowned, then said slowly, "Okay."

"Two things. First, I want players."

He brightened. "Sure. We were going to give you both one anyway."

"Second, I want to create a cylinder for Edison's ears only." I glanced at Lucien and Crow. They looked surprised.

"Why?" he asked.

I just stared at him.

"And I want a note from him that he received it," I added.

"We can cut a cylinder and ship it, but I can't guarantee he'll send you a note."

"If there's one thing Edison clearly understands," I replied. "It's a contract. Put it in writing."

"What are you going to say?" he asked.

I just stared at him again.

He sighed, and we wrote the additions in the contract margins, initialed by all, then we signed.

The recordings took us most of the day. It's a lot harder to do than you might think. It takes steady volume to cut one of them and they don't always come out right. Things don't sound exactly the same played back. We had to adjust our work to get the playback we wanted. They crushed our failed tubes to prevent their theft.

Come late afternoon, it was my turn. The tech set up my tube, then I made everyone leave the building. I knew how to do it by then. I had four minutes to say what I wanted. I did it in a minute and a half. When they came back in I had the tube in hand, in its cardboard box.

"Is there some way to seal this?" I asked.

"Yes, but the dispatch envelope is sealed."

"Someone will open that. Only Edison must open this box."

"Sure. It's just wax."

"I know that you can open this and reseal it," I said to him. "But for your own good, you shouldn't. It could end your career, or worse, if he found out."

He frowned.

"I'm not going to get in trouble for this?" he asked.

"No." I handed him the tube. "Seal it."

Three weeks later I got Edison's reply. It came in the mail. I later had it framed, the folded sheet of paper still half in the envelope. I watched the framer as he worked, putting the paper in the envelope myself so he couldn't read it. I've never told anyone everything that either of us said. I refused and refused until Aleta finally gave up asking.

We were on the train for instance.

"What did you say?"

"I told him why he was an idiot."

"But what did you say?"

"I appealed to his greed."

"Did you call him names?"

"No. That would be foolish."

I can be evasive. But this was my message to him and him alone. I hit him as hard as I could as best as I could, given that he was clearly a man who didn't care. He may have even been the type that takes pleasure in other's destruction. But, enough years have passed that I think I'm ready to tell you half of it, what he replied. Do you want to know?

Leopold taught me that it's the story behind the trophy that makes it valuable and in my own way I've learned that the beauty of art is more in the idea being expressed than the means of its delivery. In both cases, it's the idea behind the piece that's ultimately important. Inside the envelope was a blank sheet of paper. A purposeful indication of indifference. To me it felt evasive, that I had hit home, but would never know for sure. It was an enigma. He hoped to leave me hanging.

In framing it, I made it art. By not showing his reply, I implied meaning. I turned his reply into an artistic joke. The physical picture frame I put it in was just a box to hold it. The real frame I wrapped around it was the mystery of its content. I created an enigma wrapped in an enigma. A mystery within a mystery.

I hope that you read this Mr. Edison and understand what I've done, that I've turned your empty nonsense into something valuable, even famous, publically displayed for all to see. No one will ever forget what you did. Its story will slowly poison your legacy. You can't own it and you can't hide from it. It's my trophy. That is pure art. The art of revenge!

Chapter 16 – Severing Ties

We caught the Rouen Cathedral bathed in a rare burst of late afternoon winter sun. Yellow coal stained sunlight shone down under the eaves of a roof that stretched up forever. Around us, as we stood in the nave, ringed by statues, flowed shadows. They walked and stood, coming apart like smoke as we passed through them. They were too insistent, old needs and anguish unfulfilled, the air cloying thick with a fog of choking scented smoke that stung my eyes. I don't think anyone could see it but me, but it made it difficult for me to breathe. As the years have gone by, I've found cathedrals to be more and more trying, but this one was worse than most. They seem to show more on bad days as well, and this had been a very bad one. I endured until the others were satisfied and we left to find dinner and our train. Our hotel had already sent our luggage on.

Sunday was nothing but study. Poor Crow and Lucien. I knew they had to be bored, but they seemed pleased to watch us work. We did our work by the fire, sharing it sitting cross legged on the floor on pillows from our beds at the little sofa table. Outside the day was damp and cold again.

We passed the math test. Aleta had the second lowest passing score – but we passed! The whole class had suffered. Some teachers like to do that. The scores were posted next to the classroom door.

We had to dig through our purses for our paperwork to get our ID numbers. Aleta was pale, falling forward, arm extended against the wall when she saw it. I think she was crying with relief.

On Thursday, Lucien received a letter from the Crown. A summons. This wasn't just a "come back to work" one, men in derby hats come to take him away. It was official and ominous, with a seal and signatures. He sat with it open on the table, rubbing his temples. I held on to him, my head on the back of his shoulder. My poor Lucien. Would this mean another attempt on the house as well? An attack from both sides? I would die if I lost him.

And we were hardly ready for an attack. Renovations had been progressing, but we still had workmen everywhere, each one a potential assassin. The front door was always sitting open. Of course the construction had its benefits. We had heads on all three floors with sinks that had hot water and a tub downstairs! The kitchen stove had been gutted too, its interior replaced with gas burners, the coal box becoming a middle oven for braising meat. The loft was divided into two bedrooms, and all our walls were still pulled apart. Now they were stringing electricity, our main cable snaking back through the catacombs to the station three blocks away. But that was, like our water, only on for certain times of day, which was why we had the generator and a big tank of fuel. We would always have electricity as long as the fuel oil lasted. The coal scuttle was replaced with a box for ice delivery.

I never liked that coal scuttle. It let in a freezing draft and who knows what else. It was one more hole plugged. The door to the basement was replaced with a strong door also, just to make sure. No sneaking in from below!

When she saw the summons, Aleta remembered she wanted a gun. I remembered that I thought it a bad idea and we fought. The thought of us fighting even now brings tears. It didn't help that Aline sided with her. I think it was the stress of him leaving and the fear of what might be coming. Lucien tried to console me and be sympathetic without taking sides.

He left on Friday, only ten days before Valentine's Day, covered in more stupid Cali tears. Lilli, Bijou, and Dior came by later in the morning and cried with me and fed me walnuts. We had a new nut cracker and bowl. It sat on the table in the parlor.

The second try didn't hit our house at all, but waited to ambush us on the way to school. We foolishly let the drivers follow the shortest route each time. That would change.

"Cali," Aleta said. "You know Gérald from Music History?" She pulled a folded piece of paper from her purse. "Here, look at this."

It said, *Want to go out Saturday?*

"That's creepy," I said.

"I've had worse. What do you think?" she asked.

"What about Adrian and Stéphane?" They had been following her around.

"That isn't creepy?" she asked.

"True," I said. "I can't go. I'm going to try to get Paul and Henri to work together again."

She frowned at the note. "It doesn't even say day or night."

"It's up for negotiation."

Then there was a gunshot and something pulled at my hat, the one from Paul. I simply can't keep nice clothes! We dove for the floor, but we were hardly off our seats heading down towards the floor when more gunshots followed. Time seemed to slow for me. The carriage lurched, the glass in the window behind shattered in shining shards as we fell down towards the floor. Our horse was screaming and our driver yelling, wood splinters from the seat flew past me until the carriage hit something and the whole thing tipped, hitting hard, Aleta falling on top of me. The carriage dragged itself along the ground. Police whistles echoed around us as I watched the cobbles wrench past the window next to my face. It ended with a great crash as we hit a lamppost. Then nothing but police whistles and the scream of the horse. We lay there in a pile, Aleta on top of me, groaning but unhurt. Next to my head, just inches from my face, there were new blades of grass sprouting from the dirt between the street cobbles. Spring was coming.

The police caught one. The other got away. We would have to stand up in court again three weeks later. They were amateurs! They used short barrel revolvers from the side of the street. I suppose they wanted to hide them before they attacked, but they hit nothing except my hat. The bullets went everywhere. The only casualty was the carriage driver's horse, which caught a bullet and had to be killed. We paid for a new one and his repairs naturally, and bought him a heater to make up for his lost business. We declared him a hero for saving our lives, giving the newspapers lurid details we couldn't have seen from inside the cab. It was just good business. The last thing we needed was to be shunned by carriage drivers. He was brilliant though.

The strange thing is how little this affected me. I climbed out the sky side door above us and set about trying to figure out what it would take to get us the rest of the way to school. No tears or shakes. What was wrong with me? I think I had become used to death standing so near. We were becoming close. That was their second try. Sadly, the third was the charm.

Crow started riding with us to and from school after that. He would even wait for us after school, racking up carriage time, but that was the last attack for a very long time. Instead, I had people harassing me, coming to our door. I began to draw crazy people and people who wanted to sell me things or ask for money. Our address had become common knowledge.

Aleta bought it when I was away at my lunch with Paul and Henri. Aline helped her find it. It was a Webley. I wouldn't touch it. I knew that gun too well. I could see nothing but fire and death whenever it was near. It made my hand itch. Crow bought a gun too. I don't think he knew that I knew, but he favored his left arm as he watched the crowds.

The meeting with Paul and architect Henri, not to be mixed up with my painter Henri, didn't go well. They are both strong personalities. Frankly, they both walk around with chips on their shoulders. Paul wanted to manage the design while I wanted to let Henri work. Henri brought sketches which were brilliant, but inappropriate for our purposes, which got Henri angry with me. Perhaps I gave them too much wine. It was nice wine too. It ended with Henri walking out. But, as the years have gone by, I've come to realize that he does that so he won't have to worry about the tab.

Three days before Valentine's Day I received a letter from Lucien.

My Love,

167

Their plan is clear. I've been offered recognition, a place in the royal succession in return for rejecting you as a wife. Naturally, I rejected the offer in the strongest terms. In fact I was rude, which set them aback. To join them in their hypocrisy, to betray Belgium to the British is insane. But they persist. I wish you were here to help. Your vision would be invaluable.

My sister Clémentine . . .

Wait. He has a sister? I thought. She later became one of my best friends.

who is heaven sent, advises me to shun them. She feels my work has been too valuable to the crown and that necessity will prevail. I can't say more as this will surely be read. Know that I love you.

Lucien

Lucien has never been a good letter writer. I think it's all those state documents he works with or maybe he copies them out of romances. Honestly, don't hold the above against him. Aleta says that no man is entirely perfect.

By February people at school were stopping us in the hall to ask us to join their clubs. I guess they had gotten over their awkwardness and fear. We even stopped wearing Paul's dresses, and went so far as to don corsets, but it made no difference. We were clearly marked.

And so we decided to join Solidarity. We said *yes* to the hundredth girl to say "Solidarity" to us.

"What?" she said.

"Yes," I said.

"Yes?" she asked.

"Really," Aleta answered.

"Yes?" She was frowning.

"Yes," I said again, firmly. Aleta was standing there grinning at her.

"Really?" she squeaked. Her name's Anni by the way.

"Yes." I stared at her.

She twisted about clearly confused as to what to do next, then seemed to shrink. "I don't know what to do. I'm new," she said. "You need to see Jeannette."

"Jeannette?" I asked.

"She's our club president."

"Jeannette."

Jeannette, an emancipated woman who liked cigarettes, was eating in the cafeteria. Really, there's no avoiding cigarettes in public places, especially restaurants. You just have to get used to them. I will never abide cigars though. I will leave. I don't care where they came from. Once they've been lit they're horrible. Even after they've been put out they're still horrible.

We were introduced by Anni.

Jeannette looked up at us from her seat with what cannot be described as anything less than greed.

"You want to join?" she said. She leaned back with a smile.

"Please," Aleta replied.

"Well," she said, like that signified something. "Do you know what we do?" she asked.

"You stand up for the rights of women students," I replied.

"Well," she said again, and took a draw on her cigarette. "We do that. That and have fun."

"Fun?"

"Fun." It was a statement. She crossed her legs, spread like a man, showing her shoes and stockings. Taking a big a draw on her cigarette, she continued, "And we kick people who mess with us up the church steps and then back down again."

Which sounded great to me. We signed and paid our franc of annual membership fee.

Solidarity meetings, the formal ones, turned out to be big communal gripe sessions. Sympathy over unfair grades, which we get. Being forced to do partner's work in group projects was all too common and enduring advances from teachers. We kept a list of those. Teachers to avoid or not approach alone, but it was a long list and sometimes you had to. It was called the *Le Livre Bleu*, The Blue

169

Book. It was blue because that was the color of the blank notebooks in the store. It was the job of the club secretary to guard it, but it was primarily kept in the group's memory. There were many who would have loved to get ahold of that book.

We took over *Vachette*, one of the more respectable Latin Quarter coffee houses just outside of school, twice a month, always accompanied by reporters. *Portefeuille Galant* could be counted on, a paper that specializes in coffee house news, and usually one or two more. More, especially if rumors of counter action were drifting about.

Then there were the quarterly demonstrations to allow women teachers. A school that won't hire its own graduates, especially because of their sex, is pathetic. I didn't have time to attend many of these, but I did contribute substantially for placard materials and flyers. Not just for Solidarity, but other clubs as well. With our help, student demonstrations in Paris became far louder and more colorful. It gave me great leverage over other clubs and groups as well. A fact that Solidarity often used to its advantage.

We took the books back to Mr. Walker. He answered his door himself and, naturally, invited us to another party. The Left Bank expats throw a lot of them.

"Oh good, you've brought them back," he smiled. "Was it a success?"

"We. . ," I started.

"We don't know," Aleta said.

"No grades yet," I added.

"Well, try to have confidence. Although it may seem otherwise, they aren't trying to fail you."

"Perhaps," I replied.

"There's a party next Saturday night if you're interested. Just expats."

"British?" Aleta asked.

"A mix."

"England hasn't been kind to us," I said.

"No," he replied, flatly.

"Would you write about us?" Aleta asked.

"If there was something to write about."

"Would you write truthfully?" I asked.

"I try to write truthfully about everything."

I was conflicted and he saw it.

"It's sometimes nice to just hear English," he said. "Speaking French can be taxing."

"True," Aleta replied. "Where?" she asked, which surprised me.

"I'll get the address. And there are some clubs and cafés you should know about as well. Let me write them down. You can come in if you want."

Again I hesitated, but Aleta replied, "That would be very nice."

His apartment was small, but modern and quite cluttered. He had electricity and turned on some lights, moving newspapers and books to make room for us to sit on his couch.

"Now for some paper," he said. He began pulling open the drawers of a hopelessly cluttered desk, but stopped. "Oh, would you like some tea. It's straight English. No rosehips or herbs."

"That would be very nice," Aleta said. *What was she up to?*

"Excellent. I want some too. Making it for one is a chore." He then adjourned to his kitchen, leaving his last drawer sitting open.

"What are you doing?" I whispered.

"He's nice," she said.

She was angling for a date!

"He's going to write something," I hissed.

"Not if we give him nothing to write."

"News stories follow us around."

"Is everything all right?" he asked, head peeking out of the kitchen.

"We're fine," Aleta said.

Once he was back in the kitchen, I whispered, "No we're not."

"Ah, paper," we heard from the kitchen. He came back in with a sheet of school note paper and a pencil. "I keep it everywhere in case I get ideas."

Sitting on a chair, he pulled the center table close and began to write. "The party is on Rue Guillou, on the west side. And here are some clubs as well." On the list I saw, "The Jockey Club." Lucien would like that. He had circled, "Le Honky Tonk."

"What is that?" I asked.

"A black music club. But you're American. You don't know?"

"No. I'm afraid we don't spend much time on shore," I replied

That seemed to surprise him. "As musicians, you might find it interesting." He again mentioned it as we were leaving.

As far as I know. Aleta never went out with Mr. Walker and we didn't attend the party, but we did go to the Honky Tonk where we would meet Mr. Walker again. He would eventually write a biography about us. It wasn't very accurate but, to be fair, we didn't help.

Valentine's Day came. I baked Lucien a tart, just in case he came back. It was a heart. Aline helped. It had plum filling. We cooked them down the night before, then cooked the tart on Tuesday night. But he didn't appear. What was he going through? I cried myself asleep that night. I am so hopeless.

A messenger brought me flowers the next day. He had turned over the mountains of hell itself to get them to me and they were beautiful. But I watched them as they wilted and he still didn't come.

He finally showed up on the 22nd. We had to pay the carriage! He arrived practically penniless, with just the clothes on his back. Clémentine had stolen back his passport and gave him train money so he could escape from the palace. You might be asking yourself why she could only afford to give him train fare. Royalty don't actually handle money that often. Not without going through others. She had to scrape together the odd bits she could find. Things had become that crazy. It was a Tuesday so we didn't see him until he came with Crow to pick us up from school.

He was dirty, having spent two days on a slow train sleeping in a cheap seat, but he came straight to get me. You can't jump into someone's arms in a carriage. Don't try. They bounce and there are legs in the way. But we clopped home with me next to him as we listened to his story.

"You are right. It's just like the Congo," he said. "They won't move, although I don't see what use I am to them if I'm a prisoner. They might as well let me go. But the British are very clear when it comes to accounts. They feel they're owed a pound of flesh and . . . I'm afraid I'm related to a family of cowards." That last bit trailed away. I could see the shadows under his eyes. He might have even lost weight!

Then he perked up. "But you were right. Dealing with the Camorra is better. I won't go back, at least not to the palace. They'll have to arrest me." Then to himself, "Which they might. I need to talk to Jean-Paul. I'm going to need to move some bank accounts too." He checked his watch, then frowned. "Tomorrow."

It wasn't like Lucien to be so unfocused. They had been hard on him.

"You're here now," I said.

"Yes," he brightened. "If I'm exiled, then I can't think of a better place to be sentenced to. We have all of Paris and spring's coming. They can keep the rest."

He took a bath in our tub and wore some of Crow's clothes. He hadn't eaten a proper meal in two days. No coffee either! That had to be hard on him. He lives on the stuff. I pushed him into my bed and begrudgingly left him. I slept with Aleta that night over endless protests from Sarah that I should take her bed, and no offers from Aline. We really did need more room, but it would be a shame to move now that we had walls again and I'd actually hung my painting.

The next day was a school day and I didn't get anything done except to make it through the day. I gave Lucien two thousand francs. It seemed to pain him to take it, which is crazy! Why is it okay for him to give me money, but not accept it? He really needed to go to the bank, order clothes, and find a place to stay. Staying in my house was somehow scandalous, but I can't see how it was different than the hotels we stayed in. Can you see me roll my eyes? It's probably because we were a thing in the society pages and had people watching.

So Lucien started over just as I had, slowly bit by bit. It would be weeks before he recovered and looked like his old self. This time he was back for good and this is the best, he rented an apartment down the street next to the bathhouse! I could walk over and say hello whenever I wanted.

I finally made it to the bank. How long did it take me, three months? Don't laugh. I was very busy!

I had four hundred twelve thousand francs. They said that was about three hundred fifty thousand northern dollars. Crazy, huh? That bank sure did love me. Brought me tea and everything. They told me the exchange rates were very favorable if I wanted to go back to the U.S. to visit. Apparently the U.S. was experiencing runaway inflation, which made me worry about Pa. That war had to end soon.

So I was somewhat rich. That would change as I started writing checks for the store, which they gave me, along with a leather book to keep them in. Check books were very unusual in France. I had entered a different financial strata. France was on the rise, climbing out of economic depression and depositors were greatly valued by banks starved for liquidity.

I found my business manager through my future investor Fannie. She dropped by the first Saturday in March, early.

"Miss Johnson is at the door," Sarah said. She knows I'm going to say yes. I always say yes and yet we always went through the ritual, but with the rite of the door complete, Fannie came charging in clearly excited.

"I've found a manager!" she said. "He's incredible."

"Where did you find him?"

"Sabella," she replied.

"She's . . ." I was trying to remember.

"The sister of Durrell, Durrell Bonnet." Then she squinted at me. "One of your investors."

"Oh."

"Cali. You should know these things."

"I've been busy," I whined.

"I've noticed. Anyway, Sabella and I have a thing." She beamed. I was probably one of the few people in the world she could tell that to. "Her brother is a manager for Pingat." She said that like I should mean something.

I blinked at her, sitting my violin on my lap.

"Pingat. The fashion designer."

I nodded my head slightly.

"Oh Cali! How can you think of opening a design house without knowing Pingat? He rules Paris."

I needed to investigate this. "I'll look into it."

"Anyway. He's interested in your project and I want to invite him to your next meeting."

"Tomorrow."

"Tomorrow?" she winced. "That's short notice."

I shrugged.

"Would you mind if we showed up?"

"No. Please."

His name was Joseph Vidal. When Fannie had run off to find him, I told everyone I was going out. Crow was gone who knows where, so I left with no escort, which was fine by me. I didn't want to draw attention.

I had to work my way down to Rue des Martyrs to find a carriage. You don't just walk down a Paris street, especially if it's yours, to get somewhere. Not one you live on. I said hello to Mme. Touchard, M. Fouquet, and M. Delattre, then Tabby and Dior. I told the carriage driver Pingat and he knew! We clopped down towards the river to *Rue de la Paix*. What I found almost made me quit and turn around.

It's a disturbingly clean street, wide and lined with beautiful new buildings. Every shop was a designer. This was my competition! Pingat was one of the biggest. I let the carriage go and took a walk, saying over and over, I'm so crazy, I'm so crazy.

But as I walked I realized why it hurt so much to be a woman in Paris. Here were the monstrous shoulders, the corsets that bent your back, the hats big as sails, and the shoes that pinched. These were the men who did it! As I walked I grew more and more confident and maybe even just a bit angry. They were all the same. Clearly none of these men had asked a woman what she thought when they created these things. I saw a coat with at least thirty pounds of beads on it. I bet it could stop bullets! Henri was right. These were towers that needed toppling.

Chapter 17 – Égalité

We arrived at school to find that school itself had failed to show. Half our class was gone. The next nearest student was three desks away. I had to get up to walk over to ask him.

He just stared at me, like I should know. "Mardi Gras. Tomorrow is parade day. No one will be here. Not even the teachers. And only the desperate will be here Wednesday."

Really, it should have been in the school catalog. If I'd been more social I would have heard. We missed the Monday Festival of Masks sitting on our behinds in our desks at school. But Tuesday was the big party, the Procession of the Fat Ox. Don't laugh! It's crazy fun.

We gave everyone the day off which, naturally, Sarah was planning on avoiding. But we would not hear of it. I ordered her to come with us. I could see Aline over Sarah's shoulder, leaning on the counter, laughing quietly to herself. So it was all of us, except Aline, who had plans of her own, stepping out late Tuesday morning. The parade would be passing by us down on The Boulevard With Too Many Names, which was a bit of a walk. I call it that because it changes its name every two blocks. How do you cope with that?

We ran into Mme. and M. Delattre leaving for the fun. They had costumes! I think he was supposed to be a priest and her a strumpet. They were obviously homemade but it was funny as they walked with his arm around her waist.

And you can forget finding a carriage or a trolley that will get you anywhere close to the parade route. First of all, the streets become useless, full of people as you get near. Second, there are no carriage drivers because most of them are already in the crowd having fun, maybe even in the parade itself steering a float. Well, maybe not all because we caught one on Clichy and piled in – us, the Delattres, and a guy who happened to be walking by. The poor horse. We were piled up like a hay wagon. Some of us got out to push to get it moving and the driver charged us double, but it cut out half our trip which was good enough.

And the crowds were crazy and I could tell I wasn't going to see anything unless I crawled forward between legs. Especially annoying were the top hats. I understand that some people seem to feel they have to dress up for these things, but even Henri the painter can block someone's view with one of those.

So, we moved down the street looking for a way forward, enjoying people's costumes and antics. I saw a guy playing his violin like it was a mandolin, strumming it, which was weird and something I definitely had to ask at school about. Just as soon as I managed to get the confetti out of my hair. People were throwing colored paper streamers out of their windows above, which fell and draped themselves over everything. We tried to get close, but there was no making way anywhere. Lucien was talking about pushing us up on one of the statue pedestals, which would surely ruin our dresses.

"Cali! Aleta!" Someone was yelling from up above. We all looked up. It was Anni from school. "Wait there!" she called, and then disappeared.

We waited until she popped out a doorway a very long twenty feet away. "Cali, Aleta, this way!"

Luckily Crow is very good at clearing way. He needs only to loom and people move.

"Oh, hello," Anni said, when she found out we weren't alone. Which led to introductions in the hallway of her building. Her family had an apartment on the third floor.

As we made our way upstairs she whispered, "I didn't know you had a boyfriend." Which was sweet. I had to explain our relationship, which is complicated.

Upstairs, we met her parents and younger sister. Sarah just had to curtsy. All of us thanked them profusely and then they let us watch the parade from above, which was great.

There were wagons decorated with fantastic sculptures, bands, and dancers. Everyone wore beautiful costumes. Anni's family had a big bag of colored confetti which they shared.

After the parade, we offered to take them out to dinner, but they said they doubted it would be possible with the crowds and offered to feed us, but we declined. We couldn't impose more. Starting relationships is a careful, touchy business. But I would later give them tickets to the opera.

Despite the day off Mardi Gras gave us, we needed a break. The mind can only absorb so much before you begin to spend more time contemplating the wall than your books. So, come the end of February we decided to take a night off. Ah, but where to go? You can spend hours going back and forth asking each other that.

But we had that list! The one Mr. Walker had given us and the suggestion that there might be a sizable American presence in Paris. It might be fun to go visit with our fellow war refugees. That's why, dressed in our best, we were clopping towards the American left bank. We would start with The Honky Tonk. Mr. Walker had underlined it.

The American Left Bank is on the downstream end of Seine, in the southwest corner of Paris. To call it the left bank is perhaps a bit pretentious for in truth it scatters west from the left bank all the way to the walls, all over the right bank. Slavery and the war had driven a steady stream of Americans out of the country, into enclaves all over the world, Paris by far having one of the largest of any city. A great many of my fellow refugees were black, black entertainers being in great demand. According to Lilli, The Honky Tonk specialized in them, and the new black music – Rag. It was simply the newest rage in Europe.

Its front was red, the windows painted out black, except for the doors, which were brass and clear glass. Inside, through the doors, you could glimpse the stage. At least you could if you were tall enough to see over the crowd. There was a line and two doormen.

"Reservations only," I heard one of them say.

"Fifty francs?" the man replied.

"Reservations only," the doorman replied to an apparently rich young man and his date. The doorman sounded tired.

"Alie!" the man's girlfriend whined, impatient.

"A hundred?"

The doorman just stared into the distance.

"Come!" the man snapped. "We'll find something else."

"Awww . . ," his girlfriend wailed in disappointment as he pulled her down the street.

I could hear the music inside. It was like nothing I'd ever heard before. All horns and piano. They were pounding it out.

The next couple was negotiating. They had reservations, but were early.

"Cali," Aleta said. "This isn't going to work."

"We might get in," Lucien said. "You'd be amazed what doors a title can open."

That was smug, I thought. But I sure didn't mind open doors.

"Maybe," Crow said. "These French though don't seem to care about that."

They let the couple in to sit at the bar. It was our turn.

"I'm the Duke of Tervuren," Lucien said, handing him his card.

The man passed his card back without looking at it, but glanced at all of us. His eyes lingered for a second on Crow.

"Reservations only," he said.

Aleta growled then said, "Cali, tell them who you are." Then she began clawing through her purse.

"Pardon," I said. "I'm Calista Carmichael. This is my boyfriend."

Aleta handed him her card.

"And this is Aleta, and he's my uncle," I continued.

"For real?' the man said.

"Yes. He's a Crow Indian."

I finally found a card and passed it to him.

He looked at my card, then our dresses, then at Crow, and then blinked.

His friend poked his arm and said, "Go ask. I'll watch." So the doorman ducked inside and we had to wait while his friend stared at me, stroking his moustache.

I gave him a smile.

He gave it another moment, then asked, "Did you and Leopold really . . ?"

Aleta and Lucien laughed.

I rolled my eyes and then managed to laugh too, "Everyone always asks me that!" Then I sighed, "No, but he sure tried." Which got the doorman to bust up.

The first doorman returned and opened the door from inside, the music and warm air spilling out, and tipped his head to motion us in.

The inside was full of sound and smoke. I eyed the stage as we made our way between the close packed tables. The band was all black. They clearly had been having their meals and wore nice clothes. It was such a surprise that I actually stopped and stared.

The drummer tipped his head at me, which broke the spell. I gave him a grin and caught up, Lucien right behind me wondering what the problem was.

They had drums, a piano, and three horns. The piano was carrying the tune, with the horns dancing all around it, and the drums tying it all together with a simple, strangely jagged, solid beat. It was just fast enough to get the heart going. There was something strange in it. I couldn't wrap my mind around it.

We were heading for a table up front, just right of the stage. There were already two men at it, one of whom got up and left as we approached.

"Miss Carmichael, Aleta," the man said over the music. Apparently Lucien and Crow were baggage. He was elderly, graying moustache and hair. He stood and held out his hand. "Sebastian Rochefort," he said, with a slight bow.

By this point we'd been in Paris long enough to know the response and held out our hands for him to kiss, which he did quite expertly. Then he shook Lucien's and Crows hands.

"Welcome to my club. Please, can I offer you something to drink?"

"But we couldn't," I replied.

"But you can. Believe me, it costs me nothing like I charge," he smirked.

"I would like some wine," Aleta picked up.

"Of course!" he smiled, and turned to raise a finger to a waiter waiting in the shadows.

The song finished, the momentary silence suddenly loud as people realized the volume of their voices, only to be broken by the next song. They really were banging through them. It was hard to sit still, but the place had no room to move. Clubs like these needed room to dance if they were going to have music like this.

"This music is wonderful," I said.

"I wish I could say I found it," M. Rochefort replied. "But it found me. You Americans keep pouring over the sea and showing up on my doorstep."

"It's the war," I sighed.

"Yes. I hear it's bad."

"It sure is. It certainly keeps trying to kill us." I glanced at Crow, who nodded.

"My people aren't much better," Aleta said.

"And mine aren't helping," Lucien added bleakly.

"Well, cheer up," M. Rochefort smiled. "You're here now and trust me, this will all pass. We've seen so many wars."

I smiled back. "True."

"There it is," he said, smiling himself. I think he liked me smiling.

"Miss Carmichael," a voice said behind me.

I turned.

"Mr. Walker!" I exclaimed.

Aleta gave him a smile as she looked up.

"I told you to call me John," he chided.

Lucien squinted up at him, unclear if he was friend or foe. It was the English accent. "I don't believe we've been introduced."

"Yes," John said, noticing Lucien. "John Walker." They shook hands.

"English," Lucien said.

"Yes." John almost shrugged.

"John is one our regulars," M. Rochefort said.

"I'm glad you took my advice," John added.

"You sent them?" M. Rochefort asked, looking up at Mr. Walker.

He smiled back.

"I'll have to give you a commission," M. Rochefort added.

"You could offer me a seat," Mr. Walker replied, and he got one. M. Rochefort got the waiter to bring one.

And thus our evening started, our conversation limited by the noise. M. Rochefort was fascinated by Crow and wanted to hear about the West, but poor Crow was no help. He hadn't been there since he was little, being raised in Baton Rouge. None of us had really ever been there ever. So things drifted towards the sea and Red.

"Your family is currently in the Caribbean?"

"Yes. Looking for sugar. We ship it north."

"Past the South?" M. Rochefort look incredulous. Mr. Walker looked thoughtful.

"Yes."

"With the war, that has to be difficult."

"We have to sneak past. Both ways."

"There has to be a better way," M. Rochefort said.

"That's how we got in trouble. Looking for a better way."

"You mean the Congo?" M. Rochefort asked. Mr. Walker's eyes narrowed.

Aleta shuddered. Lucien looked away.

"Yes," I said, turning inward.

"Let's skip this," Aleta snapped.

M. Rochefort startled, then recovered, "Yes. Of course." He glanced at the stage for a moment. "Would you all like to come backstage? Meet some of the musicians?"

That brought back my smile. "Yes," I said.

"There it is," he said, half to himself.

The door backstage was right behind him. We rose together and followed him into the crowded hallway. It was hot from the stage limelight and gas lights in the hallway, despite the backdoor being propped open and stepping outside was a relief.

"Let's see who's here," M. Rochefort said, as he led us back. Leaning out the backdoor, he looked about.

Out back in the courtyard were weathered chairs and a table. M. Rochefort shooed away a couple of men who had been sitting on the step so we could go out.

"Boys," he said in thick-accented English. "I want to introduce you to Calista Carmichael and Aleta." It was clear that our men weren't pulling much weight at The Honky Tonk.

There were nine men and two women, all black, leaning back in chairs or standing about, most smoking. The pavement was littered with butts and the table with glasses and bottles. Several said bonjour, but I wasn't taking that.

"Hello, it's a pleasure to meet you," I said in English.

"Well," said one. "She's really American."

"Where you from, doll," said a woman, as she took a pull on her cigarette.

"Boston," I replied.

"England," Aleta added.

The other woman cooed, "Ooo . . . an Indian," as the men came down the steps. "A big one. Ain't seen one of those in an age."

"Crow," Crow said.

"You don't speak French?" she asked Crow, in French.

"He doesn't," Aleta answered.

"Honey," she said to Crow. "Do you need someone to lead you around Paris?"

Crow grinned, a rare occurrence. "Maybe."

"I'd be happy to help you climb to the top of the tower and back down again," she replied.

"Be nice," M. Rochefort chided.

"I was," the woman replied.

"I hear you're musicians," one of the men said, with a smirk at the woman, purposely changing the subject.

M. Rochefort started, looking about, then motioning with his finger at two of the sitting men to move. "Ladies, please sit," he said.

"Thank you, we would love to," I beamed. How could I turn it down?

The two of the men got up and took places leaning against the wall with their friends. M. Rochefort even held our chairs as we sat.

Then I replied, "Yes, we are," answering the man's question.

"Violin and flute?" He continued.

"Yes," I replied. "Do any of you play them?"

A couple of men snorted, then one said, "Negros don't play em."

"You don't see blacks playing them," another added, with a

glance at his friend.

"No? Why?"

"Too expensive," he replied.

"Too fragile too," another added. "A violin wouldn't last two days in the street."

"Those pieces get bent on flutes too," another said. "A horn gets bent, you just bang it back."

"Nobody steals old horns," another added.

"Yeah, a violin could get you killed."

"It's the strings too. You're always buyin them."

"That's for sure," I said.

"Strings or food."

That stopped me. The hard math of poverty. I was so lucky.

They told us how they got there, mostly by indenturing themselves, but none of them were unhappy with the deal. There were men who scouted black musicians! Those who came were living well and had money to spend. Two were even saving money to bring families over.

Apparently a rag is just a march with a "ragged" beat. They play melody in between the beat. That's why they pull you along so. It definitely deserved thought, just as soon as I had time. Maybe I could work it in to a school assignment. Back inside, I tried to listen, but everyone wanted to talk.

Before we left, Mr. Walker caught my attention and asked, "Would you be interested in telling me your story? We could try to get it right."

"I can't," I replied.

"They would just lie," Aleta snapped. "Even if you wrote the truth. They wouldn't print it."

"It's the Institution," I added.

"The what?" Mr. Walker asked.

"You don't know what that is?" I was incredulous. "Perhaps you should pursue that first." I didn't know then that we were part of a small, very tight circle, or that telling Mr. Walker might get him killed if he tried to dig too deep. I read his book years later and he didn't mention them at all, so I suppose he must have dug a bit and then chose survival.

But . . . what about you Cali? I hear you ask. *You're printing this. You're telling us.*

184

They will get me eventually. Those who published this have survived by being public. I fear that when you forget me, when I'm out of the public eye, they'll clean up the problem.

"Is something wrong?" Lucien asked, looking back to see why we paused.

"We were saying goodnight to Mr. Walker," I said.

"John," Mr. Walker corrected.

"Yes," I said, suddenly feeling very tired. "Lucien. I'm tired."

"I can help with that," he replied.

"And we have schoolwork," Aleta added.

I groaned.

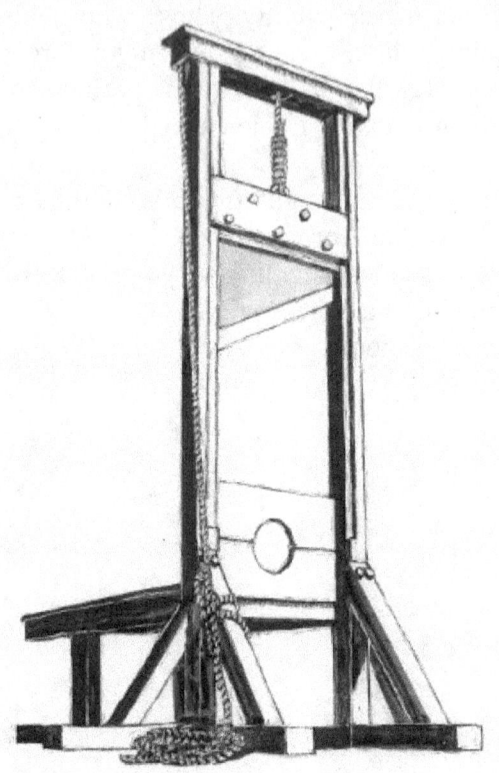

Chapter 18 – A Death in Pigalle

I received a summons to court on March 2nd, right in the middle of the term. It was Fitz's trial and I sat in there all day only to stand up twice. Once to read the deposition I gave to the police and once to answer questions. Fitz himself was sullen and withdrawn.

They chopped off his head two weeks later, but I didn't see that. I hardly noticed the reporters as I walked out of the courtroom.

Two days after my court appearance, Aliz from the mansion across and down the street, *Chat Sauvage*, was murdered. They found her body in an alley, raped and strangled. The news was all over the street.

"She was so young," Mme. Vannir said. She has the hot chestnut cart. Come spring she would be selling flowers. I buy from her sometimes, especially flowers – which I love.

"We don't know where her family is," Sable said.

"Is there going to be a funeral?" I asked.

"She had no money," Sable replied.

"How awful!" Mme. Vannir said. "The thought of her in a pauper's grave with no family." She shivered. "That's too much."

"I can help pay," I said.

"That's too much too," Mme. Vannir said. "You'll be paying for everyone's funeral."

"Someone has to," I said. "This won't do."

Sable was looking at me, but I couldn't read her expression.

"I would rather find the one who did this," I continued. "But at the very least we can show him that she wasn't alone."

"What are we talking about?" It was Pauline, M. Vaillancourt's wife. She's a really good seamstress. She comes out in the afternoon, after her nap.

"Aliz," Sable said.

"Oh," she sighed. "I should turn around. This is too sad."

"We need to have a funeral," I said.

"Does this involve money?" Pauline gave me a look. Clearly convinced that she needed to turn around.

"We need a collection," I said, my resolve firming.

Pauline sighed.

"And a wake," I continued.

"If you're sure," Sable said. "Then we'll need to get her body."

"Get her body?" I asked.

"It's on display."

"On display?" I exclaimed, surprised.

"Yes," Mme. Vannir said. "It will be at the morgue."

"On display?" I couldn't believe I was hearing this!

"They leave them out until someone claims them," Sable said.

"For everyone to see?"

"Yes," Sable said.

"That's horrible!" I don't know why, but I was starting to cry. It was the thought of everyone staring at her body before they threw her in a common pit. It was too much.

"Come!" I said to Sable. I turned and walked for the house.

"I have to go to work," she said as she jumped to catch up.

"I'll hire you."

"Are we going to the morgue?" she asked, but I said nothing. There was a great knot of anger in my throat. I wiped my tears with my handkerchief.

We passed Lilli. She was going to work.

"Lilli," I said. "Be late to work."

"Why?"

"We're going to get Aliz out of the morgue."

"Really?" she asked.

"Yes," Sable said, but I was already through the front door.

"I'm going out!" I called.

I had already turned back to the street when Crow called out behind me, "Where?"

I turned and replied, "To the morgue to rescue a friend."

"Let me get my coat."

We clopped at a brisk pace towards Notre Dame. The morgue is next door. We hurried, I paid extra. I didn't want to find the doors closed when we got there.

"They let people look at the bodies?" Crow asked. He was as incredulous as I.

"Yes," Lilli said. "They fish them out of the river and don't know who they are."

"And sometimes the police watch who comes to view them," Sable added. "Sometimes it's the murderer."

"But most come to see the naked bodies," Lillie said.

"She's naked?" I wailed. That really got me crying.

We were quiet after that, except for me. I think Crow was fuming. He had gotten to know them too.

The morgue is a wide low building. It could be a post office. Only two steps up into the crowded shallow lobby. The back wall was glass, the bodies lying naked on tables, their clothes hanging above. Pushing forward, I got close enough to see that she wasn't there.

"Where is she?" I asked.

Lilli, was right behind me. She shook her head slowly, as confused as I was. So, we turned and made our way towards the office. Inside we faced a counter and large room full of desks.

"May I help you?" said a tall man with one of those awful thin mustaches.

"We're looking for girl. Young. Maybe 18?"

"Oh yes," he said. "Very popular." She was a morgue attraction!

"Where is she?"

"The body was purchased."

"What!?" I yelled. I saw Crow's hand grip the counter.

"She was a common whore. They die all the time."

My hand whipped out before I knew it and slapped the side of his head hard from the shoulder, knocking him back behind the counter onto his coworker's desk. I was climbing the counter to jump him being pulled back by Crow and the girls.

"Whoa Missie."

"She was not common!" I yelled.

The man, back to the desk, slid to the floor and sat there stunned.

"What did you do with her!?" I was screaming.

I was arrested. They took me to the local station and locked me in a women's cell with a thief, a *putain,* who had been beaten by the way, and an old homeless woman passed out drunk, afflicted with flatulence. Lucien was there with a lawyer in two hours.

They were unlocking the cell. He looked in through the bars somewhat amused.

"Did they hurt you?" he asked.

"No. Who is that?" I nodded towards the dapper man in suit.

"Your lawyer," he said.

"These women need his help too," I said.

Lucien frowned at them. "Very well."

The guard looked up at Lucien. "What, them?"

"She was hungry!" I tipped my head towards the thief. "And she did nothing but ask for the payment she was due."

"Not the drunk sir," the guard said. "We let them go when they wake."

Lucien looked at the lawyer. "Do it. Except the drunk."

"Thank you," I said. The guard nodded.

In the office, once they had returned my purse, I gave both girls a twenty franc coin and my card, to their pleading grateful thanks. "Find a bath, some clothes, and a meal, then come to my house."

Lucien rolled his eyes.

I scowled back at him, then said, "We need to find Aliz's body."

"They told me," Lucien grimaced. "She's in the Sorbonne. They buy them for dissection."

"Dissection?" I just finally calmed down and here it was again. Where had that anger come from? It wasn't like me. I stopped for a moment to try to calm myself. One breath, then two.

"My love," Lucien said. "I understand. I remember her at Christmas. She played the violin."

I realized she had. Maybe that's why it hurt so.

"We can't do anything more today. We'll rescue her tomorrow. In the morning."

I looked up at the window. It was dark. He was right. It was too late to do anything. But that didn't stop me from sobbing into his shoulder for a bit on the carriage ride home.

Naturally there were reporters outside the jail, but they let us out the back to give a chance at avoiding them. Of course they were there too. Crow and Aleta guarded my flanks until I stopped. I realized I had to something to say.

"Cali?" It was Aleta.

"Wait," I said, then turned to the reporters. They waited, pencils poised, the flurry of questions stopped. "The displaying, buying, and selling of dead girl's bodies from Pigalle will stop." I would say no more. They swarmed around us as we walked away, backing away from Crow and Lucien as they tried to protect me as we climbed into Lucien's waiting steam carriage.

This is one of those times where something I did, small and simple as it seemed, would have a huge impact on my life later on. As you probably already know, that one sentence would change Paris and then all of France herself.

Sarah told me when we got home that there had been reporters at our doorstep, but our gendarmes, bless them, had shooed them away. I went to the kitchen to look for Aline and realized that things had changed. I'd been so focused on school that changes to the house had gone right by me. We had new counters and cupboards. Everything was painted green and yellow. There was electric light shining everywhere!

Then I saw it. When had this happened? The flagstone on the floor had been pulled up and replaced with – *linoleum*! The countertops too! I stood there stunned.

"Yes, Miss?" Aline asked, as if this were as normal as rain.

I stammered, she smirked, until I finally collected the words, "Where's my house?"

She burst into a big grin, the first time I'd ever seen one on her.

"Cali!" Aleta snapped as she walked up behind me. "You went out and got arrested without me! That is so unfair!"

"The house," I said.

"What?" Aleta replied, confused. "Is something wrong?"

"They put in linoleum."

Aline burst out laughing.

Aline is definitely evil, but I can be too.

"Aline?"

"Yes, Miss?"

"Could you use some help?"

That quieted her. She frowned. "Maybe."

"We might have company," I said.

"Who?"

"Someone who needs a job."

"Are you sure it's not a trick?" she replied.

"What happened?" Aleta asked.

"I broke some girls out of jail," I replied.

"You broke girls out of jail without me?" Aleta wailed.

Aline's grin popped back. "They'll have to sleep on the floor until we get the second house fixed Miss."

"Second house?" I squeaked.

Aline started laughing again.

On Saturday Lucien and Crow clopped with us to school. It was open and there were students. You can take classes every day but Sunday. This time we had our school catalogues and we knew where we were going. The Clinical School is on the other side of the *Pantheon Square*, on *Rue Saufflot*. But once you're there, catalogue or not, confusion, as always, sets in. School is just like that.

"Pardon," Lucien asked a passing student. "Is there a school office?"

"Lots," he replied.

"We're looking for a body," I said.

"A body? Oh! The morgue's down in the basement," and he

191

pointed down a hallway.

We found a stairway and descended. It smelled of nasty chemicals.

"The morgue?" a passerby said, when we asked. "You want the new basement. This is the old. This is specimen storage."

Up, further down the hall, and down again.

This smelled too. Something more familiar. We were faced with a far less crowded hallway. At this point it was easy, the door marked Morgue, but it wasn't a morgue. It was a butcher shop!

"Oh!" Aleta exclaimed. "Maybe it's okay to leave me home sometimes."

The smell was awful. The bodies were laying all about stacked on pushcarts. Many were pulled apart, the floor slick with "fluids." In back we could see daylight coming in from a ramp leading up to the street. Two men were sitting on a table, one eating a sandwich.

"Need help?" the chewing one said, mouth full.

"We're looking for the body of a friend," Lucien replied, trying to shield his face. I was glad he said it because I couldn't talk.

"Know when he arrived?"

"She arrived yesterday," he said.

"She?"

"Young girl."

"Oh, the new tart," the other said.

Lucien bristled and the men leaned back, hands and sandwich up. "Wait, wait. No offense meant. It's just that we get them all the time," sandwich man said.

"Sorry for the mixup," the other added. He hopped down and ambled over to a desk, opened a drawer and thumbed through a stack of forms. "Ah, here." He passed it to Lucien. "Take this up to room 210. Did you bring a coffin?"

"No."

"Can't let you have her without one," the sandwich man said. "Can't carry bodies older than a day through the streets without one, but not to worry. Most are in a rush to get here. We get that all the time."

"But she needs to be out of here today," the other added.

"Right, so where do you live?" sandwich man asked.

"Pigalle," I said.

"Makes sense. You'll want Montmartre Cemetery then. It's

early so there should be no problems. They'll have everything you need."

Upstairs we turned in the form and reimbursed the school for the body purchase. They pay the city morgue fifty centimes apiece for them! The man at the desk said as we paid, "I know, I know, half a franc. But the books must balance."

Then we clopped to the cemetery, across the river, northwest of my house. Cemetery isn't enough of a word for it. It's more of a city for the dead. It's massive. It boggles the mind that there are so many people in the world that need burying. We rolled down a short tomb lined treeless street, strangely ghost free in the hazy midday sun, past a coal pile to the cemetery workshops. They made coffins there.

"You want a coffin?" asked the old man behind the counter.

"Yes, please," I said.

"We only make state coffins here. You want a fancy one, you'll have to go outside."

"What do they look like?"

"Just a box with brass handles, and we'll want the handles back."

"We'll want a nice one," Lucien said.

"We're you from?" the man asked.

"Pigalle," I said.

"And you want a nice one?"

"Wait," I said. "Where are we burying her?"

"You have a plot yet?" the man asked.

"No."

"We have space still, but it's expensive. Better to go out of town."

This was getting complicated.

"What about the wake," I said to myself. "Aren't we supposed to have the coffin there?"

"In your house?" the man asked, incredulous. "Why'd you want to do that?"

"I thought that was how it was done," I said.

"Better to burn it. That is unless you want to build a monument."

"Burn?" I exclaimed.

"Cremate. We burn the body then give you the ashes in an urn.

A real space saver. No smell too."

"That makes sense," I replied. "Then I'd have time to organize the wake."

"Now you're thinking. Silly to burn a nice coffin too. You don't seem the high type."

I wasn't sure what would qualify me as the high type. I suppose it had to do with our clothes.

"So where's the body?" he asked.

"At the Sorbonne," I said.

He chuckled. "Didn't jump fast enough before they bought it."

We gave him the body number and description. It was only twenty francs for the box and cremation, five for the pickup and five for the urn. We were to come back at three to identify the body. So we went out for lunch.

When we saw her, she way laying on wood table, half covered with a sheet. She had been badly bruised. Afterwards we walked around, looking at the mausoleums, passing the occasional ghost. They hid in the shadows, dim outlines, shying away from the roads. It's funny where they appear, where I see them. My seeing them too had been getting worse. But, I told no one about it. It was then, as we walked about, that I realized we had no place to put her.

"Lucien?" I asked. "What are we going to do with her ashes?"

"There's no room here," Crow said. "If you keep this up like you said you would, you'll need a whole graveyard for yourself."

"It's a problem," Lucien said, but then he smiled. "Crow? How long until she figures out a solution. Before or after the wake?"

"I say before for sure."

"If you said after, I'd make it a wager." We walked for a bit, until Lucien snorted. "I think I've got it."

"What?" I asked.

"No," he replied. "It's too much fun seeing what you'll think up."

"Oh thanks," I replied, scowling.

"Put them in the catacombs," Aleta said. She looked surprised she had said it.

Lucien sighed. So much for the wager.

"We'd need Jean-Paul," I said. "He won't like people down there."

"We'd have to build some walls with gates," Lucien suggested, thoughtfully.

"Good ones," Crow added. "I bet it's against the law too."

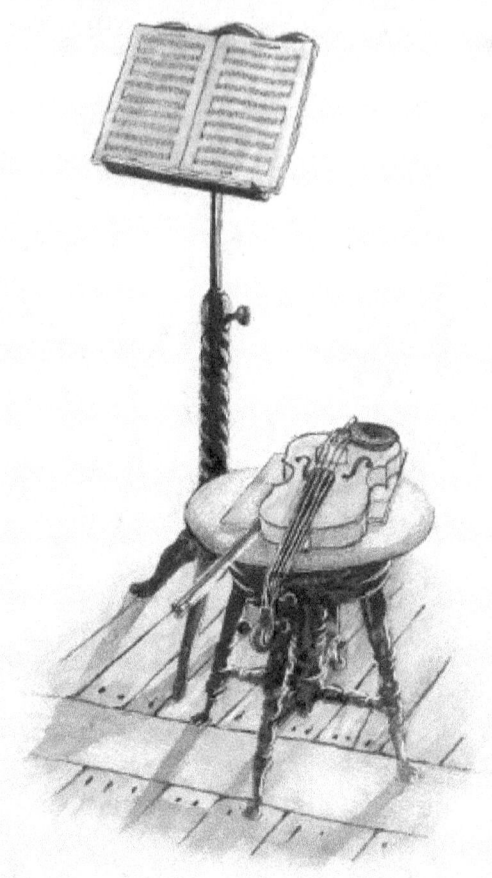

Chapter 19 – Two Deals with two Devils

"I saw your quote in the paper," Jean-Paul said.

It was Monday night. Aliz's urn was sitting on our parlor table at home. I had homework due tomorrow. But instead of being a good student I had our map open on Jean-Paul's table at La Pègre. This had to be dealt with. I was there alone. Crow was waiting back in the coat room.

"This gallery here. It's small and off a larger gallery. And we can hold wakes and services there." I pointed at a larger gallery. "If we put a gate here and opened the stairway, it would be safe."

"Yes. It's a workable plan, especially since I'm losing the house next door. I've nothing ongoing in that section. But the city won't allow it. Not publically. No new graveyards in the city limits. And I can't begin to think what the church would do."

"I can't work on that without your permission."

"I suppose I should be thankful you asked this time."

I think he meant me to laugh, but I winced instead. "Jean-Paul . . ." I was at a loss for words. How do you tell a blood-thirsty murderer that you value and need him?

"It would raise the girl's morale," he continued, with a ghost of a smile.

"And cost you nothing," I added, brightening.

"It might even make me look good in the neighborhoods." He paused. "Very well. You have my permission. You should know also that I've made it common knowledge that Carmichael contracts are forbidden."

I smiled and put my hand on his. "Thank you."

"But they ought to know that already." He smiled back. "They're all sad I'm sure. The British pay well. But I've been thinking about our favor."

Here it comes, I thought. I had figured it out from our various conversations. He was going to want to manage my debut. "Where and when?" I asked.

"You know?"

"Is it already booked?" I asked. "Please make it summer."

"Do you know any Mendelssohn?"

"No."

"Then it's good we're starting now. It's mid-September. You'll need to be ready to start working with the others late-July."

"Where?"

"Palais Garnier of course." The big opera house! "How else am I going to make back my money with reasonable profit?"

After homework, before bed that night, I wrote to M. Marmontel to ask for advice.

We scheduled the wake for Aliz that Saturday, late morning, before the *Chat* opened for business. Some, but not all of the neighborhood turned out and I told Solidarity too. Almost none of them showed. We had more press than visitors. That made me angry. But really, I'm ahead of myself again. I had a visitor of my own just as I was leaving to go across the street. M. Marmontel.

"Cali," he said as I came to the door. No hello. He was very agitated. "I can't believe you agreed to this."

"Did I do wrong?"

"Mendelssohn is very difficult. You need at least two years to master it properly and you have school! Tell me at least it's not the original."

"I don't know." Now I was worried.

He wrung his fists. "This is very bad."

"I'm going to a wake. Want to go?"

He wasn't listening, I could tell. "Of course, of course," he muttered. "Where is it?"

"Across the street."

"Across the street?" He looked around, suddenly frantic. "I'm in Pigalle." He looked at me and squinted, "This is that thing in the papers isn't it?"

"Yes."

"I can't go. I'm sorry. You must visit tomorrow . . ." He cast about, "I need my book." Then he sighed, "Ten o'clock. Yes Ten. Bring your violin."

"I will."

Then he said bye, hopping a passing carriage, muttering to himself.

What had I agreed to? But I couldn't think about it then. I had a party to attend.

Wakes in Paris start with a book covered with a black cloth by the door. You are to write last messages and thoughts in it. Past the door is the food. Usually this is provided by the family, but since she had none, I requested people bring things if they could. My thinking was that if they brought something, they would be buying in. We needed to come together as a community. At least some people came and some of them brought things. Enough to crowd the reporters outside. I had paid for more food to be delivered and we had to clear a path for it to get in. To be fair, Pigalle is not a rich neighborhood. Don't think poorly of them. Many are grateful just to get a meal.

I referred to them as "lost girls" for the papers and I told them about my hope to open a chapel and ossuary for them under Pigalle.

And you know what? Polaire showed up! Can you see me beaming? She was wearing zebra stripes with black fur, tall calf covering black boots, and a black hat. We even stood together for pictures. With her dark hair and eyes, she looked gorgeous. She gave me the name of her designer, Adolphe. He's Italian. Up and coming, just off Rue de la Paix.

Then I had my first late lunch meeting with Vidal, Henri the architect, and Paul. And Vidal was brilliant. He had a way of making suggestions that sounded like compliments.

"You can't make all that gold!" Paul snapped. "You'll blind them."

"It's the light of the modern age," Henri reposted.

"I thought you were going for motion," Vidal said. "That was a great idea."

"I am," Henri said. "Look at the strong horizontal lines."

"A long grained blond wood would give you more," Vidal suggested.

Henri frowned. "But it's supposed to be mechanical."

"Short diagonals would give it motion perhaps?"

"I could alternate them, back and forth," Henri replied thoughtfully.

"It could move like a rolling locomotive," Vidal suggested. "And Paul really only needs the stage area to be quiet don't you?"

"Yes, that's it. My clothing must sing like a performer. But to sing, it must be seen!"

"The store is its frame."

We spoke afterwards and agreed on a temporary salary that seemed too small to me.

"It's just a retainer. I'm going to want a piece of this."

I used my best poker face, but inside I was shining. The man had a silver tongue.

So I ended the day with a loss and two wins and still had time to do my math and go out with Lucien that night. He took me to the Inferno Club where we ate off the tops of coffins and watched fake ghosts. The interior ceiling and walls were sculpted with demons, fairies, and tormented spirits. And at the last we all drank "poison."

One man, I figure a plant, even gagged and "died." Altogether it was pretty funny, but I was falling asleep on Lucien's shoulder on the way home. I remember him lifting me and carrying me upstairs to my bed. Then a kiss before he left. Sarah must have undressed me because my shoes and dress were off and hung in the closet and I was tucked safe in bed.

Sunday, of course, was hard. I'd gone to bed late and had to get up, still tired from Saturday. It was a very blurry Cali, clutching her violin, clopping along to M. Marmontel's. I'd forced Crow to stay home. I didn't know when I was coming back which meant that no one else did either. There would be no ambushes and it wouldn't help me to know that poor Crow was sitting around waiting.

The driver had to wake me when we arrived. M. Marmontel's coffee was very welcome, but his stance and his eyes were grave.

"I've made some inquiries and I have some difficult news. It seems Camille will be your conductor."

I almost dropped my cup.

"I would be shocked if he went for less than the full symphony."

I could feel tears. It wasn't just the exhaustion.

"He requested the position and he has seniority. He chose the music and requested you. I can do nothing."

We sat there for a bit, until he could see that my emotions had run their course. Then he stood and clapped his hands together. "So. There's nothing for it but to get to work." He went to his desk and picked up a thick piece of sheet music.

"This is it," he said. "Don't be daunted by its intensity. I have no doubt that you can play it. But we both know there's far more to it than that."

"Let's go over what we can this morning, then I've help coming this afternoon. One of your teachers from school. You can get help from him in what free time you have there." Then he made sure he had my attention. "And Cali, know that you can count on me as well."

I was truly grateful for that but only returned a weak smile.

But you should know. The piece is crazy difficult, worse than Camille's. Mathieu came after lunch and played it all, then went over the first movement with me, but in the end it was more than clear to me that your Cali was going to look like a complete idiot in front of thousands of people and would never play the violin publicly again.

That night, with more coffee from Aline, I did as much homework as I could. Aleta was there to help.

"I can't believe that bastard did this. He set you up!" she fumed.

"Everyone already knew, even before I agreed." My concert had been in the schedule a month ago! "How did they get to Jean-Paul?" I wondered. "Did he know?"

"Cali," Aleta snapped. "He's a criminal."

They used Jean-Paul to snare me, which was very sobering. It's that he could be moved and used to move me. He was the bulwark of my defenses! Did he even know he had been used?

"I don't think he knows how risky this is," I replied. "He wouldn't have made the bet if he understood. This has to be costing everyone. I mean it's the Palais Garnier!"

Even a hug and a shoulder to cry on from Lucien didn't help.

"Quit," Lucien suggested. "This makes no sense."

"I can't."

"Why?"

"It would mean the end for me. I won't get another chance like this. Camille knew it when he set it up. My reputation is on the line."

"Your reputation," he smiled. It was funny. So many people thought so poorly of me. I had to smile too.

"My music is the one thing people still respect me for. And there are people who count on me. It's almost like my family. The girls, Paul, Henri, Fannie. They're all my friends. Even Jean-Paul." And then I realized something. "And Mrs. Hartnoll too."

"Your teacher?"

"She's counting on me to make something of myself."

"But you've done that already."

"Not musically. I know it's crazy, but it was so important to her."

"They'll all be disappointed if you fail," he noted.

"I can do it. I know I can." I was so sure, but I really didn't understand. Not yet.

"We can't run anyway. We can't go back to Belgium." He sighed. "You might as well." Then he smiled, "And I'll enjoy seeing you on stage."

The war ended March 18th with my parents still out to sea. It would be weeks, maybe even months before the killing stopped. The thought of them getting killed after the end drove me crazy. I know it worried Crow too. He paced and sent telegrams. We would just have to wait. We had no choice. We waited until we finally received word, by airmail on the last day of March.

They were laying low for a few weeks in Havana before trying to head north. Then we got another message two days later that they were heading north, leaving at night against the tide. Havana was too dangerous. And then nothing for a very long time.

April brought new buds on our trees. New growth sprouted up in the cracks between our cobbles and the wind ceased to bite every single day. The roses in the parks were no longer sticks but extended sweet dark green leaves.

Then finally, the day came when it all exploded. At first it was here and there. Clopping along to school we saw wisp's of green and pink, white and red. Little white bells had been growing out of our doorstep. That evening, on the way home, they were everywhere. Streets lined with pink foam, the sun shining, tulips climbing in rows from the ground, the gardens full of color. In French class, more than a third of the students were missing.

But again, I'm ahead of myself. One thing at a time. First we had spring break.

We got the first week in April off from school. Not that it was really off. I had homework and practice – lots of practice.

The plans for the store buildout had begun to take form. My main contribution was to whine and whinge at the cost. It was going to be very expensive. I really, really didn't want to go into debt. The total budget including six months of operating losses had to be kept below half a million or I couldn't see how we could ever expect to profit. Paul had found some thick medieval iron firebacks that were beautiful with rising suns on them. Even Henri the architect thought they were great. Gilded, they would stand as free sculptures. They fit so well with Henri's designs. I bought them and of course they had nowhere to go so they went in our basement against the wall. And we still hadn't found our storefront. I feared we would have to wait for someone on Rue de la Paix to die of old age.

But I really keep digressing! I so good at avoiding the difficult parts.

He must have known I had the week off from school.

I'd been out with Lucien when he called. We had gone to the Bois de Boulogne. It's a really big park outside the city walls. It had been warming up and we had sun. We went rowing, which is almost as romantic as a picnic, and they had a zoo! But when we got home, we found he had left his card. On the back it said, "It's time to talk. Monday morning, alone. I'll pick you up."

Lucien's eyes flared with anger when he saw it, but he was my conductor and my state of readiness was important. It was the rudeness of it I think.

Still, I've thought a lot about this. Was I wrong? Unlike in the past, my back wasn't to the wall. I had an escape. I could have turned and run and everything would have been fine. I would have finished my degree, we would have married and moved to Flanders. I would have learned German and Dutch and had kids. And yet, when Camille arrived in his steam carriage the next day, I climbed in.

He kept the heater set too warm.

We said nothing for a bit, his driver sending us forward. He didn't even look at me. I was hiding behind my violin.

"I assume you're working on it?" he said finally.

"Yes."

"You're still attending school."

"Yes."

"That will stop."

I was shocked.

"I've been following your progress. I'm going to need your full attention for the next two months. Before we start rehearsals."

"I still have all summer."

"I will not have you learning the piece while we are in rehearsal."

We rolled along for a bit. He seemed to be thinking.

"You fail to see the magnitude of the problem. It's the nature of the piece. It's the yardstick with which we measure all violinists. You will be weighed against every concert violinist that has ever existed. You will not succeed without complete commitment."

"I am committed."

"Not yet."

"Why are you doing this?"

"In the end. I will understand. We will construct this from the bottom up. I will see everything."

"And if I don't. Don't commit?"

"You would regret it, perhaps for the rest of your life. Remember, you benefit from this. Perhaps more than I. Do not claim to have the high ground. This is a more than fair trade."

"I can't drop out of school. Aleta needs me."

"Hire a tutor. Hire a carriage full. I think you can afford it. You can pick up school again next term. You're young. You have time. All the time in the world is ahead of you."

"You've never worked with an orchestra," he continued. "You must trust me in this. You'll not be learning just your part. You will learn everyone's parts. You will understand the piece as a whole."

I was silent. I had to learning everyone's part?

"You improvise. This will stop! You will concentrate on quality of sound. I will not stand for shortcuts. You will not cover your mistakes with tricks! I've noticed that you avoid vibrato on the forth finger and you need to consider more carefully when to pull it back. Your transitions need work to be truly continuous. We will work on your staccato!"

It sounded ominous.

"Then there is the question of physical training."

Physical training?

"I'm sure that you were fit when you were working on your ship, but what have you been doing lately?"

I'd been taking the carriage and sitting. He clearly knew!

"The weather is improving. We will take regular walks to start with. And no alcohol."

Henri the painter would not be pleased.

"In fact, it's not far to where we'll be working. You will walk from now on."

I was going to need a city map.

The opera house towers over the city, rising like an ornate temple. Its copper domes and gold statues adding welcome color to the gray and brown stone around it. We entered on the side, walking up swooping driveways. Inside was a beautiful circular hall with red columns and tile. They had electric light.

"We will be working in the attic."

He took me through a door and up some steps to an elevator.

"I will not give you tours," he said as we climbed. "You will see it all eventually. That or you won't." He looked squarely at me, I think for the first time. "Know this Miss Carmichael. You will give one hundred percent or I will drop you! I will not have anyone harmed by your childish antics. You will be performing for what I think may be your peers, not the society section."

The elevator door opened

I think I may have been blushing because the elevator man gave me a confused look.

"Rotunda," Camille snapped.

The operator pushed the lever forward and took us up. We turned right as we exited and then passed under an arch into a dream. Shining parquet and polished wood corridors, two stories high, lined floor to ceiling with books, manuscripts, and paintings. It was all music!

Camille must have heard me make a noise because he looked at me again with a little smile. "This is nothing."

People had been saying that to me a lot. What else could there be? I wanted to stop. It was so much.

"We will work in the Rotunda attic, when it's not in use. The acoustics are good and there is air and light. Otherwise we will go to a workroom. I will show you."

The Rotunda's domed ceiling was painted with a shining sun whose rays of sunlight rained down in a way that seemed to defy depth. The walls all around were filled with books.

We turned down another corridor to a stairway and climbed up, then up another, emerging through the floor into the building's dome itself. The walls there were lined with more bookshelves and drawers too. The floor was littered with boxes, chairs, sundry, and somehow sitting square in the center, a piano. Camille veered to the side as we entered and grabbed a music stand.

"This is the archives, currently used for storage. We will not often be bothered."

He plunked the stand down in the center of the room, next to the piano.

"I've requested lunch be brought up from the kitchens. Until it arrives we will start with a sustain. Pick a note and hold it until I tell you to stop."

Camille was right. I was out of shape and I hadn't been practicing like I should. By the time lunch arrived I was exhausted. It was just a sandwich and tea – very un-Parisian.

Before we broke at three, a man came in with a folded paper, it was a map of Paris. Camille had thought of everything.

"Tomorrow you will be here at ten. Leave early. I will not hear that you've become lost. Now shake out your arms and go walk home." Then he turned without a goodbye and left me there.

I couldn't leave though, not without wandering though the bookshelves. The desks were not empty. There were men, at least four, dressed in a mix of clothing, thumbing through books and making notes.

"May I help you?" He had snuck up behind me! Crow would not be pleased. He was a thin man in a simple but prim suit that clearly said clerk.

"I'm just looking."

"We generally don't allow the public in."

"I'm working here. I'm performing."

"Ah, you must be violinist."

I smiled, "Yes, upstairs."

"We could hear you. My name is Frédérique. Ask if you need help."

"Can you tell me about what you have?" *And where it was kept.*

"Of course," he said, brightening. "Come." He led me into the corridor. "We try to keep the Rotunda quiet."

We looked up at the shelves. "We're a branch of the National Library, keeping material having to do with the operation of opera. Music, costuming, construction, and history. We archive and document performances." Walking on he nodded towards shelves of loose cloth bound books. He looked a little smug. "These are manuscripts, early versions of scripts and scores annotated by the authors. We collect them from the performances when we can. You can plot the evolution of a work from conception to its performance."

Passing rows of little drawers, "We keep certain costumes as well, down in the vaults, but we keep the books up here. History, descriptions, drawings, plates." Then he mumbled to himself, "Costumes are very difficult to catalog." Walking along, he slid open a drawer. It was filled with paper cards. "We have a catalog of reviews here, but the papers themselves are at the main library." *I would be in that catalog!*

"Do you keep audio recordings?"

He stopped.

"No. We don't. Not yet." He sniffed. "I suggest you not worry about that. There's a great deal of controversy as to whether we should, and if so, how they should be kept."

Librarian controversy.

At home I found Lucien pacing. I was two hours beyond late. I had gotten lost several times. It was overcast so it was difficult to stay oriented in the twisting streets.

"She's home," Sarah called, as she let me in.

Lucien's head popped out from the parlor. "You're home. Finally."

There was a cold draft! We had new tarps over our carpet. It was clear that they been back at it again, knocking my house apart.

"I am," I sighed and stumbled into his arms. "I'm so tired."

Aleta came downstairs, clearly curious. "Are you okay?" she asked.

"I'm fine, but we have to make some changes."

She frowned. "Like what?"

"I'm quitting school."

"What!" She stopped at the bottom of the steps.

Lucien was frowning.

"Just for the quarter. I have to practice."

"But you have the summer," Aleta said.

"No, I don't." Looking around, I asked, "What are they doing now?"

Aleta growled, "Knocking down more walls."

"Take a look," Lucien said, then led me into the Parlor. I could hear pounding from upstairs. The wall leading to the next house had a big hole in it, the next parlor over being dark, dirty, and empty. We crunched through broken plaster through the hole into the next house where Lucien bowed and with hand out said, "The Dining Room."

"Oh," I replied, too tired to care. Really though, I couldn't ever see having time to entertain.

"This will be a closet. There, an office. The kitchen will be divided, part expanding ours, part a corridor to the courtyard, and part a larder."

"Courtyard?" That I had to see.

"Yes," Aleta said, following behind. "It's kind of plain. But the neighbors have chickens and a sheep. We'll have a new way out on the bottom floor though."

Or in, I thought.

We still had light so we went out back to see. The existing back door was flimsy. It wouldn't do. Outside, it was just a weedy square of pavers, shared with two of our neighbors. There was no exit to the street, only a stone wall. I could smell the animals. Over the wall in the distance, I could see a tree. Someone had a garden, but I didn't think we could grow one. I doubted the sun ever made it in. And then I realized that our neighbors could get to our new upper back windows by crawling from window to window!

I shivered.

"It's cold," Lucien said.

"No. It's just a thought."

Only one of the girls from jail showed up. Tisha, the thief. I have no idea where she slept. I rarely saw her. I rarely had the time.

Chapter 20 – Francesca

Walking let me watch spring unfold. Monday, I skipped class entirely and went in late to deal with school. I walked and took the trolley by the way. Camille had planned this. I did the paperwork, already approved by the department, and then spent afternoon with Grégoire working on my little finger. It wasn't just that my form was bad, which it was. I was going to have to play very high on the fingerboard.

"No, no. Keep it loose."

"I'm trying."

"Wrist up."

"It hurts."

He grunted. "Your damn violin is so long and you're hands are small." He sat back. "Here. Let me see it."

He put it under his chin and began playing with the fingering, then stopped. "What the hell is this?" Holding it by the neck he began an inspection. Peering inside at the label, he frowned and asked, "Were did you get this?"

"Cadiz, Spain."

"How did she get there?" he mumbled to himself.

He then took a sniff and then a longer sniff, ending in a frown. Handing it back to me, "It's lovely, but you'll either have to come to terms with it or find a new one. We can't change the music."

And so we worked at it. I would have to learn to bend and once bent, build strength.

I was from that day onward to see Grégoire on Mondays and Mathieu on Saturdays. My new day schedule meant that my lunch meetings had to change to dinner meetings, and that I could no longer look for storefronts. We hired a property agent. My world was becoming so full! At the edge of eighteen I had eight and a half employees to look after, which was crazy.

Lucien began to attend the store planning meetings as well, and I think he was pleased with my choices and the drawings were looking beautiful. I pinned them to the bare plaster walls at home. I couldn't attended Solidarity either, or go to demonstrations, but I could still help fund them. And I bought a painting from Cecilia, a beautiful river scene which then had to go out to be framed. But I left that to the staff to figure out. I was learning to delegate.

My plans for the ossuary had to be put on hold along with school, as I was no longer free when the government offices were open. We did go back to Rouen to make more recordings, but we flew, doing it in a single Sunday. And yes, there were photo shoots. But every scrap of time that was left went to Camille. You're laughing again. Really, he had my full and undivided attention and trust me, he used it.

"Protato, protato, protato," he said in time to my strokes, forcing me faster. "I will hear no breaks, no breaths."

But I was becoming more and more ragged instead. I bloody well hurt! That and exhaustion. I found that I'd begun to cry. I couldn't stop.

"Tears! Finally tears," he said to the ceiling. "Yes, cry Miss

Carmichael. Get it out. Shake out your hands while you're standing there. Make the time count. He was completely unfazed.

"No, wait." He pulled out his pocket watch. "It's walk time."

We took regular breaks where we walked briskly up and down the corridors which gave me a chance to gawk at the artwork and statues. But today we were going to do something different.

"I think you deserve a reward," he said, as I put my violin away. He never questioned my never letting go of it. As the years went by, the further I got from home, the more it became my anchor. I carried it with me as we descended seven floors of stairs.

"It isn't properly lit of course," he said. He clearly had something special in mind. "But I think it's time you had some idea where you will be playing."

We walked along another polished stone hallway, me counting the inlayed patterns on the floor. We turned left at the end and then stopped.

"Wait," he said. "You need to see it in the correct order." He fretted for a second, then said, "Close your eyes." He led me on through an echoing vaulting space and out into the wind and sun.

"Open them, or you'll fall down the steps."

We were in front of the theater, standing at the open gate. The guard looked amused.

"Come. We'll start down here." We headed to the center curb statue. "Now turn and look."

We were looking at the front of the theater, its green dome and golden statues towering above us.

"You've just exited your carriage, wearing your best." He looked to see if I was listening, then waved me forward. "Follow me," he said, and we started up the steps.

"It's night. Everything is lit." We passed the guard and walked through the dark brass doors. "You enter the atrium."

Its ceiling stretched above us, its vaults covered with sky, gods, and angels, all mixed with gold and cut glass. The inlayed marble floor echoed under our feet.

"This will be filled with thousands of Paris' finest. They will be checking their things."

Ahead we faced marble, a maze of carvings and statues, polished to mirror brightness, cool as a cave in the summer heat.

Sound echoed everywhere, coming in from outside. It was the city itself, people moving about. To our left and right were stairs with balustrades polished by thousands of feet and hands, rising pathways through swirls of rococo carvings, the stone itself tinted gold. I could see our familiar atriums through the corridors to either side. He saw my look and actually smiled! I was gawking. It was the great staircase. I had heard of it.

"The women will be making their way up slowly, careful of their gowns." We walked forward. Columns reached upwards toward the cavernous domed roof above as we walked past statues and huge crystal pole lights. We were ascending towards heaven.

But Camille didn't seem to notice. He was looking up at the second level. "There will be private parties up here. Celebrities and their entourages will be mingling. The bars will be busy. But many will be eager to get to their seats early to avoid the crowded stairs and climb. The truly rich though can wait. They will take the elevators from here up to their boxes."

I saw no ghosts, by the way, despite the shadows. I supposed the opera has no tombs. We climbed up into the central atrium, the painted ceiling vaulting high over us in the darkness. The light from doorways and the street behind us lit the steps.

We turned left, finishing the climb. The elevators stood in a row on our right, doors open and dark. But instead, Camille turned us left, back towards the front of the theater. Towards a sun lit room just past the little balconies. He saw me looking at them.

"People will standing in them to watch those who enter."

We entered a long columned room, almost blinding after the darkness. Everything was gold and red reflected in cut crystal chandeliers and mirrors. The Sun King himself would have felt at home.

"The parties will center here, and on the balcony if the evening is warm. It's the best place to smoke."

We reentered, heading back to the staircase. Camille picked an elevator. "Come. We'll have to do this ourselves." Closing the cage behind me, he eyed the controls. It was very dark until he switched on the light.

"I think you push it forward," I said.

"Yes. You young and your machines," he mumbled, pushing the handle carefully forward. We began to ascend.

"I prefer the second level unless I've managed to get a box," he continued. He actually did a very a good job of stopping us exactly at our floor.

Outside on the third level, looking over the railing, we could see down again at the grand staircase. I thought of all the women and their dresses spread out below like flowers in a field, but Camille did not give me a chance to gawk. He led us on, down a dark corridor.

"They could at least leave a few lights on," Camille complained. He found a door. "Of course the great chandelier isn't lit." We stepped through a short narrow red velvet corridor into steeply sloping rows of seats, four deep on each side.

"Most of these will be season ticket holders. They will know their seat mates. Some will be chatting . . . and some not." We stepped down.

Below stretched the theater itself, red and glittering gold. You could have floated a dozen clippers in it. In the dimness above was the great chandelier, now dark, but still flecked with reflected light from the stage. In front, the stage itself, curtains open, revealed a hive of activity. They were building sets.

"Have a seat," he said. "Every one of these will be full." Sitting, he pointed at the center of the stage. "That will be you."

It was huge. I would be tiny, with thousands of people watching me. I looked at the tiny figures down there and wondered why I was here.

I came home that evening, the sun low, having stopped for a cup of coffee on the way just to find the energy to keep staggering on. It was something I was doing more and more often. I opened the door to the sound of a piano. I blinked in confusion still holding my keys.

"She's home," Sarah called, as she did every night.

The piano stopped, Aleta peeking out of the parlor.

"You have to see it!" she said with glee.

"See what?"

"Our piano!"

Then I remembered. She had said something about buying one and I had said yes. I let her drag me in.

It was an upright cottage piano made of beautiful burl wood.

She had bought it used, but that made no difference. It was beautiful.

"It's lovely." I was smiling. It really was. I reached down and played a C and then a chord. Then I noticed we had new drapes. But I was so tired I didn't care. It was sad that I couldn't play it. I'd started, but as you know, I had to quit.

"Now I can practice here," she said.

"And me, once I have this damn concert done."

Lucien had come up behind me. I hadn't heard him. He put his arms around me and kissed my neck, which sent a shiver through me and got a snort out of Aleta.

"We'll have no peace here now," he said.

"You'll change your mind once I learn it," Aleta replied.

"We can turn the parlor into a beer hall," he replied.

But I didn't hear him. I just wanted him to kiss my neck some more.

My third session with Grégoire had a guest, a thin old man with knobby fingers. "This is she, Grégoire?" he asked, his voice thready.

"This is she," Grégoire replied, looking at the old man with clear respect.

"Miss Carmichael, my name is Gaston and I was wondering if I might have a look at your instrument, if I may?"

He had taken a step forward. I was standing there still in my coat and hat.

"Of course," I said, putting my violin down on the chair and heading towards the armoire to hang my things.

His voice came from behind me. "May I?" he asked. He was already standing over my case.

"Give me a minute, please," I replied. Gaston was in a hurry. Walking back at a brisk clip, I reached over the back of the chair and opened the case.

Gaston stared down into my case with rapt concentration. "Maple," he muttered. "The neck is new. But it would be wouldn't it."

This was confusing.

"May I?" he asked, hands stopped just above her.

"Yes." What was he getting at?

He picked her up carefully. "Here Grégoire, look at the back. The opposing grain."

Looking about he said, "Where did I leave my bag?"

"On the table maestro."

He put down my violin carefully, then walked to his bag. "I'm going to need some light." It was raining and dark as a dungeon.

"We're not wired yet," Grégoire said with annoyance. He picked up the lamp off the classroom desk then began patting his pockets for matches.

"Matches, matches," Gaston mumbled, patting his pockets as well. Then they both looked at me.

"We have electricity," I replied. "I've stopped carrying them."

"I'll find some," Gaston said, and started to shuffle towards the door, only to be stopped by a finger snap from Grégoire.

"Back of the textbooks," Grégoire said. "The only place students won't look."

Pulling a book from the shelf beside the desk, he reached in and felt about. "Ah!" Victory.

With the lamp lit, held up in Grégoire's hand, Gaston looked around inside my violin with a little mirror on a bent handle.

"It's a damn good one," he said. "May I clip a little piece off the label?"

"Sure." What were they getting at?

He had long tweezers and scissors, cutting and pulling out a little corner of the maker's label to stare at with a brass thing that he stuck in his eye.

"What I can't understand Grégoire is how she got from Marseilles to Cadiz." He popped the little piece of paper into a tiny bottle and pushed a cork into it.

"Marseilles?" Grégoire asked.

"We'll need a clear trail of ownership. It will have to be verified, and then verified again. She's probably one of the good copies, but young lady, I don't see why you can't call it by her name."

"She has a name?"

"Yes, Francesca. It was a monument to the maker's wife when she passed on."

Francesca.

"May I play it?" Gaston asked.

"Yes, of course."

Gaston picked it up reverently and began to play. A lonely ambling piece. It made me think of empty streets at night. We sat entranced, Gaston lost to us until he stopped mid note and took a deep breath.

"Yes," he said. "It might be real."

"What was that?" I asked.

"Tartini. It was written for this instrument."

We all sat quiet for a bit, lost in thought. At least I was. *She has a name. Francesca.* It was as beautiful as she was.

"Well," Gaston said. "I must go and make some inquiries. Take care of that young lady. If she's the real Francesca, then she's very dear to many people. They will want to know she's been found."

Sadly, once Gaston had left, we picked up again with my exercises. Francesca again became a field of toil.

"My flute needs a name," Aleta stated.

"It will never be as entirely and completely awesome as Francesca," I grinned. I was far too smug and we both knew it.

"I'll find it," she said, completely serious.

"How is school?"

"I get a lot more guys asking me out since you've left. I think you were scaring them away."

"It's just that you're alone."

She sighed, "Yes."

"You still seeing Gérald?"

She smiled, "Yes. He's fun." Then she laughed, "He's studying chemistry. He just took music to meet girls. He saw us in class and walked in."

I laughed. "I guess you're the only one in class now."

She sighed, "Yes."

"So he got lucky."

"True," she smiled again.

"Tell me if you think I should meet him."

"You know I will."

Those three months were a lonely time for us all. More than

216

anything, I missed the girls. I was out too early in the morning, home after they went to work, and asleep before they got out – except on Sunday. My day off and naturally my Lucien's favorite day. Wait. His favorite day because of me you ask? No! Because it's race day at Longchamp! They start at the end of April.

If The Moulin Rouge is the place to see and be seen at night, then Longchamp is the clear winner for the day. At least on Sunday. Which, by the way, was where I got to meet Gérald.

As you may know, my Lucien loves horses. It's just like me and ships. I'm sure his mother gave birth while riding at the club, then suckled him at the trot. And I don't mind, because being at the raceway is entirely fun, even if I don't understand half of what's going on. Just the women comparing dresses is, to be frank, a hoot. Then there are the expressions on people's faces when they win or lose. And it's nice to be out, especially when the sun is shining.

We had a box in the stands for which I was truly thankful because being short, I can't see over crowds. Heels and turf don't mix and the boxes provide a barrier to reporters as well. They can bring you lunch too, so you don't have to eat standing. Up high you can hear their hooves pounding the turf as they streak around the backstretch, all framed by the green topped city walls towering behind the track.

So much color. Dresses, flags, rainbow colored jockeys, and the horses themselves; the brown, white, and blacks of their pelts. All of it spread out against the green and black of turf, speckled with wildflowers and patches of sunshine. Paul made us hippodrome dresses with parasols, along with stacks of cards with his name and address to give to the curious.

It was in early May, my third time to the races that Aleta brought Gérald. She warned us the night before and he met us at our doorstep bright and early. Actually, he met Lucien. They arrived at the same time, both standing at the door. They were both wearing very smart suits and top hats. All the men do at the races, just so their sweethearts can't see over them.

Sarah let them in. Lucien always knocked. He had his own key, but, always a proper gentleman, he generally refrained from using it.

"Hello," Lucien called, as he handed Sarah his hat and cane.

"We have a guest."

"Gérald?" Aleta called from the parlor. We had been puzzling over her math.

"I better be," he called. "He paid for this suit."

She was up and to the door, literally in a blink.

"I can't think of a suit better filled," she replied.

Can you see me roll my eyes?

"Sorry about the draft and the plaster," she added.

"I'm not worried," he said. "The dust matches the suit."

He was wearing pale gray.

"Are we leaving?" Crow asked, in French, as he came down the stairs. The tutor was definitely helping. Crow in a suit is both amazing and just a little jarring.

"Give us a chance," I replied. "Everyone just got here."

Aline came from the kitchen with a tray. "Tea? Coffee?" Then she grinned at me, "Hashish?"

"Aline!" I snapped. Then I looked at Gérald and said, "She knows we never imbibe before noon."

"Is that why your grades were so bad?" he replied.

"How do you know my grades?" I asked.

"The Prof. was telling the class just the other day that your absence would raise the curve."

College humor.

We sat and filled ourselves with coffee and pastry, and polished our wit until I was sure I would probably not make it to Longchamp without a stop for a head. Then we wandered into the streets to find some sort of conveyance. It being Sunday morning we had to walk all the way to the boulevard, but found a car and squeezed in, my leg deliciously up against Lucien's.

Longchamp is just outside the city walls, in Bois de Boulogne. That was where Lucien and I went rowing, remember? Boats are easily as good as hayfields, especially when you find lonely inlets. Longchamp has big looping horse roads of green turf, they call them "tracks," that go this way and that, around and around, though the horses generally only use one and only make one loop. On the side, facing the city walls, is the club house, stables, and stands. They're built to look like a castle with fake towers and wattle and daub walls. It's where the races always finish. On race days, literally every flat spot that can be found is filled, even the rooves. Which is why boxes are dear.

You buy a form from one of the boys when they let you off and then head for the stables where they are showing the horses. Their trainers lead them out two or three at a time to trot them back and forth. Lucien talks about spring, and height, which I can see, and other things I can't like breed and lineage. But one thing I can see that Lucien misses is symmetry. Does it put the same weight down on both hooves? I like a good view of the rump. Is it standing straight, especially with a rider? You look at the odds, read the gossip, and compare it to what you saw. I like to bet when I disagree with the odds.

One thing I noticed that day was that Gérald knew horses and had money to bet. And he and Lucien got along very well. Maybe too well.

"But look, he was sired by Cambyse. Direct line to the Turk," Gérald said.

"But he's short, barely fifteen and a half. And Glint of Gold is a Prix winner," Lucien replied.

"Two years ago," Gérald replied is faux distain.

"They sure like their horses," Crow said to me.

"Yes," I sighed.

"Gérald," Aleta asked. "Where did you learn about horses?"

They both turned to look at us with perhaps – a bit of alarm?

"I've always liked them," Gérald said. "Been following them since I was a kid." We were all speaking English by the way. Gérald, although clearly French, speaks English with an American accent.

"What kid wouldn't?" Lucien added.

"I didn't," Crow said.

"But you're an Indian," Gérald said.

"Yup, but I don't like horses. Maybe that's why I ended up at sea."

"Amazing," Lucien said.

Crow continued, "They bite, they kick, they'll step on you, stuff gets stuck in their feet, and you end up doing a lot of shovelin."

"You're right about the shoveling," Gérald said. "I did enough of that."

"Where did you shovel stables?" Aleta asked.

Gérald frowned. "I have a rich uncle who owns horses.

219

Nephews are cheaper than stable hands."

Lucien looked amused and I realized Gérald was a bad liar. Maybe we should play cards. He and Lucien were hiding something. What were they up to?

That day ended with me a hundred and twenty francs richer.

That weekend was when I really started to worry about Ma and Pa. It had been weeks and they should have been back in Boston. Were they laying low, soaking up the sun in warm blue water or had they gone down, sunk by some coastal patrol boat that hadn't heard the war ended?

We waited for the mail, but nothing came, the postman walking right on by. The whole street knew my plight and asked when I stopped to talk. The only relief I had was when I was with Camille, who left me no energy or time to fret about anything other than meeting his next demand. I think he had noticed the change in my music. It seemed to drive him on. We had already finished Mendelsohn and had moved on to reworking Bach. I had yet to tell him I had been working on one of his pieces. I was strangely reluctant.

And then the day came when he said we were done. It was the first Friday in June. We had warm sun that day and everyone was out in the streets, except me and Camille of course. He finished without flourish or congratulations. I got no "well done." He just said, "We'll meet again next Tuesday, ten o'clock, at the stage. You do remember where that is Miss Carmichael?"

"Yes."

"Good."

And that was it. He picked up his books and walked out.

I stood there completely drained staring at the slanting sunlight until I felt a tear roll down my cheek and then another. I don't know why. Crouching down on the spot in front of my stand, I curled up and cried. Some of my tears fell on Francesca. I wiped them off carefully. I think she was weeping too.

I'm always late getting home. I never take a straight route. Sometimes I sit for a bit in the library. That evening I decided to stop and look at the trains. It's a bit out of the way, but they're fun and it's a pretty station. I was walking through the lounge when who should I spot, but Max.

Max is a German spy. He is short, thin, and not particularly handsome. I met him in the Congo. His warning saved us and, despite stern advice from others, I've always counted him as a friend.

We stopped and I think I saw a look of worry pass his eyes. I know I was worried. But then his usual grin took over.

"Miss Carmichael," he said. "It's a pleasure to see you, and you have your violin. You aren't going to play for us in the station are you?"

"No," I smiled. "That would be crazy."

"Perhaps. Once or twice wouldn't hurt, but you're right. More would be suicide."

I laughed. "I had some time, so I thought I'd look at the trains."

"That explains it."

"You're not here for me are you?"

"No," he said. It was his turn to laugh. "At least I hope not."

"Then how about some tea?"

"Tea in the evening? In Paris?"

"I'm not allowed to drink."

He thought for a moment. "Ah, your concert."

"Yes."

"I'm afraid I will most likely miss it," he said, with regret.

"I'm sorry, but if you do decide to come I might be able to get you tickets."

"I don't get much time off. I'm sure I'll be somewhere far away."

"I don't want to know why you're here."

"Yes. That's for the best," he said. Then he thought for a second. "Cali, please be careful at this concert. They'll know exactly where and when you'll be there. The stage is very exposed."

"I'm sure there will be security."

"It's a very big theater."

I frowned. "I'll make inquiries."

"That is a good start."

We stood for another moment. "No tea?" I asked.

"No. I'm expected."

"Is Emilia here?"

His eyes darted about. "I don't see why she would be."

"Maybe to look at the kimonos at the Moulin Rouge?"

He smiled. "You should carry them in your store."

"I thought of that." It meant he had been following me in the papers. Why? And he had guessed my thoughts again. He was so good at that.

"You're in the papers," he explained. "Even in Germany. But I think you're focusing too much on your playing. You should be wary. Be more suspicious." He put his hand on my shoulder. "I must go now."

I sighed, "Bye," as he walked away.

For some reason, I no longer wanted to look at the trains. I stood there for a bit, looking at the crowds, looking for Emilia I suppose, and then walked home.

Chapter 21 – The Orchestra

I had the weekend off! It was warm. No, better than warm. It was practically hot. The sun was shining and the trees were green. The gardens were full of flowers. Aleta was out of school. Lucien was bored and ready to go anywhere. I had nothing to do until Tuesday! We could have gone swimming at the river beach, I suppose, or we could throw a party!

We'll, maybe not a party. Aline demanded advanced notice of those. I guess a day to prepare wasn't enough. But we could have the girls over at least, so I left word across the street and set about shopping. Lucien took me to the flower market and it was amazing! A lot of it is roofed with glass, but the market spills out into the streets beyond. The scent is so strong that it makes your eyes water. You walk away with it in your clothes, which is kind of nice. We had the flower arrangements made for us there to save time.

Next door is the pet market. Birds, mice, rabbits, cats, dogs, and even chickens. Cages were stacked everywhere. We went walking while our flowers were being done. It's very hard to say no to a puppy, but I had too. I'm never home and I'm not sure when I might have to run for the border. But they are so sweet.

Back home we bought coffee and tea from M. Delattre, and

pastries and bread from M. Barnier. Naturally, I told them about the party. How could I not? Then produce and cheese, where we stopped to talk with neighbors about everything. Dropping things off, we headed back out for wine and beer. We had none, but we had new racks in the basement so we bought three assorted cases of wine and a case of beer. They would be delivered. And, naturally, I had to stop and talk. By this point people were stopping us to ask if they could bring anything. All this time Lucien's smile had grown until it became a chuckle as I talked.

"What?" I asked, when we were in the street.

"You've invited the entire neighborhood. Are you sure this isn't a party?"

"I can't invite some people and not others. That would be wrong."

"Then we need to warn Aline," he replied.

I snuggled up to him. "Can you do it?" I asked. She wouldn't be happy.

"I'll hold your shield for you."

But I didn't have to tell her. She already knew!

"I told you, no party!" she yelled, and slammed down a pot as we came in. Sarah had already set out the flowers.

"We've bought most of it premade," I replied.

"Did you think about cleaning?"

"Our house is already clean." Really, it was always a whole lot cleaner than I'd ever been.

"Where are we going to put things out?" I guess we needed tables. "Where will people sit?" Chairs too. "And you bought food, but not enough! And what are they going to put it on and eat it with?" She was back to yelling.

So we went back out and cleaned out every shop in the neighborhood and asked everyone about tables. That evening I asked some of the girls if they would play too. I would pay them. Money is even a better incentive than free food to a bohemian.

I said afternoon, but people started showing up early. We had nothing ready, so I put them to work, which made Aline roll her eyes. I guess you don't make guests work, but then guests shouldn't show up early! We moved furniture to make room for tables when they arrived, then blocked stairways and doors to keep people from wandering, all while more and more neighbors arrived. Far more than I invited. We had to borrow chairs from across the street so we could have a place for our "band." They set up out in the street and we set tables out when we no longer had room inside. We sent for more wine, then supplies from the next street over. Shops were opened by owners already at the party. Next came the reporters! I couldn't do anything without them of course. Our gendarmes called for extra men to cover the crowd who were dancing in the street. Come evening, people brought out lanterns. All I did was run from one thing to the next, organizing effort.

Finally, the band gave up. Seven hours is a long time to play, even with long breaks. So Aleta and I took up the job. We played ballads and jigs, shanties and reels, until we finally fell over. I was at a loss.

"Play your song," Aleta said. They'd made space for us on a sofa that was sitting out from I don't know where.

"Which?"

"The one you've been working on. I want to hear it."

I groaned. "I'm too tired," I said.

"Coffee!" Aleta shouted. "Coffee for the maestro or you'll get no more music!" And damn if coffee didn't appear. It was thick, black, and bitter. I groaned with pleasure as I drank it. And it did help. I suppose my exercise was baring fruit.

"Okay," I said. "But know that this won't be my best."

I sat up and regretted it, but stood anyway. Bending down and stretching helped.

"Mendelssohn's Violin Concerto," I called out, and got applause and cheers!

Normally the orchestra leads without introduction. We just dive in, dripping with drama and counterpoint. Perhaps too much. But as an acapella performance, it's worse. It starts off sounding like I'm crying. Maybe not the best party music I thought, as it quieted the street, dead quiet, the notes spinning away into the darkness, smooth as glass. They left webs trailing away around me, catching and drawing everything in until we were alone in the dark and the cool breeze. Francesca and I wound away the night. She was warm in my hands, glowing like moonlight. I could see ghosts edging in from the walls around us. Each note a question, asking, and then asking again, and again, faster and faster until they became a new song that marched proud and strong in darkness, standing against jeopardy, only to collapse and fall again into tired frantic tears.

Normally, I get breaks between movements during the piece, but acapella you get none. Worse, in an orchestra I don't always have the lead, which I had to compensate for with improvisation and frankly stealing from other's parts. Camille would have been livid.

I built upwards through the cadenza until I was tearing the bow across the strings. I could hear him, "Presto Carmichael, presto! You are leading the orchestra in and they will enter with no more energy than you!" Then finally landing like a lonely falling leaf, I wallowed in melancholy only to rise again in the coda.

Launching directly into the second movement, which is my least favorite part, bridging the gap with a single quiet note, I let her cry. Around me, the ghosts had begun to wander, but I ignored them as I always do, playing three and four notes at a time.

The reason I hate the second is it's the most work for the least return. It just repeats themes I've already addressed in the first movement, only they're more complicated. Worse, it's sentimental. True, the music is darker and it's a chance to show skill. This is where Francesca's deep tone really comes out. But all of this effort is expended and we learn nothing new. We just continue to mourn and struggle. But I played on, climbing each hill.

But then comes third movement. It's a frantic furious dance full of joy and celebration. I've never understood why. This though, is what everyone listens for. I turned her loose, my bow skipping and flying over the strings. She was alive in my hands.

This is the piece's center, its heart. Misery is over. Trials have been overcome. I become a fairy or a bee skipping over flowers in the spring sun. Thank God for the coffee. The ghosts remained, even more had gathered. I think they were pleased. I played for them and cried, my cheeks wet, my chin cloth damp. We danced, the crowd surging and rejoicing. The street sang of victory. The energy expended in those last six minutes could power Paris. My bow was a blur over the strings as I finished. It ended with a flourish and I bowed before anyone knew I had stopped. They all stood there, stopped in their tracks, blinking. It was funny. The entire street full of silent people.

But then came the crash. The applause that turned into a roar and a dance in the street. I just had time to give Francesca to Aleta before they came at me and picked me up to carry me about, passing me from hand to hand, which was funny. I laughed and whooped amidst the cheers.

"Down. Let me down," I finally called, stumbling back to the sofa to fall down completely spent.

I must have fallen asleep right there because I woke the next morning in bed, my shoes gone, still in my clothes. I couldn't move, I wouldn't have except for a wicked need to pee. It was Monday, thankfully without school. The house, the neighborhood, was dead quiet. Littered like a battlefield. Thankfully the front door was closed and locked, and Francesca was safe in her case. We would spend the day recovering, picking up and returning things, paying bills, promising to repair. Over the coming weeks I would buy our gendarmes presents, new leather wallets. Nice ones. And to placate Jean-Paul for wrecking his street without permission or invitation to participate, ten bottles of 88 Bordeaux. Some of the few left to be bought in Paris (I bought the rest).

All the papers covered the party the next day. I apparently danced like a puppet on strings as I played, my music "haunting." Actually, they called me "The Little Puppet", which I wasn't sure I liked.

"You will not play for anyone but me! You will not publically play until after the opening night!" Camille yelled.

He had physically pulled me aside into an office as I came in the morning of Tuesday, July 25th.

"We are working towards a peak!" He was furious. I was close to tears. "I will not see this concert compromised by tipping our hand too early. Who knows how much you have set us back. I will know. I will know how much. We will see today!" And he stormed out, leaving me there.

What was I to do? I didn't want to leave the office. How could I face them? Finally a man with a graying moustache stuck his head in and smiled. "Come on," he said quietly, and waved me forward. "Don't worry. He makes a lot of noise," he added, passing me a handkerchief.

Lucien, Aleta, and Crow had come with me, but Lucien and

Crow were nowhere to be seen. They wanted to look in on security preparations and had taken off before I'd gotten to the stage. Camille was gone too, off stomping around I'm sure.

"What a jerk," Aleta said as I emerged. "You had to put up with that all this time?"

"No. He's not like this. At least not always."

She just shook her head in disapproval.

The orchestra was there, sitting or standing in no particular order in their street clothes, some smoking. The piece is scored for a small orchestra, maybe sixteen or eighteen, but for a huge theater you need volume. Camille had at least forty! Maybe more. I couldn't count them. I'd never seen so many musicians in one place. Maybe not that many professional musicians in my entire life.

I came out clutching my violin to my chest, wiping my eyes and nose, expecting the worst, but they were all very nice. They faced me with smiles and handshakes, which got me crying again. I couldn't help it. There were too many names and too many faces.

We milled about for a bit until I heard a sharp tapping behind me. Many were already heading for their seats having seen him coming.

"Miss Carmichael, you will sit there." He pointed at a seat with his baton. He was standing front and center, his back facing the audience.

I had a stand with the music already open.

"You will listen. Follow the music and think about your part." Then he addressed the orchestra. "Gentlemen. We will begin."

He tapped out a rhythm, then started. It was strange to hear what I had only been imagining.

"Look at me, Miss Carmichael."

I'd never seen a conductor. His movements were entrancing. He marked each beat, queuing and modifying, that was until he put down his baton and yelled, "No!" He was looking at the base section. "Softly. Softly. Like pillows. We will begin again. Miss Carmichael, watch me. Watch for your queues, which he was exaggerating for me. Squinting at me like I was an idiot.

I sat there as he worked with the orchestra for two hours, until lunch. Lucien and Crow had come back by then and were sitting in the audience. They didn't look happy. There were others too, but I never learned who they were. I saw Aleta talking to Lucien and I distinctly heard the word "ass", luckily in English.

The orchestra was getting up, putting their instruments away, and I turned to leave when Camille said, "Miss Carmichael, you will eat lunch with us. You will meet the section leads and learn." Then he called out, "Be back by one thirty."

"May my friends come?" I asked.

"They may not."

But they had already gotten up and were walking forward, looking for a way across the orchestra pit.

"I can't go out," I called. "I have to meet with people."

They nodded.

Lunch was just sandwiches from the restaurant as usual. We met in back of the stage in a side room. Most of the leads seemed friendly. I felt a certain coldness from M. Vannier, the lead violinist, but it was really too soon to tell what they thought. Maybe I was expecting too much. I said nothing beyond hello. They each discussed their section's problems. Sickness, conflicting engagements complicating schedules, problems with page turns, difficult personalities and social problems. It was very strange. I could only listen. At least they had coffee.

On the way back, Camille said to me, "Be ready to play." So I set about adjusting while Camille chided latecomers. I heard an audible stirring in the orchestra when I opened my case.

Under my chin, my cloth hanging loose, the smell of her wood drifted up, distracting and soothing. I love her. She is all that I need. The rest doesn't matter.

Camille tapped.

The orchestra began.

And then I played, dancing with Camille. It all began to unroll before me. Everything that I studied was spread around me. That was, until he stopped. He was scowling at the horn section. "What are you doing?" he yelled, and he was off correcting.

"Miss Carmichael!" I started. He had caught me daydreaming. "Protato! Protato!"

Then he tapped and we started again, and again still.

We broke for the day at four. I was exhausted.

"Miss Carmichael," he snapped. "You will appear for usual practice next Thursday." No asking if I had plans. He just walked off. That was it.

"What an asshole!" Aleta spat, when we were safely outside.

"Yes," I sighed. "And no."

Aleta stared at me.

"He's rude, but he's generally right."

I was still tired from the party. Exercise be damned. Outside we called a carriage.

"They have no security," Crow said. He was clearly upset.

"That will change," Lucien added.

"Those covered boxes," Crow muttered.

"Yes, they're unacceptable." Then Lucien looked at me. "They're renovating. And we still need to see upstairs. I'll break in if I have to."

"I'm looking forward to that," Crow said. He smiled. His gold tooth showing, "They were . . ." He had to pause. There's no Indian word for it. "Unreasonable," he finally came up with.

"The problem is that the theater is a maze. A hundred policemen wouldn't be enough." Lucien growled.

"If someone does try, he'll be English," I said. "I wonder if Max would recognize him. Perhaps I can get his help."

"Max," Lucien asked. "Why would he help?"

"Who's Max?" Crow asked.

"A friend," I said.

"A German spy," Aleta added.

"Maybe we can trade favors," I explained.

I leaned forward and asked the driver to head for the German Embassy.

"This is France," Crow said. "Shouldn't we be talking to the French?"

"I will not work with the Deuxième Bureau," I replied.

"The what?" Crow asked.

"The French secret service," Lucien answered

"Child, what did you get yourself in to?" Crow asked.

"They're worse than Saint-Saëns," Aleta said.

"I admit," Lucien continued. "That I have to agree. But gendarmes will be helpful."

"With local contractors maybe, but Jean-Paul has forbidden them."

"What did you promise him for that?" Lucien sounded worried.

"Nothing. He offered. He wants his concert money. But gendarmes are no use if it's The Institution. They'd just get hurt. I won't have that."

"That explains why you think the assassin will be English. But Max alone is no use."

"Perhaps. But his advice will be useful."

"So that spy stuff in the papers really was true," Crow said, half to himself.

"Only some of it," I replied. Then I put my hand on his. "Some of it, and a lot they don't know."

"Your father isn't going to be happy."

"It's just that I've had to make deals to stay alive." I looked up at Crow. "And then once you start, it keeps on going on and on. And if you quit you'll be dead." I sighed. "If it helps, so far I've managed to stay independent. I belong to no one." Then I smiled at Lucien. "Except Lucien."

"Somehow we'll get out of this," Lucien said.

"You should go back to Boston," Crow said.

"I'm afraid I'm probably not too popular there right now," I said.

"I'm guessing I don't want to know why?" Crow asked.

"No you don't," I agreed. Phillip, an American agent, was dead. We didn't do it, but the papers thought I might have.

"They were greedy," Aleta snapped. "They didn't care who got hurt. And they blew up our zeppelin!"

"Besides," I sighed. "I love France almost as much as I love Lucien. Especially Paris. I will make my stand here. I'm not going back."

We stopped at the embassy and I dashed in and left a note for Max. I didn't know if he would get it, but it was the only thing I could think of. Then we went out for dinner because Aline still wasn't talking to us for having that giant party without her permission.

When we tried to pay the carriage, the driver waved it away. "No charge," he said in English. He had overheard everything! "No charge for a friend of France."

I had a note from Joseph waiting when we got home. He found a store front he wanted me to look at, but it was too late to reply that night. I sent one the next morning the minute that Jacques showed up. I would be there at one. That was very short notice, but I could look at the location even if he didn't show, and I wasn't sure when I'd have time in the future.

Joseph was there when I arrived. I wanted to say go, that this was it – but it wasn't. He was standing across the street, arms folded, eyeing the building, nodding as I walked up.

"What do you think?" he asked.

"It's wrong," I replied.

"Why?"

"The location." It was just off Rue de la Paix. "I don't want to be second best."

He frowned. "You'll never find an opening on the street itself."

"Then we should go elsewhere."

He was quiet for a bit. We stood there looking at it. I mean, it was nice. It would work, but . . . "I want a corner. A busy corner. With a view of the tower."

"That could bite us."

"I don't want to be associated with these men. Our philosophy is completely different and I want people to realize that. We're creating something new. And the world's fair is coming. We should be part of it. Or at least somewhere near it."

"I suppose it's foolish to compete with them head to head."

"I don't want to compete with them. I want to make them obsolete."

He laughed.

"If it's revolution, then we need a manifesto," he said.

I smiled. "In big gold letters."

"Write it," he said to me. "And I'll tell Henri. I think he'll like that."

Thursday morning, Max was waiting for me in a carriage outside. I know, I was supposed to exercise and it was a beautiful morning for a walk. But I was grateful he had showed up. So I climbed in, followed by Crow and Lucien. Aleta was going out with

Gérald.

"Hi Max!" I said.

Max eyed Crow, then said to me. "Cali. You're in trouble."

He not only knew when I was going to the theater, but why I contacted him. He told the driver in French to start.

"Don't worry," he said, looking at the three of us. "The driver doesn't understand English."

"Do you have any suggestions?" I asked.

"Cancel the concert," he replied.

I sighed.

"Move it to a more securable location," he continued.

"It is a maze," Lucien said.

"They'll use a sniper," Max said, without pause. "Probably at some loud part of the music."

"I agree," Lucien replied. "The only time they can be sure of her location is when she's on stage."

"What makes you think they'll attack at the theater?" Crow asked. "Why not somewhere else?"

"Because our dear Cali has become unpredictable and has turned Pigalle into a fortress," Max said with a smile. "She's a difficult target."

That made me feel quite proud.

"Lucien's plan is really the only one," Max continued. How did he know Lucien's plan? "At least two gendarmes at each possible shooting position, with their whistles at their lips. And all the renovation areas must be uncovered. The assassin will have at least two assistants, to unlock doors, neutralize guards, and bring in the equipment. Look for that."

"The theater won't cooperate," Crow said. "At least they didn't with us."

"They will take some convincing," Lucien said.

"You are right to be worried Cali," Max said. "What you're doing is very dangerous. And I'm afraid I can't help you directly. Germany is neutral in this case. I'm not even sure I'll be in Europe come September."

"Will they send Emilia?" I asked.

"No. She's not an assassin. They have specialists for that."

"So I won't have to worry if I see her?"

"Did you see her?"

"No."

"Good. If you do, run. She can mean nothing but trouble for you. Running is probably the one thing you can do as well as she, and she can't use her knives if she's moving."

"Lord Almighty," Crow whispered.

"I suggest staying away from well-dressed English women in general. She's not the only one of her kind."

"There are more?" I said, in almost a squeak.

"We know of six schooled agents that are active in the field, but that information might out of date. They are always women. Emilia is by far their best. Assassins though, come and go. I could think of at least eight or nine they might pick from. And they might even hire an outside contractor." Then he frowned. "I hope they don't pay us to do it."

"The British keep saying I work for you," I said. "It would be embarrassing for them if someone found out."

"Yes," Max smiled, relieved. "That's true."

"Would it help if I worked for you?" I asked.

His smile melted. "We would probably solve the problem by cancelling the concert and then sending you away to school. Are you really that desperate?"

"No. I'm not."

He took a breath. "Don't even joke about that. I like you better where you are."

"So we've accomplished nothing," Lucien said.

"I can only say that I will help if I can," Max shrugged.

I'd been so busy with the concert that I'd hardly seen Aleta in months. But I had Friday off so we could go do something together. Sadly, Lucien wasn't free. He was busy negotiating with the Opera and the *Conseil Municipal* over security issues. Aleta, though, had her Gérald. The three of us decided to go see Versailles. I had a feeling it was going to be weird having to share her.

We'd been warned by the neighbors to wear low heeled walking shoes, bring a water bottle and food, and an umbrella for the sun and the rain. And, that we had to see Marie Antoinette's private estate.

A Bad Crossing

We packed everything in our school satchels. Gérald showed up with a carriage to take us to the train station. It was warm already, which didn't bode well for the day.

Aleta gave Gérald a big kiss when she jumped in.

"Morning," Gérald managed before Aleta leapt on him. He was dressed quite casually in a loose shirt and tie, a light jacket, and a homburg. The jacket and tie would soon disappear into his satchel. We were wearing our boaters and light dresses, with ground clearance for walking. We had been warned.

He called her "My gorgeous Bavarian wench!"

She yelped and punched him. "Not in front of Cali!"

"My dangerous Bavarian wench," he smiled, but left his arm around her.

"You know she's English," I said. I was still thinking about "Bavarian."

Aleta rolled her eyes, "He's referring to the horse breed. It's my hair."

"Oooooh!" I replied, "Of course."

Gérald just smiled happily.

You can drive to Versailles, but most take the train to get there which takes less than an hour. They run extra trains in the morning and evening just to Versailles. The Versailles train station isn't pleasant like ours. It's just a bare stand sitting alone in a train yard of bare tracks. You have to step across the rails to get to the buses. Although it's very expensive and somewhat time consuming, I've since learned the best way to approach is by car, up *Avenue de Paris*.

The city of Versailles itself is a mixed bag. Near the Palace, the villas are magnificent, but the rest of the town exists just to house the workers and is far less pleasant. But then I live in Pigalle so how can I judge?

That day many of the streets were being dug up to install water and sewers. Paris was and still is the height of modernity, but I'm afraid much of my poor France still had a ways to go.

Our busses chugged down a trench, tree, and villa lined street. Technically it was in the palace grounds, but we couldn't see anything. Not until we turned right and drove around to the front. This is where the walking begins. Camille would be so happy, I got so much exercise.

They let you out at the front gates. They're big and iron and lead into a large unexciting square. You have to walk across this to a second set of gates. These are gold. Much better. Behind them, the buildings are literally covered in the stuff! That and colored stone. It hurts your eyes on a sunny day.

"You know the furniture used to be made of solid silver," Gérald said, as we walked.

"Really? That's crazy." Who polished it?

"We sold it all to pay for the revolution."

"Maybe that's for the best." I said.

"I wish we had kept some of it," Gérald continued. "It would have been something to see."

We paid the man at the gold door his franc each and entered. Gérald, by the way, lets Aleta pay for herself. They push you right through the entry hall with no bonjours into the hall of mirrors. It's quite abrupt. We were there in the morning, but it's best in the afternoon when the sunlight is shining in. Even in the morning it's ten times better than the Opera. According to the sign, Louie got mirror makers from Venice to make the mirrors, then Venice sent assassins and killed them all so they couldn't give away their mirror making secrets!

You can see a lot in those mirrors, like where Gérald's hands were headed. But Aleta didn't seem to mind and I suppose I wouldn't have minded if it were Lucien's hands on me either. Still, it was weird seeing Aleta with someone. All you can do in these situations is hope he doesn't hurt her. I mean he seemed nice. He certainly wasn't a starving artist. Chemistry probably paid pretty well. After all, Dr. Dewar did all right with it, at least until he got shot.

From the hall of mirrors you go left for the queen's wing or right for the king's. They let you wander around. There's a hall with nothing but giant paintings of battles, one after another. I mean really giant. I'd have to knock out a floor if I wanted to put one in my house. And there's a theater with more boxes than seats so all the toffs could crowd in to see performances just for them. It must have been kind of embarrassing to be stuck down in the back rows with all of them looking down on you.

But of course, that's just the big palace. The gardens go on for miles, and miles, and miles. Luckily, there are busses. They're ten centimes. Sadly, they follow no schedule. But everyone wants to see Marie's Hamlet, so it's a heavily travelled route. That and the Temple of Love.

There's a pond shaped like a cross. It goes for a mile in each direction and you can rent boats. The bus drivers point out villa of this and villa of that, and no, no, that one's a folly or a temple, you can't live in it. Then they let you out a half a mile from Marie's. You walk from there. They tell you that you have to walk around this building because it's different on each side and this garden because it represents order from chaos. Maybe I like a little chaos. I've come to realize that I'm not a fan of rococo art and baroque architecture. Their buildings and gardens are nothing but squares and their paintings have no content except syrupy color. Versailles may represent thunderous order, but that doesn't equate to interesting content. Its point is to wow. "Look, underlings, at where I live." But once an underling is wowed, there's nothing left for him or her to do but to try to find some underlings of their own to wow.

No, what I liked were the gardens around Marie's Hamlet. They meandered this way and that, always with surprises around the corner. Sure, the buildings were silly, but that's just fun. And she was a recluse, not interested in wowing anyone but her own fancy. I think Marie and I could have been friends.

And then of course, there was the temple of love which required a very long kiss from Gérald and Aleta.

Chapter 22 – A Proper Engagement

July 13th is Aleta's birthday, which warranted a special dinner – in our new dining room of course. Just so it was useful for something other than doing homework. And for once, Aline was in a good mood. Maybe it was her newer bigger kitchen, or maybe it was having a room for Tisha now.

"Sidet mon boobalinks!" she said in a schmaltzy fake Russian accent as she carried in a big dish. We were having *gratin d'endives au janbon*, which is ham wrapped around potatoes and endives with a bit of cheese grated on top.

"Wine?" Sarah was asking, walking about with the wine bottle.

"None for me," I said.

"Of course, Miss," she said with a smile.

"Some of *that* for me," Gérald said, eying the ham.

"Wait your turn," Aline replied in a graveyard rasp, then headed back towards the kitchen.

"Let me," Aleta said, being close to the dish. I think their feet were up to no good under the table.

We were going to have cake!

I sighed and smiled, truly happy. This is what family is all about.

We had birthday dinner, then Aleta played a song on the piano. Then we played some jigs. Sadly, there's no room to dance in my tiny crowded house. Then Aleta and Gérald went out for a walk. Was he going to ask for her hand? Lucien looked smug so I held my breath. But instead, Aleta came stomping back in.

"I can't believe it!" she yelled, and thumped up the stairs.

Gérald came tumbling in after her. "Aleta!" he called.

"You lied to me," she called down from above. "You never once told me the truth!"

"I didn't lie when I told you I love you!" he called back.

Her head peered over the top of the stairway. "You have no idea what love means! How can I love you if I can't trust you?"

"I warned him," Lucien said, suddenly next to me. I started. He can be very quiet when he wants to be.

"What happened?" I asked.

"He's rich."

"I kind of figured that out," I said.

"Want to go for a walk?" he asked.

"Sure."

The night would have been warm, but for the breeze. We left them to work it out. I figured it would take time.

So we were walking down our busy street. It was summer and everything was in full swing. We stopped to chuckle at Lefebvre's theoretical painting of Aleta. And you really must see that one of Sable, by the way. They clearly worked together very well. Locals tossed us cheery bonjours as we passed. This was the fat time of year for our Pigalle and there were smiles enough for everyone.

"So what is he?" I asked.

"A baron," Lucien replied.

"Really." I knew it had to be something like that.

"What gave him away?" Lucien asked.

"The horse talk."

He nodded. We walked on.

"You know I'll kill you if you lie to me," I said.

"I'll lay down and hand you the knife if I do," he replied.

That's why I love him. I took his hand and he squeezed it back.

When we got back, there was no sign of them, but Sarah met us with a smile. "They're up in her room."

He was still up there in the morning!

I was eating breakfast at our table and Aleta sat down next to me, still in her night dress.

"Cali," she said with deadly seriousness.

"You're getting married," I replied.

"You know."

"Everyone knows."

"Do you mind?" she asked.

I put down my fork and leaned over and gave her a hug. She started crying into my shoulder, then put her arms around me.

We sat like that for a bit, with Aline steering clear of the dining room, until Gérald came in and asked, "What's going on?"

We let go and I gave my napkin to her. "Gérald," I said. "You're denser even than Lucien."

"It's nothing," Aleta said. Which means, "Let it go. It's okay."

"Are you hurt?"

"No."

"Gérald, it's nothing," I said.

"Not if she's crying."

"She's happy."

Aleta nodded, but I could tell Gérald wasn't buying it. I guess he was worried something had gone wrong. He sat down next to her.

"You still love me don't you?" he asked.

She started to laugh, but it became a hiccup. Nodding her head she leaned over to hug him and hiccup into his shoulder.

"I'll get you some water." My excuse to give them room.

Sadly, it wasn't going to be that easy. Gérald, like Lucien, was ruled by his family. She would have to woo both sides if she was going to win. That would mean a trip to Delaware.

We found our storefront two days later, on a Tuesday, and it was glorious. It was expensive too, on the corner of *Rue de Grenelle* and *La Tour-Maubourg*. It used to be a sundries store driven out of business by the new franchised chain stores and rising rents. But it caught the sunlight and you couldn't help but see it.

It wasn't quite everything I wanted. Facing south on a wide busy corner fronting a little park with trees and a fountain, you sadly couldn't see the Eiffel Tower, but you could see it from across the street. It was therefore expensive. They wanted an outrageous two thousand francs per month. With buildout costs and employees I couldn't see how we could turn a profit.

Fannie said property in central Paris was a good investment. France was on the rebound and the nouveau rich were fleeing the suburbs for the delights of the central city. So I wrote to ask how much for the building. They replied half a million, which seemed crazy until you found out it's a fifth of the east side of the street and practically new. But that was way more than I had. I offered them two eighty. I was told the owner just about sneezed dust. They countered four fifty, which was a significant drop, but still outrageous. My first house only cost twenty! I realized then though, that no matter what the outcome I would need financing.

Enter a bitter acquaintance. Apparently I was on a list.

Lucien and I were sitting in the nice chairs at The Bank of France.

"Miss Carmichael and Lord Antoine. Two of our favorite customers. May I offer you some tea?"

"Yes," I said. I am after all, a bohemian and bohemians never turn down free eats. Lucien declined. He is a coffee drinker.

M. Blanc snapped his fingers, but his secretary had already left to come back shortly with a tray.

"And what do we owe the pleasure of this visit?" he asked.

"I would like a business loan," I said.

"A business loan?"

"Yes." I just said that!

"What sort of business?"

"I want to buy a building."

"Just that?" He looked worried.

"A store downstairs."

"Ah."

His secretary came in with the tea, offering us cream and sugar, even though Lucien already said he didn't want any.

"What is the address?"

When I told him, he blinked for a second. "Yes, I can see why you might be interested in a loan. It's definitely a prime area. I was thinking of investing there myself. Can you tell me about the business?"

I brought Henri's and Paul's drawings, and Joseph's buildout and cost breakpoint estimates with us, laying them out one by one on his desk.

"So you're self-funding the business, but wish to purchase the building as a separate investment. What are they asking for the building?"

"So far four hundred fifty, but I felt that I couldn't bargain in good faith without firm knowledge that I had the money," I replied.

"That is high."

"Please bear in mind as well that I'm more than willing to cosign for the loan," Lucien added.

"That won't be necessary," he smiled at Lucien. "It's a good plan. But I can't authorize this. It will have to be reviewed."

"Reviewed?" Lucien frowned. "I think we have more than ample credit."

"Yes you do, but it still has to be reviewed."

"That's unusual," Lucien replied.

"Miss Carmichael has special circumstances that have to be considered."

"Such as?" Lucien asked.

"She might die." He looked a little uncomfortable. "Give us a couple of days."

So we went home a little worried. That night Lucien took me out dancing at *Bal Mabille*. It's a big park lit with hundreds of paper lanterns and lights, and an orchestra in a little round house. On one side is a merry-go-round and it and you go around and around with the music.

The next day, Sunday, August sixth, we got a caller. It was a chauffeur, uniform and all, sent by who else but the Baron Rothschild. Apparently he wanted to see me. Almost certainly because I was trying to borrow money. Lucien was cursing when we picked him up at his apartment. The driver wanted just me, but I wouldn't go without him. I took Crow too. I'm not an idiot.

The Baron's Paris villa is right next door to Longchamp. It was odd, I thought, that we hadn't seen him at the races since he's so fond of horses. His house grounds have their own pond with streams and bridges. The road makes you drive by it on the way to the house. But for all the gardens, the house itself is pretty unimpressive. Just a big square block. It's practically pre-empire. Of course you have to walk up a bunch of stone steps to get to the front door. We waited in the entry hall while we were announced. I didn't bother with a card since this was practically an abduction.

"I knew it," said a girl's voice from the top of the stairs.

"Bertha!" I cried, then scrambled up the steps to meet her halfway down with a hug.

"What is he up to?" she asked.

"I have no idea," I replied. "But I'm so glad you're here. Did he send you away?" I asked as we walked down the steps.

"No," she said. "He was too upset."

"And you're not married."

"No. But I'm sure he's looking for the best match."

"A caring father," I smiled.

"I'm a Rothschild."

"Cali," Gustave called as he saw us at the bottom of the steps.

"Baron," Lucien said.

"And Lucien," Gustave said, a bit less enthusiastic. "And this would be Crow?" he asked.

"Yes," Crow replied, clearly unimpressed by meeting perhaps the richest man in the world.

"And you have it." He was looking at my violin. My blood ran cold.

"You can't have her," I said.

Gustave laughed.

"Papa," Bertha said, frowning.

He glanced at her with slight frown, then smiled at me. "I'm a terrible host. Come in."

We followed him into his parlor. It was completely baroque which as you know, I kind of dislike. This was probably the first of the family's many mansions.

"Coffee?" he asked as we sat. A servant entered with a tray.

"No thank you," Lucien said coldly.

I shook my head no, as did Crow. Bertha watched from the doorway.

"Bertha," he said without looking. "This is business."

"Papa. This is another mistake," she said, as she turned and headed up the stairway.

Gustave's eyes twitched. But he continued on.

"Cali, I want to buy your violin."

"No," I replied.

"You haven't heard the price."

"No."

"Gustave," Lucien said. "It's the one thing she will never sell."

"I'll give you that building."

I squinted at him. That made me angry.

"I'll make sure your store succeeds," he continued.

"Honestly sir," Crow said. "It's the one thing she won't part with. It doesn't matter to her how valuable it is."

"I'll tell you where your parents are."

Exactly the wrong thing to say! It was exactly what I had been through in the Congo. I screamed, falling backwards in my chair trying to get away.

Bertha was down the stairs and back in.

"What did you do!" she hissed.

"I made her an offer," he said. "But I think she misunderstood."

"Rothschild," Lucien spat, on his feet. "Where are they?"

"You misunderstand. I'll help find them. I don't know where they are."

But I was out the door, running. Down the steps in the bright sunshine, my feet thumping through the grass.

"Cali," someone called, far behind me.

But I was stumbling splashing through a stream and then into brush. Running, clutching Francesca. Running together, as we always had. I think I'd gone a little crazy.

They finally boxed us in against the corner of the wall. I couldn't make it to the gate and the damn wall was tall and his entire staff had been out beating the brush. There were four facing me, then six. I stood hugging Francesca.

"Stay back or I'll kill you!" I snarled.

They didn't approach, but they didn't go. Finally Crow thumped up at a run.

"Calm down Missy," he said, in out-of-breath English. "We're leaving."

"It won't stop here," I hissed. "He won't stop."

Then Lucien and Gustave trotted up on horseback.

"There she is," Gustav said.

Lucien climbed down and came towards me.

"Let's go home," he said.

"He won't stop. He'll never stop," I said. "Someone will die."

"I won't let him."

"You can't stop him." I was sobbing. "I'll have to kill him, and then they'll kill me."

"Papa," Bertha said, trotting up on her horse. "Let's go home."

"Yes," he said, backing away. He looked at me, his eyes sad, and said, "I'm sorry." Then he climbed on his horse and they both rode away.

Crow shooed the others away and then they walked me back to the car. Lucien had his arm around me as I cried, still desperately clutching Francesca.

That was the first inkling that she was truly special. My loan was approved the next day, for any amount I needed they said.

Chapter 23 – Ma and Pa

We received word that they found my family on August 20th, two days before my birthday. It was the best present. All of the old crew were alive. They found everyone but Knockers, our ship's cat, and Léon. They were still on Red. Red had been taken by pirates. They had left my family marooned! I received a letter from Ian three days later. He signed on with the pirates as crew and hadn't been able to jump ship for over a month. Then it was a long run to find any authorities who would listen.

So Red was gone. But Ma and Pa were alive! Can you see me smile? I was jumping about in the hallway.

Crow came bumping down the stairs saying, "What's up Missy?"

I thrust the message at him, still hopping.

He let out a whooping laugh, then we were both jumping and hugging.

Then Aleta, who was just back from Delaware, was there jumping too and everyone else was standing about wondering what was going on. She had been away, going here and there to meet Gérald's family, seeking their approval. It had been a hard, uphill battle for her.

My family were all in the hospital, recovering. How bad had it been? It would be weeks before I found out. Our insurance hearing wouldn't occur in Brussels until that winter and it would be more than a year before my family was back at sea.

That was it for my eighteenth birthday because Aleta and I were off to Lyon by airship, to *Usine Lumière*, to make color stills and moving pictures. I'm sure you've seen them by now, but back then both of these things were brand new and something truly incredible. The Lumière factory is dead center in the city, but the aerodrome is northeast, outside the city walls. You take a train in, just like Paris. We were met at the train station by a Lumière representative with a car who took us to our hotel. It would just be one night because I had rehearsal on Tuesday. Our schedule was so tight that we dropped off our luggage and were immediately back on the road to have lunch at the studio.

The Lumière Factory is a large walled compound, a whole block. We drove in through a big gate with guards. Inside it was like a little city, our driver taking us down dirt streets filled with workers and trucks to a barnlike building with big double doors.

"Damn it, Morin," said a man in a suit and derby. He was waiting for us out front. "You drive too fast. You're making dust."

"Sorry sir," the driver replied.

Then the man in the derby looked at us and grinned.

"Ladies, welcome. Pardon the dirt. It's been dry and we usually count on the rain to keep it down." Then he called in through the big double doors for help.

We came with trunks containing our dresses and jewelry. Men came out to take them while our host helped us down.

"Auguste Lumière. You must be Aleta and Calista." He bent to kiss our hands. "It is a pleasure to meet you."

"And it's an honor to meet you, M. Lumière."

"Auguste please."

"Auguste," Aleta said.

Inside, they had a fake parlor and a fake ship with a wheel and brinicle. It was hilarious and amazing at the same time. We played in a fake parlor, changing dresses several times. They wound the camera with a key for the moving pictures and it ticked when it was working, which was hard to ignore while we played and it only went for a minute or so, so they couldn't get an entire song. They picked the part they liked and started it then. They even recorded sound. Then we posed for stills, which was fun, but not as fun as the ship!

They cranked a big propeller to make wind and men tossed buckets of water up behind the rail while other men tipped the deck. I steered while Aleta pulled on a rope. What was she pulling? Obviously something nautical. Men ran around in what had to be pirate dress because sailors sure don't dress like that, doing who knows what while we shouted out orders and pointed. They even flashed bolts of lightning on the sky behind us. Then they flopped the big octopus over the rail. It was a puppet. Cloth filled with down, like a big tentacled pillow. We jumped on it with our "knives," which were made of wood. Men pretended to be tossed aside until we finally "killed" it. Ah, the life of a sailor.

All this took time and we didn't arrive back our hotel until late. Dinner and then bed, our night dresses already laid out. After breakfast, they took us back to the train station and then to an airship out. So what did Lyons look like you ask? Except for the usual cobble streets, I have no clue.

Once I started signing the paperwork, the store buildout blossomed with frightening speed. It's a giddy thing to see plans that existed only in drawings and diagrams take form. I caused this to happen! I didn't have a lot of time to visit, relying heavily on Joseph, now my third partner, to manage things. We expanded the storefront around the corner, knocking out a wall, incorporating the existing flower shop into the design. We wanted the extra show space to display our own lines of clothing based on the most common requests from women.

The best by far was Paul's idea for a replacement for the bodice. It was abbreviated to just beneath the sternum, with cups and under stays instead of the vertical contoured boning you have in a corset.

It left the torso completely free and deliriously cool on hot days. We called it a halter, like they put on horses, which Lucien thought terribly funny. That was until we were alone. Then they drove him crazy. They were incredibly tricky to make, but far easier than a corset. The problem was stock. Breasts come in so many shapes and sizes that we would always be scrambling to keep a reasonable selection on the shelves. But it was important that they conform comfortably to the breast, not the other way around. And Paul never left the design alone. Color, decoration, high and low front, thick and thin straps.

We were accumulating stock even while we were building the store. Our seamstresses worked steadily in an empty apartment converted to a workshop. Then we expanded it to two, knocking out the wall. Eventually I would have whole buildings full of machines and women. The equipment was new because we wanted to use electricity instead of muscle and steam and it was terribly expensive, but it definitely improved production. And every design had to have a model piece for the showroom stage. We got Lilli, Dior, Gene, Jolie, and best of all Sable for models! We picked them partly because their sizes matched.

The reporters were always underfoot. Gawkers too. There was always a crowd out front. Not just reporters, but all kinds of people seemed to follow me about. Some of them were, I think, sent by Rue de la Paix to watch what I was up to. And, of course, it was the concert as well. Paul wanted the store open by opening night. He encouraged the reporters. He may have even been tipping them off as to where I would be. Paul has always had a firm grasp on what the public wants. That's his genius; his ability to understand people. He was building it all towards an opening night peak.

In the beginning I started with only fifteen regular employees and three more under Paul, many living in our building. When the store opened we would hire ten more, with an additional eight seamstresses to be added later, before I was even out of the hospital. In less than a year I would have over a hundred. Lines of perfume, soaps, powder, and rouge appeared by the case in our storeroom. We recruited local craftsmen to build cases to display their wares. Jewelry, broaches, and watches on consignment. And it all cost money – insurance, taxes, deposits, advertising, and permits, and we had so far sold precisely nothing! My bank account dwindled as I wrote check after check, Joseph laughing at my distress. Now I know why Pa endlessly stuck to his desk, carefully counting and balancing.

The Lumière contract was good publicity, but brought in very little money. There were, at that time, very few places that could show moving pictures and color printing was still terribly slow. Jean-Paul wanted to book me at more theaters, which would bring in good steady money, but the security problems were insane. Just the Opera ran my poor Lucien ragged trying to fix them. The risk was too great.

Fannie had been talking to Edison behind my back. They had whistled up yet another deal, which I had to admit was a clever one. They wanted to record my performance! They made a new machine that recorded on disks instead of spools. Apparently they lasted a lot longer.

In between all that I still had rehearsals and practices. I no longer practiced with Camille. Just Mathieu and Grégoire. I talked to them about cancelling and they were sympathetic, but it was useless. I would meet the British no matter what, and if I quit, it would be the end of my career. I would be disgraced which probably what the British had in mind. They wanted me to quit.

Our last orchestra rehearsal was on September 7th, the theater blessedly cool. Standing like a fortress against the late summer heat and humidity. Ma and Pa came to that one. They had come by zeppelin! They arrived on the fourth.

We met at the terminal. Lufthansa has a service where they telegram you with an impending arrival time a few hours before they arrive. It's very convenient. We piled into a carriage to get to the train station and from there to the aerodrome. I was practically bouncing the whole way there. They were finally coming!

But we had to wait of course. Worse, we had to wait where we couldn't see them, in a terminal full of reporters. All we could do was eat cookies and drink coffee, which made being patient even more difficult. They had a board with flight status on it, but they called the changes out first so we knew where they were. We heard that their zeppelin was anchored, but it would be thirty tortuous minutes until they reached the terminal.

We saw the bus pull up slowly, venting steam as it stopped,

everyone crowded the windows. We had cameras in the way everywhere. It was taking so long and it was so hard to see inside through the bus windows. Crow's hand was on my shoulder. Lucien was standing beside me. Then people began to get off one at a time. No. No. No. On and on. No. Yes! It was Pa. He was helping Ma down. She had a bag.

They were thin. The war and the island had hammered gray into their hair. But they were home and I was running to the door, until the railings stopped me.

"Ma! Pa!" I called. They looked around, still blinded by the outside sun.

"Cali!" Pa called.

"Oh Hon," Ma said. They were there, their arms sweet, me crying. I couldn't stop. A dam had broken at the first sight of them. It all came spilling out, the zeppelin, Dr. Dewar, Brussels, and the attempts on my life. I clung to them and they hugged me back, perhaps a little confused.

We stood there for I don't know how long, until Ma leaned back to look at me.

"Look at you," she said, with a smile, "you've grown." She pulled out her handkerchief and dabbed my tears.

"I'm so glad you're here," I sobbed.

Pa choked back a laugh, oblivious to the stupid blitzlicht popping around us. They were good at ignoring the reporters, which was a relief.

"We missed you," Pa said. He let go of me and tugged at my dress. "It looks like Lucien has taken good care of you."

"Oh no," Lucien said, holding his hands up. "She's quite capable of taking care of herself."

Crow snorted. "It's fun to watch."

"Is it?" Ma sounded doubtful, then saw Aleta standing behind. "Hello Aleta," Ma called.

"Hello Mrs. Carmichael." She replied, almost like a child. It's funny how parents can do that.

"Have you been taking care of her?"

"We take care of each other."

"Good."

"I'm looking forward to seeing this maid of yours," Pa said.

"She has two now," Crow said.

"Does she?" Pa sounded unconvinced, still leery of my having just one.

"Sarah's here," I said, trying to regain control of myself. "She's taking care of the luggage. We should go."

Why did I feel so tired? Like I was suddenly made of lead. "We'll miss the bus. She's probably trying to hold us seats."

As we walked I started to get nervous. This was the start of inspection. I wanted to measure up. They eyed Sarah skeptically, but she smiled back and curtsied, and genuinely seemed glad to meet them.

I found out something amazing. Neither Ma nor Pa had ever been on a train. Never going inland limits one's experiences. I figured that had to change. They were in Paris and there was so much to see.

Lucien, Pa, and Crow compared Zeppelin experiences on the way in while Ma, Aleta, and I were left to our girl talk.

"You are going to like Paris, Ma," I said.

"Are you happy here?" she asked.

"Oh, yes."

"You should see the store she's opening," Aleta said.

"Your Grandpa told us about that," she said. She sounded worried.

"It's beautiful," Aleta added. I think she was defending me, just a bit.

"A week until opening," I said.

"And your concert," Ma replied. "That's too much."

"I have good help."

Thanks to Sarah, their luggage actually made it out to the carriage way. I thought about taking a car, but decided on a carriage. I didn't want to make the same mistake I made with Crow by spending too much money, but it took two carriages. Pa paid for them. He insisted.

It's only a mile to my house from the train station. Pa tested my French all the way. My speaking it never ceased to amuse him. It was late afternoon when we pulled up. Mme. Touchard called bonjour from her balcony, her Turkish cigarette trailing smoke. I called bonjour back, introducing my parents as the carriage pulled to a stop. Actually, we got curious bonjours all along the street.

Everyone would be wanting to know who these new people were.

"They will have to come and visit," Mme. Touchard said.

"They'll meet everyone," I replied.

Sarah was at the door, holding it open. Aline and Florette were at the carriages to wrestle with Pa for the luggage.

Our house had become more crowded than ever. Ma made a beeline straight for the kitchen and Pa walked about taking inventory. Aline showed rare patience, gently defending the kitchen, pushing Ma, who didn't know how to live without one, out.

"Yes Ma'am," Aline said, as Ma poked at the stove. "It's gas." And then, as Ma moved on, "Yes Ma'am, that's hot water. It comes up from the basement." Tisha stood quietly in back, staring at Ma in fear.

"And what do you do?" Ma asked Tisha, who just about bolted as Ma turned towards her.

"That's Tisha. She's our scullery maid," Aline replied, fixing Tisha in place with a hard stare.

"Scullery maid?" Ma asked.

"My assistant. You'll meet Jacques as well, if he ever gets around to coming back."

"What does he do?"

"Errands."

"It doesn't sound like you need any help," Ma said, clearly disappointed.

"No."

"I could show you my daughter's favorite foods."

"We're fine."

"Would you mind my cooking for my husband?"

"Yes."

"There's seems to be room."

"No."

It was difficult for them. Sarah and Florette gently herded and taught them as Sarah had taught me. I had extra keys made for them. I took them over the roof. And they needed to know about the catacombs.

"It's important Ma."

I don't think she liked the idea of going underground, which considering she had lived her life in the open air was understandable.

"Here Ma, try your key. Then we'll try it from below."

"Cali," Aleta called from the top of the stairs. "Let me do that. You should be practicing."

"But it's fun," I whined.

"You should," Pa said. "You've only two days."

"There, see Pa? I have lots of friends who look out for me," I sighed.

Aleta was coming down the stairs. "You won't have me much longer if Gérald has his way."

"Don't say that," I said. I couldn't conceive of life without her, but things seemed to have settled with Gérald's family.

"What are they saying?" Ma whispered to Pa, and he had to translate. We were speaking French for Aleta's sake, as always. Poor Ma was left out a lot because of that.

I was really sorry I missed Ma in the catacombs because Aleta said she was as funny as Sarah.

Our house was so crowded that I practiced in my room instead of the parlor. The windows were open and they could hear me in the street. I could see Mme. Touchard, leaning on her elbows on her railing. Many stopped to listen in addition to my usual little crowd.

Pa wanted to see the business plan and books, demanding the concert be cancelled. To quit though, would be to quit Paris. All of the things that kept me not just safe, but sane, all depended on that concert: Jean-Paul, my store, the Sorbonne, and even Mrs. Hartnoll.

I sawed away at Mendelssohn and Bach, ate meals, and took walks at all hours, never alone.

And so we come to concert day.

It was Saturday, September sixteenth, opening night. My debut. I was the second act on the opening night of opera season. The worst slot in the entire season. The rich flee Paris when they can during the heat of the summer and many weren't back yet, so the opening week is considered a warm up. A place for new talent and doubtful works. I was at the bottom of that list, and yet every performance was sold out. It had been a cunning decision on Camille's and the Opera's part to place me there. It's not often you get to witness a murder on stage.

I woke that morning, laying in my bed, looking at the crack in the ceiling in my crooked room. I could no longer see it, but I knew it was there. The paint didn't cover the fact that it was my room. My bed was new too, bigger, which made no difference because I still could not reach the edges with my feet and hands. So much room, all wasted. Outside my window I could hear the sounds of the street, my noisy Pigalle. Mme. Touchard was on her balcony with her first cigarette. M. Delattre was putting his signs out and I knew that Sarah would be waiting to buy the bread for our breakfast. Its smell drifted down the street as they baked. I could hear a rooster crowing. Our gendarme was saying hello to Sarah and Mme. Franck, who was probably standing next to Sarah, waiting for her bread too. Everyone's shutters, *persiennes,* were open to grab the night's coolness before being closed against the day's heat. Just from my bed I could see people moving about across the way. The street was stirring. Its denizen's voices echoing. I popped out of bed to use the toilet before Sarah came with my breakfast.

Back, snuggled under the covers, Lucien's head popped in the doorway looking to see if I was awake. He was up early too, tiptoeing in to say good morning before Sarah shooed him away. Good mornings are the best.

"I have your breakfast Miss, if you don't mind, my Lord."

We broke our kiss, the scent of his hair sweet.

"Of course," he smiled. We had all day. Camille told me to relax after all. It would work out or it wouldn't. There was nothing more we could do except show up. I would see tomorrow or not, but I could enjoy today. Especially since I had both orange and melon! I love Aline and Sarah.

He fed me, which was sweet, sometimes following it with a kiss.

That was until Pa interrupted.

"Cali, I want to talk to you about that loan. Your tenants . . ."

"Pa!" I was eating egg. I was almost a spit it out laughing. Lucien's hand pulled back from my breast.

"I'm sorry," Pa said. It was the first time I've ever heard him apologize. He backed towards the hallway.

"Pa!" I called.

"Cali," he said, as he stopped.

"It was to keep the loan away from the store," I said.

"You're isolating liability."

"Yes."

"Then the current tenets . . ."

"Are a problem."

"I see."

"No. You don't," I replied. "This is Paris."

He frowned.

"Go outside and buy a cup of tea, or a beer, or a turnip. Sit and listen."

"You're saying it will take time."

"Yes. Have you gone down and talked to Maurice, Ulf, and Ransu?"

"No."

"They're working today. I think you'll like them. They know you're coming."

"I'm not a smuggler."

I smiled. "No. You aren't. I just need you to know where I live."

He seemed to wilt for a moment. "I'm not used to this."

Lucien started to say something, but I gave him a look.

"Pa," I said.

"It's," he started. "It's that our home is gone. Red's gone." He looked at the window. "I don't know what to do."

I smiled. "Take the elevator up to the top of the Eiffel Tower. You can see the whole world. Reach down and pick a spot and dig in. Besides, what's wrong with smuggling?"

He brightened and chuckled. "Not a damn thing," he said, which no longer surprised me.

"Now go away," I said, tipping my head back in a swoon.

He smiled, and closed the door behind him.

Then I looked up at Lucien and gave him a mean smile. "I'm still very hungry."

We got the telegram from Max late morning. It had three names and pathetic descriptions. Too late to block their entry into the country; as if they would be using their own names.

I started dressing at four even though my part in the concert wasn't until nine. Then I was forced to take it all off to eat dinner, which I barely touched. I tried. Everyone was nervous and on edge.

Lucien was torn between spending what could be our last

moments together with me or going to the theater to supervise. He sat at the table while I was trying to eat, then stood, and then sat back down again.

"Go," I said. "To the front with you." I was trying to be funny. But it brought a tear. The first I'd ever seen from him. He kissed me savagely, gripping me in a huge hug that took my breath. Before I could look up, he was gone.

My food sat there, still on my plate.

We will make our stand, I thought. *I will not leave Pigalle.*

I dressed again for the theater. It was a brand new dress, made by Paul just for the concert. It was white, looking very much like a wedding dress and yet the hem and waist were very high, perhaps more like a flower girl's. We had a hair piece with white flowers that would fall down my back along with my hair. Sarah would put it in at the theater.

The coal-stained afternoon light shone on the walls of the houses across the street, illuminating every line and crack of every stone as I climbed into the car that practically blocked our narrow street. Sarah put down a blanket on the seat to protect my dress. The neighborhood stood out and watched. They waved as we rolled forward and shouted, *viva la France, bonne chance*, and *bien performer*, and I shouted back *France mon amour*.

Aleta and Crow sat to my sides, watching the crowd, Crow's hand half under his coat as his eyes darted about. Ma, Pa, and Sarah, sat across from us as we rattled across the cobblestones into the growing twilight.

Chapter 24 – The Theater

I chose the Napoleon entrance at random, but, to be honest, also because it's the most fun. The rotunda is beautiful and the doors are ornate brass. And the driveway is designed to avoid trouble, taking you right up next to the door. We hurriedly entered. Inside was the familiar atrium, thankfully empty. They must have blocked the inside entrance. I realized that I didn't know what to do with my family. Could they come up to my dressing room? It was only seven, too early to sit in their seats.

"Come," I said. "This way."

I led them to the elevator. Looking around, I saw no gendarmes and no operator. Where were they?

The elevator was too small for all of us. Crow growled and dashed up the stairs to guard our exit. I almost laughed, him dashing about in his new suit and shiny shoes. It was so strange. Upstairs we turned left and entered the dressing room area, which thankfully had two gendarmes standing in front of the entry door. This was correct, but what had happened to the others?

We were early and these were individual dressing rooms. Only Camille and I were using them and he was certainly downstairs organizing the Haydn opener, so we were alone in the cast wing.

"Evening, Miss," our gendarmes said.

I said hello to both, then asked, "Were there supposed to be guards at the entrance?"

"Yes Ma'am. You didn't see them?"

"No."

He frowned, just for a second, then replied, "We'll see to it. It's best if you stay in your room."

There's a pecking order to dressing rooms and being at the bottom meant that I got a very small one even though the others were empty. It was crowded, especially since Ma had worn perfume. We would all come out smelling of flowers. Crow, Ma, and Pa had to stand against the wall while we worked.

It was mostly my hair, which Sarah had very definite ideas about. The funny thing was that we were so early that we had to do it all over again an hour later. The room was stuffy, but thankfully the theater had electric light or it would have been impossibly hot as well. Of course Ma was holding back tears. She would occasionally wipe her nose and eyes.

Once coiffed and ready, there was no way I was going to sit there for an hour. Not when there was a whole theater to explore and Lucien to find.

"There's no way you're going out there," Crow said.

"Cali," Pa added. "They said to wait here."

Aleta was muttering as she worked on my hairpiece, that I didn't brush my hair enough, which was true.

I looked at Pa, dead serious, "I need to be unpredictable. If I sit here, they'll know where I am."

"Cali," he started to reply.

"Besides. I've never seen it lit up."

"She's right," Aleta said, talking around the hairpins in her mouth, backing me up, then growling at some new problem.

"Miss," Sarah said to Aleta. "Let me. Hold the flowers straight."

"And I want to see the staircase," Aleta grinned. Her dress was more formal than mine, but still that same creamy white that Paul loves. It made her look older.

"Crow," I said. "I can't be what they expect."

"I think you walking around would be just what I'd expect."

"It's a sniper. A long shot. He needs to get me in his sights, and for that I have to stay still."

"And he won't be watching the lobby," Aleta added.

"Hon," Ma said. "You should stay in here."

"He'll have a bead on me when I walk out on stage. If we force him to make his move before the concert, so much the better."

We wrestled with everything until we seemed to achieve some sort of order and then gave up.

"Pack up Sarah," I said.

"Yes, Miss."

The gendarmes outside were no better.

"Miss. You're to stay inside."

I smiled. "Come with me. I'm not coming back here tonight. I need to find Lucien."

"Our orders are clear, Miss."

"Then you'll have to arrest me," I replied. This was fun. If it was to be my last night on earth, then that was what I was going to have. "Come on," I said, and headed for the stairs. We needed to be down in the public area. Ma had to see it. Our gendarmes scowled but followed. We entered through double doors watched by a guard.

"Wait, wait," he said. "You aren't to leave the dressing rooms."

"So stop us," Aleta said.

I turned, walking backwards. "Guard the door. We may be going back this way."

"Hon, this isn't a good idea," Ma said.

"It's a better idea than staying in there. Look at the people!" I replied.

"It's beautiful. Yes. But . . ."

"Wait until you see the staircase," I said.

Walking past the stairway, we grabbed an empty balcony. The chandeliers and lights threw light everywhere, glistening like stars in the glass and polished marble. Everything was gold and golden marble, the ceiling covered in angels and gods, dripping syrupy rococo color. I looked up at them, doubting that heaven would look anything like that, but it did look good. Women and men were ascending the staircase dressed in their best, hats and bags already checked. The women's gowns flowed like rivers of color, their jewels glinting in time with the cut crystal lights that lined the stairway.

When we walked we drew stares. People weren't quite sure, even with the gendarmes and me carrying Francesca.

We simply have to walk the grand staircase, I thought. We were the only ones going down. At night it's breathtaking. We stood on marble floors staring up into a universe of gold and light, four stories high, the domain of the gods and angles. Women and men stood about in groups at the bottom, greeting acquaintances, preparing to make the climb. Women came mostly in pastels, pinks, blues, greens, creams, and whites. The men were uniformly black. It was warm but the men wore their coats. They make special dresses for the opera, made to fit the requirements of the seating. No bustles or crinolines. Trains kept to a minimum. I even saw some bare necks and shoulders, and wondered if I had been responsible for that.

At the bottom you can really see the carving in the marble at its rococo best, polished practically to mirror smoothness. The swirls, shields, angles, and nymphs, cover practically everything. We gawked until Aleta remembered that we shouldn't stay still, so we started back up. I had to show them the foyer.

We passed by the bar, none of us wanting a drink. This wasn't a night for relaxation, but it was definitely a night for gawking, which we all did. The foyer simply stopped us flatfooted, mouths open. At night it's completely different. Lit only by the chandeliers, the fireplace, and city lights from the balcony, it takes on a deep golden glow. The humming echo of the Grand Staircase hall is left to warm you from the back. People are struck dumb as they enter. They wander about with their crystal glasses in hand, heads tilted back to stare at the ceiling, the firelight dancing and shining off the floor in long lines between legs and dresses.

Ma let out a gasp, looking up with eyes wide. Pa wasn't far behind.

I'd seen this all before, several times, and had reached the point where I noticed the less pleasant things. You get drafts as the doors open and close to let people out on the balcony which can be chilly even in late summer. Up above, the ceiling panels are full of nothing but naked people. They supposedly tell different stories, but I don't know which and it's impossible to tell just by looking at them. You just see naked people. On the plus side, it's the only place you can sit outside of the theater, but the seats are usually already occupied by dames and matrons, the chairs extra wide to accommodate them.

"Cali, you were to stay in your dressing room," said a voice behind me. It was Lucien!

"It wasn't practical," I replied turning. He looked tired.

"Sorry, Sir," one of our gendarmes said.

He flashed a smile at our gendarmes. "It's fine. She's impossible to contain." Then he took my shoulders in his hands. I think he wanted a kiss, or maybe it was just that I wanted him to. "You should go back," he said.

"They'll know where I am."

"I'll know where you are," he said.

"We have protection and we're going to head backstage now anyway."

"Good. This is hardly safe," he sighed. "This place is a sniper's dream. There are holes, hidden rooms, and service access ways everywhere." He was fretting. "There aren't men enough in all of Paris to cover them and half would never come back. Lost in the maze."

He looked about. "Worse. Someone is playing pranks. Sending fake orders. Locking doors."

This should have scared me but for some crazy reason I didn't feel worried. I suppose I was completely resigned to my fate.

"At least we know they're here and not waiting outside," I replied.

"Cali. Let's stop this now," Pa said.

"I agree," Crow added.

"I'm not running," I said firmly. "Where will I go? Brazil? It will be the same there. I won't live in a hole."

"You could go back to sea," Pa said.

"They'd drop something in our cargo and we'd all die. No one would know how or where." My voice hardened. "No. I'll face them in public. In the light."

A woman reached between Aleta and Pa and took my hand. Someone else to my side said, "*Vive le Lapin.*" Another said, "*Nous sommes avec toi.*" We are with you. I had gathered a crowd.

I looked about, at their faces. They were as much my family as my parents. Their faces were as grim and determined as I felt.

"Thank you."

"Oh dear," Ma said, and started to cry. "I don't want to lose you."

I turned and gave her a long hug. "This is all my fault, Ma. I should have never sent us to the Congo."

"We didn't know," she said.

"We didn't," Aleta added. She was hugging us both. Pa's hand on Ma's back.

"They're evil," Ma said.

I thought about Mr. Walker. "No," I said. "They aren't. It's their government. Their stupid empire."

We heard the bell. Two rings, repeating. They were going to start.

"We've got to go," I said. I straightened up and began to walk. "Come on."

The stairway and halls had grown crowded and as we walked people reached out to touch me. They murmured, "*bonne chance*," and "*Vive le Lapin*." Walking down a level, we turned into the side corridor heading towards the doubled doors that led back stage.

The guards opened the door for us and we entered, walking down the stone inlayed corridor, the sound of the stage and our footsteps echoing. At the end we turned right and descended down the stairs to the stage level, entering in back.

The area back of the backdrop was a maze of construction. Set pieces, backdrops, and props for later shows. Construction of course was stopped for the duration of our performance. Materials were stacked and hung about, loose tools left to be picked up again later. We walked down the side, stepping carefully around tables of tools and paint to get to the side of the stage, to see the orchestra and curtain.

As soon as we passed the backdrop and entered the orchestra area, the sound of the audience came in to focus. The curtain in front glowed like a bed of coals in the limelight from stage front. The reality of what I was about to do hit home. What was I doing?

The orchestra was still gathering and settling itself. Camille's eyes narrowed when he saw me. Then again perhaps it was his disapproval of my bringing my family backstage.

We had reached stage wing, inside the blind edge where the audience couldn't see, when Lucien took my arm and turned me. Looking in my eyes, he moved a curl aside.

"You need to fix your hair," he said.

I tried to smile up at him and then melted in his arms with a ragged breath. He bent to kiss me.

He looked so sad.

"I'll see you again, one way or another," I said. "I swear."

"No," Pa said. "This goes no further. I won't allow it."

He took hold of my arm to drag me away. That sealed it. I wouldn't go. Not like that.

"Pa, no," I said. "There's no escape. Only delay."

"I will not lose you!"

"I will not be disgraced! Not by them."

One of our musicians was translating for the orchestra! The last thing I wanted then. It would just anger Pa.

"I have to go," Lucien said. "I have to make sure of our positions." Then he carefully pried Pa's hand from my arm. "Mr. Carmichael. Let her do this. I trust her. You must as well."

"No," Ma said. It was breathless, almost a wail.

"She has to do this," Aleta said.

"Come," Lucien said, trying to lead them away.

I looked at Crow. "Can you stay calm?"

He nodded.

"Stay close," I said. "Be ready. We have a long wait."

But Pa wouldn't be led. "Lucien," he said. "We'll stay." He looked at Ma. "We'll be quiet."

She nodded, tears in her eyes.

Lucien looked at them and then back at me. I could see the start of tears. It was just a moment, then he abruptly turned to go.

It hurt so, but I watched him leave. Aleta's arm sliding around my back. I felt utterly empty.

Half the orchestra had been watching so Camille tapped his stand to get their attention. They all turned as one, sitting straight to face him as the curtain rose like the sun, the limelight blinding, the audience a wall of applause.

Camille turned and bowed. To each side, I could see the Edison recording cones. They would start with a Haydn symphony. My part would come second.

"Miss," Sarah said. "I need to do your hair." She had her bag and had found a stool.

I was sitting facing the wrong direction so I didn't see Camille start, but heard the orchestra shift in their seats a moment before they struck the first notes. I wanted to look, but Aleta and Sarah were pulling on my hair.

And thus began the long wait. The symphony only lasts forty minutes, but each minute carried its own special kind of weight. We could do nothing. Ma and Pa sat next to me with their arms around me while I fidgeted with nervous energy.

Five minutes before they finished, I had Francesca out. She felt alive in my hands. Alive and eager, like a racehorse waiting in the gate. This was what she was made for.

I stood at the closing bars and moved to the edge to wait out the applause. It was just noise and darkness. I watched Camille. He had changed, more elemental spirit than man.

He held out his arm and motioned me forward with his fingers while he switched music. He didn't need to. He knew the piece by heart. I had long since abandoned mine.

I took a breath and strode out into the light. I could feel its heat on my face. The noise buffeted me as I took my place on Camille's left. He blessed me with a half-smile and tip of his head, while I adjusted things. He raised his eyebrows to ask if I was ready and I nodded.

Raising his baton, they started, and I followed. Their music flowed around me like water. So smooth and perfect. I swam around and through it, the audience immediately forgotten, Francesca singing in my hands.

We cried into the darkness, following the music's hills and valleys, until we came to my first break. I stood there and waited, counting time, marveling at the beauty of the music, at the orchestra. All the cacophony, the loose threads from the start had pulled together into a single being. We joined again and sang, the melancholy I'd felt in the past was gone. It was all green fields and summer rain. That is until we came to my first solo.

I was left alone on the stage. I could no longer see anything but the music and that vast cavernous blackness in front of me. My notes cut lines and shapes in the darkness. Slowly, then faster, and faster, the orchestra skipping to catch up. We charged through the night, tumbling and turning over everything like a flood.

I watched Camille as we finished the first movement and realized I had been ignoring him. He looked angry. So I took more care with the second movement, concentrating on my work, then I lead them into the third movement into that state of pure joy. He seemed to be smiling too, his baton dancing with me. We sang together in that fairyland, my bow singing across the strings, a blur of movement, my feet stepping along with the music, unable not to dance.

We finished with a final hop and a flourish. I stood there savoring it until I realized we had an audience. The applause hit me. It was a shock. I took a step back, standing there dumbfounded. People were standing. The orchestra was standing. Camille was motioning at me with a frowning smile.

"Bow," I saw him mouth.

I blinked, then bowed, smiled and bowed again. Then I was laughing and bowing to the orchestra and then to Camille. I mouthed a "thank you," to him. But he shook his head no and tapped. We were going to do Bach. This was my encore.

It was acapella. Just me alone in that empty space. It's a thoughtful winter drift, like leaves falling, turning and swaying back and forth as they leave the trees. Something to idle away time. And I drifted, ambling across the landscape, remembering each hill and valley, thinking of the Canaries and Red. The heaving sea in the misty blue twilight and the cold windswept days, the water flying like handfuls of silver coins with each dip of her bow. Sometimes I have to play two and even three parts simultaneously, weaving around and around myself, one movement after another. Each one is individual and yet they're all linked into a common whole. It's the cleverness of its construction that allows me to do this and it's why I like it. Only Bach could achieve this. A lonely gentle journey that finally, at the last note, tips into a deathly quiet. I stood their staring into the inky blackness, unsure, until a wave of sound rose up that knocked me back. I stepped back bowing, and bowed some more, marveling that I was still alive.

Then someone brought me flowers, roses without thorns, which was strange.

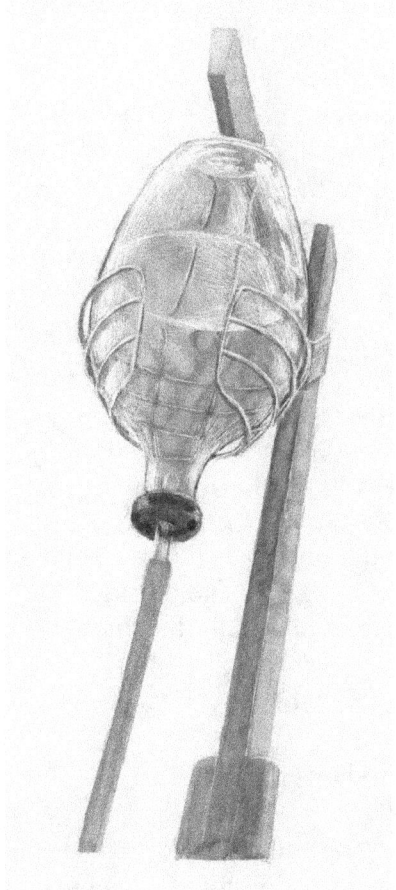

Chapter 25 – The Store

The curtain came down and Camille tapped his stand to get everyone's attention.

"Gentlemen," and then with a tip of his head towards me, "and lady. I will see you all at one, here, tomorrow."

There was a general groan.

"We have adjustments that must be attended to. And someone," he squinted at me, "needs to learn to watch the conductor," which got a general laugh.

But I didn't care. I was still in shock that I was alive. I had done it!

267

My family ran out to meet me as I walked offstage. Ma met me with a hug that knocked me back.

"I'm alive Ma," I managed to say.

I passed the flowers to Sarah just before we were swamped by musicians. They all wanted to shake my hand and pat me on the back. Even our lead violinist.

"You made it," someone said.

All I could respond was, "I can't believe I'm alive."

Then I had to break away. I was so tired. It hit me suddenly, but I had to keep going. I still had the party to attend.

"I need some coffee," I said, as we were walking.

"We should go home," Aleta said.

"No, the store."

"That store," she moaned.

"Tonight is important."

"We should count ourselves lucky and go home," she replied

Lucien came trotting up. The corridor was full of people. All the stage support were finished for the night. He picked me up in his arms.

"You're alive," he said.

"I am," I smiled.

"They appear to have retreated."

"I need coffee."

"That we have," he smiled back. "I made sure of it."

"Tell her not to go to the store," Aleta said.

He frowned. "The store," he said flatly.

"I'm going. It's important."

"Cali, we should call it a night," Pa added.

"It won't take long," I said. "I just have to show up."

We stopped at the door that led to the public side. The colors all looked so bright. Lucien asked one of the guards to fetch me coffee.

"We need to exit," he said.

"Why not the Napoleon exit again," I suggested. I frowned at my left hand and my arm. They were beginning to cramp. I shook it out. It was from the tension.

"Why not?" he asked. "I have cars waiting at all three. We need only to choose one. But when we leave the backstage, we need to go."

But we didn't because we were waiting for my coffee.

"We should go home," Aleta said again.

"We will," I replied.

The coffee came. It came quickly. It had to have been just upstairs. Some of it had sloshed into the saucer.

"Oh thank you," I said to the gendarme with a smile. He blushed. It was so good. Thick and black, although somewhat tepid. I drank it over the saucer to protect my dress. It helped.

When I had finished I told everyone that we should go. Of course everyone had different ideas as to where, but I insisted on the store.

We exited through the Napoleon exit, the car waiting just as Lucien had said. It was crowded, but we piled in. The night air was cool, but not cold. The city hummed around us. It was humid too, which didn't bode well for the coming day. And that's the last I remember.

The bullet was .303 inch round – clearly British. They wanted to leave no doubt.

It entered my middle back as I stood on the corner, in front of cameras. Thankfully, it missing my spine, instead shattering a rib, passing between my liver and lung. I lost a little of each in addition to the rib. Exiting, it hit the poor woman standing in front of me in the leg.

I was unconscious for six days, finally waking in the evening. The pain had been pulling me towards consciousness for what felt like some time, half waking then thankfully letting me sink. It hurt so much to breathe.

I moaned. Everything hurt, even the light. That's what tipped them off. They didn't want me to sink back into sleep. Someone was lifting my head, which I didn't like, trying to get me to drink, which was hard because my mouth didn't want to work.

"Come on," the woman said. "Just a bit."

I whined, but tried. My mouth was so dry.

"She's awake." It was Lucien.

The water brought pain. It hurt to swallow and hurting made me breath which made everything hurt. Then, of course, I choked, which was the worst. I tried to move, but found I was strapped down.

"Doctor," the woman said.

"Half a grain," a man said. He sounded familiar. "She needs to be calm."

The pain receded.

"Breath. Slowly," he said. "We won't tolerate popped sutures."

Sutures, oh God. I would have a scar to match Lucien's.

My eyes were dry. It was hard to see. One shape was Lucien. I tried to smile.

"There we go," the man said. It was Dr. Péan!

"Drink," the woman said. And I tried with some success.

"We're lucky," Émile said. "We've avoided infection. At least so far."

"Her waking. This is good?" Lucien asked.

"Yes. We can hydrate her naturally now. And food. She needs to eat."

The damn nurse was trying to pour more water in my mouth, but all I could do to make her stop was to let it drain out.

"No," I bubbled.

"What was that?" she said.

I tried to roll my eyes.

Lucien grinned. "I think she needs a break from the water," he said.

"Broth," Émile said. "Could you get some nurse?"

"Lucien," I said.

He moved closer, looking down at me. He seemed pleased.

"I'm an idiot."

"The store?" Lucien asked.

I blinked.

"If they missed you there, they would have come back and tried the theater later."

"Bad?" I said.

"For a bullet wound? No. But there are no nice ones."

And that was it for me. I think I fell asleep because they were lifting my head again. The nurse had a bowl of warm broth and a big rubber squeeze bulb thing for me to suck on. My arms were loose, the hanging bottle had been above me was gone.

Time went by, someone always there. They gave me pills but no more shots. I was always in agony so I wasn't good conversation and as such didn't learn about what happened for some time.

Lucien wanted me to get out on the florist side, but I insisted on the corner. I had to make my entrance. The moment I got out and stood up, they shot me – in the back. It's like they couldn't face me. It came from a window across the square. They left their rifle behind and simply got up and walked away.

Paul was unsure whether my blood staining the pavement in front of the store was a benefit or a problem. He finally had the stain ground off, which I think was best.

I had nothing to do with, nor did any of my friends have anything to do with the burning of the British Embassy. I have no quarrels with the English, just with their empire. And not even with that. Just with the pig-headed bureaucrats who run it! And the Institution, of course.

I will always be grateful to the girls, and boys, who held vigil outside the hospital. When I heard about them I wanted to go out or have them come in, but Émile wouldn't let me have any visitors but family for a long time. He was worried about infection. I'm so sorry.

Two weeks after the operation they removed the stitches. I was eating solid food by then and gaining strength. Even sitting up in bed. I had books, some of them good, but no newspapers. I didn't know about the persecution British expats endured. If I had, I would have told them to stop. It didn't help when the hospital announced that I was a virgin. Someone had checked I guess. Catholics are crazy about young virgin female martyrs and my poor France went insane.

My reviews from opening night were unanimous and glowing, but then getting shot may have had some influence on them.

Émile booted me out of the hospital after three weeks. I could barely walk, but he said hospitals are dangerous places to linger in. Too many sick people about, so we left.

Dressing was a slow, painful, process even with Lucien's and Sarah's help. What did people do when they went through this every day, without the help of a maid? It made me think about my clothing. Lifting my arms was torture, staying upright hard. Old people like the Duchess Baudouin had to be having a hard time. I had to talk to Paul about this. Clothing for the infirm.

We decided to announce our engagement then, as we left the hospital, in front of the cameras, royal family be damned. I didn't want to be photographed in a wheelchair doing it so I tried to walk out, but almost fainted. Paul made me a new dress for the occasion, by the way, and I have to say the pictures of me fainting looked good. They brought the chair for me while Lucien propped me up. We did it. It was official.

Then I was in the back of a car, in grievous pain, wishing I could take more pills, every cobblestone agony, Ma sobbing away in the seat across from me. Her daughter was getting married.

"Maybe we should take her back," Aleta said.

"I'm okay," I replied, wincing.

"You don't look okay," Aleta said.

"I'm tired of the hospital."

"That's a good sign," Lucien said. He was in a good mood.

I was leaning against him, my head on his shoulder, practically in tears with the pain.

"We should slow down," Pa said.

"No," I replied. "I want to get this over with. I just want to get home."

The neighborhood turned out when the car drove up, but it took all I had to make it in the front door and upstairs. That was it for me. They woke me for dinner and the bathroom, then I was gone again.

I woke in the dark and saw Max sitting in the chair next to the bed.

"Sorry to intrude at this awful hour, but they wouldn't let me see you."

"Max, I'll tell them."

"It doesn't matter. I have a zeppelin to catch in the morning.

"You always have a zeppelin to catch," I said.

"Yes, I'm afraid so. I'm glad you're recovering."

"I don't feel like it," I moaned.

"These sort of wounds take time."

"Max, this is dangerous. There are people here with guns. You could be shot. You should have waited until I was well."

"I thought it might cheer you up to know that the assassination team that shot you are all dead."

"You killed them?"

"No," he chuckled. "It was your Deuxième Bureau. Occasionally they're good for something. I think the British will leave you alone now."

"Why is that?"

"You're too expensive to chase."

That made me smile. They did too, that is until they started it all over again at Clémentine's wedding. But for a time we lived in peace.

"I saw your performance by the way," he said.

"You should have asked for tickets."

"I only arrived that afternoon. It was serendipitous."

"How did you get in?"

"I know you like your gendarmes, and they mean well, but you shouldn't depend on them."

I smiled again. I do love them dearly and they are *mostly* useless, at least in games like this.

"And I suggest you not play in that theater again. It's impossible to secure."

We talked a little more, and then he went back out the window, politely shutting and locking it before climbing down.

Camille never came to visit. I never found out what it was he was looking for or if he found it, but I suspect he did because of his silence. They had someone else lined up for the rest of my nights, some friend of Camille's which seemed to placate the audience, so I suppose he was good.

Which brings us to our last few loose ends. We received permission to build the ossuary in November. It was my new popularity that got the city council to pass the measure so quickly. Of course, it required the creation of a managing committee of which I was a member and would involve endless meetings and arguments. We had to solicit donations and submit our budgets for review to the city as well. Oh, the stupid parties I had to go to, then the benefit concert! There were the contracts and bids for the work which we had to be review, and more permits and inspections. Then they wanted to decorate it, starting it all over again!

Naturally, there was the definition of eligibility which required working girls to register and then be licensed, thus creating a de facto union for a profession that technically shouldn't exist. Another committee and Jean-Paul's feathers had to be smoothed. He became a legitimate brothel owner.

At least the girls got regular medical care from the government, the new hospital is right round the corner. Oh! That's a story in itself and another committee to deal with. And the church couldn't be left out. It just had to be consecrated ground which added another layer of bureaucracy and their foolish opinions. Priests can be so pig-headed! All the complications that came from that. They hid a piece of bone from some saint in there! I will never see the end of it.

I went back to school.

Aleta and I both had our weddings.

And for a little while we might have lived happily ever after – except. Except that Red was still in the hands of pirates!

A Bad Crossing

Cali`s Songs

Antonio Lucio Vivaldi - *Concerto for Flute and Violin in G minor*

The Flowers of Edinburgh

The Penny Wedding

Edvard Grieg - *Violin Sonata No. 1*

Claude Debussy - *Au Clair de la Lune*

Wolfgang Amadeus Mozart.- *Duet for flute and violin*

Joseph Bodin de Boismortier -. *Sonata I in G for flute and violin*

Jakob Ludwig Felix Mendelssohn - *Violin Concerto E Minor OP.64* – I suggest the Hillary Hahn version

Johann Sebastian Bach - *Sonata for Solo Violin No. 1* – I suggest the Fischer version, although he wrings all the sweetness out of it, unlike Pearlman who turns it into a syrupy parlor piece. Cali however plays it more like Grumiaux.

A Note about Exchange Rates

Calista more often than not has no clue as to the value of the currency she has in her purse. An excellent bargainer, she takes her queue from the person she's buying from. But you and I don't have to operate that way. Figuring out the value of money so far back through, is difficult. There were so many governments in so many different countries, sometimes differing by district. It's no small task and I have to admit that many of my sources are dubious at best. Although some may contend with this estimate, based on the price of gold I think this is about right:

7 Third Republic francs = 1 1890 U.S.dollar
4 German Imperial gold marks = 1 1890 U.S. dollar
1 1890 U.S. dollar = 30 2016 U.S. dollars

So if Calista has 2000 French francs in her purse, that's (2000 / 7) × 30 or $8,571. A lot for a seventeen year old to carry about. For a time, she was carrying over fourteen thousand or close to sixty thousand dollars, enough to buy four or five city houses in the U.S. Her fifty centime first water bath cost them together 28¢, the benefit of living in a poor part of town and being a member of the neighborhood.

But you have to balance these values with the prevailing wages of the time and the cost of living. $2000 a year salary was fabulous for the times, the salary for a full lady's maid of the highest order. Sarah's $3000 put her in a class altogether above even a head butler. But then she was Lucien's spy as well and was expected to intervene if Cali got in trouble. These are huge salaries when you consider that the average factory worker earned $15 to $20 a week and was expected to support a family!

So calculating exchange rates based on gold isn't exactly fair. 250,000 Fr in her bank is a substantial $1,041,667. More than almost any human being of the time could expect to earn in a lifetime, but still not quite truly mansion level upper class rich. Not yet, but give her time.

Turn the page for a preview
of M. Bondurant's next
Calista Antoine adventure . . .

The Sea Witch

Available Spring 2019 from
Bongo Books

Chapter 1 – Italy

Did you really think that I wouldn't tell you about my wedding? It was glorious! But because we are not Catholic we held it at *l'Oratoire* just outside of the Louvre. It's a shell of a church given to the Protestants by Napoleon. It's a bit small and there wasn't room for everyone, but it was the best we could find in Paris. Oh! The trouble I've had with the church! But really, I should start at the beginning and that would be Clémentine's wedding, in Italy. That was the event that put me squarely back in the sights of the British.

1895 was a year for marriages. In addition to mine and Clémentine's, we had Aleta's, Leopold's, and . . . Jean-Paul's!

Jean-Paul you ask? You can't be more surprised than he was. We didn't "officially" attend that one. No one did. Not officially. Jean-Paul was head of the Paris Camorra, a branch of an international crime syndicate headed by the Sicilian Mafia. He was also my stage manager. But I'm digressing again. I will tell you about all of it. I was telling you about Clémentine and Italy. One thing at a time.

We were *pas reconnu*, ostracized by Lucien's family, which is why we were living in Paris. They disapproved of me, mostly because my entanglements with the British. I see your confusion and this deserves explanation, so get ready. It's complicated, but I will try to make it all clear as quickly as I can.

Lucien, my fiancé, the Duke of Tervuren, holds several estates and a city in Flanders, Belgium. He's the unrecognized half-brother of Leopold the Third, son and heir to Leopold the Second, the current monarch of Belgium. Leopold II was a puppet of the British. Yes, that's a cruel thing to say, but I'm trying to be both frank and brief. It's important because Leopold III, my Leopold from the Congo, is not. Not since the loss of the Congo.

The British held a monopoly on trade with the Congo which they used to indirectly control the colony and their interests in it. They purposely strangled the colony's supplies to keep Belgian control weak. But they kept it too weak. The colony was unable to defend itself when the Germans invaded. The Congo was Leopold III's fief, his private playground. Its loss left him bitter and inclined to deal with the Germans to get it back. I was there, in the Congo when it all came apart. I still have nightmares.

Do not think the king a fool for siding with the British. They are dangerous. His son was playing with fire. But he wasn't king. Not yet. Just an heir.

I should explain my relationship with the British as well. Few get it right.

The loss of the Congo was a huge blow to the Empire. As you know it's now German West Africa and extends all the way to the Atlantic, cutting Africa in two. It put an end to the British dream of a Cairo to Cape Town railroad. Their investments ended at the German border. Great fortunes belonging to very powerful men were lost. They needed a scapegoat, first for an explanation to the Queen and then for the press. That's how I became *The Rabbit*. They claimed I was a seductress spy for the Germans, laying the way for the invasion.

It would have worked too, if I'd just cooperated by dying. They have tried time and again to kill me and each time I survived, my fame grew until I became too famous to kill without international repercussions. And so the British Empire and I reached a truce. We had peace, at least as long as I hid in the slums of Paris.

Lucien and Clémentine, his half sister, have always been close and royal family be damned if she was going to exclude us from her wedding, hence their choice of neutral ground in Italy. Her fiancé was Prince Napoleon Victor Bonaparte, leader of the royalist faction in France and heir to Napoleon himself. He wanted to overthrow the French Republic, by military force if necessary. Another reason to pick neutral ground.

Dark and intense, I found Napoleon lacking in humor and difficult conversation in any subject lacking in politics. My poor Clémentine. Despite our inability to communicate meaningfully, he seemed to have no problem with my proximity. I think he thought I might have political pull in France. Perhaps I did. I learned a great deal about the world I was about to enter through marriage listening to him, gathering players names, relationships, and agendas. Knowledge that would serve me well later on.

But even in Italy we were ostracized. Leopold the king would not have us sleeping in the castle where the wedding was to take place, under the same roof. We stayed in a villa close by belonging to Maria, Napoleon's sister. My room was huge! They even gave Sarah, my maid, her own room. Italian sunshine is amazing. It was early summer, just ahead of the heat, the sunlight spilling in across the sofas and tables where we were taking tea. Maria was trying to teach me to knit, but her efforts were wasted despite my being able to tie about twenty different knots with rope.

"Did you get the note about the fitting this afternoon," Maria said, looking up from her needles.

"Yes," I sighed, as much at my inability to keep proper tension as the dresses. The dresses were awful. I wished not for the last time that I had brought Paul, my dress maker.

"Oh come now," she smirked. "It's not that bad."

Maria was in her forties, but still very beautiful. I was, at that time, on the cusp of my twentieth birthday. I could see her husband, Amadeo, and Lucien outside on the balcony. Amadeo liked cigars, a smell he carried about the house with him.

I gave her a weak smile. The dresses had big puffy sleeves, a constricting neck, and worst of all – corsets.

"I would have gladly supplied them," I replied. I own a clothing factory and design house.

"Yes," she sighed back. "But your Paris fashion is a little too aggressive for Italy."

I sighed again. There was a lot of that, sighing, but it was true. They were practically living in the dark ages out in the streets.

"And outside of the wedding you can dress as you choose," she continued. "You can give all the girls in town horrid ideas."

We both smiled at that. She was in agreement with me on the subject of corsets. She was one of my customers. And there was a ball that night as well. One of the many parties before the wedding. There would be dancing and photographers! I put down my needles to take a sip of tea. The cup was beautiful. Gold gilt and pink roses.

"I don't mind wandering the town, but do I have to ride?" Lucien wanted me to learn.

She gave me a smile of sympathy and then glanced down. "You've lost your needle."

3

It had slipped out of its loops and fallen on the floor. "Oh!" I said, as I bent down to get it, catching the yarn on the brocade on my sleeve, pulling far too many of my misshapen loops loose. That dress had crazy big sleeves. It wasn't one of Paul's, but a gift from Queen Wilhelmina of Netherlands, age 13. Apparently she was a fan of mine. I had a whole cohort of fans that followed me around Paris. I enjoy their company, but it's a constant worry that they will get hurt. I mean it was a very nice dress. I liked the look, but it wasn't practical.

"Your horses try to knock me off." They do! They walk under things. Low things.

"You have to come to terms with them. Did you try bribing them?"

"Lucien says I have to learn to expect their respect first."

"It's been so long since I had to learn," she said thoughtfully. "Perhaps you need more ground time with them."

"And get kicked?"

That got a laugh from her. "I'll talk to Lucien."

Since I'd already dropped my needle I took another sip of tea before picking the needle up and threading it back in.

"It's not just the horses," I said.

It was her turn to sigh.

"I feel boxed in," I continued. "My days are planned."

"You're bored."

"Perhaps." Actually I was. It wasn't just the terrible Italian Renaissance art on her walls, blessed Virgin Mary's, pink cherubs, and baby Jesus's everywhere. My life, outside of school, had always been just a bit dangerous and eventful. My family's ship, *Red Jacket*, had taken us to fun faraway places filled with interesting people, some of them even friendly. Here though, I knew exactly when luncheon would be served and with whom. Even what I would wear was picked for me.

"Perhaps some day trips," Maria suggested.

"I've shopped everything and everywhere there is to shop. Does the castle have a dungeon?" I asked.

"No," she replied flatly

It's not a real castle. Rather it's always been a residence and social center. I didn't know it then, but they were all conspiring to keep me out of trouble. I was entirely doomed.

"Try to relax," she suggested.

Relax was the one thing I couldn't do. I couldn't sit still. I had become so used to crisis that I didn't know what to do with myself when it was gone. I desperately missed Aleta.

We were having our bridesmaid's lunch out under a tent roof in the garden of someone's villa. I knew none of them except Marguerite. All they talked about was marriage. It wasn't hard to talk with Marguerite, but the others were difficult. Aleta was marrying into her family. They would be distant cousins and I would have loved to know more about them, but she wouldn't discuss her family politics in front of others. Especially gossips like those.

"Auggie would make a terrible husband," said Princess Henriette, also known as *Henní*.

"He's rich," said Princess Joséphine, her twin sister, also known as *Finní*.

"He's losing his hair and uses so much wax in in mustache that I could use it to bend spoons," Henní replied, getting a general laugh.

"How about *Maxi*?" asked a different Princess Joséphine, also known as *Fins*. "From your letters, I thought your father likes him."

"Emmanuel? He's a cold fish."

"I'd call him calculating," Marguerite suggested.

"Maggi . . ," Henní started

"I told you not to call me that," Marguerite snapped. Marguerite is only a Marquess and born a commoner like me, albeit a very rich one.

"Calculating might be a good thing," I added.

Henní glanced at me then away, brushing me off. I was clearly only a step above servant.

"Who will keep me warm while he's calculating?" she replied with a smile, and the royals laughed.

"You might try inspiring him to do both," I said under my breath.

"Cali," Marguerite said, giving me a hard look. "I need you to look at something."

We had been through this before. I had stepped over the line.

"I forgot to tell you. There's a problem with your dress," she said as we got up.

I deserved the lecture I was about to get. The princesses began to chatter amongst themselves as we walked away. I was clearly the subject.

As we walked towards the house, she asked tiredly, "What's wrong?"

"I'm bored out of my mind."

"So you look for relief by picking fights with three possible ruling monarchs? You're smarter than that!"

"Maybe," I muttered. Then it burst out. "I'm horrible with horses. I can't knit or do needlepoint. They won't play cards. The shopping is horrible. There isn't even a cathedral and the castle is off limits, not that it matters because it doesn't have a dungeon."

"They don't need it," she shrugged. "They use the catacombs."

I lit up. "Catacombs?"

"No! I shouldn't have said that."

"You've got to go with me!" I was grinning.

"No."

"Sara won't go and it'd be dangerous to go alone. I wish Aleta was here."

"No!" she snapped. We were getting close to the house. "There could be anybody or anything in them."

"There were smugglers in the ones under my house," I said, half to myself. "Don't tell me you're happy sitting here?"

"I'm not. I'm just as bored as you are. Were there really smugglers?"

"We were captured," I replied with glee. "They threatened to kill us!"

"No!" she said, with finality.

"It will be scary," I cooed.

"No."

"You can't let me go alone. What if I fell? Who would go for help?"

"It would be your own fault. Besides, you don't know a way in."

"Do you?" I asked, drooling with anticipation.

"Of course not. Why would I know such things?"

"Because you're bored."

Marguerite has far more discipline and control than I do and she used it. I couldn't get her to budge. But the cat was out of the bag.

And so.

We were shopping in the market square.

We had ridden down. Actually, I had been led. The groom was holding our horses back at the edge of the square. My poor Lucien had business to attend to. They were sending him on errands again despite his banishment. I was ambling about, thinking of buying a melon to split with the children. They followed me around whenever I went out. They called me *La Coniglia*, The Rabbitess.

It was then that I saw a familiar face. He was walking across the square opposite me, deep in thought. It was a mistake. He should have avoided the open space. It was the man who had hired *Fitz le Couteau* to kill me, a member of The Institution, the British secret service. They are terribly dangerous people. This had to be bad.

I stood up from the melons and followed without a word. It took a few minutes for Maria to notice I'd gone, but I'm afraid it's hard to move quietly with a train of kids in tow. She saw me before I made it out of the square.

"Calista!" Maria called.

I turned and put my finger to me lips and shook my head "no", then focused again on my quarry, trying to shoo the kids back. He had turned down a side street.

"Roberto!" Maria called to our groom, then set off after me.

When I reached the corner and peeked around, kids peeking around with me, holding on to my skirts, he was gone. I took off down the street. He had to be in a doorway.

There was a short side alley that ended in crude wood door. I started down it, but the children tried to hold me back. "*No Signorina!*" I could see movement behind the door, between the boards. He was there.

"Come out!" I called, in English.

"What's going on?" It was Maria, behind me.

"Come out!" I called again, but he was gone.

"Calista?"

"Trouble," I said. "There's trouble. I have to talk to Lucien. I need the police." Then I looked at her squarely. "Tell me the truth. What's behind there?"

She thought for a second, frowning, then said, "The catacombs."

The Italian police turned out to be as useless as my gendarmes, bless them. They filled out a form. They didn't even know what The Institution was! Few did at that time. I'm sure I'm doubly marked for death for telling all of you about them. But, like the door to the catacombs, that cat is out of the bag too.

Lucien was waiting for me back at the villa. Apparently someone had sent for him. I hadn't seen him in days, but our reunion had to be subdued. He wasn't alone. There were two other men, one I recognized as Captain Hilaire in plain clothes. I knew him from the Congo.

"You've been here five days and you've already uncovered the plot," Hillaire said with a smile as I entered.

I flashed him a smile back. We were sitting in a side parlor back at the villa, me still in the clothes I wore at the police station. Lucien had ordered coffee. We waited until the servant left with his tray.

"His name is Emil Kamen. He's Bulgarian," Lucien said, continuing the conversation.

"He's not Institution?" I asked.

"Oh, he's Institution. They hire foreign agents for certain jobs for the sake of deniability. We knew he was here, somewhere."

"So we're going down to get him?" I asked, eyebrows up.

Lucien smiled. "No. We've looked into it. The catacombs here aren't the clean well-ordered ones you're familiar with from home. There are crawlways, rock falls, and badly shored soft dirt. Worse, Emil is very good at covering his tracks.

"No place for a woman. The bodies," said the unintroduced man. He was Louis Maes, head of the *Sûreté de l'État*, the Belgian State Security Service. I would get to know him later as an ineffectual bureaucrat. It was no secret why the Institution laughed at our security.

"Yes, disease," Lucien continued.

I perked up and exclaimed, "Bodies?"

Lucien gave Louis a quick scowl, then continued. "The city has, from time to time, used the tunnels for burial. Most of them are mummified, but who knows what they died of. Perhaps the Black Death? Finding Kamen in the maze will be very dangerous," which translates as *no Cali.* "Which is why we're concentrating on protecting his highness," he continued.

"They're probably after his son."

I saw his brow twitch. I do know him. "Yes," he admitted.

"I'd use gelignite." I had been reading.

Hilaire snorted. He knows me.

"Under his apartments," Lucien replied, nonplussed. "We've already blocked the tunnels underneath." Which meant they had already been in them for some time.

"She's worse than the queen," Louis mumbled. Not a pretty sound.

"Failing that," I continued, ignoring him. "I'd try at the train station or the tracks when he leaves. Either the train itself or a sniper."

"All covered," Lucien replied.

"Kamen uses local help," I suggested.

"And they will know the land better," Lucien continued. "Which is why we're minimizing our points of risk."

It hit me. "You're not using the train."

Louis' coffee cup hit his saucer loudly. "Damn!"

Hilaire chuckled.

"Cali," Lucien smiled. He has a little one that he saves just for me when he means to be upset, but is actually pleased. "This is a secret. We're airlifting him out by blimp from the garden."

"Don't tell her," Louis exclaimed. "She'll gossip it all over town!"

Lucien gathered his patience and said, "If I don't, she'll be all over town trying to figure it out. She'll draw attention."

"She won't tell," Hillaire added, with a smile. I've always liked Hillaire.

All of which meant there was nothing for your poor Cali to do. It was back to my knitting and horse lessons.

Chapter 2 – A Broken Truce

My poor Lucien was gone after that, off working. He sent me a note. There were new complications and that I was to stay in the open with people. It meant that there was danger. I found out why the next night, at the reception for Franz Joseph of Austria. It was in a tasteless too noisy hall.

She was there. The British had added a new piece to the board. We met in the middle of the reception room early in the evening, before the emperor made his entrance. She had a glass of champagne that she was only pretending to drink.

"Calista," she said, far too amiably for someone who has come close to killing me. Her voice was as perfect as her hair and dress.

"Emilia," I replied with a forced smile.

Emilia Stroud worked, probably still works for the Institution. She is a schooled agent, one of five or six in the field. Their best. Even though she's only a year or so older than me, she could easily break me like a twig.

"Is Max here?" I asked.

She laughed, "No."

That was too bad because Max, her German counterpart, was the only person on Earth who could keep her in check.

Then she ran her eyes down my dress. "You're looking interesting, as always."

I was looking better than interesting. I love Paul's work. I was all shoulder and neck with short sleeves that draped down loose from my dress straps. My short blue train was covered in embroidered silver stars and peacock feathers. On top of all of that, I was probably the most comfortable person in that room.

"I've ordered some dresses from your shop," Emilia continued. "Your Paul has intriguing ideas."

That took me by surprise. I couldn't help it. That genuinely pleased me. "Thank you."

"How is your shop doing?" She asked.

"We're having problems with production. We keep having to

expand."

"Then business is good."

"Yes, but not profitable. Is Emil going to be here?"

"Emil?" She snorted. "The idea." She waved it away. I guess she considered him the help.

"Good," I replied, grateful for any relief. Both of them would have been too much. Really, I would have bolted.

"Yes." She pretended to sip. "He's quite angry with you."

"Really?" I was surprised he even remembered me.

"First in Paris, then here. He seems to think you've damaged his manhood."

I laughed. She had surprised me again. After a thoughtful look, she laughed too and then continued. "But really." She gave me a look. "You should be careful. These southern types take things like that that seriously."

"You should too," I said, chiding. "A vendetta. He'll end up making a mistake."

"Yes," she said. I think I caught a ghost of a frown. It had been my turn to set her back. "That's true. He might." I noticed then that she absentmindedly took a real sip from her glass.

I took to exploring the house. This was difficult because someone was always keeping an eye on me. But that made the effort of exploring all that much better! They couldn't follow me everywhere. It was a matter of looking for empty rooms. That was how I found out about the secret doors the servants use. I was sitting in a room with book shelves, reading, hunched down on a sofa to avoid detection, when a bookshelf opened!

"Oh!" said a maid, in thick Italian accented French. "Miss, I didn't see you."

She bowed out with apologies. After she left, I examined the shelf. The books were false. In the middle was a peephole. The servants watched us! I was shocked. She couldn't see me because the back of the sofa faced the peephole. Searching, I found the latch. It was simple, naturally at waist height. I suppose they had to be able to use it while carrying things.

Inside I found a worn wood stairway that went up and down. I could hear her below going down the steps. I followed figuring that I would hear her say something if she passed anyone going up. Down and around she went, to a plain door that from the sound behind it led to the kitchens. The stairs kept going down, so I went on. Down to another plain door. It was dark. It opened on pitch blackness. The basement! This had to be explored, but I needed light. I would buy candles at the market.

The next day I bought three short thick hard wax candles and phosphorus matches, the merchant bobbing his head to me as I paid. I could never get them to stop doing that. These were the expensive kind and I suppose he didn't sell many. I had my largest purse just to hide them. All I could think was how much fun this was going to be, but as you will see, back then I was not in my right mind. I felt them in my purse all the way back, bouncing along on horseback.

That night I crept out of my room. I couldn't find any secret doors in my room by the way. Judging by its size compared to the adjoining rooms, I doubted that there were any, which was reassuring. I had to go back downstairs to find one, down to the room where I found my first. It was the only one I was sure went down into the basement.

No one confronted me, despite the dark creaking floors and stairs. The stairway was pitch black as I felt my way down, the kitchen quiet. Cursing the creaking door I entered and struck my match, the light feeble against the darkness. The candle was no better. I set its base on a crate by the door in case I had to find my way back in a hurry, and lit a second to carry. There were sconces and I debated lighting them, but then that would be cheating wouldn't it?

It was filled with crates and chests. The floor was swept so it wasn't abandoned. There were wine racks by another door in the back. Nothing more – except of course the trap door! Its rusty hinges were clearly unused. My smile broadened. It had to lead to the catacombs.

The latch was stuck. I had to sit and bang it with my heel. Then the door gave back reluctantly. Beneath was an old ladder leading into blackness. Carefully adding weight to the ladder, I climbed down and down to hard dirt. I knew that dusty smell, the air dead still. I would have to find one of the walls. So I wandered forward downhill, checking that I was leaving footprints I could follow back in the dirt, the trapdoor a dim square in the ceiling.

Down I went, meeting the walls to face a low passage, a few steps then up to an irregular room with just a tiny crawlway as an exit. I thought I could fit, but I couldn't explain the dirt on my clothing, so it was back to the main room to explore the walls. I found two other passages, but by then it was late and I figured this could go on for hours. And I had dress rehearsal in the morning, then the hen party which would go who knows how long.

It was late the next night before I made it back. I very rudely bowed out early. She just kept opening presents. It went on and on! That was when all the excitement happened, of course when I wasn't at my best. But I was determined to go down again.

The house was as quiet as before and the ladder just as rickety. This time I left a candle by the trap door to better find it, its square plainly visible in the black above along with the outline of a figure, looking down at me through the trapdoor.

"Miss?"

I just about jumped out of my night dress! It was Sarah, my French maid and a spy for Lucien. "Sarah?" I asked.

"Your pardon, Miss, but where are you going?"

"Out. I couldn't sleep," I replied defensively. Don't roll your eyes! It was the only thing I could think to say. I could see her face in the candle light. She looked panicked.

"I'm just going to explore for a bit," I added.

"Please don't go. Remember what happened the last time."

"I'm only going to look around a little bit, carefully. I'll be fine."

That set her to fretting, which is never a pretty sight, and set her into a stream of "please be careful"s and "oh your dress"s, and me replying over and over with "go back to bed." But to be honest, it felt better to have someone there. I really missed Aleta.

I took the first untried passage. It didn't go far before it met a room. I think it had once been a sewer, but now had both ends bricked up, perhaps for the support of buildings above. The passage continued on the other side with a crawlway off to the left. I followed the corridor for as long as I had no confusing intersections or dirty crawls, stopping every now and then to listen. I wasn't sure but I think it was heading into town. Oh what I wouldn't have given for a compass then.

I finally gave up on that one and went back to the next and called out to Sarah that I was trying the next without waiting for an answer. This one at least started towards the castle. It went up, down, and around until I had no idea where I was, stopping finally to listen. Listening until I actually heard something! There were voices, but it was coming from a crawlway down on the floor. I would definitely be dirtier than I could mend with a quick brush.

But they were voices! I mean I couldn't tell who they were or what they were saying. They could be palace guards, Lucien, smugglers, or even the enemy! Night dress be damned.

The crawlway had once been a culvert, the iron gratings long rusted away, its stonework tending to leak dust down on my hair in little streams as I pushed through. It ended in a drop, which presented a dilemma. I had no idea how far down it went or if there would be getting back up. Patience was required.

I tried to hold the candle to the side, away from my eyes. Peering in, I could see walls and shapes. Dropping stones seemed to indicate that the floor wasn't far, I was coming out near the ceiling. It was a storeroom. I was under the castle. I could climb down the shelves, but I couldn't do it head first. So I had to slide back to the entrance and go in feet first.

The sacks were soft and the shelves rickety. I was practically out when they finally broke under my weight and I fell. It all came down on me. It hurt, but I managed to stay quiet. I mean it hadn't been a huge surprise. But I was sitting there in the dark.

I needed my candle back, so I pulled out my spare and matches. I struck the match and that's when I screamed. They weren't sacks! It wasn't a storeroom. It was a burial chamber. I was buried under bones and wrappings. Flesh encrusted skulls leered at me from the floor.

I scrambled back, my match going out, only to hit another shelf that collapsed to the floor around me. I kept going back, the room no longer dark. Apparently my candle had set something alight.

Rough hands grabbed me by the arms from behind and dragged me back.

So did this sound sane to you? It doesn't to me now, as I tell it. That was a start of a dark patch in my life. When I started the talking cure. It took years to beat back the nightmares. But that's not why I'm stopping here. I'm stopping because I want to make sure you understand that my life was not the one you see in books. Foolish doesn't begin to explain it. I want you to understand that adventure isn't fun and that danger and fame come at a price, one that you pay over and over again until you break down and pray that your children don't follow you. My adventures haunt me every time I close my eyes. Please don't follow me. At this point in my life I was clearly insane and beyond lucky to have lived through it.

They had pistols and lanterns, and they dragged me along until I could stand and then made me walk while I tried to brush off the worst. Two big Italians. I had no idea what they were saying, but their intentions were clear as they shoved me along. We didn't have to go far.

A few turns and we were in a roughly cut stone room with no discernable purpose except as a hideout for spies. The floor was flat and they had brought in a couple of tables, some cots and chairs. Their packs and one suitcase were stacked open on the floor. Emil was sitting in a chair at a table, polishing a very large rifle that was sitting half apart on the tabletop. His eyes lit up, then narrowed when he saw me.

"Carmichael," he leered.

"Emil," I replied, only to be knocked from behind to the floor. My vision spun.

Emil was chuckling. Then he said, "The little tart's decided to join the party for some fun," I suppose to me because he said it in French. Then he said to his friends, "*No. No. Niente di più. Lei è mia.*"

He stood up and walked over to me as I was trying to rise, grabbing my chin and pulling my face up towards his. "Little dog. Please me and I might let you live."

I lunged toward him and managed to connect with his nose, knocking him back. That's when the beating started. I remember very little of it. It was mostly Emil while the men held me.

He had ripped off most of my clothing and sent his men away, throwing me down on a cot, which collapsed under me. I stared up at him bleeding and then behind him confused. He stopped.

"What are you looking at?"

Behind him loomed a ghost, a man dressed as a priest. There were more in the corners, others in various dress, thin and ill defined.

"A ghost," I tried to say, with difficulty.

"Where?" He glanced back.

"Behind. A priest."

He started and looked back. His pants were down and his holster loose. He had let go of an arm, so I reached over, the gun strangely lit. The priest nodded as I pulled the gun loose and shot him in the stomach in one smooth motion. The wound was bloodless for a moment as most of it went out his back. He staggered back. He looked disappointed. I could understand that. It had been so easy.

The men came running in. I shot the first, the second skidding then scrambling back out. The wounded men's screams took too long to stop. I could only lay there, too weak to move, one eye swelling shut.

Time passed. More ghosts came, waiting with me. I think the priest was pleased, but none of them moved.

"Calista?" said a female voice. Some time had passed. It took a moment, but I recognized Stroud. "Put away the gun. The game is over." She was speaking from the corridor. "Help will be here soon, but we need to talk first." Her head darted out for a glance.

I looked down and realized that I had been holding it up, pointing at the corridor. I looked up at the priest and he nodded slowly.

My hand started to shake as I tried to lower it. Both it and my hand had grown very heavy.

The shakes spread along with the pain. I started to sob.

Emilia darted her head out and back again, then came out with her hands held up, walking steadily forward.

Stopping at Emil, she picked a clean spot and prodded him with the toe of her boot in clear distaste.

"You were right," she sighed. "He made a mistake."

Then she looked at me and frowned. "You're a mess. You'll never make the wedding."

She found a bucket of painfully cold water and a shirt from Emil's suitcase and began to clean me, all the while berating me.

"It's past time you quit," she said. She carried on about responsibility to the crown, my future sister was counting on me, a selfish indulgence, needed elsewhere." On and on she chided me as she cleaned. It was unreal.

I was dressed more or less in a pair of Emil's pants and shirt. I still had my halter on. Emil had left that. I swear, men love those. When a palace guard poked his head in, then called back down the corridor, "Here!"

"Remember what we talked about," Emilia said, straightening my hair. I couldn't remember anything but hurt!

Lucien came running in followed by more troops. I was sitting at one of the tables, the gun gone.

"Cali," he said, out of breath.

I yelped as he tried to lift me. He realized it was the wrong thing to do. "Where is he?" Lucien spat, holding his hands away from me.

"Dead," I tried to say.

He saw his body on the floor, pants down and scowled. Then he looked at me and asked, "Did he?" This was not one of our better moments. Of all the things to be concerned about.

"He tried."

Hillare snorted, then said, "Sir?" He was standing at the table with the rifle.

Lucien glanced at it, then looked harder, scowling again.

"An anti-aircraft rifle," he said. Then he looked up at Emilia. "You knew. How?"

She smiled as she said, with a wave of her hand, "Casual gossip."

Then he looked at me again. "We'll need a stretcher."

"I can walk," I said and tried to stand, but groaned and sat back down. "I'll walk when it's time." It was my gut. He had hit me hard.

Emilia said to me, "You need a stretcher." Then she sighed, "At least until we get up top."

A runner was sent. More people came asking stupid questions. I was taken up to the palace wrapped in a blanket and left in a bed.

The next I remember was the face of a strange man in a suit working at my clothing. I started back, too shocked to scream. Then I saw Lucien.

"You need to leave," the doctor said to him, as he tried to hold me down.

"It would be better if I stayed," Lucien replied. "She'll be calmer."

"It's unseemly," the doctor replied. We weren't married yet.

My eyes were darting between them. I was trying to stay calm. "Don't go," I said.

"He must," the doctor said. "We're in the palace." Too many witnesses, too much gossip and propriety. Lucien finally left with only a squeeze of my hand. I think he was afraid to kiss me with all the bruises.

The doctor examined me. My virginity was intact. Can you see me roll my eyes? They had to wrap my chest. Apparently I had rebroken some ribs. Ice packs were thrust at me that I had to hold on my face! And there I sat, time passing. Me in a half doze wondering where they had gotten the ice.

When Lucien came back, he held my hand, first with one and then both, holding it up to kiss it.

"This has to stop," he said. There were the start of tears in his eyes.

"I know. Emilia said so too."

He looked grim. "I hate owing her anything, but I suppose I should thank her."

"She could have killed me."

"Yes," he said bleakly. "Any of them could have."

"Is my nose broken?" I asked.

He smiled. There were tears. "No," he said.

"It sure feels like it. My whole face feels broken." My words sounded funny too.

"No. He used the flat of his hand." He voice caught.

"Well, he's dead."

"Yes."

Then I started to cry. It just bubbled up and came tumbling out. I held out my good arm and he held me while each sob shot pain through my side.

I missed the papers again. I'm never allowed to see them. Naturally they, as they always do, got the story completely wrong. The Rabbit had foiled an anarchist plot to murder the king. The British were never mentioned. The truth of it though, at least something closer to the truth, was spelled out plainly I'm told in the broadsheets. The British were not pleased.

He never visited me by the way, the king. Clementine did though. She brought me dinner.

"Lucien said this would happen," she said.

"I'm sorry."

"You and he both. You're like moths to a flame. At least though, he can temper it with common sense."

"Yes."

"Now I'm short a bridesmaid," she said with fake severity. "This will definitely be the last time I ever ask you to do this again."

That got a snort out of me, which hurt. I do love her.

"And it will be unbalanced. Can you kill one of Victor's?"

It was so cruel, but she kept trying to make me laugh. She got Fins' little sister to take my place. It was so good of her to visit on the eve of her wedding. She had to have been very busy. She even fed me.

Then who should visit but Emilia herself, the morning after the wedding. You have no idea how confusing and distressing this was. Why did she leave me alive?

"Oh good. You're awake," she said, as she peeked in. "And healing."

"It hurts."

"Yes. These things do. Try to roll with them next time. Let them connect with the back of your cheekbone. It will keep your ear and nose clear."

She shooed Sarah out then stood there for a moment to give me quick assessment.

"At least he went easy on you," she said.

"Easy?" I exclaimed.

"He definitely wanted you conscious. As you pointed out, one mistake after another."

"He almost failed there."

"Perhaps," she said quietly. Then she took a breath before continuing, "But I came here for a quick talk before I leave."

She sat and looked at me while I waited. The seconds passed.

"What?" I asked.

She gave a little nod and finally continued. "I have your

undivided attention?"

"Yes."

"It has come to my attention that you have no idea where you stand in the game."

"You said the game was over," I replied, confused.

That might have angered her. "You obviously don't."

Then she paused again, looking at me strangely. "Do you intend to marry the duke?" she asked.

"Lucien? Of course."

"Will you continue to side with the heir?" Leopold III.

"If it's a question of his being murdered."

She gave a quick nod as if that confirmed all.

"Then you are definitely in the game and definitely a fair target."

That crazy anger of mine began to bubble. "That is so unfair!"

"But it isn't," she lectured. "Let me explain. You have designs on the throne."

"I do not!" I snapped. "That's the last thing I want."

"You do!" she snapped back. "It would only take Leopold ascending to the throne then recognizing the duke as his brother to make you second in line. He needs allies and your Lucien is probably the most powerful man in Belgium. And then there's Victor, looking for Belgian support in France. And who could sway France?" she said, looking at me accusingly. "We see the foundation of a strong anti-British coalition forming. A German backed Belgium with you sitting in its center, waiting for a chance to tip the balance of power in the Atlantic." This is what Marguerite had been trying to warn me about.

"No!"

"You have no interest in expanding Belgian colonial interests?"

"The Congo?" I asked, incredulous.

"Perhaps the Boers might be interested in Belgian support as well?"

"You are out of your mind."

"Revenge perhaps?" she said accusingly.

"No."

"Then let things go. Go back to your little house in Pigalle."

"It's not little!"

I think she almost stomped her foot in frustration, but stood up instead. "You've been warned." Then she left without another word.

How was I supposed to cope with this? I had just survived a beating and attempted rape and here I was being accused of attempting to overthrow the British Empire. I needed to talk to Lucien.

When we finally did talk we were at a loss. It's really hard to find privacy in a palace by the way. But these issues were so large and lives were at stake. All we wanted was a Belgium free of the British, and we were definitely not willing to let them kill Leopold.

We stayed at the palace an extra two weeks. Until the worst of the swelling and dizziness left, and I could walk on my own. Sarah fluttered about me day and night. There were reporters at the station, but with a touch of powder I looked passable under the shade netting on my hat. Blitzlicht popped as we boarded the train to the Milan aerodrome. Even with all of that they still picked up on my inability to climb into the coach unassisted. Speculation on my wounds was rampant.

And on the train together, we both agreed to accept help with our nightmares.

Review
ME!

If you liked the story, and want to help the author, then please rate it, or even better - review it - on Amazon.com

PURE AMERICAN STEAMPUNK
ON SALE NOW AT AMAZON.COM
THE ROSE OF THE WEST

www.ingramcontent.com/pod-product-compliance
Lightning Source LLC
Chambersburg PA
CBHW071106250626
47159CB00002B/626